Samuel Smiles

Brief Biographies

Samuel Smiles

Brief Biographies

ISBN/EAN: 9783743306714

Manufactured in Europe, USA, Canada, Australia, Japa

Cover: Foto ©Raphael Reischuk / pixelio.de

Manufactured and distributed by brebook publishing software
(www.brebook.com)

Samuel Smiles

Brief Biographies

BRIEF BIOGRAPHIES

BY

SAMUEL SMILES

NEW YORK
AMERICAN BOOK EXCHANGE
764 BROADWAY
1881

NOTE.

The first edition of this work appeared in 1860; and as the biographical sketches of persons then living have of course become incomplete and inadequate, they have been omitted in the present issue.

CONTENTS

JAMES WATT.

THE inventor of the steam-engine, now so extensively applied to production in all the arts of industry, is entitled to be regarded as one of the most extraordinary men who has ever lived. Steam is the very Hercules of modern mythology. In the manufactures of Great Britain alone, the power which it exercises is estimated to be equal to the manual labor of four hundred millions of men, or more than double the number of males supposed to inhabit the globe. Steam has become the universal lord. It impels ships in every sea, and drags tram-loads of passengers and merchandise in all lands. It pumps water, drives mills, hammers iron, prints books and newspapers, and works in a thousand ways with an arm that never tires. All this marvelous and indescribable power has flowed from the invention of one man, the subject of the following memoir.

JAMES WATT was born at Greenock on the Clyde, on the 19th of January, 1736. His parents were of the middle class,—honest, industrious people, with a character for probity which had descended to them from their "forbears," and was the proudest inheritance of the family. James Watt was thus emphatically well-born. His grandfather was a teacher of navigation and mathematics in the village of Cartsdyke, now part of Greenock, and dignified himself with the name of "Professor." But as Cartsdyke was as yet only a humble collection of thatched hovels, and the shipping of the Clyde was confined principally to fishing-boats, the probability is, that his lessons in navigation were of a very humble order. He was, however, a dignitary of the place, being Bailie of the Barony, as well as one of the parish elders. His son, James Watt, the father of the engineer, settled at Greenock as a carpenter and builder. Greenock was then little better than a fishing-village, consisting of a single row of thatched cottages lying parallel with the sandy beach of the

Frith of Clyde. The beautiful shore, broken by the long, narrow sea-lochs running far away among the Argyleshire hills, and now fringed with villages, villas, and mansions, was then as lonely as Glencoe; and the waters of the Frith, now daily plashed by the paddles of almost innumerable Clyde steamers, were as yet undisturbed, save by the passing of an occasional Highland cobble. The prosperity of Greenock was greatly promoted by Sir John Shaw, the feudal superior, who succeeded in obtaining from the British Parliament, what the Scottish Parliament previous to the Union had refused, the privilege of constructing a harbor. Ships began after 1740 to frequent the pier, and then Mr. Watt added ship-carpentering and dealing in ships' stores to his other pursuits. He himself held shares in ships, and engaged in several foreign mercantile ventures, some of which turned out ill, and involved him in embarrassments. A great deal of miscellaneous work was executed on his premises,—household furniture and ship's carpentry,—chairs and tables, figure-heads and capstans, blocks, pumps, gun-carriages, and dead-eyes. The first crane erected on the Grenock pier, for the convenience of the Virginia tobacco-shops, was supplied from his stores. He even undertook to repair ships' compasses, as well as the commoner sort of nautical instruments then in use. These multifarious occupations were the result of the smallness of the place, while the business of a single calling was yet too limited to yield a competence. That Mr. Watt was a man of repute in his locality is shown by his having been elected one of the trustees to manage the funds of the borough in 1741, when Sir John Shaw divested himself of his feudal rights, and made them over to the inhabitants. Mr. Watt subsequently held office as town-treasurer, and as a bailie or magistrate.

Agnes Muirhead, the bailie's wife, and the mother of James Watt, was long remembered in the place as an intelligent woman, bountifully gifted with graces of person as well as of mind and heart. She was of a somewhat dignified appearance; and it was said that she affected a superior style of living to her neighbors. One of these, long after, spoke of her as "a braw, braw woman, none like her nowadays," and commented on the extraordinary fact of her having on one occasion no fewer than "two lighted candles on the table at the same time"! The bailie's braw wife was, perhaps, the only lady in Greenock who then dressed à-la-mode—the petticoat worn over a hoop, and curiously tucked up behind, with a towering head-dress over her powdered hair. This pretentious dame, as she appeared, probably did no more than adapt her mode of living to Mr. Watt's circumstances, which seem to have enabled him to adopt a more generous style than was usual in small Scottish towns, where the people were for the most part very poor, and accustomed to slender fare.

From childhood, James Watt was of an extremely fragile constitution, requiring the tenderest nurture. Unable to join in the rude play of healthy children, and confined almost entirely to the house, he acquired a shrinking sensitiveness which little fitted him for the rough battle of life ; and when he was sent to the town school it caused him many painful trials. His mother had already taught him reading, and his father a little writing and arithmetic. His very sports proved lessons to him. His mother, to amuse him, encouraged him to draw with a pencil upon paper, or with chalk upon the floor, and he was supplied with a few tools from the carpenter's shop, which he soon learned to handle with considerable expertness. The mechanical dexterity he acquired was the foundation upon which he built the speculations to which he owes his glory, nor without this manual training is there the least likelihood that he would have become the improver and almost the creator of the steam-engine. Mrs. Watt exercised an influence no less beneficial on the formation of his moral character ; her gentle nature, strong good sense, and earnest, unobtrusive piety, strongly impressing themselves upon his young mind and heart. Nor were his parents without their reward ; for as he grew up to manhood he repaid their anxious care with warm affection. Mrs. Watt was accustomed to say that the loss of her only daughter, which she had felt so severely, had been fully made up to her by the dutiful attentions of her son.

From an early period he was subject to violent headaches, which confined him to his room for weeks together. It is in such cases as his that indications of precocity are generally observed, and parents would be less pleased at their appearance did they know that they are generally the symptoms of disease. Several remarkable instances of this precocity are related of Watt. On one occasion, when he was bending over a marble hearth, with a piece of chalk in his hand, a friend of his father said, "You ought to send that boy to a public school, and not allow him to trifle away his time at home." "Look how my child is occupied," replied the father, "before you condemn him." Though only six years of age, he was trying to solve a problem in geometry. On another occasion, he was reproved by Mrs. Muirhead, his aunt, for his indolence at the tea-table. "James Watt," said the worthy lady, "I never saw such an idle boy as you are ; take a book, or employ yourself usefully ; for the last hour you have not spoken one word, but taken off the lid of that kettle and put it on again, holding now a cup, and now a silver spoon, over the steam, watching how it rises from the spout, catching and counting the drops it falls into ; are you not ashamed of spending your time in that way?" In the view of M. Arago, "the little James before the tea-kettle becomes the mighty engineer preparing the discoveries which were to immortalize him." In our opinion, the judgment of the aunt was the truest. There is no reason to suppose that the mind of little James was occupied with philosophical considerations on the condensation of steam. This is an after-thought borrowed from his subsequent discoveries. Nothing is commoner than for children to be amused with such phenomena, in the same way that they will form air-bubbles in a cup of tea, and watch them sailing over the surface till they burst ; and the probability is that little James was quite as idle as he seemed.

At school, where a parrot-power of learning what is set down in the lesson-book is the chief element of success, Watt's independent observation and reflection did not enable him to distinguish himself, and he was even considered dull and backward for his age.— He shone as little in the playground as in the class. The timid and sensitive boy found himself completely out of place in the midst of the boisterous juvenile republic. Against the tyranny of the elders he was helpless; their wild play was completely distasteful to him; he could not join in their sports, nor roam with them along the beach, nor take part in their hazardous exploits in the harbor. Accordingly, they showered upon him contemptuous epithets; and, the school being composed of both sexes, the girls joined in the laugh. Continual ailments, however, prevented his attendance for weeks together.

When not yet fourteen, he was taken by his mother for change of air to some relatives at Glasgow, then a quiet place, without a single long chimney, somewhat resembling a rural market-town of the present day. He proved so wakeful during his visit, and so disposed to indulge in that story-telling which even Sir Walter Scott could admire at a late period of his life, that Mrs. Watt was entreated to take him home. "I can no longer bear the excitement in which he keeps me," said Mrs. Campbell; "I am worn out for want of sleep." Every evening, before our usual hour of retiring to rest, he adroitly contrives to engage me in conversation, then begins some striking tale, and, whether it is humorous or pathetic, the interest is so overpowering, that all the family listen to him with breathless attention; hour after hour strikes unheeded, but the next morning I feel quite exhausted. You must really take home your son." His taste for fiction never left him; and to the close of his days he took delight in reading a novel.

James Watt, having finished his education at the grammar-school of his native town, received no further instruction. As with all distinguished men, his extensive after-acquirements in science and literature were entirely the result of his own self-culture. Towards the end of his school career his strength seems to have grown; his progress was more rapid and decided; and before he left he had taken the lead of his class. But his best education was gathered from the conversation of his parents. Almost every cottage, indeed, in Scotland, is a training-ground for their future men. How much of the unwritten and traditionary history which kindles the Scotchman's nationality, and tells upon his future life, is gleaned at his humble fireside! Moreover, the library shelf of Watt's home contained well-thumbed volumes of Boston, Bunyan, and "The Cloud of Witnesses," with Harry the Rhymer's "Life of Wallace," and old ballads tattered by frequent use. These he devoured greedily, and re-read them until he had most of them by heart.

During holiday times, he indulged in rambles along the Clyde, sometimes crossing to the north shore, and strolling up the Gare Loch and Holy Loch, and even as far as Ben Lomond itself. He was of a solitary disposition, and loved to wander by himself at night amidst the wooded pleasure-grounds which surrounded the old mansion-house overlooking the town, watching through trees the mysterious movements of the stars. He became fascinated by the wonders of astronomy, and was stimulated to inquire into the sciences by the nautical instruments which he found amongst his father's ship-stores. It was a peculiarity which characterized him through life, that he could not look upon any instrument or machine without being seized with a determination to unravel its mystery, and master the *rationale* of its uses. Before he was fifteen, he had twice gone through, with great attention, S'Gravesande's Elements of Natural Philosophy, which belonged to his father. He performed many chemical experiments, and even contrived to make an electrical machine, much to the marvel of those who felt its shocks. Like most invalids, he read eagerly such books on medicine as came in his way. He went so far as to practice dissection; and on one occasion he was found carrying off the head of a child who had died of some uncommon disease. "He told his son," says Mr. Muirhead, "that, had he been able to bear the sight of the sufferings of patients, he would have been a surgeon." In his rambles, his love of wildflowers and plants lured him on to the study of botany. Ever observant of the aspects of nature, the violent upheavings of the mountain ranges on the northern shore of Loch Lomond next directed his attention to mineralogy. He devoured all the works which fell in his way; and on a friend advising him to be less indiscriminate, he replied, "I have never yet read a book, or conversed with a companion, without gaining information, instruction, or amusement." This was no answer to the admonition of his friend, who merely recommended him to bestow upon the best books the time he devoted to the worse. But the appetite for knowledge in inquisitive minds is, during youth, when curiosity is fresh and unslaked, too insatiable to be fastidious, and the volume which gets the preference is usually the first which comes in the way.

Watt was not a mere bookworm. In his solitary walks through the country, he would enter the cottages of the peasantry, gather their local traditions, and impart to them information of a similar kind from his own ample stores. Fishing, which suited the tranquil character of his nature, was his single sport. When unable to ramble for the purpose, he could still indulge the pursuit while standing in his father's yard, which was open to the sea, and the water of sufficient depth, at high tide, to enable vessels of fifty or sixty tons to lie alongside.

Watt, as we have seen, had learnt the use of his hands, a highly serviceable branch of education, though not taught at schools or colleges. He could ply his tools with considerable dexterity, and he was often employed in the carpenter's shop in making miniature cranes, pulleys, pumps, and capstans. He could work in metal, and a punch-ladle of his manufacture, formed out of a large silver coin, is still preserved. His father had originally intended him to follow his own business of a merchant, but having sustained several heavy losses about this time,—one of his ships having foundered at sea,—and observing the strong bias of his son towards mechanical pursuits, he determined to send him to Glasgow, to learn the trade of a mathematical-instrument maker.

In 1754, when he was in his eighteenth year, he accordingly set out for Glasgow, which was as different from the Glasgow of 1860 as it is possible to imagine. Little did he dream, when he entered it a poor prentice lad, what it was afterwards to become, through the result of his individual labors. Not a steam engine or a steamboat then disturbed the quiet of the town. There was a little quay on the Broomielaw, partly covered with broom ; and this quay was fitted with a solitary crane, for which there was but small use, as boats of more than six tons could not ascend the Clyde. Often not a single masted vessel was to be seen in the river. The chief magnates of the place were the tobacco-merchants and the Professors of the College. Next to tobacco, the principal trade of the town with foreign countries was in grindstones, coals, and fish,—Glasgow herrings being in great repute.

Inconsiderable though Glasgow was at the middle of last century, it was the only place in Scotland which exhibited signs of industrial prosperity. About the middle of last century Scotland was a poor and haggard country. Nothing could be more dreary than those Lowland districts which now perhaps exhibit the finest agriculture in the world. Wheat was so rare a plant, that a field of eight acres within a mile of Edinburgh attracted the attention of the whole neighborhood. Even in the Lothians, Roxburgh, the Lanarkshire, little was to be seen but arid, bleak moors and quaking bogs, with occasional patches of uninclosed and ill-cultivated land. Where manure was used, it was carried to the field on the back of the crofter's wife ; the crops were carried to market on the back of the plow-horse, and occasionally on the backs of the crofter and his family. The country was without roads, and between the towns there were only rough tracks across moors. Goods were conveyed from place to place on pack-horses. The trade between Glasgow and Edinburgh was conducted in the same rude way ; and when carriers were established, the time occupied going and coming between Edinburgh and Selkirk—a distance of only thirty-eight miles—was an entire fortnight. The road lay along Gala Water, and in summer the driver took his rude cart along the channel of the stream, as being the most level and easiest path. In winter the road was altogether impassable. Communication by coach was scarcely anywhere known. A caravan, which was started between Glasgow and Edinburgh in 1749, took two days to perform the journey. For practical purposes, these towns were as distant from London as they now are from New York. As late as 1763 there was only one stage-coach which ran to London. It set out from Edinburgh once a month, and the journey occupied from fifteen to eighteen days. Letters were mostly sent by hand, and after mails were established the post-bags were often empty. Sir Walter Scott knew a man who remembered the London post-bag, which contained the letters from all England to all Scotland, arriving in Edinburgh with only one letter. In 1707 the entire post-office revenue of Scotland was only £1,194 ; in 1857, the penny-postage of Glasgow alone produced £68,877. The custom dues of Greenock now produce more than five times the revenue derived from the whole of Scotland in the times of the Stuarts. The Clyde, which less than a century ago could scarcely admit the passage of a herring-boat, floats down with almost every tide vessels of thousands of tons burden, capable of wrestling with the hurricanes of the Atlantic. The custom-duties levied at the port of Glasgow have been increased from £125 in 1796, to £718,835 in 1856. The advance has been nearly the same in all the other departments of Scotch industry.

At Glasgow, Watt in vain sought to learn the trade of a mathematical-instrument maker. The only person in the place dignified with the name of "Optician" was an old mechanic who sold and mended spectacles, constructed and repaired fiddles, tuned the few spinnets of the town and neighborhood, and eked out a slender living by making and selling fishing-rods and fishing-tackle. Watt was as handy at dressing trout and salmon-flies as at most other things, and his master no doubt found him useful enough ; but there was nothing to be learned in return. Profesor Dick, having been consulted as to the best course to be pursued, recommended the lad to proceed to London. Watt accordingly set out for the metropolis in June, 1755, in the company of a relative, Mr. Marr, the captain of an East-Indiaman. The pair traveled on horseback, and performed the journey in thirteen days. Arrived in town, they went from shop to shop without success. Instrument-makers were few in number, and the rules of the trade, which were then very strict, only permitted them to take into their employment apprentices who should be bound for seven years, or journeymen who had already served their time. "I have not," said Watt, writing to his father about a fortnight after his arrival, "yet got a master ; we have tried several, but they all make some objection or other. I find that, if any of them agree with me at all, it will not be for less than a year, and even for that time they will be expecting some money." At length, one Mr. Morgan, an instrument-maker in Finch Lane, consented to take him for twelvemonth, for a fee of twenty guineas. He soon proved himself a ready learner and skillful workman. The division of labor, the result of an extensive trade, which causes the best London-built carriages to be superior to any of provincial construction, was even then applied to mathematical instruments. "Very few here," wrote Watt, "know any more than how to make a rule, others a pair of dividers and such like." His discursive mind would under no circumstances have allowed him to rest content with such limited proficiency, and he probably contemplated setting up in Scotland, where every branch of the business would have to be executed by himself. He resolved to acquire the entire art, and from brass scales and rules proceeded to Hadley's quadrants, azimuth-compasses, brass sectors, theodolites, and the more delicate sort of instruments. By the end of the year he wrote to his father that he had "just made a brass sector with a French joint, which is reckoned as nice a piece of framing work as is in the trade." To relieve his father of the expense of his maintenance, he wrought after-hours on his own account. His living cost him only eight shillings a week; and lower than that, he wrote, he could not reduce it, "without pinching his belly." When night came, "his body was wearied and his hand shaking from ten hours' hard work." His health suffered. His seat in Mr. Morgan's shop during the winter being close to the door, which was frequently opened and shut, he caught a severe cold. But in spite of sickness and a racking cough, he stuck to his work, and still earned money in his morning and evening hours.

Another circumstance prevented his stirring abroad during the greater portion of his stay in London. A hot press for sailors was then going on, and as many as forty press-gangs were out. In the course of one night they took a thousand men. Nor were the kidnappers idle. These were the agents of the East India Company, and had crimping-houses, or depots, in different parts of metropolis, to receive the men whom they secured for the Indian army. When the demand for soldiers slackened, they continued their trade, and sold the poor wretches to the planters in Pennsylvania and other North American colonies. Sometimes severe fights took place between the press-gangs and the kidnappers for the possession of the unhappy victims who had been seized. "They now press anybody they can get," wrote Watt in the spring of 1756, "landsmen as well as seamen, except it be in the liberties of the city, where they are obliged to carry them before the Lord Mayor first; and unless one be either a prentice or a creditable tradesman, there is scarce any getting off again. And if I was carried before my Lord Mayor, I *durst not* avow that I worked in the city, it being against their laws for any non-freeman to work, even as a journeyman, within the liberties." What a curious glimpse does this give us into the practice of man-hunting in London in the eighteenth century!

When Watt's year with Mr. Morgan was up, his cold had assumed a rheumatic form. Distressed by a gnawing pain in his back, and depressed by weariness, he determined to leave London, although confident that he could have found remunerative employment, and seek for health in his native air, among his kinsfolk at Greenock. After spending about twenty guineas in purchasing tools, together with the materials for making many more, and buying a copy of Bion's work on the construction and use of mathematical instruments, he set off for Scotland, and reached Greenock in the autumn of 1756. Shortly after, when his health had been somewhat restored by rest, he proceeded to Glasgow and commenced business on his own account, at twenty years of age.

In endeavoring to establish himself in his trade, Watt encountered the same obstacle which, in London, had almost prevented his learning it. Although there were no mathematical instrument makers in Glasgow, and it must have been a public advantage to have him settle in the place, he was opposed by the corporation of hammermen, on the ground that he was neither the son of a burgess, nor had served an apprenticeship within the borough. He had been employed, however, to repair some mathematical instruments bequeathed to the University by a gentleman in the West Indies; and the Professors, having an absolute authority within the area occupied by the college buildings, determined to give him an asylum, and free him from the incubus of Guilds. By the midsummer of 1757 he was securely established within the College precincts, where his room, which was only about twenty feet square, is still to be seen, and is the more interesting that its walls remain in as rude a state as when he left it. It is entered from the quadrangle by a spiral stone stair-case, and over the door in the court below Watt exhibited his name, with the addition of "Mathematical-Instrument Maker to the University."

Though his wants were few, and he subsisted on the humblest fare, Watt had a hard struggle to live by his trade. After a year's trial of it, he wrote to his father, in September, 1758, "that unless it be the Hadley's instruments, there is little to be got by it, as at most other jobs I am obliged to do the most of them myself; and as it is impossible for one person to be expert at everything, they very often cost me more time than they should do." Of the quadrants, he could make three in a week, with the assistance of a lad, and the profit upon the three was 40s. But the demand was small, and, unless he could extend his market, "he must fall," he said, "into some other way of business, as this will not do in its present situation." Failing sufficient customers for his instruments in Glasgow, he sent them to Greenock and Port Glasgow, where his father helped him to dispose of them. Orders gradually flowed in upon him, but his business continued to be very small, eked out though it was by map and chart selling.

The most untoward circumstances have often the happiest results. It is not Fortune that is blind, but man. The fame and success of Watt were probably due to his scanty trade, which made him glad to take any employment requiring mechanical ingenuity. A Mason's lodge in Glasgow desired to have an organ, and he was asked to build it. He was totally destitute of a musical ear, and could not distinguish one note from another. But he accepted the offer. He studied the philosophical theory of music, and found that science would be a substitute for his want of ear. He commenced by building a small organ for Dr. Black, and then proceeded to the large one. He was always, he said, dissatisfied both with other people's work and his own, and this habit of his mind made him study to improve upon whatever came before him. Thus in the process of building his organ he devised a number of novel expedients, such as indicators and regulators of the strength of the blast, with various contrivances for improving the efficiency of the stops. The qualities of the organ when finished are said to have e cited the surprise and admiration of musicians. He seems at one period to have been almost as much a maker of musical as of mathematical instruments. He constructed and repaired guitars, flutes, and violins, and had the same success as with his organ.

Small as was Watt's business, there was one circumstance connected with his situation which must have been peculiarly grateful to a man of his accomplishments and thirst for knowledge. His shop, being conveniently situated within the College, was a favorite resort for professors as well as students. Amongst his visitors were the famous Dr. Black, Professor Simson, the restorer of the science of geometry, Dr. Dick, and Dr. Moor; and even Dr. Adam Smith looked in occasionally. But of all his associates none is more closely connected with the name and history of Watt than John Robison, then a student at Glasgow, and afterwards Professor of Natural Philosophy at Edinburgh University. He was nearer Watt's own age than the rest, and stood in the intimate relation of bosom friend as well as fellow-inquirer in science. Robison was a prepossessing person, frank and lively, full of fancy and good humor, and a general favorite in the college. He was a capital talker, an extensive linguist, and a good musician; yet, with all his versatility, he was a profound thinker and a diligent student, especially of mathematical and mechanical philosophy, as he afterwards abundantly proved in his able contributions to the "Encyclopædia Britannica," of which he was the designer and first editor.

Robison's introduction to Watt has been described by himself. After feasting his eyes on the beautifully finished instruments, Robison entered into conversation with him Expecting to find a workman, he was surprised to discover a philosopher. "I had the vanity," said Robison, "to think myself a pretty good proficient in my favorite study (mathematical and mechanical philosophy), and was rather mortified at finding Mr. Watt so much my superior. But his own high relish for these things made him pleased with the chat of any person who had the same tastes with himself; and his innate complaisance made him indulge my curiosity, and even encourage my endeavors to form a more intimate acquaintance with him. I lounged much about him, and, I doubt not, was frequently teasing him. Thus our acquaintance began." Shortly after, Robison, who had been originally destined for the Church, left College. Being of a roving disposition, he entered the navy as a midshipman, and was present at some of the most remarkable actions of the war; and, amongst others, at the storming of Quebec. Robison was on duty in the boat which carried Wolfe to the point where the army scaled the heights the night before the battle, and, as the sun was setting in the west, the General, doubtless from an association of ideas which was suggested by the dangers of the coming struggle, recited Gray's Elegy, and declared that "he would prefer being the author of that poem to the glory of beating the French on the morrow."

When Robison returned from his voyagings in 1763, a traveled man,—having had the advantage during his absence of acting as confidential assistant of Admiral Knowles in the course of his marine surveys and observations,—he reckoned himself more than on a par with Watt; but he soon found that his friend had been still busier than himself, and was continually striking into new paths, where Robison was obliged to be his follower. The extent of the mathematical instrument maker's investigations was no less remarkable than the depth to which he pursued them. Not only did he master the principles of engineering, civil and military, but he diverged into studies in antiquity, natural history, languages, criticisms, and art. Every pursuit became science in his hands, and he made use of this subsidiary knowledge as stepping-stones towards his favorite objects. Before long he was regarded as one of the ablest men about the College; and "when," said Robison "to the superiority of knowledge, which every man confessed, in his own line, is joined the native simplicity and candor of his character, it is no wonder that the attachment of his acquaintances was so strong. I have seen something of the world and I am obliged to say that I never saw such another instance of general and cordial attachment to a person whom all acknowledged to be their superior. But this superiority was concealed under the most amiable candor, and liberal allowance of merit to every man. Mr. Watt was the first to ascribe to the ingenuity of a friend things which were very often nothing but his own surmises followed out and embodied by another. I am well entitled to say this, and have often experienced it in my own case." There are few traits in biography more charming than these generous recognitions of merit, mutually attributed by the one friend to the other. Arago, in quoting the words of Robison, has well observed that it is difficult to determine whether the honor of having uttered them be not as great as that of having inspired them.

By this high-minded friend the attention of Watt was first directed to the subject of the steam-engine. Robison in 1759 suggested to him that it might be applied to the moving of wheel-carriages. The scheme was not matured, and indeed science was not yet ripe for the locomotive. But after a short interval Watt again reverted to the study of steam, and in 1761 he was busily engaged in performing experiments with the humble aid of apothecaries' phials and a small Papin's digester. There were then no museums of art and science to resort to for information, and he perhaps cultivated his own powers the more thoroughly, that he had no such easy methods of acquiring knowledge. He mounted his digester with a syringe a third of an inch in diameter. containing a solid piston, When he turned a cock the steam rushed from the digester against the lower side of the piston in the syringe, and by its expansive power raised a weight of fifteen pounds with which the piston was loaded. Then again turning the cock, which was arranged so as to cut off the communication with the digester, and open a passage to the air, the steam escaped; and the weight upon the piston, being no longer counteracted, forced it to descend. He saw it would be easy to contrive that the cocks should be turned by the machinery instead of by the hand, and the whole be made to work of itself with perfect regularity. But there was no objection in the method. Water is converted into vapor, as soon as its elasticity is sufficient to overcome the weight of the air which keeps it down. Under the ordinary pressure of the atmosphere the water acquires this necessary elasticity at 212°; but as the steam in Papin's digester was prevented from escaping, it acquired increased heat, and by consequence increased elasticity. Hence it was that the steam which issued from the digester was not only able to support the piston and the air which pressed upon its upper surface, but the additional load with which the piston was weighted. With the imperfect mechanical construction, however, of those days there was a risk that the boiler in which the high-pressure steam was generated would be burst by its expansive power, which also enabled it to force its way through the ill-made joints of the engine. This, conjoined with the great expenditure of steam, led Watt to abandon the plan. The exigencies of business did not then allow him to pursue his experiments, and the subject again slept till the winter of 1763—64.

The College at Glasgow possessed a model of one of Newcomen's engines, which had been sent to London for repair. It would appear that the eminent artificer to whom it had been intrusted paid little attention to it, for at a University meeting in June, 1760, a resolution was passed to allow Mr. Anderson "to lay out a sum not exceeding two pounds sterling to recover the steam-engine from Mr. Sisson, instrument maker, at London." In 1763 this clumsy little engine, destined to become so famous, was put in the hands of Watt. The boiler was somewhat smaller than an ordinary tea-kettle, the cylinder two inches in diameter, and the mathematical-instrument maker merely regarded it as "a fine plaything." When, however, he had repaired the machine and set it to work, he found that the boiler, though apparently sufficiently large, could not supply steam fast enough, and only a few strokes of the piston could be secured. The fire under it was stimulated by blowing, and more steam was produced, but still the machine would not work properly. Exactly at the point where another man would have abandoned the task in despair, the mind of Watt became thoroughly roused. "Everything," says Professor Robison, "was to him the beginning of a new and serious study; and we knew he would not quit it till he had either discovered its insignificance, or had made something out of it." Thus it happened with the phenomenon presented by the model of the steam-engine. He endeavored to ascertain from books by what means he was to remedy the defects; and when books failed to aid him, he commenced a course of experiments, and resolved to work out the probelm himself. In the course of his inquiries he came upon a fact which more than any other led his mind into the train of thought which at last conducted him to the invention of which the results were destined to prove so stupendous. This fact was the existence of latent heat. But before we go on to state his proceedings, it is necessary to describe the condition at which the steam-engine had arrived when his investigations commenced.

Steam had not then become a common mechanical power. The sole use to which it was applied was to pump water from mines. A beam, moving upon a center, had affixed to it a chain, which was attached to the piston of the pump ; to the other end of it a chain, which was attached to a piston that fitted a cylinder. It was by driving this latter piston up and down the cylinder that the pump was worked. To communicate the necessary movement to the piston, the steam generated in a boiler was admitted to the bottom of the cylinder, forcing out the air through a valve and by its pressure upon the under side of the piston counter balancing the pressure of the atmosphere upon its upper side. The piston, thus placed between two equal and two opposite forces, was then drawn up to the top of the cylinder by the greater weight of the pump-gear at the opposite extremity of the beam. The steam, so far, only discharged the office which was performed by the air it displaced ; but if the air had been allowed to remain, the piston once at the top of the cylinder could not have been returned, being pressed as much by the atmosphere underneath as by the atmosphere above it. The

steam, on the contrary, could be conden　　, by injecting cold
water through the bottom of the cylinder. This caused a vacuum
below the piston, which was now unsupported, and descended by
the pressure of the atmosphere upon its upper surface. When the
piston reached the bottom, the steam was again let in, and the process was repeated.

This was the machine in use when Watt was pursuing the investigations into which he was led by the litttle model of the Newcomen
engine. Among other experiments, "he constructed a boiler which
showed, by inspection, the quantity of water evaporated in a given
time, and thereby ascertained the quantity of steam used in every
stroke of the engine." He was astonished to discover that a *small*
quantity of water, in the form of steam, heated a *large* quantity of
water injected into the cylinder for the purpose of cooling it ; and
upon further examination, he ascertained that steam heated six times
its weight of well-water to 212°, which was the temperature of the
steam itself. Unable to understand so remarkable a circumstance,
he mentioned it to Dr. Black, who then expounded to him the theory
of latent heat, which this great chemist had already taught his
pupils, unknown to Watt. This vast amount of heat stored up in
steam, and not indicated by the thermometer, involved a propor-
tionate consumption of coals. When Watt learned that water, in its
conversion into vapor, became such a reservoir of heat, he was more
than ever bent upon economizing it, striving, with the same
quantity of fuel, at once to augment its production and diminish its
waste. "He greatly improved the boiler," says Professor Robison,
"by increasing the surface to which the fire was applied ; he made
flues through the middle of the water, and made his boiler of wood,
as a worse conductor of heat than the brick-work which surrounds
common furnaces. He cased the cylinder and all the conducting-
pipes in materials which conducted heat very slowly ; he even made
them of wood." But none of these contrivances were effectual ; for
it turned out that the chief expenditure of steam, and consequently
of fuel, was in the re-heating the cylinder after it had been cooled
by the injection of the cold water. Nearly four-fifths of the whole
steam employed was condensed on its first admission, before the
surplus could act upon the piston. Watt therefore came to the conclusion, that, to make a perfect steam-engine, it was necessary that
the cylinder should be always as hot as the steam that entered it ;
but it was equally necessary that the steam should be condensed
when the piston descended,—nay, that it should be cooled down
below 100°, or a considerable amount of vapor would be given off,
which would resist the descent of the piston and diminish the
engine.* The two conditions seemed quite incompatible. The

---

* Since the more the pressure upon the water is diminished. the lower the
temperature at which it boils, water at any temperature less than 100° gives
off vapor in the vacuum of the cylinder.

cylinder was never to be at a less temperature than 212°, and yet at each descent of the piston it was to be less than 100°.

" He continued," he says, "to grope in the dark, misled by many an ignis fatuus." At length, as he was taking a walk one Sunday afternoon, in the spring of 1765, the solution of the problem suddenly flashed upon his mind. As steam was an elastic vapor, it would expand and rush into a previously exhausted space. He had only to produce a vacuum in a separate vessel; and open a communication between the vessel and the cylinder of the steam-engine at the moment when the piston was required to descend, and the steam would disseminate itself and become divided between the cylinder and the adjoining vessel. But as this vessel would be kept cold by an injection of water, the steam would be annihilated as fast as it entered, which would cause a fresh outflow of the remaining steam in the cylinder till nearly the whole of it was condensed without the cylinder itself being chilled in the operation. An air-pump, worked by the steam-engine, would pump from the subsidiary vessel the heated water, air, and vapor, accumulated by the condensing process. Great and prolific ideas are almost always simple. What seems impossible at the outset appears so obvious when it is effected, that we are prone to marvel that it did not force itself at once upon the mind. Late in life, Watt, with his accustomed modesty, declared his belief that, if he has excelled, it had been by chance, and the neglect of others. But mankind has been more just to him than he had been to himself. There was no accident in the discovery. It had been the result of close and continuous study, and the idea of the separate condenser, which flashed upon him in a moment, and filled him with rapture, was merely the last step of a long journey,—a step which could not have been taken unless the previous road had been traversed.

The steam in Newcomen's engine was only employed to produce a vacuum. The working power of the engine was in the down stroke, which was effected by the pressure of the air upon the piston ; hence it is now usual to call it the atmospheric engine. Watt perceived that the air which followed the piston down the cylinder would cool the latter, and that steam would be wasted in reheating it. To effect a further saving, he resolved "to put an air-tight cover upon the cylinder, with a hole and stuffing-box for the piston-rod to slide through, and to admit steam above the piston, to act upon it instead of the atmosphere." When the steam had done its duty in driving down the piston, a communication was opened between the upper and lower part of the cylinder, and the same steam, distributing itself equally in both compartments, sufficed to restore equilibrium. The piston was now drawn up by the weight of the pump-gear, the steam beneath it was then condensed to leave a vacuum, and a fresh jet of steam from the boiler was let in above the piston, and forced it again to the bottom of the cylinder. From an atmospheric it had thus become a true steam-engine, and with a much greater economy of steam than when the air did half the duty. But it was not only important to keep the air from flowing down the inside of the cylinder. The air which circulated without cooled the metal, and condensed a portion of the steam within. This Watt proposed to remedy by a second cylinder, surrounding the first, with an interval between the two which was to be kept full of steam. "When once," he says, "the idea of separate condensation was started, all these improvements followed as corollaries in quick succession, so that in the course of one or two days the invention was thus far complete in my mind."

But although the engine was complete in his mind, it cost Watt many long and laborious years before he could perfect it in execution. One source of delay was the numerous expedients which sprung up in his fertile mind, "which," he said, "his want of experience in the practice of mechanics in great flattered him would prove more commodious than his matured experience had shown them to be. Experimental knowledge is of slow growth, and he tried too many fruitless experiments on such variations." One of his chief difficulties was to find mechanics to make his large models for him. The beautiful metal workmanship which has been called into being by his own invention did not then exist. The only available hands in Glasgow were the blacksmiths and tinners,—little capable of constructing articles out of their ordinary walk. He accordingly hired a small work-shop in a back street of the town, where he might himself erect a working model, with the aid of his assistant, John Gardiner. His mind, as may be supposed, was absorbed in the desire to realize his beautiful conception. "I am at present," he wrote to his friend Dr. Lind, "quite barren on every other article, my whole thoughts being bent on this machine." The first model, on account of the bad construction of the larger parts, was only partially successful, and then a second and bigger model was commenced in August, 1765. In October it was at work ; but the machine leaked in all directions, and the piston proved not steam-tight. To secure a nice-fitting piston, with the indifferent workmanship of that day, taxed his ingenuity to the utmost. At so low an ebb was the art of making cylinders, that the one he employed was not bored but hammered, the collective mechanical skill of Glasgow being then unequal to the casting and boring of a cylinder of the simplest kind. In the Newcomen engine a little water was poured upon the upper surface of the piston, and filled up the interstices between the piston and the cylinder. But when Watt employed steam to drive down the piston, he was deprived of this resource ; for the water and the steam could not coexist. Even if he had retained the agency of the air above, the drip of water from the crevices into the lower part of the cylinder would have been incompatible with keeping the surface hot and dry, and, by turning into vapor as it fell upon the heated metal, it would have impaired the vacuum during the descent of the piston. To add to Watt's troubles, while he was busied with his model, the tinner, who was his leading mechanic, died. *"My old white-iron man is dead,"* he wrote to Dr. Roebuck in December,—an almost irreparable loss ! By the addition of collars of varnished cloth the piston was made steam-tight, and the machine went cleverly and successfully on trials, at a pressure of ten to fourteen pounds on the square inch. Thus inch by inch Watt battled down difficulty, held good the ground he had gained, verified the expectations he had formed, and placed the advantages of the invention, to his own mind, beyond the reach of doubt.

Watt's means were small, and there were no capitalists in Glasgow likely to take up the steam-engine. Commercial enterprise had scarcely begun, or was still confined to the trade in tobacco. To give a fair trial to the new apparatus would involve an expenditure of several thousand pounds ; and who on the spot could be expected to invest so large a sum in trying a machine so entirely new, and depending for its success on physical principles very imperfectly understood ? But he had not far to go for an associate. "Most fortunately," says Professor Robison, "there was in the neighborhood such a person as he wished—Dr. Roebuck, a gentleman of very uncommon knowledge in all the branches of civil engineering, familiarly acquainted with the steam-engine, of which he employed several in his collieries, and deeply interested in this improvement. He was also well accustomed to great enterprises, of an undaunted spirit, not scared by difficulties, nor a niggard of expense." He was born at Sheffield in 1718, and practiced as a physician at Birmingham with distinguished success, had made many improvements in various manufacturing arts, and was now engaged in the double task of carrying on iron-works at Carron and sinking coal-mines at Borrowstoness.

As early as August, 1765, Watt was in full correspondence with Roebuck on the subject of the engine. No partnership was entered into till 1778 ; but it is evident, from the nature of Watt's letters, that Roebuck took the greatest interest in the project, and had probably pledged himself to engage in it if the experiments promised success. In November, Watt sent detailed drawings of a covered cylinder and piston to be cast at the Carron works. Though the cylinder was the best that could be made there, it was so ill-bored as to be useless. The piston-rod was constructed at Glasgow, under his own supervision ; and when it was completed, he was afraid to send it in a cart, lest the work-people should see it, which would "occasion speculation." "I believe," he added, "it will be best to send it in a box." These precautions would seem to have been dictated by a fear of piracy. The necessity of acting by stealth increased the difficulties arising from the clumsiness and inexperience of the mechanics. There is a gap in the correspondence of Watt with Roebuck from May, 1766, to January, 1768, and we hear no more of this piston-rod or of its worthless cylinder. Something, however, must have occurred in the interval to inspire Roebuck with confidence, for, in 1767, he undertook to pay a debt of £1,000 which Watt had contracted in prosecuting his project, to provide the money for the further experiments, and to pay for the patents. In return for this outlay he was to have two-thirds of the property in the invention.

In April, 1768, Watt made trial of a new model. The result was not altogether satisfactory. Roebuck, in reply to the announcement, asked Watt to meet him at Kilsythe, a place about half-way between Carron and Glasgow, and talk the matter over. "I would," says Watt, in his answer, "with all my heart, wait upon you on Friday, but am far from being well, and the fatigue of the ride would disable me from doing anything for three or four days ; besides, I hope by that time to have a more successful trial, without which I cannot have peace in my mind to enjoy anything." After various contrivances, a trial which he made on the 24th of May answered to his heart's content. "I intend," he wrote, to Dr. Roebuck, "to have the pleasure of seeing you at Kinneil on Saturday or Friday. I sincerely wish you joy of this successful result, and hope it will make you some return for the obligation I ever will remain under to you." Kinneil House, where Watt hastened to pay his visit of congratulation to Dr. Roebuck, was a singular old edifice, a former country seat of the Dukes of Hamilton, finely situated on the shores of the Forth, with large apartments and stately staircases, and an external style of architecture which resembles the old French château. The mansion has become rich in classical associations, having been inhabited, since Roebuck's time, by Dugald Stewart, who wrote in it his "Philosophy of the human Mind." There he was visited by Wilkie, the painter, when in search of subjects for his pictures, and Dugald Stewart found for him, in an old farm-house in the neighborhood, the cradle-chimney which is introduced in the "Penny Wedding." But none of these names can stand by the side of that of Watt, and the first thought at Kinneil, of every one who is familiar with his history, would be of the memorable day when he rode over in exultation to Dr. Roebuck to wish him joy of the success of the steam-engine. His date of triumph was, however, premature. He had yet to suffer many sickening delays, and many bitter disappointments ; for though he had contrived to get his model executed with fair precision, the skill was still wanting for manufacturing the parts in their full size with the requisite nicety, and his present conquest was succeeded by discomfiture.

The model went so well that it was now determined to take out a patent, and in August, 1768, Watt went to London for the purpose. After transacting his business he proceeded home by way of Birmingham, then the best school of mechanics in England. He here saw his future partner, Mr. Boulton, for the first time, and they at once conceived for each other a hearty regard. Mr. Boulton, in particular, was strongly impressed both by the character and genius of Watt. They had much conversation respecting the engine, and it cheered its inventor that the sagacious and practical Birmingham manufacturer augured well of its success. Watt seems, however, to have been seized with low spirits on his return to Glasgow ; his heart probably aching with anxiety for his family, whom it was hard to maintain upon hope so often deferred. The more sanguine Doctor was elated with the good working of the model, and he was impatient to put the invention in practice. "You are letting," he wrote to Watt, October 30, 1768, "the most active part of your life insensibly glide away. A day, a moment, ought not to be lost. And you should not suffer your thoughts to be diverted by any other object, or even improvement of this, but only the speediest and most effectual manner of executing one of a proper size, according to your present ideas." This was an allusion to the fresh expedients which were always starting up in Watt's brain, and which appeared endlessly to protract the consummation of the work ; but it was by never resting satisfied with imperfect devices that he attained to perfection. Long after, when a noble Lord was expressing his admiration at his great achievement, Watt replied, "The public only look at my success, and not on the intermediate failures and uncouth constructions which have served as steps to climb to the top of the ladder." As to the lethargy of which Roebuck spoke, it was merely the temporary reaction of a mind strained and wearied with long-continued application to a single subject.

The patent was dated January 5, 1769, a year also memorable as that in which Arkwright took out the patent for his spinning-machine, and Watt by the law had four months in which to prepare his specifications. To render it as perfect as possible, he commenced a series of fresh experiments, and all his spare hours were devoted to making various trials of pipe-condensers and drum condensers,—trying to contrive new methods of securing tightness of the piston, and devising steam-jackets to prevent the waste of heat,—inventing oil-pumps, gauge-pumps, and exhausting-cylinders,—loading valves, beams, and cranks.

He commenced at Kinneil the construction of a steam-engine on a larger scale than he had yet attempted. It had been originally intended to erect it in the small town of Borrowstoness; but as he wished to avoid display, being determined, as he said, "not to puff," he put it up in an outhouse at Kinneil, close by the burnside in the glen, where there was abundance of water and secure privacy. The materials were brought partly from Glasgow and partly from Carron, where the cylinder had been cast. The process of erection was

tedious, for the mechanics were unused to the work. Watt was occasionally compelled to be absent on other business, and he generally on his return found the men at a stand-still, not knowing what
to do next.   As the engine neared completion "his anxiety for his
approaching doom kept him from sleep," for his fears, he says, were
at least equal to his hopes.   The whole was finished in September,
1769, and proved a "clumsy job."   One of his new contrivances did
not work well; and the cylinder, having been badly cast, was almost
useless. Watt again was grievously depressed.   "It is a sad thing,"
he wrote to his friend, Dr. Small of Birmingham, in March, 1770,
"for a man to have his all hanging by a single string.   If I had
wherewithal to pay the loss, I don't think I should so much fear
a failure; but I cannot bear the thought of other people becoming
losers by my scheme, and I have the happy disposition of always
painting the worst."   His poverty was already compelling him to
relinquish his experiments for employment of more pecuniary profit.

Watt had married his cousin, Miss Miller, in July, 1764.   His expenses were thus enlarged almost at the very moment when his
invention began to fill his mind, and distracted his attention from
his ordinary calling.   His increasing family led him before long to
seek employment as a land-surveyor, or, as it was called in Scotland,
a "land-louper."   Much of his business was of the class which now
belongs to the civil engineer, and in 1767 he laid out a small canal
to unite the rivers Forth and Clyde.   There was a rival scheme,
cheaper and more direct, which was espoused by the celebrated
Smeaton, and Watt had to answer before a Committee of the House
of Commons to defend his plan.   "I think," he wrote to Mrs. Watt,
April 5, 1767, "I shall not long to have anything to do with the House
of Commons again: I never saw so many wrong-headed people on
all sides gathered together."   The fact that they decided against him
had probably its share in producing this opinion of their wrong-
headedness.

In April, 1769, when he was busily engaged in erecting the Kinneil engines, he heard that a linen-draper in London, of the name
of Moore, had plagiarized his invention, and the reflections which
this drew forth from him is an evidence of the settled despondency
which clouded his mind, and even cramped his faculties.

I have resolved, unless these things that I have now brought to some perfection reward me for the time and money I have lost on them, if I can
resist it, to invent no more. Indeed, I am not near so capable as I once was;
I find that I am not the same person that I was four years ago, when I invented the fire-engine, and foresaw, even before I made a model, almost every
circumstance that has since occurred. I was at that time spurred on by the
alluring hope of placing myself above want, without being obliged to have
much dealing with mankind, to whom I have always been a dupe. The necessary experience in great * was wanting; in acquiring which I have met with

* The expression "in great" means machines upon a large scale, instead
of the small models with which his experiments had been made.

many disappointments. I must have sunk under the burden of them if I had not been supported by the friendship of Dr. Roebuck. I have now brought the engine near a conclusion, yet I am not in idea nearer that rest I wished for than I was four years ago. However, I am resolved to do all I can to carry on this business, and if it does not thrive with me I will lay aside the burden I cannot carry. OF ALL THINGS IN LIFE THERE IS NOTHING MORE FOOLISH THAN INVENTING.

It is nevertheless a remarkable proof of his indefatigable perseverance in his favorite pursuit, that at this very time, when apparently sunk in the depths of gloom, he learned German for the sole purpose of getting at the contents of a curious book, the "Theatrum Machinarum" of Leupold, which just then fell into his hands, and which contained an account of the machines, furnaces, methods of working, profits, etc., of the mines in the Upper Hartz. His instructor on the occasion was a Swiss dyer settled in Glasgow. With the similar object of gaining access to untranslated books in French and Italian, —then the great depositories of mechanical and engineering knowledge,—Watt had already mastered both these languages.

Mrs. Watt had on one occasion written to him, "If the engine will not do, something else will : never despair." The engine did not do for the present, and he was compelled to continue his surveying. Instead of laying aside one burden he was constrained to add a second. In September, 1769, just when he tried the Kinneil engine, he was employed in examining the Clyde with a view to improve the navigation,—for the river was still so shallow as to prevent boats of more than ten tons burden ascending to the Broomielaw. Watt made his report, but no steps were taken to execute his suggestions until several years later, when the commencement was made of a series of improvements, which have resulted in the conversion of the Clyde from a pleasant trouting-stream into one of the busiest navigable highways in Europe.

I would not have meddled with it, he wrote to Dr. Small, had I been certain of bringing the engine to bear; but I cannot, on an uncertainty, refuse any piece of business that offers. I have refused some common fire-engines, * because they must have taken up my attention so as to hinder my going on with my own. However, if I cannot make it answer soon, I shall certainly undertake the next that offers, for I cannot afford to trifle away my whole life, which God knows may not be long. Not that I think myself a proper hand for keeping men to their duty; but I must use my endeavor to make myself square with the world if I can, though I much fear I never shall.

"To-day," he again wrote to Dr. Small on the 31st of January, 1770, "I enter in the thirty-fifth year of my life, and I think I have hardly

---

* The fire-engine was the name given in those days to the atmospheric engines of Newcomen. Watt says elsewhere that "he was concerned in making some," but whether previous or subsequent to this letter of September 30, 1769, does not appear.

done thirty-five pence worth of good in the world; but I cannot
help it."

The people of Glasgow decided upon making a canal for coal traffic to the collieries at Monkland, in Lanarkshire; "and having," says
Watt, "conceived a much higher idea of my abilities than they merit,
they resolved to encourage a man that lived among them rather than
a stranger." He made the survey in 1769, and the air and exercise
acted like a cordial upon him. " The time," he wrote to Dr. Small,
January 3, 1770, "has not been thrown away, for the vaguing (wandering) about the country, and bodily fatigue, have given me
health and spirits beyond what I commonly enjoy at this dreary
season, though they would still *thole amends* (bear improvement).
Hire yourself to somebody for a plowman,—it will cure ennui."
He made another survey of a canal from Perth to Cupar in the spring
of 1770, with a less favorable result. The weather was inclement,
and the wind and snow and cold brought back his low spirits and
ill health. When the Act for the Monkland Canal was obtained, he
was invited to superintend the execution of it, and "had to select
whether to go on with the experiments on the engine, the event of
which was uncertain, or to embrace an honorable and perhaps profitable employment." His necessities decided him. " I had a wife
and children, and saw myself growing gray without having any settled way of providing for them." He determined, however, not to
drop the engine, but to proceed with it the first spare moments he
could find. In December, 1770, he made a report to Dr. Small of
his experience in canal-making, and it was not very favorable. His
constant headaches continued, but in other respects he had gained
in vigor of mind and body. "I find myself more strong, more
resolute, less lazy, less confused than I was when I began it." His
pecuniary affairs were alone more prosperous. "Supposing the
engine to stand good for itself, I am able to pay all my debts, and
some little thing more, so that I hope in time to be on a par with the
world." But there was a dark side to the picture. His life was one
of vexation, fatigue, hunger, wet, and cold. The quiet and secluded
habits of his early life did not fit him for the out-door work of the
engineer. He was timid and reserved, and wanted that rough
strength,—that navvy sort of character,—which enables a man to
deal with rude laborers. He was nervously fearful lest his want of
experience should betray him into scrapes, and lead to impositions
on the part of the workmen. He hated higgling, and declared that
he would rather "face a loaded cannon than settle an account or
make a bargain." He acted as surveyor, engineer, superintendent
and treasurer, with only the assistance of one clerk; and had been
"cheated," he said, "by undertakers, and was unlucky enough
to know it." His men were so inexperienced; that he had to watch
the execution of every piece of work that was out of the common
track. Yet, with all this, "the work done was slovenly, the work-

men bad, and he himself not sufficiently strict." The defect which he charged on himself was merely the want of training and experience in the laborers. When Telford afterwards went into the Highlands to construct the Caledonian Canal, he encountered the same difficulty. The men were unable to make use of the most ordinary tools; they had no steadiness in their labor; and they had to be taught, and drilled, and watched like children at school. In fact, every great undertaking in engineering may be regarded in the light of a working academy in which men are trained to the skillful use of tools and the habit of persistent industry; and the Scotch laborers were only then passing through the elementary discipline. Watt determined he would not continue a slave to this hateful employment. He was willing to act as engineer, but not as manager, and said he would have nothing to do "with workmen, cash, or workmen's accounts."

His superintendence of the Monkland Canal, for which he received a salary of £200 a year, lasted from June, 1770, to December, 1772. Before that period had expired, a commercial crisis had arrived; and Dr. Roebuck, whose unremunerative speculations had already brought him to the verge of ruin, was unable to weather the storm. All the anxieties of Watt were revived, and more for Roebuck than for himself. But an extract from his letter to Dr. Small, on the 30th of August, 1772, will best speak his sentiments:—

I pursued my experiments till I found that the expense and loss of time lying wholly upon me, through the distress of Dr. Roebuck's situation, turned out to be a burden greater than I could support, and not having conquered all the difficulties that lay in the way of the execution, I was obliged for a time to abandon the project. Since that time I have been able to extricate myself from some part of my private debts, but am by no means yet in a situation to be the principal in so considerable an undertaking. The Doctor's affairs, being yet far from being reinstated, give me little hope of help from that quarter: in the mean time the time of the patent is running on. It is a matter of great vexation to me that the Doctor should be out so great a sum upon this affair, while he has otherwise such pressing occasion for the money. I find myself unable to give him such help as his situation requires; and what little I can do for him is purchased by denying myself the conveniences of life my situation requires, or by remaining in debt where it galls me to the bone to owe.

He repeated in November, that nothing gave him so much pain as having entangled Dr. Roebuck in the scheme, and that he would willingly have resigned all prospect of profit to himself, provided his associate could have been indemnified. He regarded the considerable sum which he had sunk on his own part, "as money spent upon his education," and looked for scarce any other recompense "for the anxiety and ruin in which the engine had involved him." These are the sentiments of a mind of sensitive honor, as well as scrupulous integrity. In the issue, the embarrassments of Roebuck proved the making of the steam-engine and of Watt.

The association of Watt with Dr. Roebuck was in many respects fortunate, for the latter possessed the qualities in which the former was deficient. "I find myself," Watt wrote, "out of my sphere when I have anything to do with mankind ; it is enough for an engineer to force Nature, and to bear the vexation of her getting the better of him. Give me a survey to make, and I think you will have credit of me ; set me to contrive a machine, and I will exert myself." To invent was Watt's faculty ; to push an invention was entirely contrary to his temperament. Not only was he averse to business, but he was easily depressed by little obstructions, and alarmed at unforeseen expense. Roebuck, on the contrary, was sanguine, adventurous, and energetic. The disposition of Watt to despond under difficulties, and his painful diffidence in himself, were frequent subjects of friendly merriment at Kinneil House ; and Mrs. Roebuck said one evening : "Jamie is a queer lad, and without the Doctor his invention would have been lost ; but Dr. Roebuck won't let it perish." Watt always acknowledged the debt he owed him, and declared he had been to him "a most sincere and generous friend." The alliance, however, was not without its drawbacks. The extensive undertakings of Dr. Roebuck absorbed both his capital and his time. He was unable to pay, according to the terms of his engagement, the expenses of the patent, and Watt had to borrow the money from Dr. Black. His coal and iron-works required incessant superintendence, and the management of the business connected with the steam-engine chiefly devolved upon Watt, who said he "was incapable of it from his natural inactivity, and want of health and resolution." When he passed through Birmingham on his way from London, in October, 1768, Mr. Boulton, who then knew nothing of Watt's agreement with Roebuck, offered to be concerned in the speculation. This gave "great joy" to Watt, and he wished Dr. Roebuck to consent. But the latter "grew more tenacious of the project the nearer it approached to certainty," and he only proposed to Boulton to allow him a share in the engine for the counties of Warwick, Stafford, and Derby. The letter which Boulton wrote to Watt upon the occasion (Feb. 7, 1769) shows how clearly he saw what was required to render the invention available :—

I was excited by two motives to offer you my assistance,—which were, love of you, and love of a money-getting, ingenious project. I presumed that your engine would require money, very accurate workmanship, and extensive correspondence, to make it turn out to the best advantage ; and that the best means of keeping up the reputation, and doing the invention justice, would be to keep the executive part out of the hands of the multitude of empirical engineers, who, from ignorance, want of experience, and want of necessary convenience, would be very liable to produce bad and inaccurate workmanship,—all which deficiencies would affect the reputation of the invention. To remedy which, and to produce the most profit, my idea was to settle a manufactory near to my own, by the side of our canal, where I would erect all the conveniences necessary for the completion of engines, and from which manufactory we would serve all the world with engines of all sizes. By these means, and your assistance, we would engage and instruct some excellent workmen, who (with more excellent tools than would be worth any man's while to procure for one single engine) could execute the invention twenty per cent cheaper than it would be otherwise executed, and with as great a difference of accuracy as there is between the blacksmith and the mathematical-instrument maker. It would not be worth my while to make for three counties only; but I find it very well worth my while to make for all the world.

This was precisely the plan which was ultimately adopted. Watt, when he read it, must have been more than ever urgent to have Boulton for a coadjutor, and he again, in September, 1769, pressed upon Roebuck the wisdom of admitting him into the partnership. In November, Roebuck proposed to make over a third of the patent to Mr. Boulton or Dr. Small for any sum, not less than £1,000, which they should think reasonable, after the experiments on the engine were finished. They were to take their final resolution at the end of a year; but though they assented to the terms, no agreement seems to have been made at the conclusion of the twelve-month; and it was not till ruin drove Roebuck to sell his share, that the bargain was struck. Then he transferred his entire property in the patent to Mr. Boulton in the latter half of 1773, in consideration of being released from a debt of £630, and receiving the first £1,000 of profit from the engine. "My heart bleeds for his situation," Watt wrote to Boulton, "and I can do nothing to help him. I stuck by him till I have much hurt myself. I can do so no longer; my family calls for my care to provide for them. Yet, if I have, I cannot see the Doctor in want, which I am afraid will soon be the case." The situation of this able, upright, and enterprising man, who deserved a better fate, was not, in the opinion of his assignees, rendered worse by the sale of his share in the steam-engine, for they did not value it at a single farthing. Even Watt said that Boulton had got one bad debt in exchange for another.

This was the turning-point in Watt's fortunes. It was the imperfect workmanship, and ineffective superintendence, which had caused the failure of so many experiments, and the wise and vigorous management of Mr. Boulton was soon to show the engine in its true powers. But before Watt enjoyed this triumph, he had another bitter cup to drink. He was suddenly summoned to Glasgow in the autumn of 1773, when on a survey of the Caledonian Canal, by intelligence of the illness of his wife. The journey was dreary, through a country without roads. "An incessant rain," said he, "kept me for three days as wet as water could make me; I could hardly preserve my journal book." On reaching home he found his wife had died in childbed. She had struggled with him through poverty, had often cheered his fainting spirit when borne down by doubt, perplexity, and disappointment; and often afterwards he paused on the threshold of

his house, unable to summon courage to enter the room where he
was never more to meet "the comfort of his life." "Yet this misfortune," he wrote to Small, "might have fallen upon me when I
had less ability to bear it, and my poor children might have been
left suppliants to the mercy of the wide world. I know that grief
has its period ; but I have much to suffer first." "None of the many
trying calamities," he said, fifteen years afterwards, "to which
human nature is subjected, bears harder or longer on a thinking
mind than that grief which arises from the loss of friends. But,
like other evils, it must be endured with patience. The most powerful remedy is to apply to business or amusements which call the
mind from its sorrows and prevent it from preying on itself. In the
fullness of our grief we are apt to think that allowing ourselves to
pursue objects which may turn our minds from the object it is but
too much occupied with, is like a kind of insult or want of affection
for the deceased, but we do not then argue fairly ; our duty to the
departed has come to a period, but our duty to our living family, to
ourselves, and to the world, still subsists, and the sooner we can
bring ourselves to attend to it the more meritorious. Upon these
wise sentiments he endeavored, though not very successfully, to
act. To work was in some degree within the power of his will, but
to regain the elasticity of the mind was beyond the reach of self-
control. "Man's life, you say," he wrote to Dr. Small, in December, 1773, "must be spent either in labor or ennui ; mine is spent
in both. I am heart-sick of this country ; I am indolent to excess,
and, what alarms me most, I grow stupider. My memory fails me
so as often totally to forget occurrences of not very ancient dates. I
see myself condemned to a life of business ; nothing can be more
disagreeable to me ; I tremble when I hear the name of a man I
have any transactions to settle with. The engineering business is
not a vigorous plant ; we are in general very poorly paid. This last
year my whole gains do not exceed £200." But the darkest hour,
it is said, is nearest the dawn. Watt had passed through a long
night, and a gleam of sunshine was at hand. He was urged to proceed to Birmingham to superintend the manufacture of his engines,
one of which was nearly completed. He arrived at Birmingham in
the summer of 1774, and in December he wrote to his father, now
an old man, still resident at Greenock : "The business I am here
about has turned out rather successful ; that is to say, that the fire-
engine I have invented is now going, and answers much better than
any other that has yet been made, and I expect that the invention
will be very beneficial to me." Such was Watt's modest announcement of the practical success of the greatest invention of the eighteenth century !

His partner, who proved himself such an able second, had the rare
quality of a first-rate man of business. Mr. Boulton was not a mere

buyer and seller, but a great designer, contriver, and organizer. His own original trade was that of a manufacturer of plated goods, ormolu, and works in steel. He subsequently turned his attention to improving the machinery for coining, and attained, says M. Arago, to such rapidity and perfection of execution, that he was employed by the British Government to recoin the whole copper specie of the kingdom. His methods were established, under his superintendence, in several mints abroad, as well as in the National Mint of England. With a keen eye for details, he combined a large and comprehensive grasp of intellect. Whilst his senses were so acute that, sitting in his office at Soho, he could at once detect the slightest derangement in the machinery of his vast establishment, his power of imagination enabled him to look along extensive lines of possible action throughout Europe, America, and the Indies. He was equally skillful in the fabrication of a button and in the establishment of the motive power that was to revolutionize the industrial operations of the world. In short, he was a man of various gifts, nicely balanced and proportioned,—the best of tradesmen, a patron of art and science, the friend of philosophers and statesmen. With all his independent titles to distinction, he esteemed the steam-engine of his friend the pride of his establishment. Once, when he was in the company of Sir Walter Scott, he said, in reply to some remark: "That's like the old saying, In every corner of the world you will find a Scot, a rat, and a Newcastle grindstone." This touched the national spirit of the novelist, and he retorted, "You should have added, *and a Brummagem button.*" "We make something better in Birmingham than buttons," replied Boulton,—"we make steam-engines;" and when he next met Scott, he showed that he had not forgiven the disparaging remark. Boswell, who visited Soho in 1776, shortly after the manufacture of steam-engines had been commenced there, was struck by the vastness and contrivance of the machinery. "I shall never forget," he says, "Mr. Boulton's expression to me, when surveying the works: 'I sell here, sir, what all the world desires to have,—POWER.'" "He had," continues Boswell, "about seven hundred people at work. I contemplated him as an iron chieftain; and he seemed to be a father of his tribe. One of the men came to him complaining grievously of his landlord for having distrained his goods. 'Your landlord is in the right, Smith,' said Boulton; 'but I'll tell you what,—find you a friend who will lay down one-half of your rent, and I'll lay down the other, and you shall have your goods again.'" Mrs. Schimmel-Penninck, a native of Birmingham, gives, in her autobiography, a lively description of his person. "He was tall, and of a noble appearance; his temperament was sanguine, with that slight mixture of the phlegmatic which imparts calmness and dignity; his manners were eminently open and cordial; he took the lead in conversations, and, with a social heart, had a grandiose manner like that arising from position, wealth, and habitual command. He went among his people like a monarch bestowing largess."

Not long after Watt settled at Birmingham, he married his second wife, Miss Macgregor, the daughter of a citizen of Glasgow. The precise date of the marriage is not stated by Mr. Muirhead, but it seems to have been in 1776, and at any rate took place too early to render possible an incident told by Mrs. Schimmel-Penninck, that when Watt was mourning the loss of his first wife, Miss Macgregor —then a girl, according to the story, three or four years old —"came up to his knee, and looking in his face, begged him not to grieve, for she would be his little wife, and make him happy." This lady was a thrifty Scotch housewife, and such was her passion for cleanliness, that she taught her pet dogs to wipe their feet upon the doormat. Her propensity was carried to a pitch which often fretted her son by the restraints it imposed; and once when a lady apologized to him for the confusion in which he found her house, he exclaimed, "I love *dirt !*" But Mrs. Watt was a partner worthy of her husband, and with the revival of his domestic felicity, and surrounded by all the appliances for perfecting his steam-engine, he was for a brief space in a happier position than he had enjoyed for many years past.

The mechanics of Birmingham were the chief workers in metal in England. The best tools and arms of the kingdom had been manufactured there almost from time immemorial, and the artisans possessed an aptitude for skilled manipulation which had descended to them from their fathers, like an inheritance. Watt, as we have seen, had found to his sorrow that there was no such class of workmen in Scotland. The consequence was, that the very first engine erected at Soho was a greater triumph than all that Watt had previously been able to accomplish. Some of the most valuable copper mines in Cornwall had been drowned out ; Boulton immediately wrote to the miners, and informed them of the success of the new invention. A deputation of Cornish miners went down to Birmingham to look at the engine. There could be no doubt as to its efficiency, but it was dear, and it was some time before any orders were given. Boulton saw that, to produce any large result, he must himself supply the capital, and he entered into an arrangement with the miners; by which he agreed to be at the whole cost, provided he was allowed as royalty *one-third* of the value of the ascertained saving of coal, as compared with Newcomen's best engine. The bargain having been struck, Watt went into Cornwall to superintend the work. The impression produced by one of the earliest engines he erected is thus described in one of his letters to Mr. Boulton: "The velocity, violence, magnitude, and horrible noise of the engine, give unusual satisfaction to all beholders, believers or not. I have once or twice trimmed the engine to end its strokes gently and make less noise ; but Mr. ——— cannot sleep unless it seems quite furious, so I have left it to the engineman. And, by the by, the noise seems to convey great ideas of its power to the ignorant, who seem to be no more taken with modest merit in an engine than in a man." Whilst in Cornwall Watt, whose mechanical ingenuity was inexhaustible, invented a counter to ascertain the saving effected. It was attached to the main beam and marked the number of strokes, which was the measure of the payment. The register, which was contrived to keep the record for an entire year, was inclosed in a locked box, and thus fraud was prevented. It was shortly found that the saving of coal by the new engine was nearly three-fourths of the whole quantity formerly consumed, or equal to an annual saving on the Chacewater engine of £7,200. Such a result did not fail to tell, and orders for engines soon came in at Soho; but the capital invested by Mr. Boulton amounted to some £47,000, before any profits began to be derived from their sale.

As some years had been expended in unremunerative experiments one of the first necessities, when it was apparent that the engine could be made to answer, was to obtain an extension of the patent, and in 1775 an Act of Parliament was passed to preserve the rights of the patentees till the year 1800, in consideration of the great utility of the invention, and the trouble and expense incurred in completing it. It was long before it yielded any return. In 1780 Watt and Boulton were still out of pocket, and in 1783 they had not realized a profit. But the extension of the patent gave a stimulus to the busy brain of the inventor; and he continued to devise improvement upon improvement. The application of the powers of steam to give a rotatory motion to mills, had from the first formed the subject of his particular attention, and in his patent of 1769 he described a method of producing continued movement in one direction, which Mr. Boulton proposed to employ for working boats along the canals. A continuous movement of machinery had indeed to some extent been secured by the use of the steam-engine, which was employed to pump up water, the fall of which turned water-wheels in the usual way. But Watt's object was to effect this by the direct action of the engine itself, and thus to supersede, in a great measure, the use of water, as well as of animal power. This he at length accomplished by contrivances which are embodied in the patents he took out between the years 1781 and 1785. Among other devices, these patents include the rotatory motion of the sun and planet-wheels, the expansive principle of working steam, the double engine, the parallel motion, the smokeless furnace, and the governor,—the whole forming a series of beautiful inventions, combining the results of philosophical research and mechanical ingenuity to an extent, we believe, without a parallel in modern times.

The idea of the double-acting engine occurred to Watt in 1767, but he kept it back in consequence of the difficulty "he had encountered in teaching others the construction and use of the single engine

and in overcoming prejudices;" in the single engine the force
which drew up the piston was the counterpoise on the pump-
gear, which merely sufficed to put the piston in a position for the
effective down-stroke. The working powers of the engine were
therefore idle during half the time, or while the piston was ascending. By making the upper part of the cylinder as well as the lower
communicate with the condenser, he alternately formed a vacuum
above and below, and the piston in its ascending stroke, beyond the
addition of its own weight, experienced no more resistance than it
had previously done in the down-stroke. While the steam was condensing at the top of the cylinder fresh steam was let in below, and
drove the piston up. The process was then reversed. The steam at
the bottom of the cylinder was condensed, and fresh steam was let
in at the top to drive the piston down. Thus every movement was
one of working power, and time was no longer lost while the engine
was employed, as it were, in gathering up its strength for the stroke.
The expansive principle, which effects an immense saving of steam,
also occurred to Watt as early as 1767. It simply consists in cutting off the flow of steam from the boiler when the cylinder is partly
filled, and allowing the rest of the stroke to be accomplished by the
expansive power of the steam already supplied. As the elastic or
moving force of the steam diminishes as it expands, a stroke of the
piston upon this plan is not as powerful as a stroke upon the old;
but the saving of steam is in a much greater proportion than the
diminution of the power.

The circumstances connected with the invention of the sun and
planet motion are illustrative of Watt's fertility of resources. The best
method of securing continuous rotation which occurred to him was
the crank, —not, as he says, an original invention, for "the true inventor of the crank rotative motion was the man, who unfortunately has
not been deified, that first contrived the common foot-lathe. The
applying it to the engine was merely taking a knife to cut cheese
which had been made to cut bread." Models of a plan for adapting
it to the steam-engine were constructing at Soho, when one Saturday
evening a number of the workmen, according to custom, proceeded
to drink their ale at the Wagon and Horses, a little low-browed, old-
fashioned public-house, still standing in the village of Handsworth,
close to Soho. As the beer began to tell, one Cartwright, a pattern-
maker, who was afterwards hanged, talked of Watt's contrivance for
producing rotatory motion, and to illustrate his meaning proceeded
to make a sketch of the crank upon the kitchen table with a bit of
chalk. A person in the assumed garb of a workman, who sat in the
kitchen corner and greedily drank in the account, posted off to
London, and forthwith secured a patent for the crank, which Watt,
"being much engaged in other business," had neglected to do at the
moment. He was exceedingly wroth at the piracy, averring that
Wasbrough had "stolen the invention from him by the most

infamous means;" but he was never at fault, and, reviving an old idea he had conceived, he perfected in a few weeks his Sun and Planet motion. Eventually, however, when Wasbrough's patent had expired, Watt reverted to the employment of the simpler crank, because of its less liability to get out of order. Its mere adaptation to the steam-engine ought not to have been protected by a patent at all, any more than the knife which was made to cut bread should be capable of being patented for every new substance to which its edge is applied.

The mode by which Watt secured the accurate rectilinear motion of the ascending and descending piston-rod, by means of the Parallel Motion, has been greatly and justly admired. "My soul," he said, "abhors calculations, geometry, and all other abstract sciences;" but when an end was to be gained, he could apply the principles of geometry with exquisite skill. The object was to contrive that, whilst the end of the beam was moving alternately up and down in part of a circle, the end of the piston-rod connected with it should preserve a perfectly perpendicular direction. This was accomplished by means which can hardly be made intelligible in mere verbal description; but so beautiful is the movement, that Watt said that when he saw his device in action he received from it the same pleasure that usually accompanies the first view of the invention of another person. "Though I am not over anxious after fame," he wrote in 1808, "yet I am more proud of the parallel motion than of any other mechanical contrivance I have ever made."

In spite of the outward success which attended Watt, his disposition did not permit him to be happy in the midst of bustle and rivalries. "The struggles," he wrote to Dr. Black in December, 1778, "which we have had with natural difficulties, and with the ignorance, prejudices, and villainies of mankind, have been very great; but I hope are now nearly come to an end." In this hope he was disappointed, for they continued unabated. The perpetual thought which the engine required to bring it to perfection, and the large correspondence in which the business of the establishment involved him, had to be performed under the oppression of those sick-headaches which were the bane of his existence. He was sometimes so overcome by them, that he would sit by the fireside for hours together, with his head leaning on his elbow, and scarcely able to utter a word. In 1782 his father died, and his inevitable absence from his bedside weighed upon his spirits. His despondency gathered strength with years, till in 1786 it appeared to have reached its climax. "In the anguish of his mind, amid the vexations occasioned by new and unsuccessful schemes, like Lovelace, I 'curse my inventions,' and almost wish, if we could gather our money together, that somebody else should succeed in getting our trade from us." So he wrote to Mr. Boulton in April, and in June his account of himself was sadder still: "I have been quite effete and listless, neither daring to face business nor capable of it; my head and memory failing me much; my stable of hobby-horses pulled down, and the horses given to the dogs for carrion. I have had serious thoughts of throwing down the burden I find myself unable to carry, and, perhaps, if other sentiments had not been stronger, should have thought of throwing off the mortal coil. Solomon said that in the increase of knowledge there is increase of sorrow: if he had substituted *business* for knowledge it would have been perfectly true." These wailing notes of a mind radically wretched were renewed by the attempts to pirate his inventions. Watt was so fruitful in contrivances, that the fortunes of many ordinary mechanicians were made by their pickings and stealings from him. When he was an unknown Glasgow artisan, his drawing-machine had been boldly appropriated by a London mathematical-instrument maker; his micrometer had been purloined by another pilferer of the same class; his crank had been stolen from him through the instrumentality of his own workmen; and now the pirates were endeavoring to make a prize of the condensing-engine itself; which had cost him full twenty years of anxiety and labor. The Cornish miners especially, who had derived immense pecuniary advantages from its adoption, sought on the most frivolous pretenses to evade the payment of that portion of the saving which they had stipulated to pay to Boulton and Watt. A baser instance of unprincipled greediness is hardly to be found in the annals of trade. "We have been so beset with plagiaries," Watt wrote to Dr. Black, "that, if I had not a very good memory of my doing it, their impudent assertions would lead me to doubt whether I was the author of any improvement on the steam-engine, and the ill-will of those we have most essentially served, whether such improvements have not been highly prejudicial to the commonwealth!" Though the patentees were invariably successful, the vindication of their rights proved a heavy fine; their legal expenses during only the last four years of their patent having amounted to between five and six thousand pounds. The peace of mind which the lawsuits cost Watt was far more serious than the cost in money. His feelings during the pending trial of 1796 are described by himself as less acute than what he had been accustomed to undergo on more insignificant occasions. "Yet I remained," he says, "after the trial, nearly as much depressed as if we had lost it. The stimulus to action was gone, and but for the attentions of my friends I ran some risk of falling into stupidity." In 1803, "after he had retired with a very moderate fortune that he might enjoy the quiet for which alone he was fitted," he ascribed his incapacity for further exertion "to the vexation he had endured for many years from his harassing lawsuit." Whoever is tempted to envy a great inventor would surely be cured of his passion by the contemplation of the life of him who was the chief of the race. Whilst he was struggling with difficulties at Glasgow, his friend Dr. Hutton had strongly dissuaded him from proceeding further with his unprofitable and distressing work. "Invention," said he, "is only for those who live by the public; or who, from pride, would choose to leave a legacy to the public. It is not a thing that will pay, under a system where the rule is to be best paid for the thing that is easiest done." But to invent was the habitual operation of Watt's intellect, and neither the admonitions of friends, nor his experience of the miseries it entailed upon him, could turn his mind aside from its natural bent.

Among his minor works, the contrivance of which formed the pastime of his leisure hours, were his machine for copying letters, his instrument for measuring the specific gravity of fluids, his regulator lamp, his plan of heating buildings by steam, and his machine for drying linen, invented for his father-in-law, Mr. Macgregor, a dyer at Glasgow. He was also occupied with speculations respecting an arithmetical machine, and early threw out the suggestion of a spiral oar for the propulsion of ships. His specification of the steam-engine included a steam-carriage for use on common roads, and he had many discussions with his assistant, William Murdock, and his friend, Lovell Edgeworth, on the subject.

His residence at Birmingham was greatly cheered by the society of men of eminence in science, literature, and art. Boulton and himself formed a center of attraction to many kindred minds, and the meetings of the Lunar Society, at Soho House, were long remembered as among the most delightful things of their kind. Lovell Edgeworth, himself a member, has thus described the group: "Mr. Keir, with his knowledge of the world and good sense; Dr. Small, with his benevolence and profound sagacity; Wedgwood, with his unceasing industry, experimental variety, and calm investigation; Boulton, with his mobility, quick perception, and bold adventure; Watt, with his strong inventive faculty, undeviating steadiness, and large resources; Darwin, with his imagination, science, and poetical excellence; and Day, with his unwearied research after truth, his integrity, and eloquence,—formed, altogether, such a society as few men have had the good fortune to live with,—such an assemblage of friends as fewer still have had the happiness to possess and keep through life." To these distinguished members others were afterwards added, among whom may be mentioned Dr. Priestley, the discoverer of oxygen and other gases; Mr. Galton the ornithologist, and Dr. Withering, the botanist. In the meetings of this society originated Watt's experiments on water; and it is now placed beyond a doubt, that he was the first to promulgate the true theory of its composition, though Cavendish had arrived, by independent research, at the same result.

The designation of "Lunar Society" was converted into "Lunatic Society" by the people, and when the riots of 1791 broke out, one of the watchwords of the mob was, "No philosophers!" Sir Samuel Romilly says that some persons even painted the denunciation on their houses. The Birmingham folks, during the last century, were certainly good haters. When the firebrand Dr. Sacheverell went down to Birmingham and called upon the people to "build up Zion," they responded to the exhortation by gutting a Dissenters' meeting-house in the neighborhood. So, again, at the public dinner which was held in the town to celebrate the anniversary of the French Revolution, the mob, who took the loyal side of the question, rose, pulled down two dissenting meeting-houses, and burned or sacked the houses of some of the principal inhabitants;—among others, those of Mr. Taylor, one of the chief employers of skilled labor in the town; Mr. Hutton, the bookseller and historian; and several more. But their principal fury was directed against the "philosophers,"—especially Dr. Priestley, whose house and library they destroyed, and were busily engaged in plundering the house of Dr. Withering when the military arrived. Watt was included in the proscription, and, apprehending an attack upon his house, he had the Soho workmen armed for Mr. Boulton's defense and his own. "Though our principles," said he, writing to his friend De Luc, "are well known, as friends to the established government and enemies to republican principles, and should have been our protection from a mob whose watchword was 'Church and King,' yet our safety was principally owing to most of the Dissenters living on the south of the town; for, after the first moments, they did not seem over nice in their discrimination of religion or principles. I, among others, was pointed out as a Presbyterian, though I never was in a meeting-house in Birmingham, and Mr. Boulton is well known as a Churchman. We had everything most portable packed up, fearing the worst; however, all is well with us." The circumstance is worth recording, not only as an incident in the life of Watt, but as a specimen of the insane and ignorant ideas which animate mobs.

Watt's later years were years of comparative peace, but of bereavement. One by one his early friends dropped away; the pride and hope of his heart, his son Gregory, died also; and the old man was left almost alone. Fragile though his frame had been through life, he survived the most robust among his associates. Roebuck, Boulton, Darwin, and Withering went before him, as well as his dear friends Robison and Black. Black had watched to the last, with tender interest, the advancing reputation and prosperity of his protégé. When Robison returned from London, and told him of the issue of Watt's suit with Hornblower, for the protection of his patent-right, the kind old Doctor was delighted even to tears. "It's very foolish," he exclaimed, "but I can't help it when I hear of anything good to Jamie Watt." Watt, in his turn, said of Black, "To him I owe, in great measure, my being what I am; he taught me to reason and experiment in Natural Philosophy." Dr. Black expired so peacefully, that his servant, in describing his death, said that he had "given over living." having departed with a basin of milk upon his knee, which remained unspilled. "We may all pray," was the comment of Watt, "that our latter end may be like his; he has truly gone to sleep in the arms of his Creator."

Towards the close of his life, Watt was distressed by the apprehension that his mental faculties were deserting him, and remarked to Dr. Darwin, "Of all the evils of age, the loss of the few mental faculties one possessed in youth is the most grievous." To test his memory, he again commenced the study of German, which he had allowed himself to forget; and speedily acquired such proficiency as enabled him to read the language with comparative ease. But he gave stronger evidence of the integrity of his powers. When, in his seventy-fifth year, he was consulted by a company at Glasgow as to the mode of conveying water from a peninsula across the Clyde to the company's engines at Dalmarnock, a difficulty which appeared to them almost insurmountable, the plan suggested by Watt proved that his remarkable ingenuity remained unimpaired by age. It was necessary to fit the pipes through which the water passed to the uneven and shifting bed of the river, and Watt, taking the tail of the lobster for his model, forwarded a plan of a tube of iron similarly articulated, which was executed and laid down with complete success.

A few years later, when close upon his eightieth year, the aged mechanician formed one of a party assembled in Edinburgh, at which Sir Walter Scott was present. He delighted the Northern literati with his kindly cheerfulness, not less than he astonished them by the extent and profundity of his information. "The alert, kind, benevolent old man," says Scott, "had his attention alive to every one's question, his information at every one's command. His talents and fancy overflowed on every subject. One gentleman was a deep philologist,—he talked with him on the origin of the alphabet, as if he had been coeval with Cadmus; another, a celebrated critic,—you would have said the old man had studied political economy and belles-lettres all his life; of science it is unnecessary to speak,—it was his own distinguished walk." The vast extent of his knowledge was remarked by all who came in contact with him. "It seemed," says Jeffrey, "as if every subject that was casually started had been that which he had been occupied in studying." Yet, though no man was more ready to communicate knowledge, none could be less ambitious of displaying it. "He was," says Mrs. Schimmel-Penninck, in the vivid portrait she has drawn of him in her Autobiography, "one of the most complete specimens of the melancholic temperament. His head was generally bent forward or leaning on his hand in meditation, his shoulders stooping and his chest falling in, his limbs lank and unmuscular, and his complexion sallow. His utterance was slow and unimpassioned, deep and low in tone, with a broad Scottish accent; his manners gentle, modest, and unassuming. In a company where he was not known; unless spoken to, he might have tranquilly passed the whole time in pursuing his own meditations. When he entered a room, men of letters, men of science, nay, military men, artists, ladies, even little children, thronged round him. I remember a celebrated Swedish artist having been instructed by him that rats' whiskers make the most pliant painting-brushes; ladies would appeal to him on the best means of devising grates, curing smoking chimneys, warming their houses, and obtaining fast colors. I can speak from experience of his teaching me how to make a dulcimer and improve a Jew's-harp." What Jeffrey said of the steam-engine may be applied to the conversation of its parent, that, like the trunk of an elephant, it could pick up a pin or rend an oak.

Watt returned to his little workshop at Heathfield, to proceed with the completion of his diminishing-machine for copying busts and statues. His habit was, immediately on rising, to answer all letters requiring attention; then, after breakfast, to proceed into the workshop adjoining his bedroom, attired in his woolen surtout, his leather apron, and the rustic hat which he had worn some forty years, and there go on with his machine. He succeeded with it so far as to produce specimens of its performances, which he distributed amongst his friends, jocularly describing them as "the productions of a young artist just entering into his eighty-third year." But the hand of the workman was stopped by death. The machine remained unfinished, and, what is a singular testimony to the skill and perseverance of a man who had invented so much, it is almost his only unfinished work.

He was fully conscious of his approaching end, and expressed from time to time his sincere gratitude to Divine Providence for the blessings which he had been permitted to enjoy, for his length of days, and his exemption from the infirmities of age. "I am very sensible," said he, to the mourning friends who had assembled round his death-bed, "of the attachment you show me, and I hasten to thank you for it, as I am now come to my last illness." He passed quietly away from the world on the 19th of August, 1819, in his eighty-third year. A statue by Chantrey—perhaps the greatest work of that master—has been placed in Handsworth Church, where Watt lies buried, and justifies the compliment paid to the sculptor, that he "cut breath;" for when uncovered before the old servants assembled round it at Soho, it so powerfully reminded them of their master, that they "lifted up their voices and wept." Watt has been fortunate in his monumental honors. The colossal statue in Westminster Abbey, also from the chisel of Chantrey, bears upon it an epitaph from the pen of Brougham, which is beyond all comparison the finest lapidary inscription in the English language, and among its other signal merits has one which appertains rather to its subject than its author, that, lofty as is the eulogy, every word of it is strictly true.

ROBERT STEPHENSON.

ABOUT forty years since, a little boy, the son of a colliery engineman at Killingworth, dressed in a suit of homely gray stuff, cut out by his father, was accustomed to ride to Newcastle daily upon a donkey, for the purpose of attending school there. Years passed, and the boy became a man knownto world-wide fame as Robert Stephenson, the engineer. He died, and on the 14th of October, 1859, he was laid to rest in Westminster Abbey, side by side with the departed kings, statesmen, and great men of his country.

Only ten years before, the remains of George Stephenson, the father, were quietly interred in a small church on the outskirts of the town of Chesterfield, followed to the grave principally by his own work-people. The event excited little interest beyond the bounds of that secluded locality. Yet George Stephenson, thus obscurely buried, was the inventor of the passenger locomotive, and the founder of the now gigantic railway system of England, and of the world: and it is only within the last few years that the public have learned from his biography how great a man then passed from the earth. But the honors which George Stephenson failed to receive during his life and at his death, and which, in the strength of his self-dependence, he would have been the last to seek, have at length not unworthily been reflected upon his eminently meritorious son; and those who hereafter read his tablet and contemplate his monument in Westminster Abbey will probably not fail to remember that Robert Stephenson was himself one of the best products of his great father's manly affection, his noble character, and his indefatigable industry.

Every reader now knows the story of the father's life,—his early encounter with poverty and difficulty, his strenuous endeavors after self-education, his determination to gain "insight," into all the details of his business, his patience, his bravery, his self-discipline and self-reliance. But greatest of all was his manly love for his only son;

and his resolution, formed almost as soon as the boy was born, and
steadily acted out in his life, that no labor, nor pains, nor self-denial
should be spared to furnish him with the best education that it was
in his power to bestow. His own words on the subject are memorable. "In the earlier period of my career," said he, "when Robert
was a little boy, I saw how deficient I was in education, and I made
up my mind that he should not labor under the same defect, but
that I would put him to a good school, and give him a liberal training. I was, however, a poor man; and how do you think I managed?
I betook myself to mending my neighbors' clocks and watches at
nights, after my daily labor was done, and thus I procured the means
of educating my son."

The father, moreover, taught the son to work with him, and
trained him as it were to educate himself. When a little fellow not
big enough to reach so high as to put a clock-head on, his father
would make him mount a chair for the purpose; and to "help father," became the proudest work which the boy then, and ever after,
could take part in. This daily and unceasing example of industry
and application, working on before the boy's eyes in the person of a
loving and beloved father, imprinted itself deeply upon his mind,
in characters never to be effaced. A spirit of self-improvement took
possession of him, which continued to influence him through life;
and to the close of his career he was proud to confess that, if his success had been great, it was mainly to the example and training of
his father that he owed it.

When Robert went to Mr. Bruce's school at Newcastle, he was a
rough, unpolished country lad, speaking the broad dialect of the
pitmen; and the other boys would tease him occasionally, for the
purpose of provoking an outburst of his Killingworth Doric. But he
was kindly of disposition, and a diligent pupil; Mr. Bruce frequently holding him up to the laggards of the school as an example of
good conduct and industry. He was accustomed to spend much of
his spare time at the rooms of the Literary and Philosophical Institute; and when he went home in the evenings he would recount to his
father the results of his reading. Sometimes he was allowed to take
to Killingworth a volume of the "Repertory of Arts and Sciences,"
which the father and son studied together, George laying great stress
upon his son's being able to read and understand the plans and di-
agrams without reference to the written descriptions. Sometimes
they tried chemical experiments together, assisted by Wigham, a
neighboring farmer's son; and occasionally Robert experimented on
his own account, as, for instance, upon the cows in Wigham's inclosure, which he electrified by means of his electric kite, making
them run about the field with their tails on end, and on an other occasion upon his father's Galloway when standing at the cottage door
nearly knocking the pony down by the smartness of the shock,

George was about this time occupied with the invention of his safety lamp, and Robert was present and assisted in making many of the experiments upon the fire-damp brought from Killingworth pits. On one occasion, George was engaged in experimenting by means of a gasometer and glass receivers borrowed from the Newcastle Institute; Nicholas Wood being appointed to turn the cocks, and Robert to time the experiment. The flame being observed to descend in the tube, the word was given to turn the cock, but unfortunately Wood turned it the wrong way, the gas exploded, and the apparatus was blown to pieces, though fortunately no one was hurt. At other times, Robert was engaged in embodying in a practicl shape the drawings of machines and instruments which he found described in the books he read ; among other things, constructing a theodolite spirit-lever, on which he engraved the words, "Robert Stephenson, fecit." Another of his works, while he was at Bruce's school, was the sun-dial, the joint work of father and son, constructed after much study and labor, and eventually fixed over the cottage door at Killingworth, where it is still to be seen. Not long since Mr. Stephenson visited the place with some friends, and pointed out the very desk in the little room of the cottage at which he had studied the plan of the dial and calculated the latitude of his village.

The youth left school well grounded in the ordinary branches of education, and an adept in arithmetic, geography, and algebra. In his after life, he with good reason attached much importance to the thorough training in mathematics which he received at Bruce's school, and considered that it had been the foundation of much of his success as an engineer in the higher walks of the profession. His father at first destined him for the business of a coal-miner, and with that object apprenticed him to Nicholas Wood, then chief viewer of Killingworth. While thus engaged, Robert acquired a familiarity with underground work, which afterwards proved of much value to him; and, in the evenings, after the day's work was over, he pursued his studies in mechanics under the eye of his father, who had by this time been advanced to the post of chief engine-wright of the colliery.

The Killingworth locomotive was now in full work, and Robert became familiar with its every detail. The possible adaptation of the engine to more important uses than the hauling of coal to the shipping-place, the improvement of the steam-blast (employed in all the engines constructed by Stephenson subsequent to the year 1815), and the enlargement of the heating surface, so as to produce a more rapid supply of steam, formed the subject of repeated evening discussions in the cottage of the Stephensons. Of the two, the youth was at that time by much the most sanguine, his father "holding him back" by setting up all manner of objections for him to answer, and thus in the most effectual way cultivating his faculties and stimulating his inventiveness. It was a happy time for both, full of discipline, co-operation, self-improvement, and steadily advancing mechanical ability.

The father, however, was not satisfied with the knowledge which h's son might thus laboriously acquire by studying in company with himself at Killingworth. He was fully conscious of his own want of scientific knowledge, which had hampered him at every stage of his career. Above all things, he desired that Robert should be well grounded in the principles of natural science ; for which purpose he felt it would be necessary to place him under disciplined teachers. He resolved, accordingly, to send Robert to Edinburgh University, where he spent the winter and summer sessions of 1820-21, attending the classes of Natural Philosophy under Sir John Leslie, Mineralogy under Professor Jamieson, and Chemistry under Dr. Hope. Young Stephenson was one of the most diligent and hardworking students of his year. He took copious notes of all the lectures, which he was accustomed carefully to write out, and afterwards to consult, even to the close of his life. One evening, a few years ago, an engineering friend was discussing with him in his library in Gloucester Square some scientific point, when Mr. Stephenson rose, and took down from the shelves a thick volume, for the purpose of consulting it. On the question being asked, " What have we here?" he replied, "When I went to college, I knew the difficulty my father had in collecting money to send me there; before going I studied shorthand, and while at Edinburgh I took down verbatim every lecture I attended ; every evening before I went to bed I transcribed those lectures word for word, and you see the result in that range of books."

It was a good custom of Professor Jamieson, at the close of each session, to select the most diligent and meritorious of his pupils to accompany him in a botanical and geological excursion over some of the most interesting parts of Scotland; and Robert Stephenson was one of these favored pupils at the close of the session of 1820-21. Only about a year before his death, when he was making an excursion in his yacht with a party of friends through the Caledonian Canal, he took occasion to point out some of the ground which he had gone over during that delightful excursion with his professor, and he then expressed the practical advantages which he had derived from studying the great works of the Creator upon the chart of Nature itself. The student's excursion ended, Robert returned to Killingworth; and his father was a proud man when his son reported the progress he had made, and, above all, when he laid before him the prize for mathematics which he had won at the University. The cost of the year's education was about eighty pounds ; but though a large sum in the estimation of both father and son at the time, George then and afterwards declared that it was one of the best investments of money which he had ever made.

We have been thus particular in describing the several stages in the education of Robert Stephenson, and the active part which his father took in the process, because it was thus that the foundations of his character were laid. The young man was now to enter by himself upon the road of life, fortified by good example, his habits well trained, his faculties well disciplined, and fully conscious that the issue rested mainly with himself. For several years more, however, he remained under his father's eye, passing through the admirable discipline of the workshop, to which he himself in after years was accustomed to attach the greatest importance. At the meeting of Mechanical Engineers, held at Newcastle, in August, 1858, he used these words: "Having been brought up originally as a mechanical engineer, and seen perhaps as much as any one of the other branches of the profession, I feel justified in insisting that the civil engineering department is best founded upon the mechanical knowledge obtained in the workshop. I have ever been fully conscious how greatly my civil engineering has been modified by the mechanical knowledge which I acquired from my father; and the further my experience has advanced, the more have I been convinced that it is necessary to educate an engineer in the workshop. That is the education emphatically which is calculated to render the engineer most intelligent, most useful, and the fullest of resources in times of difficulty."

In 1824 George Stephenson was busily engaged in the construction of the Stockton and Darlington Railway; and at the same time Robert was employed in the locomotive manufactory already commenced at Newcastle, in superintending the construction of No. 1 engine, the "Active," for that railway; the same engine that was lately placed upon a pedestal in front of the Darlington station. He was also busy designing the fixed engine for the Brusselton incline, which he completed by the end of the year, when he left England for a time to take charge of the engines and machinery of a mining company newly established in Colombia, South America. Severe study and close application had begun to tell upon his health, and his father consented that he should accept the situation which had been offered him, in the hope that the change of scene and occupation might restore him to health and strength, though ill able to dispense with his valuable assistance at that important crisis in his own career.

The Darlington line was finished and opened, and its success was such as to encourage the Liverpool merchants shortly after to project their undertaking of a railway between that town and Manchester. The difficulties encountered in obtaining the act, and in constructing the railway across Chat Moss, are among the most interesting chapters in George Stephenson's life, and need not be adverted to here. Then began the battle of the locomotive, and the keen discussions between the advocates of fixed and traveling engines, George Stephenson standing almost alone in his advocacy of the latter. At this juncture he wrote to his son, urging him to return home, as the fate of the locomotive hung upon the issue. Accordingly we find Robert Stephenson again returned to England, and in charge of the locomotive manufactory at Newcastle, by the end of the year 1827. From this time forward Robert was as his father's right hand, fortifying his arguments, illustrating his views, embodying his ideas in definite shapes, writing his reports to the directors, exposing the fallacies contained in the arguments put forward by the advocates of fixed engines, and in all ways energetically fighting by the side of his father the battle of the locomotive. At length their joint perseverance produced its effect; a prize was offered for the best locomotive, and George and Robert Stephenson's engine, the "Rocket," won the prize at Rainhill. Mr. Booth furnished the idea of the multitubular boiler; George Stephenson furnished the general plan of the engine; but the working out of the whole details, on which so much depended, was carried out by Robert Stephenson himself in the manufactory at Newcastle. Successful, however, though the performances of that engine were, it was but the beginning of Robert Stephenson's labors. For many years after, he continued to devote himself to perfecting the locomotive in all its details; and it was astonishing to observe the rapidity of the improvements effected, every engine turned out of the Stephenson workshops exhibiting an advance upon its predecessor in point of speed, power, and working efficiency.

The success of railways being now proved, railway projects multiplied in all directions, and Mr. Stephenson then decided to enter upon the business of a civil engineer; the first railway laid out by him being the Leicester and Swanington line; after which, in conjunction with his father, he was appointed engineer of the London and Birmingham Railway. It is related as an illustration of his conscientious perseverance in laying out this line, that, in the course of his examination of the country between London and Birmingham, he walked over the whole intervening districts upwards of twenty times. The difficulties encountered in carrying out this undertaking in those early days of railway-making were of the most formidable kind, the most important being the construction of the Kilsby Tunnel; but by perseverance and skill added to his previous knowledge of mining operations, which proved of great service to him, they were all surmounted; and the success of the London and Birmingham Railway speedily introduced our young engineer to a vast and prosperous business, in which he continued to hold the very first place to the close of his life. It was stated in his presence at the celebration of the opening of the High Level Bridge at Newcastle a few years ago, that not less than eighteen hundred and fifty miles of railway had then been constructed after his designs and under his superintendence, at an outlay of seventy millions sterling.

His Parliamentary business was necessarily extensive. In the session of 1846 he appeared as the engineer for no fewer than thirty-three schemes; and he might have been engineer for as many more, if he would have allowed his name to appear in connection with them. On all questions of railway working and railway construction, his evidence was eagerly sought and highly valued. Into the controversy respecting the comparative merits of the narrow and broad gauges, and the locomotive as compared with the atmospheric system, he threw himself with more than ordinary scientific keenness. He was the head and front of the opposition to his friend Brunel's innovations, and the result proved that his views were correct. The most vehement Parliamentary struggle of this kind occurred in the session of 1845, when the rival schemes of Brunel and Stephenson were before Parliament,—the one promoting the Northumberland Atmospheric, and the other the Newcastle and Berwick (locomotive) line. The former was recommended to the Commons Committee by Mr. Sergeant Wrangham, as calculated to be "a *respectable* line, and not one that was to be converted into a road for the accommodation of the coal-owners of the district;" and Mr. Brunel summed up his evidence in these words: "In short, rapidity, comfort, safety, and economy are its recommendations." Mr. Stephenson was examined at great length, and his evidence must have had its due weight with the Committee, who passed the preamble of his bill; and the shareholders were thus saved much useless expenditure, for after the lapse of a few years the atmospheric system was everywhere abandoned.

The High Level Bridge at Newcastle formed part of the east coast system of railways, of which Mr. Stephenson was then the engineer, extending from London to Berwick. This noble work occupied three years in construction, and it was opened by her Majesty on the 19th of August, 1849. It is a much finer architectural structure than any of the great iron bridges subsequently erected by Mr. Stephenson; combining, also, in a remarkable degree, the qualities of strength, rigidity, and durability. The bridge and viaduct approaching it are of great length, being, together, about four thousand feet. The bridge spans the Tyne between Newcastle and Gateshead, and passes completely over the roofs of the houses which fill the valley on either side the river. The prospect from the bridge is most striking; the Tyne, full of shipping, lies a hundred and thirty feet below, the funnels and masts of steamers being visible, when the smoke allows, far down the river. Seen from beneath, the bridge is very majestic, the impress of power being grandly stamped upon it. One of the most important features of the bridge—characteristic of all Mr. Stephenson's structures, but especially so in this case—is its utility. It is a double bridge, forming a direct road, connecting the busy towns of Newcastle and Gateshead with each other, at the same time that it is an integral part of the railway system along which the traffic by the east coast between England and Scotland is enabled to pass without break of gauge; and it will probably remain, for many

centuries to come, the finest and most appropriate monument in
Newcastle to the native genius of the Stephensons.

Another of Mr. Stephenson's great structures is his well-known
Britannia Bridge across the Menai Straits,—a masterly work, the result
of laborious calculation, founded on painstaking experiment, combined with eminent constructive genius and high moral and intellectual courage. The original idea embodied by Mr. Stephenson in
this bridge was the application of wrought-iron tubes in the form of
an aerial tunnel, for the purpose of spanning this arm of the sea at
such a height as to enable vessels of large burden to pass underneath in full sail. The arch was rejected, as incompatible with the
requirements of the Act of Parliament, and the engineer was thrown
upon his own resources to overcome the apparently insurmountable difficulties of the passage. After much reflection and study, the
scheme of a wrought-iron hollow beam, of gigantic dimensions, was
adopted; Mr. Stephenson feeling satisfied that the principles on which
the idea was founded was nothing more than an extension of those in
daily use in the profession of the engineer. While his mind was
still occupied with the subject in its earlier stages, an accident occurred to the *Prince of Wales* iron steamship, at Blackwall, which
singularly corroborated Mr. Stephenson's views as to the strength
of wrought-iron beams of large dimensions. While launching this
vessel, the cleat of the bow gave way, in consequence of the bolts
breaking, and let the vessel down so that the bilge came in contact
with the wharf, and she remained suspended between the water
and the wharf for a distance of about one hundred and ten feet,
without injury to the plates of the ship, thus proving her great
strength. The illustration was well-timed, and so fully confirmed
the calculations which Mr. Stephenson had already made on the
strength of tubular structures, that it greatly relieved his anxiety,
and converted his confidence into a certainty that he had not un-
dertaken an impracticable task. Then commenced a series of elaborate experiments, in which the engineer was ably assisted by Professor Hodgkinson, Mr. Fairbairn, and Mr. E. Clarke, to determine
the best form, thickness, and dimensions of the required tubes, so
that assurance might be made doubly sure. Every detail was carefully attended to, and not a point was neglected that could add to
the efficiency and security of the structure. As Mr. Stephenson
himself said, at the opening of the bridge for traffic: "The true and
accurate calculation of all the conditions and elements essential to
the safety of the bridge had been a source not only of mental, but
of bodily toil; including, as it did a combination of abstract thought
and well-considered experiment adequate to the magnitude of the
project." Mr. Stephenson's anxiety was very great during the arduous process of raising the tubes, and it is said that for three weeks
he was almost sleepless. Sir F. Head, however, relates, that on the
morning following the raising of the final tube, when about to leave

the scene of so many days harassing operations, he observed, sitting on a platform which had been erected to enable some of the more favored spectators to command a good view of the preceding day's operations, a gentleman reclining entirely by himself, smoking a cigar, and as if almost indolently gazing at the aerial gallery before him. It was the father looking at his new-born child! He had strolled down from the neighboring village, after his first sound and refreshing sleep for weeks; to behold in sunshine and solitude that which, during a weary period of gestation, had been either mysteriously moving in his brain, or, like a vision,—sometimes of good omen, and sometimes of bad,—had, by night as well as by day, been flitting across his mind.

The Victoria Bridge, across the St. Lawrence, near Montreal, is constructed on the same principle as the Britannia Bridge, but on a much larger scale; the Victoria Bridge, with its approaches, being only sixty yards short of two miles in length. In its gigantic strength and majestic proportions, there is no structure to compare with it in ancient or modern times. It consists of not less than twenty-five immense tubular bridges joined into one; the great central span being three hundred and thirty feet, the others two hundred and forty-two feet in length. The weight of wrought-iron in the bridge is about ten thousand tons; and the piers are of massive stone containing some eight thousand tons each of solid masonry. Of this last and greatest of his works, it is to be lamented that the engineer did not live to see the completion.

For many years his time was completely occupied with the promotion of railway bills, the surveying of new lines for many companies, and giving evidence for those companies in Parliament, as well as superintending the construction of railway works in progress. During this busy period of his life his income was very large, and his accumulation of property was rapid,—far beyond any previous example of engineering gain. And when his father died, in 1848, bequeathing to him his valuable collieries, his share in the engine manufactory at Newcastle, and his accumulated savings, Robert Stephenson occupied the position of an engineer millionaire,—the first of the race. He continued, however, to live in a quiet style, and although he bought pictures, and indulged in the luxury of a yacht, he did not live up to his income, which went on accumulating. He had no family to inherit his fortune, and he could, therefore, afford to be generous—which he was, to his honor—to the educational institutions of his native town. The Newcastle and Literary Institute had liberally assisted his father and himself with books and apparatus in the days of their obscurity; and he accordingly presented the Institute, during his lifetime, with a sum of above £3,000, towards paying off the debt which lay heavily upon the institution, conditional on its local supporters finding the remaining half of the debt, which they did. It is well to see men of wealth thus mindful of the educational claims of the localities to which they belong, and of the institutes which helped them in their youth.

Mr. Stephenson was greatly esteemed in his profession, and when any difficulty arose, he was prompt to render his best advice and assistance. When Mr. Brunel was occupied with his first fruitless efforts to launch the Great Eastern, at the close of one most disheartening day's work, he wrote Mr. Stephenson, urging him to come down to Blackwall on the following morning, and confer with him as to further measures. Next morning Mr. Stephenson was in the yard at Blackwall shortly after six o'clock, and he remained there until dusk. While superintending the operations about midday, he came to the end of a balk of timber which canted up, and he fell up to his middle in the Thames mud. He was merely in his ordinary dress, without any great coat (though the weather was bitter cold) and with only thin boots upon his feet. He was urged to leave the yard and change his dress, but, with his usual disregard of health, his reply was, "O, never mind me, I'm quite used to this sort of thing," and he went paddling about in the mud, smoking his cigar until almost quite dark, when the work of the day was completed. The consequence of this exposure was an inflammation of the lungs, which kept him to his bed for a fortnight.

No man could be more beloved than Mr. Stephenson was by a wide circle of friends. His pupils and juniors in the profession regarded him with a sort of worship; and he even ran some risk of being spoiled by the adulation with which they surrounded him. But he preserved his simplicity, his modesty, and his manliness, through all. He was a kind and pleasant companion, very unaffected, cordial, and communicative. Possessing ample means, he was enabled to do many benevolent acts, particularly to those who had worked with him in the early part of his career; and he was always ready to help on the deserving and the industrious.

He was greatly honored in his life, though he died untitled. Like his father, he was offered knighthood, and declined it; but he accepted the honors of foreign potentates for whom he had performed important services. By the King of the Belgians he was made Knight of the Order of Leopold; the King of Sweden presented him with the Grand Cross of Olaf; and the Emperor of the French decorated him with the Order of the Legion of Honor. In 1857 the University of Oxford conferred on him the honor of D. C. L.; and for many years he represented Whitby in Parliament. The greatest honor of all, however, was reserved for his death, when he was laid to rest amidst the great departed of England in Westminster Abbey.

Among those who stood beside his grave were many of the friends of his boyhood and his manhood. William Kell, Philip Staunton, and Joseph Glynn, his schoolfellows; Nicholas Wood, his first master in the business of life; Joseph Sandars, the projector of the Liverpool and Manchester Railway; Henry Booth, his coadjutor in designing the "Rocket," which won the prize at Rainhill; Joseph Locke and John Dixon, his early professional companions ; Mr. Glyn, Mr. Ellis, and Mr. Joseph Pease, fast friends of his father, as well as himself; down to Henry Weatherburn, driver of the "Harvey Combe," beside whom the engineer stood on the foot-plate of the locomotive at the opening of the London and Birmingham Railway. Besides these were many of the greatest living men of thought and action, assembled at that solemn ceremony to pay their last mark of respect to this illustrious son of one of England's greatest workingmen. Requiescat!

DR. ARNOLD.

IT does one's heart good to contemplate the life of such a man as Dr. Arnold of Rugby. He possessed that quality of earnestness which gives force to every purpose in life. He was full of strong sympathy for all that was true and good in our modern social movements, and of as strong antipathy for all that he conceived to be false and unjust. He did battle in the cause that he conscientiously felt to be right, with his whole heart and soul; and waged an uncompromising war against what seemed to him to be shams and falsities. He was of the stern stuff of which martyrs are made; for when he saw his way clear, and his conscience approved, he never hesitated at once to act boldly and energetically. We may not agree with him in all the views that he held and advocated; but we never fail to admire the undeviating and high-minded consistency of his life, and the purity of the motives on which he acted.

The history of Dr. Arnold contains comparatively few incidents. He was a scholar and a thinker, acting upon the world through his school and his study, rather than taking an active part in its practical movements and struggles. He influenced it from without, and spoke to the men in action, as if from a higher sphere. Thomas Arnold was born at West Cowes, in the Isle of Wight, in 1795. His father, who was the collector of customs at that place, died suddenly in 1801, and left a large family to be provided for, Thomas (the youngest) being then only six years old. His aunt undertook the care of his education, and sent him to Warminster School in 1803, where he remained four years, and then removed to Winchester, leaving that seminary in 1811. As a boy, he was shy and retiring, but he then formed numerous warm friendships, which continued through life. He was fond of ballad poetry, and while at Winchester wrote a long poem on the subject of Simon de Monfort, which obtained for him the appellation of "Poet Arnold." But in his school career there was, on the whole, nothing remarkable.

He entered Corpus Christi College, Oxford, in 1811; was elected a Fellow of Oriel College, in 1815; and subsequently obtained the Chancellor's prize for the University essays in Latin and English. He often looked back with delight to his residence at Oxford, and trod over again in fancy the beautiful scenery of the neighborhood, —Bagely Wood, and Shotover, with Horspath nestling under it; Elsfield, with its green slope, and all the variety of Cumnor Hill. He had an intense love of nature in all its aspects, and quite reveled amongst the beautiful scenery of Westmoreland, where he had his rural home during the later years of his life. While at College his inquiries became directed upon religious subjects, and he was early beset by doubts and scruples, through which most strong minds have vigorously to struggle. But Arnold succeeded in at length reaching what he felt to be firm ground, his nature strengthened by the struggles which he had undergone.

In December, 1818, he was ordained deacon at Oxford; in 1819 he settled at Laleham with his mother, aunt, and sister, taking in pupils to prepare them for the Universities; and in 1820 he married Mary Penrose, the youngest daughter of the Rector of Fledborough, Lincolnshire. He remained at Laleham for nine years, diligently improving his mind, engaged in the study of Greek and Roman history, learning German in order to read Niebuhr, searching out the deep meaning of the Scriptures, and devoting himself to the improvement and culture of the minds of his pupils. He loved teaching, and seemed to live for it, entering into the pursuits of his scholars, making them feel in love with knowledge and virtue, giving them new views of life and action, and discovering to them the means of being useful and truly happy. He loved his pupils, and they loved him warmly in turn. He bathed with them, leaped with them, sailed and rowed with them, and entered into all their amusements, as well as intellectual occupations.

His success at Laleham, and the high opinion which began to be entertained of him by leading minds, directed attention to Dr. Arnold as the proper person to fill the office of Head Master of Rugby School, on the resignation of Dr. Wool, for a long time master of that academy; and on presenting himself as a candidate, he was at once elected to the office in December, 1827. In the following year he received priest's orders; shortly after, he took his degree of B. D., and D. D., and entered upon his duties in August, 1828. He commenced his work with the ardent zeal of a reformer. He had long deplored the state of the public schools of England, holding many of them to be seminaries of vice rather than of virtue, and he longed to try "whether his notions of Christian education were really impracticable, and whether our system of public schools had not in it some noble elements which might produce fruit, even to life eternal."

Many have expressed a regret that Arnold, with his fine powers of mind, should have devoted his main energies through life to the performance of the duties of a schoolmaster. But he himself had the proper notions of this high calling, and he felt that in forming, influencing, and directing the minds of hundreds of young men, who were to occupy, many of them, prominent places in society, at the same time that he was laboring to reform and to elevate the entire system of school education, he was really engaged in a noble and elevating work. He threw himself into this work with great zeal, at first feeling his way, but gradually acting with greater boldness and decision. He succeeded in enlisting the boys themselves in his labors, made them co-operators with himself in the improvements he sought to introduce, and the result was, that, in the course of a very few years, Rugby School was rendered one of the most famous and successful in England.

It would occupy too much space to detail the tenderness, the firmness, the judgment, the kindness, and the Christian zeal which the master displayed in carrying out his great purpose, and to exhibit by what means he fired his pupils with the love of truth, virtue, and integrity,—teaching them to do for themselves rather than to depend upon others for success,—treating them as gentlemen, and thus making them such,—trusting them, confiding in them, stimulating them, and encouraging them. But, as was to have been expected, there were many unruly spirits to be dealt with among an indiscriminate mass of three hundred boys; and mischievous tendencies and bad feeling could not be altogether repressed among them. On one of these occasions he exclaimed: "Is this a Christian school? I cannot remain here if all is to be carried on by constraint and force; if I am to be here as a jailer, I would rather resign my office at once." And on another occasion, when he had found it necessary to send away some unruly boys, he said: "It is not necessary that this should be a school of three hundred, or of one hundred, or of fifty boys; but it is necessary that it should be a school of Christian gentlemen." And such stirring appeals to the generous nature of his boys rarely failed in their effect.

What Dr. Arnold mainly aimed at, was to promote the self-development of the young minds committed to his charge, by encouraging them to cultivate their own intellects. "I am sure," he used to say: "the temptations of intellect are not comparable to the temptations of dullness;" and he often dwelt on "the fruit which he above all things longed for,—moral thoughtfulness,—the engrossing love of truth going along with the devoted love of goodness;" and again he said: "I am quite sure that it is a most solemn duty to cultivate our understandings to the uttermost, for I have seen the evil moral consequences of fanaticism to a greater degree than I ever expected to see them realized; and I am satisfied that a neglected intellect is far oftener the cause of mischief to a man than a perverted or over-valued one." He longed to train men so that they should form their own opinions honestly, and entertain them decidedly. He could not bear that nondescript in society,—the *neutral* character. " Neutrality, however," he observed, "seems to me a natural state for men of fair honesty, moderate wit, and much indolence; they cannot get strong impressions of what is true and right, and the weak impression, which is all that they can take, cannot overcome indolence and fear; I crave a strong mind for my children, for this reason,—that they then have a chance, at least, of appreciating truth keenly, and when a man does that, honesty becomes comparatively easy." " I would far rather," he said, send a boy to Van Dieman's Land, where he must work for his bread, than send him to Oxford to live in luxury, without any desire in his mind to avail himself of his advantages. Childishness in boys, even of good abilities, seems to me to be a growing fault, and I do not know to what to ascribe it, except to the greater number of exciting books of amusement, like 'Pickwick' and 'Nickleby,' 'Bentley's Miscellany,' etc., etc. These completely satisfy all the intellectual appetites of a boy, which is rarely very voracious, and leave him totally palled, not only for his regular work, which I could well excuse in comparison, but for good literature of all sorts, even for history and poetry."

At the same time, for mere cleverness, whether in men or boys, without moral goodness, and mental strength, he had very little esteem. "Mere intellectual acuteness," he used to say, in speaking of lawyers, for example, "divested as it is, in too many cases, of all that is comprehensive and great and good, is to me more revolting than the most helpless imbecility, seeming to be almost like the spirit of Mephistophiles." Again, "If there be one thing on earth which is truly admirable, it is to see God's wisdom blessing an inferiority of natural powers, where they have been honestly, truly, and zealously cultivated." In speaking of a pupil of this character, he said, "I would stand to that man *hat in hand*." Once, at Laleham, when teaching a rather dull boy, he spoke rather sharply to him, when the pupil looked up in his face and said, "Why do you speak angrily, sir? *indeed* I am doing the best I can." Years afterwards he used to tell the story to his children, and said, "I never felt so much in my life,—that look and that speech I have never forgotten." In such a spirit did Dr. Arnold enter and proceed upon his work of educating young minds, and the success that attended his efforts was immense. He excited quite an enthusiastic admiration among his pupils, and many there are who confess that they owe to him the main bent of their lives and actions, and all the good which they have accomplished. This feeling has by no means been exaggerated by Mr. Hughes in his celebrated "Tom Brown's School Days."

While thus diligently occupied among his pupils, and superintending, with an anxious eye, the whole business of his great school, Dr. Arnold took the most eager interest in the ongoings of the busy world without. He followed the public movements of the day with enthusiasm; he was a man who could not possibly be neutral, and he at once took his side with the cause of progress. In his youth, Arnold had been a conservative; but the reading of history, of the Bible, and Aristotle, with a free mind, soon led him entirely the other way. His feelings were most intense, as to the neglect of the poor by the rich, and the injustice and want of sympathy exercised toward the multitudinous classes. "It haunts me," he said, "almost night and day. It fills me with astonishment to see antislavery and missionary societies so busy with the ends of the earth, and yet all the worst evils of slavery and heathenism existing among ourselves."

Again, in 1840, he says: "The state of the times is so grievous, that it really pierces through all private happiness, and *haunts me daily like a personal calamity.*" Again and again does he give expression to similar desponding views in his letters to his intimate friends. "It seems to me," he said, "that people are not enough aware of the monstrous state of society, absolutely without a parallel in the history of the world; with a population poor, miserable, and degraded, both in body and mind as much as if they were slaves, and yet called freemen, and having a power as such of concerting and combining plans of risings, which makes them ten times more dangerous than slaves. And the hopes entertained by many, of the effects to be wrought by new churches and schools, while the social evils of their condition are left uncorrected, appear to me to be utterly wild." The Corn Laws and the Debt, the increasing mortgages on land and industry, oppressed his mind like a nightmare. He could not rid himself of the thought of these things. He feared that "too late" were the words which must be affixed to every plan of reforming society in England. "The English nation," he observed, "are like a man in a lethargy; they are never roused from their conservatism till mustard poultices are put to their feet." The conduct of the higher classes, at the same time roused his extreme ire. "There is," said he, "no earthly thing more mean and despicable in my mind than an English gentleman destitute of all sense of his responsibilities and opportunities, and only reveling in the luxuries of our high civilization, and thinking himself a great person."

He endeavored to give his views on these subjects a practical direction, and labored to organize a society "for drawing public attention to the state of the laboring classes throughout the kingdom." But the plan never come to maturity. He tried to establish a newspaper, but it failed after a few numbers. He wrote letters in the Sheffield Courant and the Herts Reformer, and thus endeavored to rouse the public attention. "I have a testimony to deliver," he said; "*I must write or die.*" His scholastic studies were all prosecuted with the same views. His Greek and Roman History was "not an idle inquiry about remote ages and forgotten institutions, but a living picture of things present, fitted not so much for the curiosity of the scholar, as for the instruction of the statesman and the scholar." "My abhorance of conservatism," he observed at another time, "is not because it checks liberty,—in an established democracy it would favor liberty; but because it checks the growth of mankind in wisdom, goodness, and happiness, by striving to maintain institutions which are of necessity temporary, and thus never hindering change, but often depriving the change of half its value." Yet Dr. Arnold, decided though his views were, might be said to belong to no "party," either in the State or in the Church. His independence was too great,— his opinions were so entirely self-formed and elaborated, and held with such tenacity, that he was not a man who could jog quietly along in the train of any "party." He was strongly in favor of Catholic emancipation, and wrote an eloquent pamphlet in its favor; but strange to say, for reasons which he stated equally strongly, he was opposed to the emancipation of the Jews.

On Church questions, his views were equally bold and decided. He stood quite aloof from High Church and Low Church alike. He was strongly impressed with a sense of what he termed the "corruption of the Church," which, he maintained, had been ''virtually destroyed;'' for by the Church was now understood only "the Clergy," the Laity being excluded from all share in its administration. He inveighed, in an article of his in the Edinburgh Review, "On the Fanaticism which has been the Peculiar Disgrace of the Church of England,"—"a dress, a ritual, a name, a ceremony, a technical phraseology,—the superstition of a priesthood without its power,— the gown of Episcopal government, without its substance,—a system imperfect and paralyzed, not independent, not sovereign,— afraid to cast off the subjection against which it was perpetually murmuring,—objects so pitiful, that, if gained ever so completely, they would make no man the wiser, or the better : they would lead to no good, intellectual, moral, or spiritual." For this article he was taken to task by Earl Howe, one of the trustees of Rugby School, and called upon to confess whether he were the author. He replied that the authorship of the article was well known,—that he had spoken undisguisedly of it to his friends, but he refused to give a direct answer to his Lordship's interrogatory, which would be "to acknowledge a right which I owe it," he said, "not only to myself, but to the master of every endowed school in England, absolutely to deny " The result was a meeting of the trustees, but Dr. Arnold was retained in his office without any further communication being made to him.

Dr. Arnold had an intense sense of the true religious life, and this it was which shocked him at its shams, and at the virtual Atheism in which men lived. "I cannot," he said, "understand what is the good of a national church, if it be not to Christianize the nation, and introduce the principles of Christianity into men's social and civil relations, and expose the wickedness of that spirit which maintains the Game Laws, and, in agriculture and trade, seems to think that there is no such sin as covetousness; and, that if a man is not dishonest, he has nothing to do but to make all the profit of his capital that he can." He deplored that religion had become, among us, an affair of clergy, not of people; of preaching and ceremonies, not of living; of Sundays and synagogues, instead of one of all days and all places, houses, streets, town, and country." "Alas!" he exclaimed, "when will the church ever exist more than in name, so that this profession might have that zeal infused into it which is communicated by an esprit de corps; and, if the 'Body' were the real church, instead of our abominable sects, with their half-priest-craft, half-profaneness, its 'Spirit' would be one that we might receive into all our hearts and minds."

Into the questions raised by the Oxford Controversy, also, he entered with great warmth. He saw in it the essence of "priest-craft," which he hated, characterizing Newmanism as "the great Anti-Christian heresy;" but into his views on this subject we need not enter. Speaking thus strongly, it will be obvious that he could not fail to rouse a strong feeling of hostility against himself. At London, where he wished religious, not sectarian, examination to be introduced into the University, he was regarded as a bigot; while at Oxford he was regarded as an extreme latitudinarian. "If I had two necks," said he, "I think I had a very good chance of being hanged by both sides." Nor would he aid the Sabbatarians in stopping railway traveling on Sundays, holding that the Jewish law of the Sabbath was not binding on Christians. Loud outcry was raised against him in many and various quarters, but still he was nothing daunted, even though old friends grew cool and new ones fell away. The truth which he felt, he uttered, and never ceased till his last breath to do so. In course of time, however, as the rancor of the strife subsided, and the great success of his manage-ment and teaching at Rugby became apparent, and, as his works on Greek and Roman history made their appearance, to show the mag-nificent caliber of his mind, new and powerful friends came around him, and his fame spread wider than before. Lord Melbourne offered him the vacant chair of History at Oxford, in 1841, which he joyfully accepted, though he lived only to deliver the introductory course of lectures on his favorite theme.

It will be observed, from what we have said, that the prominent characteristic of the man was intense earnestness. He felt life keenly, its responsibilities as well as its enjoyments. His very pleasures were earnest; he was indifferent or neutral in nothing. He was always full of work, learning some new language, studying some fresh historical subject, or cheering on by his pen the progressive movements of the age. "It boots not," he said, "to look backward: forward, forward, forward, should be our motto." "I covet rest neither for my friends nor yet for myself, so long as we are able to work;" but, again he would say, "work after all is but half the man, and they who only work together, do not truly live together." "Instead of feeling my mind exhausted," he would say, after the day's business in the school was over, "it seems to have quite an eagerness to set to work. I feel as if I could dictate to twenty secretaries at once." He was a thoroughly "go-ahead" man, and rejoiced at all the signs of work and progress in this busy age. The delight with which he regarded the power of the railway was quite characteristic of him. "I rejoice to see it," he said, as he stood on one of the arches of the London and Birmingham line, and watched the train flash along through the distant hedgerows,—"I rejoice to see it, and think that feudality is gone forever. It is so great a blessing to think that any one evil is really extinct."

He was a great lover of men. When he met with one earnest and zealous as himself,—and such was rare,—he loved him with his whole heart. Chevalier Bunsen and Niebuhr were objects of his high admiration. Carlyle, too, was a great favorite. "What I daily feel more and more to need,' he said, "as life every year rises more and more before me in its true reality, is to have intercourse with those who take life in earnest. It is very painful to me to be always on the surface of things, and I think that literature, science, politics, many topics of far greater interest than mere gossip, or talking about the weather, are yet, as they are generally talked about, still on the surface; they do not touch the real depths of life." And again: "Differences of opinion give me but little concern; but it is a real pleasure to be brought into communication with any one who is in earnest, and who really looks to God's will as his standard of right and wrong, and judges of actions according to their greater or less conformity." Hence Arnold disliked the mere theologians. "There appears to me," he said, "in all the English divines a want of believing, or disbelieving anything, because it is true or false." And again: "I have left off reading our divines, because, as Pascal said of the Jesuits, if I had spent my time in reading them fully, I should have read a great many very indifferent books. But if I could find a great man amongst them, I would read him thankfully and earnestly. As it is, I hold John Bunyan to have been a man of incomparably greater genius than any of them, and to have given a far truer and more edifying picture of Christianity. His 'Pilgrim's Progress' seems to be a complete reflection of Scripture, with none of the rubbish of the theologians mixed up with it."

Interested as Arnold was in the ongoings of the outer world, he intensely enjoyed his own family and fireside. At Laleham, at Rugby, but above all, in his country home at Fox How, near Rydal, in Westmoreland, his heart ran over with expressions of joy and deep delight. Fox How was the paradise to which he retreated from the turmoil of the world. "It is with a mixed feeling of solemnity and tenderness," he said, "that I regard our mountain nest, whose surpassing sweetness, I think I may safely say, adds a positive happiness to every one of my waking hours passed in it." When absent from Fox How, it "dwelt on his memory as a vision of beauty, from one vacation to another;" and when present there, he felt that "no hasty or excited admiration of a tourist could be compared with the quiet and homely delight of having the mountains and streams as familiar objects, connected with all the enjoyments of home, one's family, one's books, and one's friends." Among the delicious scenery of Italy, he said, that "if he stayed more than a day at the most beautiful spot in the world, it would only bring on a longing for Fox How;" and it was his repeated wish that, when he died, "his bones should go to Grasmere churchyard, to lie under the yews which Wordsworth planted, and to have the Rotha, with its deep and silent pools, passing by."

This true and noble man died too soon for himself and the world. He was suddenly cut off, in the midst of his labors, on the morning of the 12th of June, 1842, in the forty-seventh year of his age. He died, but he left a legacy of pure thoughts, earnest impulses, and noble aspirations to his race, and which, it is to be hoped, the world will not willingly let die.

HUGH MILLER.

MEN may learn much that is good from each other's lives,—especially from good men's lives. Men who live in our daily sight, as well as men who have lived before us, and handed down illustrious examples for our imitation, are the most valuable practical teachers. For it is not mere literature that makes men,—it is real, practical life, that chiefly molds our nature, enables us to work out our own education, and to build up our own character.

Hugh Miller has very strikingly worked out this idea in his admirable autobiography, entitled, "My Schools and Schoolmasters." It is extremely interesting, even fascinating, as a book; but it is more than an ordinary book,—it might almost be called an institution. It is the history of the formation of a truly noble and independent character in the humblest condition of life,—the condition in which a large mass of the people of this country are born and brought up; and it teaches all, but especially poor men, what it is in the power of each to accomplish for himself. The life of Hugh Miller is full of lessons of self-help and self-respect, and shows the efficacy of these in working out for a man an honorable competence and a solid reputation. It may not be that every man has the thew and sinew, the large brain and heart of a Hugh Miller,—for there is much in what we may call the *breed* of a man, the defect of which no mere educational advantages can supply; but every man can at least do much, by the help of such examples of his, to elevate himself, and build up his moral and intellectual character on a solid foundation.

We have spoken of the *breed* of a man. In Hugh Miller we have an embodiment of that most vigorous and energetic element of English national life,—the Norwegian and Danish. In times long, long ago, the daring and desperate pirates of these nations swarmed along the eastern coasts. In England they were resisted by force of arms, for the prize of England's crown was a rich one; yet, by dint of numbers, valor, and bravery, they made good their footing in England, and even governed the eastern part of it by their own kings until the time of Alfred the Great. And to this day the Danish element amongst the population of the east and northeast of England is by far the prevailing one. But in Scotland it was different. They never reigned there; but they settled and planted all the eastern coasts. The land was poor and thinly peopled; and the Scottish kings and chiefs were too weak—generally too much occupied by intestine broils—to molest or dispossess them. Then these Danes and Norwegians led a seafaring life, were sailors and fishermen, which the native Scots were not. So they settled down in all the bays and bights along the coast of Scotland, and took entire possession of the Orkneys, Shetland, and Western Isles, the Shetlands having been held by the crown of Denmark down to a comparatively recent period. They never amalgamated with the Scotch Highlanders; and to this day they speak a different language, and follow different pursuits. The Highlander was a hunter, a herdsman, a warrior, and fished in the fresh waters only. The descendants of the Norwegians, or the Lowlanders, as they came to be called, followed the sea, fished in salt waters, cultivated the soil, and engaged in trade and commerce. Hence the marked difference between the population of the town of Cromarty—where Hugh Miller was born, in 1802—and the population only a few miles inland; the townspeople speaking Lowland Scotch, and being dependent for their subsistence mainly on the sea,—the others speaking Gaelic, and living solely upon the land.

These Norwegian colonists of Cromarty held in their blood the very same piratical propensities which characterized their forefathers who followed the Vikings. Hugh Miller first saw the light in a long, low-built house, built by his great-grandfather, John Feddes, "one of the last of the buccaneers;" this cottage having been built, as Hugh Miller himself says he has every reason to believe, with "Spanish gold." All his ancestors were sailors and seafaring men; when boys they had taken to the water as naturally as ducklings. Traditions of adventures by sea were rife in the family. Of his grand-uncles, one had sailed round the world with Anson, had assisted in burning Paeta, and in boarding the Manilla galleon; another, a handsome and powerful man, perished at sea in a storm; and his grandfather was dashed overboard by the jib-boom of his little vessel when entering the Cromarty Firth, and never rose again. The son of this last, Hugh Miller's father, was sent into the country by his mother to work upon a farm, thus to rescue him, if possible, from the hereditary fate of the family. But it was of no use. The propensity for the salt water, the very instinct of the breed, was too powerful within him. He left the farm, went to sea, became a man-of-war's man, was in the battle with the Dutch off the Dogger Bank, sailed all over the world, then took "French leave" of the royal navy, returned to Cromarty with money enough to buy a sloop and engage in trade on his own account. But this vessel was one stormy night knocked to pieces on the bar of Findhorn, the master and his men escaping with difficulty; then another vessel was fitted out by him, by the help of his friends, and in this he was trading from place to place when Hugh Miller was born.

What a vivid picture of sea life, as seen from the shore at least, do we obtain from the early chapters of Miller's life! "I retain," says he, "a vivid recollection of the joy which used to light up the household on my father's arrival, and how I learned to distinguish for myself his sloop when in the offing, by the two slim stripes of white that ran along her sides, and her two square topsails." But a terrible calamity —though an ordinary one in sea-life—suddenly plunged the sailor's family in grief; and he, too, was gathered to the same grave in which so many of his ancestors lay,—the deep ocean. A terrible storm overtook his vessel near Peterhead; numbers of ships were lost along the coast; vessel after vessel came ashore, and the beach was strewn with wrecks and dead bodies, but no remnant of either the ship or bodies of Miller and his crew were ever cast up. It was supposed that the little sloop, heavily laden, and laboring in a mountainous sea, must have started a plank and foundered. Hugh Miller was but a child at the time, having only completed his fifth year. The following remarkable "appearance," very much in Mrs. Crowe's way, made a strong impression upon him at the time. The house-door had blown open, in the gray of evening, and the boy was sent by his mother to shut it.

"Day had not wholly disappeared, but it was fast posting on to night, and a gray haze spread a neutral tint of dimness over every more distant object, but left the nearer ones comparatively distinct, when I saw at the open door, within less than a yard of my breast, as plainly as ever I saw anything, a dissevered hand and arm stretched towards me. Hand and arm were apparently those of a female; they bore a livid and sodden appearance; and directly fronting me, where the body ought to have been, there was only blank, transparent space, through which I could see the dim forms of the objects beyond. I was fearfully startled, and ran shrieking to my mother, telling what I had seen; and the house-girl, whom she next sent to shut the door, apparently affected by my terror, also returned frightened, and said that she, too, had seen the woman's hand; which, however, did not seem to be the case. And finally, my mother going to the door, saw nothing, though she appeared much impressed by the extremeness of my terror, and the minuteness of my description. I communicate the story as it lies fixed in my memory, without attempting to explain it; its coincidence with the probable time of my father's death, seems at least curious."

The little boy longed for his father's return, and continued to gaze across the deep, watching for the sloop with its two tripes of white along the sides. Every morning he went wandering about the little harbor, to examine the vessels which had come in during the night; and he continued to look out across the Moray Frith long after anybody else had ceased to hope. But months and years passed, and the white stripes and square topsails of his father's sloop he never saw again. The boy was the son of a sailor's widow, and so grew up, in sight of the sea, and with the same love of it that characterized his father. But he was sent to school; first to a dame school, where he learned his letters; he then worked his way through the Catechism, the Proverbs, and the New Testament, and emerged into the golden region of "Sinbad the Sailor," "Jack the Giant-Killer," "Beauty and the Beast," and "Aladdin and the Wonderful Lamp." Other books followed,—the Pilgrim's Progress, Cook's and Anson's Voyages, and Blind Harry the Rhymer's History of Wallace; which first awoke within him a strong feeling of Scottish patriotism. And thus his childhood grew, on proper child-like nourishment. His uncles were men of solid sense and sound judgment, though uncultured by scholastic education. One was a local antiquary, by trade a working harness-maker; the other was of a strong religious turn: he was a working cartwright, and in early life had been a sailor, engaged in nearly all Nelson's famous battles. The examples and the conversation of these men were for the growing boy worth any quantity of school primers: he learned from them far more than mere books could teach him.

But his school education was not neglected either. From the dame's school he was transferred to the town's grammar-school, where, amidst about one hundred and fifty other boys and girls, he received his real school education. But it did not amount to much. There, however, the boy learned life,—to hold his own,—to try his powers with other boys,—physically and morally, as well as scholastically. The school brought out the stuff that was in him in many ways, but the mere book-learning was about the least part of the instruction.

The school-house looked out on the beach, fronting the opening of the Frith, and not a boat or a ship could pass in or out of the harbor of Cromarty without the boys seeing it. They knew the rig of every craft, and could draw them on their slates. Boats unloaded their glittering cargoes on the beach, where the process of gutting afterwards went busily on ; and to add to the bustle, there was a large killing-place for pigs not thirty yards from the school door, "where from eighty to a hundred pigs used sometimes to die for the general good in a single day ; and it was a great matter to hear, at occasional intervals, the roar of death rising high over the general murmur within, or to be told by some comrade, returned from his five minutes' leave of absence, that a hero of a pig had taken three blows of a hatchet ere it fell, and that, even after its subjection to the sticking process, it had got hold of Jock Keddie's hand in its mouth, and almost smashed his thumb." Certainly it is not in every grammar-school that such lessons as these are taught.

Miller was put to Latin, but made little progress in it,—his master had no method, and the boy was too fond of telling stories to his schoolfellows in school hours to make much progress. Cock-fighting was a school practice in those days, the master having a perquisite of twopence for every cock that was entered by the boys on the days of the yearly fight. But Miller had no love for this sport, although he paid his entry money with the rest. In the meantime his miscellaneous reading extended, and he gathered pickings of odd knowledge from all sorts of odd quarters,—from workmen, carpenters, fishermen and sailors, old women, and, above all, from the old boulders strewed along the shores of the Cromarty Frith. With a big hammer, which had belonged to his great-grandfather, John Feddes, the buccaneer, the boy went about chipping the stones, and thus early accumulating specimens of mica, porphyry, garnet, and such like, exhibiting them to his Uncle Alexander, and other admiring relations. Often, too, he had a day in the woods to visit his uncle, when working as a sawyer,—his trade of cartwright having failed. And there, too, the boy's attention was excited by the peculiar geological curiosities which lay in his way. While searching among the stones and rocks on the beach, he was sometimes asked, in humble irony, by the farm servants who came to load their carts with sea-weed, whether he "was gettin' siller in the stanes," but was so unlucky as never to be able to answer their question in the affirmative. Uncle Sandy seems to have been a close observer of nature, and in his humble way had his theories of ancient sea-beaches, the flood, and the formation of the world, which he duly imparted to the wondering youth. Together they explored caves, roamed the beach for crabs and lobsters, whose habits Uncle Sandy could well describe; he also knew all about moths and butterflies, spiders, and bees,—in short, was a born natural-history man, so that the boy regarded him in the light of a professor, and, doubtless, thus early obtained from him the bias toward his future studies.

There was the usual number of hair-breadth escapes in Miller's boy-life. One of them, when he and a companion had got cooped up in a sea cave, and could not return because of the tide, reminds us of the exciting scene described in Scott's Antiquary. There were school-boy tricks, and school-boy rambles, mischief-making in companionship with other boys, of whom he was often the leader. Left very much to himself, he was becoming a big, wild, insubordinate boy; and it became obvious that the time was now come when Hugh Miller must enter that world-wide school in which toil and hardship are the severe but noble masters. After a severe fight and wrestling-match with his schoolmaster, he left school, avenging himself for his defeat by penning and sending by the teacher that very night, a copy of satiric verses, entitled "The Pedagogue," which occasioned a good deal of merriment in the place.

His boyhood over, and his school training ended, Hugh Miller must now face the world of toil. His uncles were most anxious that he should become a minister; and were even willing to pay his college expenses, though the labor of their hands formed their only wealth. The youth, however, had conscientious objections: he did not feel *called* to the work; and the uncles, confessing that he was right, gave up their point. Hugh was according apprenticed to the trade of his choice,—that of a working stone-mason; and he began his laboring career in a quarry looking out upon the Cromarty Frith. This quarry proved one of his best schools. The remarkable geological formations which it displayed awakened his curiosity. The bar of deep-red stone beneath, and the bar of pale-red clay above, were noted by the young quarryman, who, even in such unpromising subjects, found matter for observation and reflection. Where other men saw nothing, he detected analogies, differences, and peculiarities, which set him a-thinking. He simply kept his eyes and his mind open; was sober, diligent, and persevering; and this was the secret of his intellectual growth.

Hugh Miller takes a cheerful view of the lot of labor. While others groan because they have to work hard for their bread, he says that work is full of pleasure, of profit, and of materials for self-improvement. .He holds that honest labor is the best of all teachers, and that the school of toil is the best and noblest of all schools, save only the Christian one,—a school in which the ability of being useful is imparted, and the spirit of independence communicated, and the habit of persevering effort acquired. He is even of opinion that the training of the mechanic, by the exercise which it gives to his observant faculties, from his daily dealings with things actual and practical, and the close experience of life which he invariably acquires, is more favorable to his growth as a man, emphatically speaking, than the training which is afforded by any other condition of life. And the array of great names which he cites in support of his statement is certainly a large one. Nor is the condition of the average well-paid operative at all so dolorous, according to Hugh Miller, as many modern writers would have it. "I worked as an operative mason," says he, "for fifteen years,—no inconsiderable portion of the more active part of a man's life; but the time was not altogether lost. I enjoyed in those years fully the average amount of happiness, and learned to know more of the Scottish people than is generally known. Let me add, that from the close of the first year in which I wrought as a journeyman, until I took final leave of the mallet and chisel, I never knew what it was to want a shilling: that my two uncles, my grandfather, and the mason with whom I served my apprenticeship—all working-men—had had a similar experience;

and that it was the experience of my father also. I cannot doubt that deserving mechanics may, in exceptional cases, be exposed to want; but I can as little doubt that the cases *are* exceptional, and that much of the suffering of the class is a consequence either of improvidence on the part of the completely skilled, or of a course of trifling during the term of apprenticeship,—quite as common as trifling at school,—that always lands those who indulge in it in the hapless position of the inferior workman."

There is much honest truth in this observation. At the same time, it is clear that the circumstances under which Hugh Miller was brought up and educated are not enjoyed by all workmen,—are, indeed, experienced by comparatively few. In the first place, his parentage was good, his father and mother were a self-helping, honest, intelligent pair, in humble circumstances, but yet comparatively comfortable. Thus his early education was not neglected. His relations were sober, industrious, and "God-fearing," as they say in the north. His uncles were not his least notable instructors. One of them was a close observer of nature, and in some sort a scientific man, possessed of a small but good library of books. Then Hugh Miller's own constitution was happily framed. As one of his companions once said to him, "Ah, Miller, you have stamina in you, and will force your way; but I want strength; the world will never hear of me." It is the *stamina* which Hugh Miller possessed by nature, that were born in him, and were carefully nurtured by his parents, that enabled him as a working-man to rise, while thousands would have sunk or merely plodded on through life in the humble station in which they were born. And this difference in *stamina* and other circumstances is not sufficiently taken into account by Hugh Miller in the course of the interesting, and, on the whole, exceedingly profitable remarks, which he makes in his autobiography on the condition of the laboring poor.

We can afford, in our brief space, to give only a very rapid outline of Hugh Miller's fifteen years' life as a workman. He worked away in the quarry for some time,· losing many of his finger-nails by bruises and accidents, growing fast, but gradually growing stronger, and obtaining a fair knowledge of his craft as a stone-hewer. He was early subjected to the temptation which besets most young workmen,—that of drink. But he resisted it bravely. His own account of it is worthy of extract :—

When overwrought, and in my depressed moods, I learned to regard the ardent spirits of the dram-shop as high luxuries; they gave lightness and energy to both body and mind, and substituted for a state of dullness and gloom one of exhilaration and enjoyment. Usquebhae was simply happiness doled out by the glass, and sold by the gill. The drinking usages of the profession in which I labored were at this time many; when a foundation was laid the workmen were treated to drink; they were treated to drink when the walls were leveled for laying the joists; they were treated to drink when the building was finished; they were treated to drink when an apprentice joined the squad; treated to drink when his 'apron was washed'; treated to drink when his 'time was out'; and occasionally they learned to treat one another to drink. In laying down the foundation stone of one of the larger houses built this year by Uncle David and his partner, the workmen had a royal 'founding pint,' and two whole glasses of the whisky came. to my share. A full-grown man would not have deemed a gill of usquebhae an overdose, but it was considerably too much for me; and when the party broke up, and I got home to my books, I found, as I opened the pages of a favorite author, the letters dancing before my eyes, and that I could no longer master the sense. I have the volume at present before me, a small edition of the Essays of Bacon, a good deal worn at the corners by the friction of the pocket, for of Bacon I never tired. The condition into which I had brought myself was, I felt, one of degradation. I had sunk, by my own act, for the time, to a lower level of intelligence than that on which it was my privilege to be placed, and though the state could have been no very favorable one for forming a resolution, I in that hour determined that I should never again sacrifice my capacity of intellectual enjoyment to a drinking usage; and, with God's help, I was enabled to hold my determination.

A young working mason, reading Bacon's Essays in his by-hours, must certainly be regarded as a remarkable man ; but not less remarkable is the exhibition of moral energy and noble self-denial in the instance we have cited.

It was while working as a mason's apprentice, that the lower Old Red Sandstone along the Bay of Cromarty presented itself to his notice; and his curiosity was excited and kept alive by the infinite organic remains, principally of old and extinct species of fishes, ferns, ammonites, which lay revealed along the coasts by the washings of waves, or were exposed by the stroke of his mason's hammer. He never lost sight of this subject; went on accumulating observations and comparing formations, until at length, when no longer a working mason, many years afterwards, he gave to the world his highly interesting work on the Old Red Sandstone, which at once established his reputation as an accomplished scientific geologist. But this work was the fruit of long years of patient observation and research. As he modestly states in his autobiography, "the only merit to which I lay claim in the case is that of patient research,—a merit in which whoever wills may rival or surpass me; and this humble faculty of patience, when rightly developed, may lead to more extraordinary developments of idea than even genius itself." And he adds how he deciphered the divine ideas in the mechanism and framework of creatures in the second stage of vertebrate existence.

But it was long before Hugh Miller accumulated his extensive geological observations, and acquired that self-culture which enabled him to shape them into proper form. He went on diligently working at his trade, but always observing and always reflecting. He says he could not avoid being an observer; and that the necessity which made him a mason, made him also a geologist. In the winter months, during which mason-work is generally superseded in country places, he occupied his time with reading, sometimes with visiting country friends,—persons of an intelligent caste,—and often he strolled away amongst old Scandinavian ruins and Pictish forts, speculating about their origin and history. He made good use of his leisure. And when spring came round again, he would set out into the Highlands, to work at building and hewing jobs with a squad of other masons,—working hard, and living chiefly on oatmeal brose. Some of the descriptions given by him of life in the remote High-and districts are extremely graphic and picturesque, and have all the charm of entire novelty. The kind of accommodation which he experienced may be inferred from the observation made by a High-land laird to his uncle James, as to the use of a crazy old building left standing beside a group of neat modern offices. "He found it of great convenience," he said, "every time his speculations brought a drove of pigs, or a squad of masons, that way." This sort of life and its surrounding circumstances were not of a poetical cast; yet the youth was now about the poetizing age, and during his solitary rambles after his day's work, by the banks of the Conon, he medi-ated poetry, and began to make verses. He would sometimes write them out upon his mason's kit, while the rain was dropping through the roof of the apartment upon the paper on which he wrote. It was a rough life of poetical musing, yet he always contrived to mix up a high degree of intellectual exercise and enjoyment with what-ever manual labor he was employed upon; and this, after all, is one of the secrets of a happy life. While observing scenery and natural history, he also seems to have very closely observed the characters of his fellow-workmen, and he gives us vivid and life-like portaits of some of the more remarkable of them in his Autobiography. There were some rough and occasionally very wicked fellows among his fellow-workmen, but he had strength of character, and sufficient inbred sound principle, to withstand their contamination. He was also proud,—and pride in its proper place is an excellent thing,—particularly that sort of pride which makes a man revolt from doing a mean action, or anything which would bring discredit on the family. This is the sort of true nobility which serves poor men in good stead sometimes, and it certainly served Hugh Miller well.

His apprenticeship ended, he "took jobs" for himself,—built a cottage for his Aunt Jenny, which still stands, and after that went out working as journeyman-mason. In his spare hours, he was improv-ing himself by the study of practical geometry, and made none the worse a mason on that account. While engaged in helping to build a mansion on the western coast of Ross-shire, he extended his geologi-cal and botanical observations, noting all that was remarkable in the formation of the district. He also drew his inferences from the condition of the people,—being very much struck, above other things, with the remarkably contented state of the Celtic popu-lation, although living in filth and misery. On this he shrewdly observes: "it was one of the palpable characteristics of our Scottish

Highlanders, for at least the first thirty years of the century, that they were contented enough, as a people, to find more to pity than to envy in the condition of their Lowland neighbors; and I remember that at this time, and for years after, I used to deem the trait a good one. I have now, however my doubts on the subject, and am not quiet sure whether a content so general as to be national may not, in certain circumstances, be rather a vice than a virtue. It is certainly no virtue, when it has the effect of arresting either individuals or peoples in their course of development ; and is periously allied to great suffering, when the men who exemplify it are so thoroughly happy amid the mediocrities of the present that they fail to make provision for the contingencies of the future."

Trade becoming slack in the North, Hugh Miller took ship for Edinburgh, where building was going briskly on (in 1824), to seek for employment there as a stone-hewer. He succeeded, and lived as a workman at Niddry, in the neighborhood of the city, for some time ; pursuing at the same time his geological observations in a new field, Niddry being located on the carboniferous system. Here also he met with an entirely new class of men,—the colliers,—many of whom, strange to say, had been *born slaves;* the manumission of the Scotch colliers having been effected in comparatively modern times,—as late as the year 1775 ! So that, after all, Scotland is not so very far ahead of the serfdom of Russia.

Returning to the North again, Miller next began business for himself in a small way, as a hewer of tombstones for the good folks of Cromarty. This change of employment was necessary, in consequence of the hewer's disease, caused by inhaling stone-dust, which settles in the lungs, and generally leads to rapid consumption, afflicting him with its premonitory symptoms. The strength of his constitution happily enabled him to throw off the malady, but his lungs never fairly recovered their former vigor. Work not being very plentiful, he wrote poems, some of which appeared in the newspapers; and in course of time a small collection of these pieces was published by subscription. He very soon, however, gave up poetry writing, finding that his humble accomplishment of verse was too narrow to contain his thinking ; so next time he wrote a book it was in prose, and vigorous prose too, far better than his verse. But Miller had meanwhile been doing what was better than either cutting tombstones or writing poetry : he had been building up his *character*, and thereby securing the respect of all who knew him. So that, when a branch of the Commercial Bank was opened in Cromarty, and the manager cast about him to make selection of an accountant, whom should he pitch upon but Hugh Miller, the stone-mason? This was certainly a most extraordinary selection ; but why was it made? Simply because of the excellence of the man's character, He had proved himself a true and a thoroughly excellent and trustworthy man in a humble capacity of life, and the

Inference was, that he would carry the same principles of conduct into another and higher sphere of action. Hugh Miller hesitated to accept the office, having but little knowledge of accounts, and no experience in book-keeping ; but the manager knew his pluck and determined· perseverance in mastering whatever he undertook ; above all, he had confidence in his character, and he would not take a denial. So Hugh Miller was sent to Edinburgh to learn his new business at the head bank.

Throughout life Miller seems to have invariably put his conscience into his work. Speaking of the old man with whom he served his apprenticeship as a mason, he says : "*He made conscience of every stone he laid.* It was remarked in the place, that the walls built by Uncle David never bulged nor fell ; and no apprentice nor journeyman of his, was permitted, under any plea, to make 'slight work.'" And one of his own Uncle James's instruction to him on one occasion was, "In all your dealings, give your neighbor *the cast of the bauk*,—'good measure, heaped up and running over,'— and you will not lose by it in the end." These lessons were worth far more than what is often taught in schools, and Hugh Miller seems to have framed his own conduct in life on the excellent moral teaching which they conveyed. Speaking of his own career as a workman, when on the eve of quitting it, he says : "I do think I acted up to my uncle's maxim ; and that, without injuring my brother workmen by lowering their prices. I never yet charged an employer for a piece of work that, fairly measured and valued, would not be rated at a slightly higher sum than that at which it stood in my account."

Although he gained some fame in his locality by his poems, and still more by his "Letters on the Herring Fisheries of Scotland," he was not, as many self-raised men are, spoiled by the praise which his works called forth. "There is," he says, "no more fatal error into which a working-man of a literary turn can fall, than the mistake of deeming himself too good for his humble employments ; and yet it is a mistake as common as it is fatal. I had already seen several poor wrecked mechanics, who, believing themselves to be poets, and regarding the manual occupation by which they could alone live in independence as beneath them, had become in consequence little better than mendicants,—too good to work for their bread, but not too good virtually to beg it ; and looking upon them as beacons of warning, I determined that, with God's help, I should give their error a wide offing, and never associate the idea of meanness with an honest calling, or deem myself too good to be independent." Full of this manly and robust spirit, Hugh Miller pursued his career of stone-hewing by day, and prose composition when the day's work was done, until he entered upon his new vocation of banker's accountant. He showed his self-denial, too, in waiting for a wife until he could afford to keep one in respectable comfort,—

his engagement lasting over five years, before he was in a position to fulfill his promise.   And then he married, wisely and happily.

At Edinburgh, by dint of perseverance and application, Mr. Miller shortly mastered his new business, and then returned to Cromarty, where he was installed in office.   His "Scenes and Legends of the North of Scotland" were published about the same time, and were well received ; and in his leisure hours he proceeded to prepare his most important work, on "The Old Red Sandstone."   He also contributed to the "Border Tales," and other periodicals.   The Free-Church movement drew him out as a polemical writer : and his Letter to Lord Brougham on the Scotch Church Controversy excited so much attention, that the leaders of the movement in Edinburgh invited him to undertake the editing of the Witness newspaper, the organ of the Free-Church party.   He accepted the invitation, and continued to hold the editorship until his death, in 1856.

The circumstances connected with his decease were of a most distressing character.   On entering his room one morning, he was found lying dead, shot through the body, and under circumstances which left no doubt that he had died by his own hand.   He had for some time been closely applying himself to the completion of his "Testimony of the Rocks," without rest or relaxation, or due attention to his physical health.   Under these circumstances, overwork of the brain speedily began to tell upon him.   He could not sleep, —if he lay down and dozed, it was only to wake in a start, his head filled with imaginary horrors; and in one of these fits of his disease he put an end to his life;—a warning to all brain-workers, that the powers of the human constitution may be strained until they break, and that even the best and strongest mind cannot dispense with the due observance of the laws which regulate the physical constitution of man.

FRANCIS JEFFREY.

SOME thirty years since, we happened to visit the High Courts of Session, held in Edinburgh, in the purlieus of the old Scotch Parliament-House. These are the chief law courts of Scotland; and though they are always objects of interest to a visitor, they were perhaps more so at that time than they are now, in consequence of their being then professionally frequented by several men of world-wide reputation.

We remember well the striking entrance to those courts; they occupy one side of a square, opposite to the old cathedral church of St. Giles's, where Jenny Geddes initiated the great Rebellion of two centuries back, by hurling her "cutty-stool" at the head of the officiating bishop, on his proposing to read the collect for the day. "Diel colic the wame o' thee!" shouted Jenny, as she hurled her stool at the bishop; and from that point the Revolution began. John Knox, at an earlier period, used to deliver his thrilling harangues in the same church; and in the space now forming the square—which was used as a cemetery previous to the Reformation—the mortal remains of that undaunted reformer were laid; of whom the Regent Murray said, as he was lowered into his grave, "There lies one who never feared the face of man." Another portion of the square was formerly occupied by the old jail or Tolbooth of Edinburgh, celebrated throughout the world by Scott's novel of "The Heart of Mid-Lothian."* But it had been demolished some years before the period of our visit.

Entering the courts by a door in the southwest corner of the square, and crossing a spacious vestibnle, we passed through a pair of folding doors, and found ourselves in the famous Parliament-

---

* A popular orator from the South once greatly disturbed the complacency of an Edinburgh audience, by addressing them as "Men of the Heart of Mid-Lothian"!

House. It is a noble hall, upwards of one hundred and twenty feet long, and about fifty wide. Its lofty roof is oak, arched with gilt pendants, in the style of Westminster Hall. This was the place in which the Scottish Parliament held its sittings for about seventy years previous to the Union. It was in a bustle, as it usually is during the sittings of the court, with advocates promenading in their wigs and gowns; writers (*Anglice*, solicitors), with their blue and red bags crammed with bundles of legal documents, scudding hither and thither; litigants, with anxious countenances, collected in groups, anxiously discussing the progress of their "case;" whilst above the din and hum which filled the hall there occasionally rose the loud voice of the criers, summoning the counsel in the different causes to appear before their lordships.

All the courts open into this hall, and we entered one of these; we think it was the Justiciary Court. We have no recollection of the cause that was being tried; some petty horse-warranty affair or other, about which a great deal of clever sarcasm and eloquence was displayed. But though we have forgotten the cause that was tried, we have not forgotten the pleader. He rose immediately after his burly opponent had seated himself,—Patrick Robertson, for a long time the wit of the Parliament-House,—the author of a book of poems, published a few years ago, full of gravity, but without poetry,— afterwards Lord Robertson. The advocate who rose to reply was a man the very opposite in feature, form, and temperament to Patrick Robertson. A little, slender, dark-eyed man, of a highly intellectual appearance; his head was small,—indeed, the opponents of phrenology have asserted that his head was *so* small, that it was enough of itself to overthrow that science,—but then it was exquisitely formed, the organs were beautifully balanced, the bulk of the brain lay over the forehead, and the outline was such as to give one the impression of the finest possible organization. He wore no wig; and his black hair was brushed straight up from his beautiful forehead.

When he rose to his feet, the hum of the court was stilled into silence ; and one who accompanied us said, "You see that little man there going to speak?" "Yes." "That's FRANCIS JEFFREY, of the Edinburgh Review." And Jeffrey went on with his speech in a high-keyed, sharp, clear, and acute strain, not rising into eloquence, but running on in a smart and copious, yet somewhat precise, manner : indeed, one might have denominated his style of speech and of argument as a little *finical;* yet it was unusually complete and highly finished, like everything else that he did.

But there was in the same court that day one whose reputation and whose genius infinitely transcended Jeffrey's, great though these may have been. Sitting immediately under the Lord President, at the clerk's table, were two men, one on each side,—the clerks of the Court of Session. "You see that man at the table

there,—the one with the white hair and the overhanging brow?,.
"Yes, I see *two;* they have both white hair, and are both heavy-
browed." "Yes; but I mean the one to the Lord President's right,—
immediately before Patrick Robertson there." "The one with his
head stooping over his papers, writing?" "Yes: see, he is now
rising up, and going across the room." "I see him,—surely I know
that face; I must have seen the man before." "You may have seen
the portrait of him often enough,—it is Sir Walter Scott!" In a
moment we recognized the Great Wizard of the North, whose magical pen had quickened into life the long dead and buried past, and
created shapes of magical beauty by the aid of his wonderful
fancy,—the greatest literary celebrity of the age! His face, as we
saw it then, presented but few indications of those remarkable intellectual powers, which might almost be said to *blaze* in the features
of Jeffrey. It was heavy, solid, *lourd,* and homely,—somewhat like
the face of a country-bred farmer's man, grown old in harness, and
rather "back" with his rent. He limped across the court to one of
the advocates or writers to the signet, to whom he delivered a paper,
and then returned to his seat. The terrible crash of Sir Walter
Scott's fortunes had occurred, through the failure of his publisher,
but a few years before; and here was the hard-working man, still
toiling at his post of clerk of court during the day,—to enter upon
his laborious literary labors on returning home,—all with the view
of desperately retrieving the loss of his fortune and estate.

One other man we may mention,—then a comparatively young
advocate in good business. His eye, of all his features, struck us
the most. Never did we see a more beautiful, piercing eye before.
Keen, black, and penetrating, it seemed to look through you. Once
afterwards, we encountered the eye in Princes' Street, and recognized the man on the instant. It was Henry Cockburn, the author
of the "Life of Jeffrey." He had the look of a man of genius; and
was long afterwards known as a highly acute and able lawyer. But
he had never before done anything in literature that we know of,
until he wrote the life of his friend Jeffrey; yet we mistake much if
it do not take its place among the best standard biographies of our
time. We should not be surprised if, like Boswell's Johnson, it
were read when the books of the author whose life is commemorated
are allowed to lie on the shelf.

Not that there is any vivid interest in Jeffrey's life; happy and
prosperous people have usually little history. Life flows on in a
smooth current; everything succeeds with them; they gather wealth
and fame with years, and die full of honors, which are recorded on
a mausoleum. But certainly there was about the life of Jeffrey—
even independently of the literary merits of Lord Cockburn's por-
traiture of him, much that is instructive, interesting, and delightful.

Jeffrey was a man full of bonhomie. He was an honest minded,
independent man; a most industrious, hard-working, and persever-

ant man ; and, withal, a genuinely loving man. But above all, he was the founder of the "Edinburgh Review." This was the great event of his life. By means of that eminently able organ of opinion, he elevated criticism into a magistrature. He invested it with dignity, and administered it like a judge, according to certain laws. He became an oracle of taste in poetry, literature, and art. He did not merely follow the literary fashion of the day, but he directed it, and for many years presided over the highest critical organ in the country. Yet it will be confessed, that, if we look into the collected edition of his works, they have comparatively little interest for us. Even the most effective criticism is necessarily of an ephemeral character. Like a thrilling Parliamentary speech, its chief interest consists in its appropriateness to the time, the circumstances, and the audience to whom it is addressed. At best, literary criticism is but a clever and discriminating judgment upon books. The books so criticised are now either dead and forgotten, or they have secured a footing, and live on independent of all criticism. Yet criticism is not without its value, as Jeffrey and his fellow laborers amply proved.

The leading incidents of Francis Jeffrey's life are soon told. He was born in Charles street, George's square, in the old town of Edinburgh, on the 22d of October, 1773. His father was a depute clerk, in the Court of Session. His mother was an amiable, intelligent woman, who died when Francis was but a boy. The youth was educated at the Edinburgh High School, where he remained for six years. Here is an incident of his boyhood :—

"One day in the winter of 1786-87, he was standing in the high street, staring at a man whose appearance struck him ; a person standing at a shop door tapped him on the shoulder, and said, 'Ay, laddie ! ye may weel look at that man ! that's ROBERT BURNS.' He never saw Burns again.

From Edinburgh High School, Jeffrey proceeded to Glasgow University where he studied with distinction during two sessions. In the Historical and Critical Club, he astonished the members by the force and acuteness of his criticisms on the essays submitted for discussion. Thus early did the peculiar bent of his mind display itself. He worked very hard,—was a systematic student,—took copious notes, cast into his own forms of expression, of all the lectures,—and read largely on all subjects. He returned to Edinburgh, and attended the law classes there in the ,two sessions of 1789-91, still studying and composing essays on various subjects, but chiefly on life and its philosophy.

"It was about this time (1790 or 1791) that he had the honor of assisting to carry the biographer of Johnson, in a state of great intoxication, to bed. For this he was rewarded next morning by Mr. Boswell, who had learned who his bearers had been, clapping his head, and telling him that he was a very promising lad, and that, 'If you go on as you've begun, you may live to be a Bozzy yourself yet."

He next went to Oxford to study, and remained there for a season, but he never entered fully into the life of the place, and evidently detested it. He did not find a single genial companion. He says of the meetings of the students, "O these blank parties!—the quintessence of insipidity,—the conversation dying from lip to lip,—every countenance lengthening and obscuring in the shade of mutual lassitude,—the stifled yawn contending with the affected smile on every cheek,—and the languor and stupidity of the party gathering and thickening every instant, by the mutual contagion of embarrassment and disgust......In the name of heaven, what do such beings conceive to be the order and use of society? To them, it is no source of enjoyment; and there cannot be a more complete abuse of time, mind, and fruit." He detests the law, too. "This law," he says, "is vile work. I wish I had been born a piper." There was only one thing that he hoped to learn at Oxford, and that was the English pronunciation. And he certainly succeeded in acquiring it after a sort, but he never spoke it as an Englishman is wont to do. As Lord Holland said of him afterwards, "he lost the *broad Scotch* at Oxford, but he gained only the *narrow English* in its place.

He returned to Edinburgh in July, 1792, and again attended the law lectures there. He joined the Speculative Society, then numbering among its active members many afterwards highly celebrated men,—Scott, Brougham, Grant (afterwards Lord Glenelg), Petty (afterwards Marquis of Lansdowne), Francis Horner, and others. Jeffrey distinguished himself by several admirable papers which he read before the society; and also by the part which he took in the discussions. But, like many susceptible young minds, at this time, he was haunted by fits of despondency. He could not take the world by storm : few knew that he lived. How was he to distinguish himself? He would be *a Poet!* Writing to his sister about this time, he said, "*I feel I shall never be a great man, unless it be as a Poet!*" But afterwards he says more calmly, "My poetry does not improve ; *I think it is growing worse every week.* If I could find the heart to abandon it, I believe I should be the better for it." He nevertheless went on writing tragedies, love poems, sonnets, odes, and such like ; but they never saw the light. Once, indeed, he went so far as to leave a poem with a bookseller, to be published,— and fled to the country ; but finding some obstacle had occurred, he returned, recovered the manuscript,—rejoicing that he had been saved,—and never repeated so perilous an experiment.

In 1794, Jeffrey was called to the Scotch bar. The times were sick and out of joint. The French Revolution was afoot, and its violence tended to drive some men sternly back upon the past, and to impel others wildly forward into the future. Some took a middle course ; and, while they discountenanced all violent change, sought after constitutional progress and social improvement. To this middle party, Jeffrey early attached himself. He joined himself to the

Whigs, though to do so at that day was to erect a lofty barrier in the way of his own success. Yet he did so, courageously and resolutely ; and he held to his course. He had several noble allies ; among whom may be named Brougham, Horner, and Erksine (the brother of the Lord Chancellor). At the bar, Jeffrey got on very slowly. Very few fees came in, and these were chiefly from his father's connections. He began to despair of success, and even went to London with the object of becoming a literary "grub." He was furnished with letters to authors, newspaper editors, and publishers. But, fortunately, they received him coldly, and he returned to Edinburgh to reoccupy himself with essay writing, translating from the Greek, and waiting for clients. The clients did not come yet, and he began seriously to despair of ever achieving success in his profession.

"I cannot help," he wrote at this time, "looking upon a slow, obscure, and philosophical starvation at the Scotch bar, as a destiny not to be submitted to. There are some moments when I think I could sell myself to the minister or to the devil, in order to get above these necessities." He also entertained the idea of trying the English bar, or going out to India, like so many other young Scotchmen of his day. He had now been five years at the bar, and could not yet, as the country saying goes, "make saut to his kail." In the seventh year of his practice, he says, "My profession has never yet brought me £100 a year." But this is the history of nearly all young men in their first ascent of the steeps of professional enterprise.

Yet Jeffrey's poor prospects did not prevent him falling in love with a girl as poor as himself, and he married her. The young lady was, however, of good family: she was the daughter of Dr. Nelson, Professor of Church History at St. Andrew's. The young pair settled down in Buccleuch Place, in the Old Town ; and the biographer informs us that "his own study was only made comfortable at the cost of £7 18s.; the banqueting-hall rose to £13 8s.; and the drawing-room actually rose to £22 19s." He made a careful inventory of all the costs of furnishing, which is still preserved.

But his marriage seemed to have been the starting-point of Jeffrey's success. He devoted himself sedulously to his profession. Clients appeared in greater numbers; he began to be looked upon as a rising man; and when once the ball is fairly set a-rolling, it goes on comparatively easy. Shortly after, the famous Edinburgh Review was projected by himself and Sydney Smith, though the merit of suggesting the work is undoubtedly due to the latter. Sydney Smith's account of its origin is this: "One day we happened to meet in the eighth or ninth story, or flat, in Buccleuch Place, the elevated residence of the then Mr. Jeffrey. I proposed that we should set up a review; this was acceded to with acclamation. I was appointed editor, and remained long enough in Edinburgh to edit the first number of the Edinburgh Review." But Jeffrey's aptness for editorial work, his peculiar critical ability, together with the fact of his being the only settled man of the lot permanently located in Edinburgh, soon led to his undertaking the entire control of the Review, and furnishing the principal part of the writing.

The first number of the Edinburgh Review appeared in October, 1802, and the effect produced by it was almost electrical. It was so bold, so novel, so spirited and able, –so unlike anything of the kind that had heretofore appeared,—that its success from the first was decided. It afforded a gratifying proof of the existence of liberal feeling in a part of the country where before one dull, dead uniform level of slavish obsequiency had prevailed. It gave a voice to the dormant feeling of independence which nevertheless still survived. The effect upon public opinion was most wholesome, and the influence of the Review went on increasing from year to year. Horner, Sydney Smith, and Brougham soon left Edinburgh for England, to enter upon public life; but Jeffrey stood by the Review, and continued its main-stay. When Horner left Edinburgh, he made a present of his bar wig to Jeffrey, who "hoped that in time it would attract fees" besides admiration. But Jeffrey never liked to wear a wig, and soon abandoned it for his own fine black hair. Among the greatest bores which he experienced was attending Scotch appeals in the House of Lords in London, when he had to sit under a great load of serge and horsehair, perhaps in the very height of the dog-days!

His practice increased, while his fame in connection with the Review spread his name abroad. His severe handling of many of the writers of the day, brought down upon him a good deal of bitter speech,—such as Lord Byron's "English Bards and Scotch Reviewers." His severe review of Moore's lascivious love poems brought him into collision with that gentleman, and an innocuous duel was the consequence; but after that they remained warm friends. There was little of interest in Jeffrey's life for many years after this occurrence. It flowed on in an equable and widening current of steady prosperity. His wife died in 1805, and was sincerely lamented by him. The letter which he wrote to his brother on the occasion is exceedingly beautiful,—full of affectionate and deep feeling for the departed. "I took no interest," he says, "in anything which had not some reference to her. I had no enjoyment away from her, except in thinking what I should have to tell or to show her on my return; and I have never returned to her, after half a day's absence, without feeling my heart throb and my eye brighten with all the ardor and anxiety of a youthful passion. All the exertions I ever made in the world were for her sake entirely. You know how indolent I was by nature, and how regardless of reputation and fortune; but it was a delight to me to lay these things at the feet of my darling, and to invest her with some portion of the distinction she deserved, and to increase the pride and vanity she felt for her

husband, by accumulating these public tests of his merit. She had
so lively a relish for life, too, and so unquenchable and unbroken a
hope in the midst of protracted illness and languor, that the stroke
which cut it off forever appears equally cruel and unnatural.
Though familiar with sickness, she seemed to have nothing to do
with death. She always recovered so rapidly, and was so cheerful
and affectionate and playful, that it scarcely entered into my
imagination that there could be one sickness from which she would
not recover." But Jeffrey did not remain single. A few years after,
in 1813, we find him on his way to the United States, to bring home
his second wife,—a grand-niece of the famous John Wilkes. He
wooed and won her, and an admirable wife she made him.

There are only a few other prominent landmarks in Jeffrey's
career, which we would note in the midst of his prosperous life. In
1820 he was elected Lord Rector of the University of Glasgow, and
delivered a noble speech on his installation. In 1829 he was elected
Dean of the Faculty of Advocates, a post of high honor in the profession. On being elected, he gave up the editorship of the Review,
after superintending it for a period of twenty-seven years. In 1830
the Whigs came into office, and Jeffrey was appointed Lord Advocate,—the first law officer of the Crown for Scotland. This was the
height of his ambition. He could only climb a step higher, which
he did a few years later, when he was made a judge, and died Lord
Jeffrey, in January, 1850.

His friend and fellow-judge has admirably depicted Jeffrey as he
lived,—in his home life, which was beautiful, and in his public
career, which was honorable, useful, and meritorious. He was a
most affectionate man. In one of his letters,—and they are, perhaps, the most charming portions of the work,—he says, "I am
every hour more convinced of the error of those who look for happiness in anything but concentered and tranquil affection." His intellect was sharp and bright,—not so powerful as keen. His
knowledge was various rather than profound. His taste was exquisite ; his sense of honor very fine ; and his manner was full of gentleness and kindness. Withal, he was an earnest, resolute man,
whose heart glowed in the conflicts of the world. In conclusion we
may add, that Lord Jeffrey, in his valuable life, has furnished a further illustration of what honorable, persistent industry and application will do for a man in this life ; for it was mainly this that
raised him from obscurity and dependence to a position of afflu-
ence and worldly renown.

EBENEZER ELLIOTT.

EBENEZER ELLIOTT, the Sheffield iron-merchant, a poet of no mean fame, was extensively known beyond the bounds of his own locality as "the Corn-Law Rhymer." Though for a time identified with a political movement, to which he consecrated the service of his lyre, he had nevertheless the world-wide vision of the true poet, who is of no sect nor party. Any one who reads his poems will not fail to note how closely his soul was knit to universal nature—how his pulse beat in unison with her,—how deeply he read and how truly he interpreted her meanings. With a heart glowing for love of his kind, out of which indeed his poetry first sprung, and with a passionate sense of wrongs inflicted upon the suffering poor, which burst out in words of electric, almost tremendous power, there was combined a tenderness and purity of thought and feeling, and a love for Nature in all her moods, of the most refined and beautiful character. In his scathing denunciations of power misused, how terrible he is ; but in his expression of beauty, how sweet! Bitter and fierce though his rhymes are when his subject is "the dirt-kings,—the tax-gorged lords of land," we see that all his angry spirit is disarmed when he takes himself out to breathe the fresh breath of the heavens, in the green lane, on the open heath, or up among the wild mountains. There he takes Nature to his bosom,—calls her by the sweetest of names, pours his soul out before her, gives her his whole heart, and yields up to her his manly adoration. You see this beautiful side of the poet's character in his exquisite poems entitled "The Wonders of the Lane," "Come and Gone," "The Excursion," "The Dying Boy to the Sloe Blossom," "Flowers for the Heart," "Don and Rother," and even in "Winhill," that most powerful of his odes. The utterance is that of a man, but the heart is tender as that of a woman. These exquisite little poems of Elliott, in their terseness and vividness of expression, and their sweetness and delicacy of execution, cannot fail to remind one of the kindred magical power and genius of Robert Burns.

Elliott's life proved, what is still a disputed point, that the culti-
vation of poetic tastes is perfectly compatible with success in trade
and commerce. It is a favorite dogma of some men, that he who
courts the Muses must necessarily be unfitted for the practical business of life; and that to succeed in trade, a man must live altogether for it, and never rise above the consideration of its little
details. This is, in our opinion, a notion at variance with actual
experience. Generally speaking, you will find the successful literary man a man of industry, application, steadiness, and sobriety.
He must be a hard worker. He must apply himself. He must
economize time, and coin it into sterling thought, if not into sterling money. His habits tell upon his whole character, and mold it
into consistency. If he be in business, he must be diligent to succeed in it; and his intelligence gives him resources which to the
ignorant man are denied. It may not have been so in the last century, when the literary man was a rara avis, a world's wonder, and
was fêted and lionized until he became irretrievably spoiled; but
now, when all men have grown readers, and a host of men have become writers, the literary man is no longer a novelty : he drags quietly along in the social team, engages in business, succeeds, and
economizes, just as other men do, and generally to much better purpose than the illiterate and the uncultivated. Some of the most successful men in business, at the present day, are men who regularly
wield the pen in the intervals of their daily occupations, – some for
self-culture, others for pleasure, others because they have something
cheerful or instructive to utter to their fellow-men ; and shall we
say that those men are less usefully employed than if they had been
cracking filberts over their wine, sleeping over a newspaper, gadding
at clubs, or engaging in the frivolity of evening parties?

Ebenezer Elliott was a man who profitably applied his leisure
hours to the pursuit of literature, and, while he succeeded in business, he gained an eminent reputation as a poet. After a long life
spent in business, working his way up from the position of a laboring man to that of an employer of labor, a capitalist, and a merchant,
he retired from active life, built a house on a little estate of his own,
and sat under his "vine and fig-tree" during the declining years of
his life; cheered by the prospect of a large family of virtuous sons
and daughters growing up around him in happiness and usefulness.

We enjoyed the pleasure of a visit to this gifted man, at his own
fireside, little more than a month before his death. It was one of the
last lovely days of autumn, when the faint breath of summer was
still lingering among the woods and fields, as if loath to depart from
the earth she had gladdened; the blackbird was still piping his
mellifluous song in the hedges and coppice, whose foliage was tinted
in purple, russet, and brown, with just enough of green to give that
perfect autumnal tint, so beautifully pictorial, but impossible to
paint in words. The beech-nuts were dropping from the trees, and

crackled under foot, and a rich, damp smell rose from the decaying leaves by the road-side. After a short walk through a lovely, undulating country, from the Darfield station of the North Midland Railway, along one of the old Roman roads, so common in that part of Yorkshire, and which leads into the famous Watling Street, near the town of Pontefract, we reached the village of Old Houghton, at the south end of which stands the curious Old Hall,—an interesting relic of Middle-Age antiquity. Its fantastic gable-end, projecting windows, quaint doorway, diamond "quarrels," and its great size looming up in the twilight, with the well-known repute which the house bears of being "haunted," made us regard it with a strange, awe-like feeling; it seemed like a thing not of this every-day world; indeed, the place breathes the very atmosphere of the olden time, and a host of associations connected with a most interesting period of old English history are called up by its appearance. It reminds one of the fantastic old Tabard, in Dickens's "Barnaby Rudge" (we think it is); and the resemblance is strengthened by the fact of this Old Hall being now converted into a modern public-house, the inscription of "Licensed to be drunk on the premises," etc., being legibly written on a sign-board over the fantastic old porch. "To what base uses," alas! do our old country-houses come at last! Being open to the public, we entered; and there we found a lot of the village laborers, ploughmen, and delvers, engaged, in a boxed-off corner of the Old Squire's Hall, drinking their Saturday night's quota of beer, amidst a cloud of tobacco-smoke; while the mistress of the place, seated at the tap in another corner of the apartment, was dealing out her potations to all comers and purchasers. A huge black deer's head and antlers projected from the wall, near the door, evidently part of the antique furniture of the place; and we had a glimpse of a fine broad stone staircase, winding up in one of the deep bays of the hall, leading to the state apartments above. Though strongly tempted to seek a night's lodging in this haunted house, as well as to explore the mysteries of the interior, we resisted the desire, and set forward on our journey to the more inviting house of the poet.

We reached Hargate Hill, the house and home of Ebenezer Elliott, in the dusk of the autumn evening. There was just light enough to enable us to perceive that it was situated on a pleasant height, near the hill-top, commanding an extensive prospect of the undulating and finely-wooded country towards the south; on the north stretched away an extensive tract of moorland, covered with gorse-bushes. A nicely-kept flower-garden and grass-plot lay before the door, with some of the last of the year's roses still in bloom. We had a cordial welcome from the poet, his wife, and two interesting daughters,— the other members of his large family being settled in life for themselves,—two sons, clergymen, in the West Indies, two in Sheffield, and others elsewhere. Elliott looked the wan invalid that he was, pale and thin; and his hair was nearly white. Age had deeply marked his features since last we saw him; and, instead of the iron-framed, firm-voiced man we had seen and heard in Palace Yard, London, some eleven years before, and in his own town of Sheffield at a more recent date, he now seemed a comparatively weak and feeble old man. An anxious expression of face indicated that he had suffered much acute pain,—which indeed was the case. After he had got rid of that subject, and begun to converse about more general topics, his countenance brightened up, and, under the stimulus of delightful converse, he became, as it were, a new man. With all his physical weakness, we found that his heart beat as warm and true as ever to the cause of human kind. The old struggles of his life were passed in review, and fought over again; and he displayed the same zeal and entertained the same strong faith in the old cause which he had rhymed about so long before it seized hold of the public mind. He mentioned, what I had not before known, that the Sheffield Anti-Corn-Law Association was the first to start the system of operations afterwards adopted by the League, and that they first employed Paulton as a public lecturer; but to Cobden he gave the praise of having popularized the cause, knocked it into the public head by dint of sheer hard work and strong practical sense, and to Cobden he still looked as the great leader of the day,—one of the most advanced and influential minds of his time. The patriotic struggle in Hungary had enlisted his warmest sympathies; and he spoke of Kossuth as "cast in the mold of the greatest heroes of antiquity." Of the Russian Emperor he spoke as "that tremendous villain, Nicholas," and he believed him to be so infatuated by his success in Hungary, that he would not know where to stop, but would rush blindly to his ruin.

The conversation then led towards his occupations in this remote country spot, whither he had retreated from the busy throng of men, and the engrossing pursuits and anxieties of business. Here he said he had given himself up to meditation and thought; nor had he been idle with his pen either, having a volume of prose and poetry nearly ready for publication. Strange to say, he spoke of his prose as the better part of his writings, and, as he himself thought, much superior to his poetry. But he is not the first instance of a great writer who has been in error as to the comparative value of his own works. On that question the world, and especially posterity, will pronounce the true verdict.

He spoke with great interest of the beautiful scenery of the neighborhood, which had been a source to him of immense joy and delight; of the two great old oaks, near the old Roman road, about a mile to the north, under the shade of which the Wapontake formerly assembled, and in the hollow of one of which, in more recent times, Nevison the highwayman used to take shelter, but it was burnt down in spite, after his execution, by a band of gypsies; of the glorious wooded country which stretched to the south,—Wentworth, Wharncliffe, Conisborough, and the fine scenery of the Dearne and the Don ; of the many traditions which still lingered about the neighborhood, and which, he said, some Walter Scott, could he gather them up before they died away, would make glow again with life and beauty.

"Did you see," he observed, "that curious Old Hall on your way up? The terrible despot Wentworth, Lord Strafford, married his third wife from that very house, and afterwards lived in it for some time ; and no wonder it is rumored among the country folks as 'haunted ;' for if it be true that unquiet, perpetual spirits have power to wander over the earth, after the body to which they had been bound is dead, *his* could never endure the peaceful rest of the grave. After Wentworth's death it became the property of Sir William Rhodes, a stout Presbyterian and Parliamentarian. When the great civil war broke out, Rhodes took the field with his tenantry, on the side of the Parliament, and the first encounter between the two parties is said to have taken place only a few miles to the north of Old Houghton. While Rhodes was at Tadcaster with Sir Thomas Fairfax, Captain Grey (an ancestor of the present Earl Grey), at the head of a body of about three hundred Royalist horse, attacked the Old Hall, and, there being only some thirty servants left to defend it, took the place and set fire to it, destroying all that would burn. But Cromwell rode down the cavaliers with his plowmen at Marston Moor, not very far from here either, and then Rhodes built the little chapel that you would still see standing apart at the west end of the Hall, and established a godly Presbyterian divine to minister there ; forming a road from thence to Driffield, about three miles off, to enable the inhabitants of that place to reach it by a short and convenient route. I forget how it happened," he continued, "I believe it was by marriage,—but so it was that the estate fell into the possession, in these later days, of Moncktown Milnes, to whom it now belongs. But as Monk Frystone was preferred as a family residence, and was in a more thriving neighborhood, the chief part of the land about was sold to other proprietors, and only some three holdings were retained, in virtue of which Mr. Milnes continues lord of the manor, and is entitled to his third share of the moor or waste lands in the neighborhood, which may be reclaimed under Inclosure Acts. But the Old Hall has been dismantled, and all the fine old furniture and tapestry and paintings have been removed down to the new house at Monk Frystone."

And then the conversation turned upon Monckton Milnes, his fine poetry, and his "Life of Keats,"—on Keats, of whom Elliott spoke in terms of glowing eulogy as that great "resurectionized Greek,"—on Southey, who had so kind proffered his services in advancing the interests of Elliott's two sons, the clergymen, whose livings he obtained for them,—on Carlyle, whom he admired as one of the greatest of living poets, though writing not in rhyme,—and on Longfellow, whose "Evangeline" he had not yet seen, but longed to read. And thus the evening stole on with delightful converse in the heart of that quiet, happy family, the listeners recking not that the lips of the eloquent speaker would soon be moist with the dews of death. Shortly after the date of this visit, we sent the poet a copy of "Evangeline," of which he observed, in a letter written after a delightful perusal of it : "Longfellow is indeed a poet, and he has done what I deemed an impossibility,—he has written English hexameters, giving our mighty lyre a new string ! When Tennyson dies, he should read 'Evangeline' to Homer." Poor Elliott ! That task, if a possible one, be now his !

We cannot better conclude this brief sketch than by giving the last lines which Elliott wrote, while autumn was yet lingering round his dwelling, and the appearance of the robin red-breast near the door augured the approach of winter. They were written at the request of the poet's daughter (who was married only about a fortnight before his death), to the air of "'Tis time this heart should be unmoved" :—

> Thy notes, sweet Robin, soft as dew,
>   Heard soon or late, are dear to me ;
> To music I could bid adieu,
>   But not to thee.

> When from my eyes this life-full throng
>   Has past away no more to be ;
> Then, Autumn's primrose, Robin's song,
>   Return to me.

GEORGE BORROW.

SINCE the publication of "The Bible in Spain," a singularly interesting and fascinating book, few English writers have excited so deep a personal interest as George Borrow,—Gypsy George,—Don Giorgio,—the Gypsy Hogarth. The writer projected so much of *himself* into that book, as well as into his "Gypsies of Spain," his first published work, and gave us such delightful glimpses of his own life and experience, as keenly to whet our curiosity, and make us eagerly long to know more about him.

Here was a traveling missionary of the Bible Society, who knew all about gypsy life and lingo, was familiar with the lowest haunts of field thieves and mendicants, and up to all their gibberish ; a horse-sorcerer and whisperer, a student of pugilism under Thurtell, and himself no mean practioner in "the noble art of self-defense," but withal a man of the most varied gifts and accomplishments,—a philologist or "word-master," knowing nearly every language in Europe and the East,—a racy and original writer, with the force of Cobbett and the learning of Parr,—the translator of the Bible, or parts of it, into Mantchou, Basque, Rommaney, or Gypsy-tongue, and many other languages, and of old Danish ballads into English, a person of fascinating conversation and of powerful eloquence. Fancy these varied gifts embodied in a man standing six feet two in his stocking-soles, his frame one of iron, his daring and intrepidity unmatched, and you have placed before your mind's eye George Borrow, the Bible missionary,—the Gypsy Hogarth,—the emissary of Exeter Hall,—the quondam pupil of Thurtell,—Lavengro, the Word-master !

One wishes to know much of this extraordinary being. What is his history? What has been his life? It must be full of novel experiences, the like of which was never before written. Well, he has written a book called "Lavengro," in which he proposes to satisfy the public curiosity about himself, and to illustrate his biography as "Scholar, Gypsy, and Priest." The book, however, is not all

fact ; it is fact mixed liberally with fiction,—a kind of poetic rhapsody ; and yet it contains many graphic pictures of real life,—life
little known of, such as exists to this day among the by-lanes and
on the moors of England.   One thing is obvious, the book is thoroughly original, like all Mr. Borrow has written.   It smells of the
green lanes and breezy downs,—of the field and the tent ; and his
characters bear the tan of the sun and the marks of the weather
upon their faces.   The book is not written as a practiced book-
maker would write it ; it is not pruned down to suit current tastes.
Borrow throws into it whatever he has picked up on the high-ways
and by-ways, garnishing it up with his own imaginative spicery ad
libitum, and there you have it,—"Lavengro ; the Scholar, the Gypsy,
the Priest!"   But the work is not yet completed, seeing that he has
only as yet treated us to the two former parts of the character ;
"The Priest" is yet to come, and then we shall see how it happened
that Exeter Hall was enabled to secure the services of this gifted
missionary.

From his childhood George Borrow was a wanderer, and doubtless his early associations and experiences gave their color to his future life.   His father was a captain of militia about the beginning
of the present century, when the principal garrison duties of the
country were performed by that force.   The regiment was constantly
moving about from place to place, and thus England, Scotland, and
Ireland passed as a panorama before the eyes of the militia officer's
son.   He was born at East Dereham, in Norfolk, when the regiment
was lying there in 1803.   Borrow claims the honor of gentle birth,
for his father was a Cornish gentillatre, and by his mother he was
descended from an old Huguenot family, who were driven out of
France at the Revocation of the Edict of Nantes, and, like many
other of their countrymen, settled down in the neighborhood of
Norwich.   Borrow the elder was a man of courage, and though
never in battle, he fought with his fists, and vanquished "Big Ben
Brain," in Hyde Park, a feat of which his son thinks highly, and
the more so, as Big Ben Brain, four months after the event, "was
champion of England, having vanquished the heroic Johnson.
Honor to Brain, who, at the end of four other months, worn out by
the dreadful blows which he had received in his many combats, expired in the arms of my father, who read the Bible to him in his
later moments,—Big Ben Brain."   Such are the son's own words in
his autobiographic "Lavengro."

Borrow had one brother older than himself, an artist, a pupil of
Haydon, the historical painter.   He died abroad in comparative
youth, but after he had given promise of excellency in his profession.
This elder brother was the father's favorite; for George, when a child,
was moody and reserved,—a lover of nooks and retired corners,
shunning society, and sitting for hours together with his head upon
his breast.   But the family were constantly wandering and shifting

about, following the quarters of the regiment, sometimes living in barracks, sometimes in lodgings, and sometimes in camp. At a place called Pett, in Sussex, they thus lived under canvas walls, and here the first snake-charming incident in the child's life occurred:

"It happened that my brother and myself were playing one evening in a sandy lane, in the neighborhood of this Pett camp; our mother was at a slight distance. All of a sudden a bright yellow, and, to my infantine eye, beautiful and glorious object, made its appearance at the top of the bank from between the thick quickset, and, gliding down, began to move across the lane to the other side, like a line of golden light. Uttering a cry of pleasure, I sprang forward, and seized it nearly by the middle. A strange sensation of numbing coldness seemed to pervade my whole arm, which surprised me the more, as the object, to the eye, appeared so warm and sunlike. I did not drop it, however, but, holding it up, looked at it intently, as its head dangled about a foot from my hand. It made no resistance; I felt not even the slightest struggle; but now my brother began to scream and shriek like one possessed. 'O mother, mother!' said he, 'the viper! my brother has a viper in his hand!' He then, like one frantic, made an effort to snatch the creature away from me. The viper now hissed amain, and raised its head, in which were eyes like hot coals, menacing, not myself, but my brother. I dropped my captive, for I saw my mother running towards me; and the reptile, after standing for a moment nearly erect, and still hissing furiously, made off, and disappeared. The whole scene is now before me as vividly as if it occurred yesterday,—the gorgeous viper, my poor, dear, frantic brother, my agitated parent, and a frightened hen clucking under the bushes,—and yet I was not three years old."

Borrow cites this as an instance of the power which some persons possess of exercising an inherent power or fascination—call it mesmeric, if you will—over certain creatures; and he afterwards cites instances of the same kind, or the taming of wild horses by the utterance of words or whispers, or by certain movements, which seemed to have power over them.

Thus the family wandered through Norfolk, Suffolk, Essex, and Kent. At Hythe, the sight of a huge Danish skull, the headpiece of some mighty old Scandinavian pirate, lying in the old penthouse adjoining the village church, struck the boy's imagination with awe; and, like the apparition of the viper in the sandy lane, it dwelt in his mind, affording copious food for thought and wonder. "An indefinable curiosity for all that is connected with the Danish race began to pervade me; and if, long after, when I became a student, I devoted myself, with peculiar zest, to Danish lore, and the acquirement of the old Norse and its dialects, I can only explain the matter by the early impression received at Hythe from the tale of the old sexton beneath the penthouse, and the sight of the huge Danish skull."

Borrow's acquaintance with books began with the most fascinating of all boys' books,—and which has preserved its popularity
undiminished far more than a hundred years, and, while boys's
nature remains as now, will hold a high place in English literature,
—the entrancing, fascinating, delightful "Robinson Crusoe." He
afterwards fell in with another almost equally interesting book, by
the same writer, "Moll Flanders," which an old apple-woman on
London Bridge lent him to read while he sat behind her stall there;
but "Robinson" exercised by far the greatest influence on his
mind, and probably helped in no slight degree, to give a direction
to his after career.

His child-wanderings continued ; Winchester, Norman's Cross
near Peterborough (where French prisoners were then kept', and
many other places, passed before his eyes. At Norman's Cross
when he was seven years of age, he met with a serpent-charmer ; the
man was catching vipers among the woods, and the boy accompanied
him in his wanderings, learning from him his art of catching vipers.
When the old man left the neighborhood, he made the boy a present
of one of those reptiles, which he had tamed, and rendered quite
harmless by removing the fangs.

Three years passed at Norman's Cross, during which the boy
learned Lilly's Latin grammar.   Then the regiment removed
towards the north, halting, for a time, first in one town and then in
another,—in Yorkshire, in Northumberland, and then beyond the
Tweed, at Edinburgh, where the regiment was quartered in the
Castle, standing high upon its crag, overlooking all the other houses
in that interesting city.   Here he was initiated into the boy-life of
Edinburgh,—the "bickers" on the North Loch and along the Castle
Hill, between the New Town and the Old, already immortalized by
Sir Walter Scott.   He entered a pupil in the High School, and
gathered, before he left, some further acquaintance with Latin and
other tongues.   Oddly enough, one of the cronies whom he picked
up when residing in the Castle, or engaged in "bickers" on the face
of the crag, was David Haggart, then a drummer-boy, afterwards the
most notorious of Scotch criminals, and hanged for murdering the
jailer at Dumfries, in a desperate attempt to escape.   But Borrow's
sympathies are so entirely with the criminal and Gypsy class, that
he does not hesitate to compare Haggart with Tamerlane!—the only
difference being that "Tamerlane was a heathen, and acted according to the lights of his country,—he was a robber while all around
were robbers, whereas Haggart"—then after a strange eulogium of
the "strange deeds" of Haggart, he concludes, "Thou mightest
have been better employed, David ! but peace be with thee, I repeat,
and the Almighty's grace and pardon !"

Two years passed in Edinburgh, during which time the young
Borrow acquired, to his father's horror, the unmistakable dialect of
"the High School callant."   Then they left ; the militia corps

returned to England, and were disbanded. Another year passed in quiet life; 1815 arrived, and Napoleon's return from Elba again threw the whole isle into consternation. The militia were raised anew, and though the French were quelled, disturbances were threatened in Ireland, and thither the corps with which Borrow's father, and now his eldest brother, were connected, were shipped from a port in Essex, and landed at Cork, in Ireland, in the autumn of the year above named. Up the country they went; it became wilder as they proceeded,—the people along the road-sides, with whom the soldiers jested in the patois of East Anglia, answered them in a rough, guttural language, strange and wild. The soldiers stared at each other, and were silent. It was Irish-Celtic that the people spoke, and soon, when the regiment got settled in quarters, young Borrow set to work, and learned it from one of his school-fellows, taking lessons in Irish from him in exchange for a pack of cards.

Borrow's brother having been sent up to the country with a small detachment of men, the younger brother went to visit him in his quarters,—crossed the bogs, passed many old ruined castles far up on the heights, on many of which "the curse of Cromwell" fell. He was overtaken by a snow-storm when crossing a bog, and had nearly been devoured by a wild smuggler and his dog, when a few words of Irish uttered by him at once cleared his road. At length he reached his brother, in a wild out-of-the-way place, " the officer's" apartments being in a a kind of hay-loft, reached by a ladder. Young Borrow now learned to ride; and it is delightful to hear him when he breaks out in praise of horse-flesh. One morning a horse is led out by a soldier, that the youth might "give him a breathing:" he thus describes the horse:

"The cob was led forth; what a tremendous creature! I had frequently seen him before, and wondered at him; he was barely fifteen hands, but he had the girth of a metropolitan dray-horse; his head was small in comparison with his immense neck, which curved down nobly to his wide back; his chest was broad and fine, and his shoulders models of symmetry and strength. He stood well and powerfully upon his legs, which were somewhat short. In a word, he was a gallant specimen of the genuine Irish cob, a species at one time not uncommon, but at the present day nearly extinct."

He mounted, and the horse set off, the youth on its bare back. In two hours he made the circuit of the Devil's Mountain, and was returning along the road bathed with perspiration, but screaming with delight,—the cob laughing in his quiet, equine way, scattering foam and pebbles to the left and right, and trotting at the rate of sixteen miles an hour. Hear his enthusiasm on the subject of the First Ride!—

"O, that ride! that first ride! most truly it was an epoch in my existence, and I still look back to it with feelings of longing and regret. People may talk of first love—it is a very agreeable event, I dare say,—but give me the flush, and triumph, and glorious sweat of a first ride, like mine on the mighty cob! My whole frame was shaken, it it true ; and during one long week I could hardly move foot or hand, but what of that? by that one trial I had become free, as I may say, of the whole equine species. No more fatigue, no more stiffness of joints, after the first ride round the Devil's Hill on the cob."

His passion for horses seems almost equal, indeed, to his passion for boxing, for Bibles, for languages, and for Gypsy life. His sense of physical life is intense ; and wherever muscular energy has full play, he seem to be in his native element. Afterwards, when in the middle of one of his sermons at Cordova (see his "Gypsies of Spain") it occurs to him that the breed of horses of that ancient city is first-rate, and off he goes at full gallop, like a hunter who hears a horn, into a masterly sketch of the Andalusian Arab, and how to groom him! But one day, while in Ireland, an accident occurred which introduced him to his first lesson in "horse-whispering :"

"By good luck a small village was at hand, at the entrance of which was a large shed, from which proceeded a most furious noise of hammering. Leading the cob by the bridle, I entered boldly. 'Shoe this horse, and do it quickly, a-gough,' said I to a wild, grimy figure of a man, whom I found alone, fashioning a piece of iron.

"'Arrigod yuit?' said the fellow, desisting from his work, and staring at me.

"'O, yes ; I have money,' said I, 'and of the best,' and I pulled out an English shilling.

"'Tabhair chugam?' said the smith, stretching out his grimy hand.

"'No, I sha'n't,' said I ; 'some people are glad to get their money when their work is done.'

"The fellow hammered a little longer, and then proceeded to shoe the cob, after having first surveyed it with attention. He performed his job rather roughly, and more than once appeared to give the animal unnecessary pain, frequently making use of loud and boisterous words. By the time the work was done, the creature was in a state of high excitement, and plunged and tore. The smith stood at a short distance, seeming to enjoy the irritation of the animal, and showing, in a remarkable manner, a huge fang, which projected from the under jaw of a very wry mouth.

"'You deserve better handling,' said I, as I went up to the cob, and fondled it ; whereupon it whinnied, and attempted to touch my face with its nose.

"'Are ye not afraid of that beast?' said the smith, showing his fang ; 'arrah! it's vicious that he looks.'

"'It's at you, then ; I don't fear him ;' and thereupon I passed under the horse, between its hind legs.

"'And is that all you can do, agrah?' said the smith.

"'No,' said I, 'I can ride him.'

"'Ye can ride him ; and what else, agrah?'

"'I can leap him over a six-foot wall,' said I.

"'Over a wall ; and what more, agrah?'

"'Nothing more,' said I ; 'what more would you have?'

"'Can you do this, agrah?' said the smith ; and he uttered a word, which I had never heard before, in a sharp, pungent tone. The effect upon myself was somewhat extraordinary, a strange thrill ran through me ; but with regard to the cob it was terrible ; the animal forthwith became like one mad, and reared and kicked with the utmost desperation.

"'Can you do that, agrah?' said the smith.

"'What is it?' said I, retreating ; 'I never saw the horse so before.'

"'Go between his hind legs, agrah,' said the smith,—'his hinder legs ;' and he again showed his fang.

"'I dare not,' said I ; 'he would kill me.'

"'He would kill ye ! and how do ye know that, agrah?'

"'I feel he would,' said I ; 'something tells me so.'

"'And it tells ye truth, agrah ; but it's a fine beast, and it's a pity to see him in such a state ; Io again airt leigeas ;' and here he muttered another word, in a voice singularly modified, but sweet and almost plaintive. The effect of it was almost instantaneous as that of the other, but how different! the animal lost all its fury, and became at once calm and gentle. The smith went up to it, coaxed and patted it, making use of various sounds of equal endearment ; then turning to me, and holding out once more the grimy hand, he said, 'And now ye will be giving me the Sassanach tenpence, agrah !'"

But at length the militia were all disbanded, and the Borrows returned to England, where they settled down at Norwich. The two boys were now growing up, and the elder was put to study painting; the second, George, was still at his books and rambles. His thoughts were in the fields, but he learned French, Italian, and German. His spare hours were spent in fishing or shooting, and sometimes in the practice of the "noble art of self-defense." One day, when attending the horse-fair at Norwich, attracted thither by the sight of the fine animals which he so much admired, he fell in with the son of the Gypsy man he had before met in the lane at Norman's Cross, and shortly after he followed him to his tent beyond the moor. The father and mother, described in our previous extract, had by this time been "bitchadey pawdel," that is, "banished beyond seas for crime," and their son, Jasper Pentulengro, now the Pharaoh of the Gypsies, had to shift for himself. From this time Borrow's intercourse with the wandering Gypsies was frequent ; he accompanied them to fairs, learned their language, acquired the art of horse-shoeing, familiarized himself with their ways of living,—much to the horror of his parents, who were disgusted with his loose and wandering habits.

But the boy was now fast growing up into the man, and something must be done to break him into the ways of civilized life; his father accordingly cast about for him, and at length succeeded in getting the young man articled to a lawyer in Norwich. But he hated the drudgery of the desk, and made no progress in the study of the law. Blackstone was neglected for Danish ballads and Welsh poems. He made the grossest blunders in his business, and his master wished to get rid of him; but time sped on, and he remained, alternating his studies of Ab Gwilym by readings of the life of Moore Carew, "the King of the Beggars," and Murray and Latroon's histories of illustrious robbers and highwaymen. Then a celebrated fight would come off in the neighborhood, and be sure our youth was present there. Extraordinary it is, how Borrow, the missionary, should be the one man living to eulogize this pastime in his books! but he does it, both in his "Gypsies in Spain" and in "Lavengro." In both he tells us how Thurtell, the murderer, taught him the use of "the gloves"; and there is one famous fight, which he has described in glowing language in both these books, which was got up by Thurtell and Gypsy Will, the latter his instructor in horse-riding.

"I have known the time," he says, "when a pugilistic encounter between two noted champions was almost considered in the light of a national affair; when tens of thousands of individuals, high and low, meditated and brooded upon it, the first thing in the morning and the last at night, until the great event was decided. But the time is past, and many people will say, Thank God that it is; all I have to say is; that the French still live on the other side of the water, and are still casting their eyes hitherward; and that, in the days of pugilism, it was no vain boast to say, that one Englishman was a match for two of t' other race; at present it would be a vain boast to say so, for these are not the days of pugilism."

And again he says: "What a bold and vigorous aspect pugilism wore at that time! and the great battle was just then coming off; the day had been decided upon, and the spot, a convenient distance from the old town;—and to the old town were now flocking the bruisers of England, men of tremendous renown. Let no one sneer at the bruisers of England; what were the gladiators of Rome, or the bull-fighters of Spain in its palmiest days, compared to England's bruisers? Pity that corruption should have crept in amongst them, —but of that I wish not to speak; let us still hope that a spark of *the old religion, of which they were the priests*, still lingers in the hearts of Englishmen." No, Mr. Borrow, the glories of pugilism, like those of dueling, bull-baiting, and bull-running, have all departed, and yet England stands where it did; nay, we are even strongly of opinion that the English race, instead of retrograding thereby, has achieved an unquestionable moral advancement. But we willingly pass over this part of Mr. Borrow's confessions, which, though racily written, have a very unhealthful tendency.

At length Borrow's father dies; his articles have expired, and he is thrown upon the world on his own resources. He went to London, like most young men full of themselves and yet wanting help. He packed up his translations of the Danish ballads, and of Ab Gwilym's Welsh poetry, and sought for a publisher on his arrival in London. Of course he failed, but he got an introduction to Sir Richard Phillips, and through his instrumentality Borrow obtained some task-work from a publisher, though the remuneration derived from it was so trifling that he could scarcely subsist. He compiled lives of highwaymen and criminals, and at length, when reduced to his last shilling, wrote a story, which enabled him to raise sufficient cash to quit the metropolis, which he did on the instant, and started on a pedestrian excursion through the country. His life in London occupies the second volume of "Lavengro;" it seems spun out, and reads heavy,—very inferior in interest to the first volume, which contains the cream of the book. In the country he falls in with a disconsolate tinker, who has been driven off his beat by the "Flaming Tinman," a gigantic and brutal ruffian. "Lavengro" buys the tinker's horse, cart, and equipment, and enters upon a life of savage freedom, many parts of which are most graphically depicted. At length he falls in with the "Flaming Tinman," and a desperate fight takes place between them; he vanquishes the tinman, and gains also one of the tinman's two wives, who remains with him in the Mumper's Dingle, where they encamp; and here "Lavengro" ends.

He does not tell us whether his encounter with the "Flaming Tinman," or his knowlegde of gypsy and hedge life, had anything to do with his after career ; or how it was that he became a Bible society's agent ; probably he may tell us something more of that by and by.

In the meantime we may add what we know of his public history in connection with the Bible society, who, in engaging him, possibly had an eye more to the end than the means. Specimens of his "Kaempe Viser," from the Danish, were printed at his native place, Norwich, in 1825, and, shortly after, he was selected by the Bible society to introduce the Scriptures into Russia. He resided there for several years, during which time he mastered its language, the Sclavonian, and its Gypsy dialects. He then prepared an edition of the entire Testament in the Tartar Mantchou, which was published at St. Petersburg, in 1835, in eight volumes. It was at St. Petersburg that he published versions into English from thirty languages. In the meantime he had been in France, where he was a spectator, if not an actor, in the Revolution of the Barricades. Then he went to Norway, crossed into Russia again, sojourned among the Tartars, among the Turks, the Bohemians, passed into Spain, from thence into Barbary,—in short, the sole of his foot has never rested; his course has been more erratic than that of any Gypsy, far more eccentric than that of his brother missionary, Dr. Wolff, the wandering Jew. In his "Bible in Spain" occurs the following passage, which flashes a light upon his remarkably varied history:

"I had returned from a walk in the country, on a glorious sunshiny morning of the Andalusian winter, and was directing my steps towards my lodging. As I was passing by the portal of a large gloomy house near the gate of Xeres, two individuals, dressed in zamarras, emerged from the archway, and were about to cross my path, when one, looking in my face, suddenly started back, exclaiming in the purest and most melodious French, 'What do I see? if my eyes do not deceive me, it is himself. Yes, the very same, as I saw him first at Bayonne; then, long subsequently, beneath the brick wall at Novogorod; then beside the Bosphorus; and last, at—at—O my respectable and cherished friend, where was it that I had last the felicity of seeing your well-remembered and most remarkable physiognomy?'

"*Myself.*—'It was in the south of Ireland, if I mistake not; was it not there that I introduced you to the sorcerer who tamed the savage horses by a single whisper into their ear? But tell me, what brings you to Spain and Andalusia,—the last place where I should have expected to find you?'

"*Baron Taylor.*—'And wherefore, my most respectable B——? Is not Spain the land of the arts; and is not Andalusia of all Spain that portion which has produced the noblest monuments of artistic excellence and inspiration? But first allow me to introduce you to your compatriot, my dear Monsieur W——,' turning to his companion (an English gentleman, from whom, and from his family, I subsequently experienced unbounded kindness and hospitality on various occasions and at different periods, at Seville), 'allow me to introduce to you my most cherished and respectable friend; one who is better acquainted with Gypsy ways than the Chef de Bohémiens à Triana; one who is an expert whisperer and horse-sorcerer; and who, to his honor I say it, can wield hammer and tongs, and handle a horse-shoe with the best of the smiths amongst the Alpujarras of Granada.'"

From his great knowledge of languages, physical energies, and extraordinary intrepidity, it will be clear enough that Mr. Borrow was not ill adapted for the dangerous mission on which he was engaged; indeed, he seems to have been pointed out as the very man for the work. It is not child's play to go into foreign countries, such as Russia and Spain, and distribute Bibles. Fortunately for his success in Spain, the country was in a state of great disorder and turbulence at the time of his mission there, so that his movements were not so much watched as they would otherwise have been;

yet, as it was, he became familiar with the interiors of half the jails in the Peninsula. There he cultivated his acquaintance with the Gypsies and other vagabond races, and gathered new words for his Rommany vocabulary.

While in Spain, however, he did more than cultivate Rommany and distribute Bibles; he brought out Bishop Scio's version of the New Testament in Spanish; he translated St. Luke into the Gypsy language, and edited the same in Basque,—one of the languages most difficult of attainment, because it has no literature; it has other difficulties, for it is hard to learn,—and the Basque people tell a story of the Devil (who does not lack abilities) having been detained among them seven years trying to learn the language, which he at last gave up in despair, having only been able to learn three words. Humboldt also tried to learn it, with no better success than his predecessor. But no difficulty was too great for Borrow to overcome; he acquired the Basque, thus vindicating his claim to the title of "Lavengro," or word-master.

If any of our readers should happen not yet to have read "The Bible in Spain," we advise them to read it forthwith. Though irregular, without plan or order, it is a thoroughly racy, graphic, and vigorous book, full of interest, honest, and straightforward, and without any cant or affectation in it; indeed, the man's prominent quality is honesty, otherwise we should never have seen anything of that strong love of pugilism, horsemanship, Gypsy life, and physical daring of all kinds, of which his books are full. He is a Bible Harry Lorrequer,—a missionary Bampfylde Moore Carew,—an Exeter Hall bruiser,—a polyglot wandering Gypsy. Fancy these incongruities, —and yet George Borrow is the man who embodies them in his one extraordinary person!

AUDUBON THE ORNITHOLOGIST.

THE great naturalist of America, John James Audubon, left behind him, in his "Birds of America" and "Ornithological Biography," a magnificent monument of his labors, which through life were devoted to the illustration of the natural history of his native country. His grand work on the Biography of Birds is quite unequaled for the close observation of the habits of birds and animals which it displays, its glowing pictures of American scenery, and the enthusiastic love of nature which breathes throughout its pages. The sunshine and the open air, the dense shade of the forest, and the boundless undulations of the prairies, the roar of the sea beating against the rock-ribbed shore, the solitary wilderness of the Upper Arkansas, the savannas of the South, the beautiful Ohio, the vast Mississippi, and the green steeps of the Alleghanies,—all were as familiar to Audubon as his own home. The love of birds, of flowers, of animals,—the desire to study their habits in their native retreats,—haunted him like a passion from his earliest years, and he devoted almost his entire life to the pursuit.

He was born to competence, of French parents settled in America, in the state of Pennsylvania,—a beautiful green undulating country, watered by fine rivers, and full of lovely scenery. "When I had hardly yet learned to walk," says he, in his autobiography prefixed to his work, "the productions of nature that lay spread all around were constantly pointed out to me. They soon became my playmates; and before my ideas were sufficiently formed to enable me to estimate the difference between the azure tints of the sky and the emerald hue of the bright foliage, I felt that an intimacy with them, not consisting of friendship merely, but *bordering on frenzy*, must accompany my steps through life ; and now, more than ever, am I persuaded of the power of those early impressions. They laid such hold of me, that, when removed from the woods, the prairies, and the brooks, or shut up trom the view of the wide Atlantic, I experienced none of those pleasures most congenial to my mind. None but aerial companions suited my fancy. No roof seemed so secure to me as that formed of the dense foliage under which the feathered tribes were seen to resort, or the caves and fissures of the massy rocks to which the dark-winged cormorant and the curlew retired to rest, or to protect themselves from the fury of the tempest."

Audubon seems to have inherited this intense love of nature from his father, who eagerly encouraged the boy's tastes, procured birds and flowers for him, pointed out their elegant movements, told him of their haunts and habits, their migrations, changes of livery, and so on,—feeding the boy's mind with vivid pleasure and stimulating his quick sense of enjoyment. As he grew up towards manhood, these tastes grew stronger within him, and he longed to go forth amid the forests and prairies of America to survey the native wild birds in their magnificent haunts. But, meanwhile, he learned to draw ; he painted birds and flowers, and acquired a facility of delineation of their forms, attitudes, and plumage. Of course he only reached this through many failures and defeats ; but he was laborious and full of love for his pursuit, and in such a case ultimate success is certain.

His education was greatly advanced by a residence in France, whither he was sent to receive his school education, returning to America at the age of seventeen. In Paris, he had the advantage of studying under the great David. He revisited the woods of the New World with fresh ardor and increased enthusiasm. His father gave him a fine estate on the banks of the Schuylkill ; and amidst its beautiful woodlands, its extensive fields, its hills crowned with evergreens, he pursued his delightful studies. Another object about the same time excited his passion, and he soon rejoiced in the name of husband. But though Audubon loved his wife most fondly, his first ardent love had been given to nature. It was his genius and destiny, which he could not resist, and he was drawn on towards it in spite of himself.

He engaged, however, in various branches of commerce, none of which succeeded with him, his mind being preoccupied by his favorite study. His friends called him "fool,"—all excepting his wife and children. At last, irritated by the remarks of relatives and others, he broke entirely away from the pursuits of trade, and gave himself up wholly to natural history. He ransacked the woods, the lakes, the prairies, and the shores of the Atlantic, spending years away from his home and family. His object, at first, was not

to become a writer ; but simply to indulge a passion,—to enjoy the
sight of nature. It was Charles Lucian Bonaparte, an accomplished
naturalist, who first incited him to arrange his beautiful drawings
in a form for publication, and to enter upon his grand work, "The
Birds of America." He now explored over and over again the woods
and the prairies, the lakes, the rivers, and the sea-shore, with this
object in view ; but when he had heaped together a mass of information, and collected a large number of drawings an untoward
accident occurred to his collection, which we cannot help relating
in his own words :

. "I left the village of Henderson, in Kentucky, situated on the
banks of the Ohio, where I resided for several years, to proceed to
Philadelphia on business. I looked to all my drawings (ten hundred in number) before my departure, placed them carefully in a
box, and gave them in charge to a relative with injunctions to see
that no injury happened to them. My absence was of several
months; and when I returned, after having enjoyed the pleasures of
home for a few days, 1 inquired after my box, and what I was pleased
to call my treasure. The box was produced, and opened, but,
reader, feel for me,—a pair of Norway rats had taken possession of
the whole, and had reared a young family amongst the gnawed bits
of paper, which, but a few months ago had represented nearly a
thousand inhabitants of the air! The burning heat which instantly
rushed through my brain was too great to be endured, without affecting the whole of my nervous system. 1 slept not for several nights,
and the days passed like days of oblivion, until the animal powers
being recalled into action, through the strength of my constitution,
I took up my gun, my note-book, and my pencils, and went forth to
the woods as gayly as if nothing had happened. I felt pleased that
I might now make much better drawings than before, and ere a
period not exceeding three years had elapsed, I had my portfolio
filled again."

While you read Audubon's books, you feel that you are in the
society of no ordinary naturalist. Everything he notes down is the
result of his own observation. Nature, not books, has been his teacher.
You feel the fresh air blowing in your face, scent the odor of the
prairie-flowers and the autumn-woods, and hear the roar of the surf
along the sea-shore. He takes you into the squatter's hut in the lonely
swamp, where you listen to the story of the wood-cutter's life, and
sally out in the night to hunt the cougar ; or he launches you on the
Ohio in a light skiff, where he paints for you in glowing words
the rich autumnal tints decorating the shores of that queen of
rivers,—every tree hung with long and flowing festoons of different
species of vines, many loaded with clustered fruits of varied brilliancy, their rich bronzed carmine mingling beautifully with the
yellow foliage predominating over the green leaves,—gliding down
the river, under the rich and glowing sky which characterizes what

is called the "Indian summer," and reminding you of the delicious description in Longfellow's "Evangeline:"

Now through rushing chutes, among green islands, where, plum-like,
Cotton-trees nodded their shadowy crests, they swept with the current,
Then emerged into broad lagoons, where silvery sandbars
Lay in the stream, and along the wimpling waves of their margin,
Shining with snow-white plumes, large flocks of pelicans waded.
Over their heads the towering and tenebrous boughs of the cypress
Met in a dusky arch, and trailing mosses in mid-air
Waved like banners that hang on the walls of ancient cathedrals.
Then from a neighboring thicket the mocking-bird, wildest of singers,
Swinging aloft on a willow-spray that hung o'er the water,
Shook from his little throat such floods of delirious music,
That the whole air, and the woods, and the waves, seemed silent to listen.

In one of his excursions on the Ohio, Audubon was accompanied by his wife and eldest son, then an infant; and they floated on from Pennsylvania to Kentucky, sleeping and living in the boat, under the Indian summer sun and the mellowed beauty of the moon, skirting the delicious shores, so picturesque and lovely at that autumn season, gliding along the stream, and meeting with no other ripple of the water than that formed by the propulsion of the boat. The margins of the river were at that time (for this voyage took place about forty years ago) abundantly supplied with game, and occasionally the party landed at night on the green shore; a few gunshots procured a wild turkey or grouse, or a blue-winged teal; a fire was struck up, and a comfortable repast secured; after which the family again proceeded quietly on their way down stream. The following is only one of the many lovely pictures sketched by Audubon of this enchanting sail, which probably Longfellow had in his eye when he penned the charming description in his "Evangeline."

" As night came, sinking in darkness the broader portions of the river, our minds became affected by strong emotions, and wandered far beyond the present moments. The tinkling of the bells told us that the cattle which bore them were gently roving from valley to valley in search of food, or returning to their distant homes. The hooting of the great owl, or the muffled noise of its wings as it sailed smoothly over the stream, were matters of interest to us; so was the sound of the boatman's horn, as it came more and more softly from afar. When daylight returned, many songsters burst forth with echoing notes, more and more mellow to the listening ear. Here and there the lonely cabin of a squatter struck the eye, giving note of commencing civilization. The crossing of the stream by a deer foretold how soon the hills would be covered with snow."

The scene is greatly changed since then. The shores are inhabited; the woods are mainly cleared away; the great herds of elk, deer, and buffalo have ceased to exist; villages, farms, and towns margin the Ohio; hundreds of steamboats are plying up and down the river, by night and by day; and thousands of British and American emigrants have settled down, in all directions, to the pursuits of agriculture and commerce, where only forty years ago was heard the hoot of the owl, the cry of the whip-poor-will, and the sharp stroke of the squatter's axe.

Or, he takes you into the Great Pine Swamp, like a "mass of darkness," the ground overgrown by laurels and pines of all sorts; he has his gun and note-book in hand, and soon you have the woodthrush, wild turkeys, pheasants, and grouse lying at his feet, with the drawings of which he enriches his portfolio; or you are listening to his host, while he reads by the log fire the glorious poetry of Burns. Again, you are with him on the wild prairie, treading some old Indian track, amid brilliant flowers and long grass, the fawns and their dams gamboling along his path, and across boundless tracts of rich lands as yet almost untrodden by the foot of the white man, and then only by the Canadian trappers or Indian missionaries. Or he is on the banks of the Mississippi, where the great magnolia shoots up its majestic trunk, crowned with evergreen leaves, and decorated with a thousand beautiful flowers, that perfume the air around; where the forests and fields are adorned with blossoms of every hue; where the golden orange ornaments the gardens and the groves; where the white-flowered Stuartia and innumerable vines festoon the dense foliage of the magnificent woods, shedding on the vernal breeze the perfume of their clustered flowers; there, by the side of deep streams, or under the dense foliage, he watches by night the mocking-bird, the whip-poor-will, the yellow-throat, the humming-bird, and the thousand beautiful songsters of that delicious land. Then a crevasse, or sudden irruption of the swollen Mississippi, occurs, and forthwith he is floating over the submerged lands of the interior, nature all silent and melancholy, unless when the mournful bleating of the hemmed-in deer reaches the ear; or the dismal scream of an eagle or a raven is heard, as the bird rises from the carcass on which it had been allaying its appetite.

How gloriously Audubon paints the eagle of his native land! The American white-headed eagle, that haunts the Mississippi, stands sculptured before your eyes in his book. See! he takes wing, and there you have him whirling up into the air as a noble swan comes in sight, and now there is the screaming pursuit and the fatal struggle.

"Now is the moment to witness the display of the eagle's powers. He glides through the air like a falling star, and, like a flash of lightning, comes upon the timorous quarry, which now, in agony and despair, seeks by various maneuvers, to elude the grasp of his cruel talons. It mounts, doubles, and willingly would plunge into the stream, were it not prevented by the eagle, which, long possessed of the knowledge that by such a stratagem the swan might escape him, forces it to remain in the air, by attempting to strike it with his talons from beneath. The hope of escape is soon given up by the swan. It has already become much weakened, and its strength fails at the sight of the courage and swiftness of its antagonist. Its last gasp is about to escape, when the ferocious eagle strikes with his talons the under side of its wing, and, with unresisted power, forces the bird to fall in a slanting direction upon the nearest shore."

Then we have the same bird on the Atlantic shore in pursuit of the fish-hawk. "Perched on some tall summit, in view of the ocean, or of some watercourse, he watches every motion of the osprey while on wing. When the latter rises from the water with a fish in its grasp, forth rushes the eagle in pursuit. He mounts above the fish-hawk, and threatens it by actions well understood, when the latter, fearing perhaps that his life is in danger, drops its prey. In an instant the eagle, accurately estimating the rapid descent of the fish, closes his wings, follows it with the swiftness of thought, and the next moment grasps it. The prize is carried off in silence to the woods and assists in feeding the ever-hungry brood of the eagle."

But Audubon did not like the white-headed eagle, no more than did Franklin, who, in common with the ornithologist, regretted its adoption as the emblem of America, because of its voracity, its cowardice, and its thievish propensities. Audubon's favorite among the eagles of America was the great eagle or "The Bird of Washington," as he named it. He first saw this grand bird when on a trading voyage with a Canadian, on the Upper Mississippi, and his delight was such that he says, "Not even Herschel when he discovered the planet that bears his name, could have experienced more rapturous feelings." But the bird had soon flown over the heads of the party and became lost in the distance. Three years elapsed before he saw another specimen; and then it was when engaged in collecting cray-fish on one of the flats which border and divide Green River, in Kentucky, near its junction with the Ohio, that he discerned, up among the high cliffs which there follow the windings of the river, the marks of an eagle's nest. Climbing his way towards it, he lay in wait for the parent: two hours elapsed, and then the loud hissing of two young eagles in the nest announced the approach of the old bird, which drew near and dropped in among them a fine fish. "I had a perfect view," he says, "of the noble bird as he held himself to the edging rock, hanging like the barn, bank, or social swallow, his tail spread, and his wings partly so. In a few minutes the other parent joined her mate, and from the difference in size (the female of rapacious birds being much larger) we knew this to be the mother bird. She also had brought a fish, but, more cautious than her mate, she glanced her quick and piercing eye around, and instantly perceived that her abode had been discovered. She dropped her prey, with a loud shriek communicated the alarm to her mate, and, hovering with him over our heads, kept up a growling cry, to intimidate us from our suspected design. This watchful solicitude I have ever found peculiar to the female ; must I be understood to speak only of birds?"

Two years more passed in fruitless efforts to secure a specimen of this rare bird; but at last he was so fortunate as to shoot one; and then gave it the name it bears, "The Bird of Washington," the noblest bird of its genus in the States. Why he so named the bird he thus explains : "To those who may be curious to know my reasons, I can only say, that, as the New World gave me birth and liberty, the great man who insured its independence is next to my heart. He had a nobility of mind and a generosity of soul such as are seldom possessed. He was brave, so is the eagle; like it, too, he was the terror of his foes; and his fame, extending from pole to pole, resembles the majestic soarings of the mightiest of the feathered tribes. If America has reason to be proud of her Washington, so has she to be proud of her Great Eagle."

In the course of his extensive wanderings, Audubon experienced all sorts of adventures. Once he was within an inch of his life in a solitary squatter's hut in one of the wide prairies of the upper Mississippi; in one of the extensive swamps of the Choctaw territory in the state of Mississippi, he joined in the hunt of a ferocious cougar or *painter* (panther) which had been the destruction of the flocks in that neighborhood; in the Banem of Kentucky he was once surprised by an earthquake, the ground rising and falling under his terrified horse like the ruffled waters of a lake; he became familiar with storms and hurricanes, which only afforded new subjects for his graphic pen; he joined in the Kentucky hunting sports, or with the Indian expeditions on the far prairie; he witnessed the astounding flights of wild pigeons in countless multitudes, lasting for whole days in succession, so that "the air was literally filled with pigeons, the light of noonday obscured as by an eclipse, the dung fell in spots not unlike melting flakes of snow, and the continued buzzing of the millions of wings had a tendency to lull the senses to repose,"—one of these enormous flocks extending, it is estimated by Audubon, over a space of not less than 180 miles; then he is on the trail of the deer or the buffalo in the hunting-grounds of the Far West, he misses his way, and lies down for the night in the copse under the clear sky, or takes shelter with a trapper, where he is always welcome; then he is in the Gulf of Mexico, spending weeks together in the pursuit of birds, or observing their haunts and habits; then he is in the thick of a bear-hunt. Such is the rapid succession of objects that passes before you in the first volume of the "Birds of America," interspersed with delicious descriptions of such birds as the mocking-bird, whip-poor-will, humming-bird, wood-thrush. and other warblers of the forest.

In his description of the wood-thrush, which he confesses to be

his "greatest favorite of the feathered tribes," you see something of
the hardships to which he exposed himself by the enthusiasm with
which he followed his exciting pursuit.. "How often," he says,
"has it revived my drooping spirits when I have listened to its wild
notes in the forest, after passing a restless night in my slender shed,
so feebly secured against the violence of the storm as to show me the
futility of my best efforts to rekindle my little fire, whose uncertain
and vacillating light had gradually died away under the destruct-
ive weight of the dense torrents of rain that seemed to involve the
heavens and the earth in one mass of fearful murkiness, save when
the red streaks of the flashing thunderbolt burst on the dazzled
eye, and, glancing along the huge trunk of the stateliest and noblest
tree in the immediate neighborhood, were instantly followed by an
uproar of crackling, crashing, and deafening sounds, rolling their
volumes in tumultuous eddies far and near, as if to silence the very
breathings of the unformed thought. How often, after such a night,
when far from my dear home, and deprived of the presence of those
nearest and dearest to my heart, wearied, hungry, drenched, and so
lonely and desolate as almost to question myself why I was thus
situated ; when I have seen the fruits of my labors on the eve of
being destroyed, as the water collected in a stream, rushed through
my little camp, and forced me stand erect, shivering in a cold fit,
like that of a severe ague ; when I have been obliged to wait with
the patience of a martyr for the return of day, trying in vain to
destroy the tormenting mosquitoes, silently counting over the years
of my youth, doubting, perhaps, if ever again I should return to my
home, and embrace my family,—how often, as the first glimpses of
morning gleamed doubtfully amongst the dusky masses of the forest-
trees, has there come upon my ear, thrilling along the sensitive
cords which connect that organ with the heart, the delightful music
of this harbinger of day ; and how fervently, on such occasions,
have I blessed the Being who formed the wood-thrush, and placed
it in those solitary forests, as if to console me amidst my privations,
to cheer my depressed mind, and to make me feel, as I did, that
never ought man to despair, whatever may be his situation, as he
can never be certain that aid and deliverance are not at hand."

After many years of persevering toil, when he had collected a
rich treasure of original drawings of the birds of America, many of
which up to that time were altogether unknown, and had never
been described, Audubon proceeded to the then two chief cities of
the States, Philadelphia and New York, and endeavored to find a
publisher. He sought for one in vain ! Some said his book would
never sell, others that his drawings could never be engraved. Audubon was of a resolute spirit, and had learned to brave all manner
of difficulties in the pine-woods and the prairies, and he determined
that he *would* find a publisher. America was not the world ; he
would carry his collections to Europe, and try and find a publisher
there.

He came to England in 1827, and was welcome
Many yet remember the glowing enthusiasm
Woodsman," and the ardent eloquence of his d
glorious rivers, the wide prairies, the magnifice
the ornithological treasures of his native countr
love a lover," and here was one of the most ar
hearts with a generous glow. His drawings w
greatly admired. From Liverpool, where he lanc
to Scotland, the land of Burns, for he "longed 1
scenes immortalized by his fervid strains." Here
and was "received as a brother" by the most disti
and literary men of that metropolis. There he 1
in Adam Black, with Lizars for his engraver. T
his magnificent illustrations appeared in 1825, a
plete volume of the "Ornithological Biography" i:
was received with general laudations. Nothing o
it in riveting interest had appeared before; and i
rivaled. He proposed to devote the remainder
completion of his work. Sixteen years was the
mated as required for the preparation and produc
Observing on the time remaining for its completio
all, it will be less than the period frequently giver
to the maturation of certain wines placed in the
not thus that men generally write nowadays, 1
railroad speed. Audubon's object was to do his
thoroughly and well, so as to leave nothing to b
and he has done it gloriously.

In the introduction to his third volume, pub
said: "Ten years have now elapsed since the fi
'Illustrations of the Birds of America' made its
that period, I calculated that the engravers would
in accomplishing their task; and this I announce
tus, and talked of to my friends." At that tim
single individual who encouraged him to procee
him "rash," advised him to abandon his plan
drawings, and give up the project. When he
drawings to the engraver, he had not a single subs
determined on success, and he persevered. "To w
the maxim, and it was Audubon's. "My heart
says, "and my reliance on that Power on whon
brought bright anticipations of success. I worke
and glad I was to perceive that the more I labor
proved." Subscribers at length supported him,
him, when they saw he was bent on success, and a
four years of great anxiety, his engraver, Mr. Hav
with the first volume of his "Birds of America."

In the interval he made several voyages between

and England, pursuing his ornithological observations there, and superintending his publication here. In 1828 he visited the illustrious Cuvier at Paris. He spent the winter in England, and went out to the States in April, 1829. "With what pleasure," he says, "did I gaze on each setting sun, as it sank in the far distant west! With what delight did I mark the first wandering American bird that hovered over the waters! and how joyous were my feelings when I saw a pilot on our deck! I leaped on the shore, scoured the woods of the Middle States, and reached Louisiana in the end of November." Louisiana was one of his favorite localities for the study of birds; and Audubon often lingered there. In his description of the "great blue heron" and other birds which frequent that state, he shows how familiar he is with its luxuriant swamps. "Imagine, if you can," he says, "an area of some hundred acres overgrown with huge cypress-trees,—the trunks of which, rising to a height of perhaps fifty feet before they send off a branch, spring from the midst of the dark muddy waters. Their broad tops, placed close together with interlaced branches, seem intent on separating the heavens from the earth. Beneath their dark canopy scarcely a stray sunbeam ever makes its way; the mire is covered with fallen logs, on which grow matted grasses and lichens, and the deeper parts with nympheal and other aquatic plants. The Congo-snake and water-moccasin glide before you as they seek to elude your sight; hundreds of turtles drop, as if shot, from the floating trunks of the fallen trees, from which also the sullen alligator plunges into the dismal pool. The air is pregnant with pestilence, but alive with mosquitoes and other insects. The croaking of the frogs, joined with the hoarse cries of the anhingas and the screams of the herons, forms fit music for such a scene. Standing knee-deep in the mire, you discharge your gun at one of the numerous birds that are brooding high overhead, when immediately such a deafening noise arises, that, if you have a companion with you, it were quite useless to speak to him. The frightened birds cross each other in their flight; the young attempting to secure themselves, some of them lose their hold and fall into the water with a splash; a shower of leaflets whirls downwards from the tree-tops, and you are glad to make your retreat from such a place."

Accompanied by his wife, Audubon left New Orleans in January, 1830, proceeded to New York, and from thence again to England, where he arrived to receive a diploma from the Royal Society, which he esteemed as a great honor conferred on an American woodsman. Returning to the States in 1831, he took with him two assistants, his work assuming an importance not before dreamed of. The American government now aided him, and he was provided with letters of protection along the frontiers, which proved valuable helps. His chief field of investigation this year was Florida,—full of interest and novelty to the ornithologist. It was, comparatively, a new field and

Audubon explored it with his usual enthusiasm. There, along the reef-bound coast about Key West, and among the islets of coral that everywhere rise from the surface of the ocean like gigantic water-lilies, he cruised in his bark, often under a burning sun, pushing for miles over soapy flats, tormented by myriads of insects, but eager to procure some new heron, the possession of which would at once compensate him for all his toils. There, in these native haunts, he studied the habits of the sandpiper and the cormorant, and scoured the billows after the fulmar and the frigate-bird. There, along the shore, among its luxuriant fringe of flowers, plants, and trees, georgeously luxuriant, he followed after birds nearly all of which were new to him, and which filled him with boundless delight.

On the east coast of Florida, he was surprised and delighted at the wild orange-groves through which his steps often led him; the rich perfume of the blossoms, the golden hue of the fruits that hung on every twig and lay scattered on the ground, and the deep green of the glossy leaves which sometimes half concealed the golden fruit. Audubon used sometimes to pass through orange-groves of this kind a full mile in extent, quenching his thirst with the luscious fruit, and delighted at the rich variety of life with which the woods were filled.

Having received letters from the Secretaries of the Navy and Treasury of the United States to the commanding officers of the vessels of war and of the reserve service, directing them to afford assistance to Audubon in his labors, he on one occasion embarked at St. Augustine, in the schooner *Spark*, for St. John's River, a little to the north. He now studied, amid their haunts along the coast, the snowy pelican, cormorants, sea-eagles, and blue herons; and sailed for one hundred miles up the river, between banks swarming with alligators, where he landed and made familiar acquaintance with beautiful humming-birds, and the other frequenters of the groves and thickets in that tropical region. Here is an ugly phase of the naturalist's life :

"Alligators were extremely abundant, and the heads of the fishes which they had snapped off lay floating around on the dark waters. A rifle-bullet was now and then sent through the eye of one of the largest, which, with a tremendous splash of its tail, expired. One morning we saw a monstrous fellow lying on the shore. I was desirous of obtaining it, to make an accurate drawing of his head, and, accompanied by my assistant and two of the sailors, proceeded cautiously towards him. When within a few yards, one of us fired and sent through his side an ounce ball, which tore open a hole large enough to receive a man's hand. He slowly raised his head, bent himself upwards, opened his huge jaws, swung his tail to and fro, rose on his legs, blew in a frightful manner, and fell to the earth. My assistant leaped on shore, and, contrary to my injunctions, caught hold of the animal's tail; when the alligator, awaking

from its trance, with a last effort crawled slowly towards the water,
and plunged heavily into it. Had he once thought of flourishing
his tremendous weapon, there might have been an end of his assail-
ant's life; but he fortunately went in peace to his grave, where we
left him, as the water was too deep. The same morning another of
equal size was observed swimming directly for the bows of our vessel, attracted by the gentle rippling of the water there. One of the
officers, who had watched him, fired and scattered his brains through
the air, when he trembled and rolled at a fearful rate, blowing all
the while most furiously. The river was bloody for yards round;
but although the monster passed close by the vessel, we could not
secure him, and after a while he sank to the bottom."

At other times, Audubon was carried out beyond the coral reef
which surrounds the Floridan coast, to the Keys, or islands standing out a little to sea. These were covered with rich vegetation, and
full of life. The shores were also swarming with crabs and shell-
fish of all kinds. "One of my companions thrust himself into the
tangled groves that covered all but the beautiful coral beach that in
a continued line bordered the island, while others gazed on the
glowing and diversified hues of the curious inhabitants of the deep.
I saw one rush into the limpid element to seize on a crab, that, with
claws extended upwards, awaited his opponent, as if determined
not to give way. A loud voice called him back to the land, for
sharks are as abundant along those shores as pebbles, and the hungry prowlers could not have got a more dainty dinner." Flamin-
goes, ibises, pelicans, cormorants, and herons frequent those islands
in vast numbers, and turtles and sea-cows bask along their shores.
The party landed at night on the Indian Key, where they were
kindly welcomed; and while the dance and the song were going on
around him, Audubon, his head filled with his pursuit, sat sketch-
ing the birds that he had seen, and filling up his notes respecting
the objects witnessed in the course of the day. Thus it is that his
descriptions have so strong and fresh a flavor of nature, and that to
read them is like being present at the scenes he so graphically de-
picts. After supper, the lights were put out, the captain returned
to his vessel, and the ornithologist, with his young men, "slept in
light swinging hammocks under the leaves of the piazza." It was
the end of April, when the nights are short there and the days long;
so, anxious to turn every moment to account, they were all on board
again at three o'clock next morning, and proceeded outwards to sea.
He thus briefly describes a sunrise on one of those early April
mornings :

"The gentle sea-breeze glided over the flowing tide, the horizon
was clear, and all was silent save the long breakers that rushed over
the distant reefs. As we were proceeding towards some Keys seldom
visited by man, the sun rose from the bosom of the waters with a
burst of glory that flashed on my soul the idea of that Power which

called into existence so magnificent an object. The moon, thin and pale, as if ashamed to show her feeble light, concealed herself in the dim west. The surface of the waters shone in its tremulous smoothness, and the deep blue of the clear beams was pure as the world that lies beyond them. The heron flew heavily towards the land, like the glutton retiring at daybreak, with well-lined paunch, from the house of some wealthy patron of good cheer. The night-heron and the owl, fearful of day, with hurried flight sought safety in the recesses of the deepest swamps; while the gulls and terns, ever cheerful, gamboled over the waters, exulting in the prospect of abundance. I also exulted in hope; my whole frame seemed to expand; and our sturdy crew showed, by their merry faces, that nature had charms for them too. How much of beauty and joy is lost to those who never view the rising of the sun, and of whose waking existence the best half is nocturnal!"

They landed on Sandy Island, which lies about six miles from the extreme point of South Florida, stretching away down into the Gulf of Mexico; they laid themselves down in the sand to sleep, the waters almost bathing their feet; the boat lay at their side, like a whale reposing on a mud-bank. Birds in myriads fed around them,—ibises, godwits, herons, fish-crows, and frigate pelicans. Having explored the island, and shot a number of birds, they proceeded back to land through the tortuous channels among the reefs, and were caught by one of those sudden hurricanes which so often sweep across the seas. And here is Audubon's picture of the storm:

"We were not more than a cable's length from the shore, when, with imperative voice, the pilot said to us; 'Sit quite still, gentlemen, for I should not like to lose you overboard just now; the boat can't upset, my word for that, if you but sit still. *Here you have it!*' Persons who have never witnessed hurricanes such as not unfrequently desolate the sunny climates of the south, can scarcely form an idea of their terrific grandeur. One would think that, not content with laying waste all on land, it must needs sweep the waters of the shallows quite dry to quench its thirst. No respite for an instant does it afford to the objects within the reach of its furious current. Like the scythe of the destroying angel, it cuts everything by the roots, as it were, with the careless ease of the experienced mower. Each of its revolving sweeps collects a heap that might be likened to the full sheaf which the husbandman flings by his side. On it goes, with a wildness and fury that are indescribable; and when at last its frightful blasts have ceased, Nature, weeping and disconsolate, is left bereaved of her beauteous offspring. In some instances even a full century is required before, with all her powerful energies, she can repair her loss. The planter has not only lost his mansion, his crops, and his flocks, but he has to clear his lands anew, covered and entangled as they are with the trunks and branches of trees that are everywhere strewn. The bark, overtaken by the storm, is cast on the lee-shore, and, if any are left to witness the fatal results, they are the 'wreckers' alone, who, with inward delight, gaze upon the melancholy spectacle. Our light bark shivered like a leaf the instant the blast reached her sides. We thought she had gone over, but the next instant she was on the shore. And now, in contemplation of the sublime and awful storm, I gazed around me. The waters drifted like snow, the tough mangroves hid their tops amid their roots, and the loud roaring of the waves driven among them blended with the howl of the tempest. It was not rain that fell; the masses of water flew in a horizontal direction, and when a part of my body was exposed, I felt as if a smart blow had been given to it. But enough!—in half an hour it was over. The pure blue sky once more embellished the heavens, and although it was now quite night, we considered our situation a good one. The crew and some of the party spent the night in the boat. The pilot, myself, and one of my assistants, took to the heart of the mangroves, and having found high land, we made a fire as well as we could, spread a tarpauling, and, fixing our insect bars over us, soon forgot in sleep the horrors that had surrounded us."

Audubon returned to Charleston with a store of rich prizes for his work, and from thence proceeded to Philadelphia, New York, and Boston, greatly enjoying the lavish hospitality of the last-named city. Then he proceeded, still on his industrious explorations, to Moose Island, in the Bay of Fundy (situated between Nova Scotia and New Brunswick), where he continued to extend his observations on altogether different classes of birds from those in the South. He afterwards explored New Brunswick and Maine, increasing his collections, and returned to Boston, where he was a witness to the melancholy death of the great Spurzheim, the phrenologist. He was himself seized with illness, the result of close application to his work, but he soon after resolved to set out again in quest of fresh materials for his pencil and pen.

This time, it was the grand, rocky coasts of Labrador, haunted by innumerable sea-birds, that attracted him. At Eastport, in Maine, he chartered a beautiful and fast-sailing schooner, the *Ripley*, and set sail, with several friends, on his delightful voyage. He passed out of the port under a salute of honor from the guns of the fort, and of the revenue-cutter at anchor in the bay. Touching islands in the St. Lawrence Gulf, each haunted by its peculiar tribes of birds, a heavy gale came on, and the vessel sped away, under reefed sails, to the coast of Labrador. Masses of drifting ice and snow, filling every nook and cove of the rugged shores, came in sight; they neared the coast at the place called the "American Harbor," and there Audubon landed. Large patches of unmelted snow dappled the face of the wild country; vegetation had scarcely yet commenced; the chilliness of the air was still penetrating; the absence of trees, the barren aspect of all around, the somber mantle of the mountainous distance that hung along the horizon, excited melancholy feelings. But hist! what is that? It is the song of the thrush,—the first sound that meets Audubon's ear,—and the delightful associations it called up at once reconciled him to the comparative miseries of the locality, so different from the glowing luxuriance of Florida and his favorite Louisiana. Robins, hopping about amid the blossoms of the dogwood; black-poll warblers, and numerous other birds, some of them entirely new, began to appear; and soon Audubon was fully absorbed in his delightful pursuit. The *Ripley* sailed further north, and entered the harbor of Little Macatina, of which this is his description:

"It was the middle of July: the weather was mild, and very pleasant; our vessel made her way, under a smart breeze, through a very narrow passage, beyond which we found ourselves in a small, circular basin of water, having an extent of seven or eight acres. It was so surrounded by high, abrupt, and rugged rocks, that, as I glanced around, I could find no apter comparison for our situation than that of a nut-shell at the bottom of a basin. The dark shadows that overspread the waters, and the mournful silence of the surrounding desert, sombered our otherwise glad feelings into a state of awe. The scenery was grand and melancholy. On one side hung over our heads, in stupendous masses, a rock several hundred feet high, the fissures of which might to some have looked like the mouths of a huge, undefined monster. Here and there a few dwarf pines were stuck, as if by magic, to this enormous mass of granite; in a gap of the cliff, the brood of a pair of grim ravens shrunk from our sight, and the gulls, one after another, began to wend their way overhead towards the middle of the quiet pool, as the furling of the sails was accompanied by the glad cries of the sailors. The remarkable land-beacons erected in that country to guide vessels into the harbor, looked like so many figures of gigantic stature, formed from the large blocks that lay on every hill around. A low valley, in which meandered a rivulet, opened at a distance to the view. The remains of a deserted camp of seal-catchers was easily traced from our deck, and as easily could we perceive the innate tendency of man to mischief, in the charred and crumbling ruins of the dwarf-pine forests. But the harbor was so safe and commodious, that, before we left it to find shelter in another, we had cause to be thankful for its friendly protection."

Thus coasting along Labrador, peeping into its bays and inlets,—through bogs, and ice, and fishing-smacks, pursuing their vocations,—landing here and there along the coast, and penetrating into the interior,—the summer of 1833 passed joyously and profitably. Audubon enriched his portfolio with drawings of new birds, and his note-book with numerous fine descriptions of Labrador coast-life and scenery. He describes cod-fishing in glowing colors; devotes a chapter each to the "eggers of Labrador," and the "squatters of

Labrador;" and enlivens his details of the natural history, haunts, and habits of birds by a thousand interesting adventures and reflections. He makes you feel the enthusiasm he felt himself, and shares with you the delight he experienced in the course of his cruisings and journeyings. He returned to the States in autumn, touching at Newfoundland, Nova Scotia, and New Brunswick, and thence on to Boston. "One day only was spent there, when the husband was in the arms of his wife, who, with equal tenderness, embraced his beloved child." For Audubon's eldest son had accompanied him in this last-named voyage.

Subscribers to the "Birds of America" now increased; friends multiplied in all quarters; and he proceeded again to England to superintend the continued publication of his work. There he extended his friendships and enlarged his knowledge, comparing his experience with that of the greatest authorities in natural history. His third volume of "Ornithological Biography" was published in 1835; and in it he gives a graphic sketch of an interview he had with Thomas Bewick, the famous wood-engraver and naturalist, at Newcastle-on-Tyne. This volume is quite equal in interest to the first two and greatly added to his reputation as a writer. In it he describes birds of North and South, of Labrador and Florida, of the Great Pine Forest of Pennsylvania, and of the swamps along the Mississippi, with marvelous picturesque power and fidelity. He returned to the States in 1836, again to pursue his studies; again he visited the western coast of Florida, and sailed through the Gulf of Mexico to New Orleans; then explored the coast of Texas to the Bay of Galveston, traveled across Texas, and returned again to New Orleans. Crossing the country by Mobile, Pensacola, and Augusta, he again reached Charleston, and thence northwards by Washington to New York. He embarked again for England in 1837, where new honors and diplomas awaited him, bringing out his fourth volume of "Ornithological Biography" at the end of 1838. He was now sixty-three years of age, but, speaking of himself, he observed: "The adventures and vicissitudes which have fallen to my lot, instead of tending to diminish the fervid enthusiasm of my nature, have imparted a toughness to my bodily constitution, naturally strong, and to my mind, naturally buoyant, an elasticity such as to assure me that, though somewhat old, and considerably denuded in the frontal region, I could yet perform on foot a journey of any length, were I sure that I should thereby add materially to our knowledge of the ever-interesting creatures which have for so long a time occupied my thoughts by day, and filled my dreams with pleasant images." In the following year, 1839, he published his fifth and last volume, and was then as full of hope and life as ever. His only regret, in parting with his readers, was that he could not transfer to them the whole of the practical knowledge which he had acquired during so many years of enthusiastic devotion to the study of nature.

"Amid the tall grass," said he, "of the far-extended prairies of the West, in the solemn gusts of the North, on the heights of the midland mountains, by the shores of the boundless ocean, and on the bosom of the vast lakes and magnificent rivers, have I sought to search out the things which have been hidden since the creation of this wondrous world, or seen only by the naked Indian, who has, for unknown ages, dwelt in the gorgeous but melancholy wilderness. Who is the stranger to my own dear country that can form an adequate conception of its primeval woods,—of the glory of those columnar trunks that for centuries have waved in the breeze and resisted the shock of the tempest,—of the vast bays of our Atlantic coasts, replenished by thousands of streams, differing in magnitude as differ the stars that sparkle in the expanse of the pure heavens,— of the density of aspect in our Western plains, our sandy Southern shores, interspersed with reedy swamps, and the cliffs that protect our Eastern coasts,—of the rapid currents of the Mexican Gulf, and the rushing tide-streams of the Bay of Fundy,—of our ocean lakes, our mighty rivers, our thundering cataracts, our majestic mountains, rearing their snowy heads into the calmest regions of the clear cold sky? Would that I could delineate the varied features of that loved land!"

As he lived, so he died, full of love for nature. He went on observing, comparing, and noting down his experience, to the last. On the 27th of January, 1851, at his home in New York, at the advanced age of seventy-six, "the American woodsman," to use his own words in one of his volumes, "wrapped himself in his blanket, closed his eyes, and fell asleep."

WILLIAM MACGILLIVRAY.

ENGLAND has as yet produced no naturalist so distinguished as Audubon in his particular department of science. Wilson, the Paisley weaver, published an admirable work on the birds of America, and, having settled in that country, he came to be regarded as an American rather than as a British writer. Macgillivray, perhaps, stands at the head of English writers on British birds. His history is similar to that of many other ardent devotees of science and art. His early life was a long and arduous struggle with difficulties, poverty, and neglect; and it was only towards the close of his career, when he had completed the last volume of his admirable work, that he saw the clouds which had obscured his early fortunes clearing away and revealing the bright sky and sunshine beyond,—but, alas! the success came too late: his constitution had given way in the ardor of the pursuit, and the self-devoted man of science sank lamented into an early grave.

William Macgillivray was born at Aberdeen, the son of comparatively poor parents, who nevertheless found the means of sending him to the University of his native town, in which he took the degree of Master of Arts. It was his intention to take out a medical degree, and he served an apprenticeship to a physician with this view; but his means were too limited, and his love of natural history too ardent, to allow him to follow the profession as a means of support. He accordingly sought for a situation which should at the same time enable him to subsist and to pursue his favorite pursuit.

Such a situation presented itself in 1823, when he accepted the appointment of assistant and secretary to the Regius Professor of Natural History, and Keeper of the Museum, of the Edinburgh University. The collection of natural history at that place is one of peculiar excellence, and he was enabled to pursue his studies there with increased zest and profit;—not, however, as regarded his purse, for the office was by no means lucrative; but, having the charge of this fine collection, he was enabled to devote his time exclusively to the study of scientific ornithology during the winter, whilst during the summer vacation he made long excursions in the country in order to investigate and record the habits of British birds. He was afterwards appointed Conservator to the Museum of the Royal College of Surgeons at Edinburgh, where we have often seen him diligently poring over, dissecting, and preparing the specimens which, from time to time, were added to that fine collection. It was while officiating in the latter capacity that he wrote the first three volumes of his elaborate work. His spare time was also occupied in the preparation of numerous other works on natural history, some of them of standard excellence; by which he was enabled to eke out the means of comfortable subsistence.

Mr. Macgillivray was a man of indefatigable industry, of singular order and method in his habits, a strict economist of time, every moment of which he turned to useful account. Although he studied and wrote upon many subjects,—zoology, geology, botany, mollusca, physiology, agriculture, the feeding of cattle, soils and subsoils,—ornithology was always his favorite pursuit. He accompanied Audubon in most of his ornithological rambles in Scotland, and doubtless imbibed some portion of the ardent enthusiasm with which the American literally burned. Mr. Macgillivray wrote the descriptions of the species, and of the alimentary and respiratory organs, for Audubon's work. His own "British Birds" reminds us in many parts of the enthusiasm of Audubon, and of the graces of that writer's style. Like him, Macgillivray used to watch the birds of which he was in search by night and day. Wrapped in his plaid, he would lie down upon the open moor or on the hill-side, waiting the approach of morning to see the feathered tribes start up and meet the sun, to dart after their prey, or to feed their impatient brood. We remember one such night spent by him on the side of the Lammermoor hills, described in one of his early works, which is full of descriptive beauty, as well as of sound information upon the subject in hand. There is another similar description of a night spent by him among the mountains of Braemar. He had been in search of the gray ptarmigan, whose haunts and habits he was engaged in studying at the time, and had traced the river Dee far up to its sources among the hills, where all traces of the stream became lost: clouds began to gather; nevertheless he pressed on towards the hill-top, until at length he found himself on the summit of a magnificent precipice, several hundred feet high, and at least half a mile in length. "The scene," he says, "that now presented itself to my view was the most splendid that I had then seen. All around rose mountains beyond mountains, whose granite ridges, rugged and tempest-beaten, furrowed by deep ravines worn by the torrents, gradually became dimmer as they receded, until at length on the verge of the horizon they were blended with the clouds or stood abrupt against the clear sky. A solemn stillness pervaded all nature; no living creature was to be seen: the dusky wreaths of vapor rolled majestically over the dark valleys, and clung to the craggy summits of the everlasting hills. A melancholy, pleasing, incomprehensible feeling creeps over the soul when the lone wanderer contemplates the vast, the solemn, the solitary scene, over which savage grandeur and sterility preside.

"The summits of the loftier mountains, Cairngorm on the one hand, Ben-na-muic-dui and Benvotran on the other, and Loch-na-gar on the south, were covered with mist; but the clouds had rolled westward from Ben-na-buird, on which I stood, leaving its summit entirely free. The beams of the setting sun burst in masses of light here and there through the openings in the clouds, which exhibited a hundred varying shades. There, over the ridges of yon brown and torrent-worn mountain, hangs a vast mass of livid vapor, gorgeously glowing with deep crimson along all its lower-fringed margin. Here the white shroud that clings to the peaked summits assumes on its western side a delicate hue, like that of the petals of the pale-red rose. Far away to the north glooms a murky cloud, in which the spirits of the storm are mustering their strength, and preparing the forked lightnings, which at midnight they will fling over the valley of the Spey."

The traveler, seeing night coming on, struck into a corry, down which a small mountain streamlet rushed; and having reached the bottom of the slope, he began to run, starting the ptarmigans from their seats and the does from their lair. It became quite dark; still he went on walking for two hours, but all traces of the path became lost, and he groped his way amid blocks of granite, ten miles at least from any human habitation, and "with no better cheer in my wallet," he says, "than a quarter of a cake of barley and a few crumbs of cheese, which a shepherd had given me. Before I resolved to halt for the night, I had, unfortunately, proceeded so far up the glen that I had left behind me the region of heath, so that I could not procure enough for a bed. Pulling some grass and moss, however, I spread it in a sheltered place, and after some time succeeded in falling into a sort of slumber. About midnight I looked up on the moon and stars that were at times covered by the masses of vapor that rolled along the summits of the mountains, which, with their tremendous precipices, completely surrounded the hollow in which I cowered, like a ptarmigan in the hill-corry. Behind me, in the west, and at the head of the glen, was a lofty mass enveloped in clouds; on the right a pyramidal rock, and beside it a peak of less elevation; on the left a ridge from the great mountain, terminating below in a dark conical prominence; and straight before me, in the east, at the distance apparently of a mile, another vast mass. Finding myself cold, although the weather was mild, I got up and made me a couch of larger stones, grass, and a little short heath; unloosed my pack, covered one of my extremities with a nightcap, and thrust a pair of dry stockings on the other, ate a portion of my scanty store, drank two or three glasses of water from a neighboring rill, placed myself in an easy posture, and fell asleep. About sunrise I awoke, fresh, but feeble; ascended the glen; passed through a magnificent corry, composed of vast rocks of granite; ascended the steep with great difficulty, and at length gained the summit of the mountain, which was covered with light gray mist that rolled rapidly along the ridges. As the clouds cleared away at intervals, and the sun shone upon the scene, I obtained a view of the glen in which I had passed the night, the corry, the opposite hills, and a blue lake before me. The stream which I had followed I traced to two large fountains, from each of which I took a glassful, which I quaffed to the health of my best friends.

"Descending from this summit, I wandered over a high moor, came upon the brink of rocks that bounded a deep valley, in which was a black lake; proceeded over the unknown region of alternate bogs and crags; raised several flocks of gray ptarmigans, and, at length, by following a ravine, entered one of the valleys of the Spey, near the mouth of which I saw a water-ouzel. It was not until noon that I reached a hut, in which I procured some milk. In the evening, at Kingussie, I examined the ample store of plants that I had collected in crossing the Grampians, and refreshed myself with a long sleep in a more comfortable bed than one of the granite slabs with a little grass and heather spread over them."

Macgillivray's description of the golden eagle of the highlands, in its eloquence, reminds one of the splendid descriptions of his friend Audubon. We can only give a few brief extracts.

"The golden eagle is not seen to advantage in the menagerie of a zoölogical society, nor when fettered on the smooth lawn of an aristocratic mansion, or perched on the rockwork of a nursery-garden ; nor can his habits be well described by a cockney ornithologist, whose proper province it is to concoct systems, 'work out' analogies, and give names to skins that have come from foreign lands carefully packed in boxes lined with tin. Far away among the brown hills of Albyn is thy dwelling-place, chief of the rocky glen ! On the crumbling crag of red granite—that tower of the fissured precipices of Loch-na-gar—thou hast reposed in safety. The croak of the raven has broken thy slumbers, and thou gatherest up thy huge wings, smoothest thy feathers on thy sides, and preparest to launch into the aerial ocean. Bird of the desert, solitary though thou art, and hateful to the sight of many of thy fellow-creatures, thine must be a happy life ! No lord hast thou to bend thy stubborn soul to his will, no cares corrode thy heart ; seldom does fear chill thy free spirit, for the windy tempest and the thick sleet cannot injure thee, and the lightnings may flash around thee, and the thunders shake the everlasting hills, without rousing thee from thy dreamy repose.

"See how the sunshine brightens the yellow tint of his head and neck, until it shines almost like gold! There he stands, nearly erect, with his tail depressed, his large wings half raised by his side, his neck stretched out, and his eye glistening as he glances around. Like other robbers of the desert, he has a noble aspect, an imperative mien, a look of proud defiance; but his nobility has a dash of churlishness, and his falconship a vulturine tinge. Still he is a noble bird, powerful, independent, proud, and ferocious ; regardless of the weal or woe of others, and intent solely on the gratification of his own appetite; without generosity, without honor; bold against the defenseless, but ever ready to sneak from danger. Such is his nobility, about which men have so raved. Suddenly he raises his wings, for he has heard the whistle of the shepherd in the corry; and bending forward, he springs into the air. O that this pencil of mine were a musket charged with buckshot.! Hardly do those vigorous flaps serve at first to prevent his descent; but now, curving upwards, he glides majestically along. As he passes the corner of that buttressed and battlemented crag, forth rush two ravens from their nest, croaking fiercely. While one flies above him the other steals beneath, and they essay to strike him, but dare not, for they have an instinctive knowledge of the power of his grasp ; and after following him a little way they return to their home, vainly exulting in the thought of having driven him from their neighborhood. Bent on a far journey, he advances in a direct course, flapping his great wings at regular intervals, then shooting along without seeming to move them.

"Over the moors he sweeps, at the height of two or three hundred feet, bending his course to either side, his wings wide spread, his neck and feet retracted, now beating the air, and again sailing smoothly along. Suddenly he stops, poises himself for a moment, but recovers himself without reaching the ground. The objects of his regards, a golden plover, which he had espied on her nest, has eluded him, and he cares not to pursue it. Now he ascends a little, wheels in short curves,—presently rushes down headlong,—assumes the horizontal position,—when close to the ground, prevents his being dashed against it by expanding his wings and tail,—thrusts forth his talons, and, grasping a poor terrified ptarmigan that sits cowering among the gray lichen, squeezes it to death, raises his head exultingly, emits a clear, shrill cry, and, springing from the ground, pursues his journey.

"In passing a tall cliff that overhangs a small lake, he is assailed by a fierce peregrine falcon, which darts and plunges at him as if determined to deprive him of his booty, or drive him headlong to the ground. This proves a more dangerous foe than the raven, and the eagle screams, yelps, and throws himself into postures of defiance; but at length the hawk, seeing the tyrant is not bent on plundering his nest, leaves him to pursue his course unmolested. Over woods and green fields and scattered hamlets speeds the eagle; and now he enters the long valley of the Dee, near the upper end of which is dimly seen through the thin gray mist the rock of his nest. About a mile from it he meets his mate, who has been abroad on a similar errand, and is returning with a white hare in her talons. They congratulate each other with loud yelping cries, which rouse the drowsy shepherd on the strath below, who, mindful of the lambs carried off in spring-time, sends after them his malediction. Now they reach their nest, and are greeted by their young with loud clamor."

His descriptions of the haunts of the wild birds of the North are full of picturesque beauty. Those of the grouse, the ptarmigan, the merlin, are full of memorable pictures, and here is a brief sketch of the haunts of the common snipe, which recalls many delightful associations. "Beautiful are those green woods that hang upon the craggy sides of the fern-clad hills, where the heath-fowl threads its way among the tufts of brown heath, and the cuckoo sings his ever-pleasing notes as he balances himself on the gray stone, vibrating his fan-like tail. Now I listen to the simple song of the mountain blackbird, warbled by the quiet lake that spreads its glittering bosom to the sun, winding far away among the mountains, amid whose rocky glens wander the wild deer, tossing their antlered heads on high as they snuff the breeze tainted with the odor of the slow-paced shepherd and his faithful dog. In that recess, formed by two moss-clad slabs of mica-slate, the lively wren jerks up its little tail, and chits its merry note, as it recalls its straggling young ones that have wandered among the bushes. From the sedgy slope, sprinkled with white cotton-grass, comes the shrill cry of the solitary curlew; and there, high over the heath, wings his meandering way the joyous snipe, giddy with excess of unalloyed happiness.

"'There another has sprung from among the yellow-flowered marigolds that profusely cover the marsh. Upwards slantingly, on rapidly vibrating wings, he shoots, uttering the while his shrill, two-noted cry. Tissick, tissick, quoth the snipe, as he leaves the bog. Now in silence he wends his way, until at length, having reached the height of perhaps a thousand feet, he zigzags along, emitting a louder and shriller cry of zoo-zee, zoo-zee, zoo-zee; which over, varying his action, he descends on quivering pinions, curving towards the earth with surprising speed, while from the rapid beats of his wing the tremulous air gives to the ear what at first seems the voice of distant thunder. This noise some have likened to the bleating of a goat at a distance on the hill-side, and thus have named our bird the Air-goat and Air-bleater."

In his latter volumes, the naturalist gives many admirable descriptions of the haunts of sea-birds along the rock-bound shores of his native Highlands. He loves to paint the coast of the lonely Hebrides, where he often resorted in the summer months to watch and study the divers and plungers of the sea. Here, for instance, is a picture of the gray heron on a Highland coast :

"The cold blasts of the north sweep along the ruffled surface of the lake, over whose deep waters frown the rugged crags of rusty gneiss, having their crevices sprinkled with tufts of withered herbage, and their summits covered with stunted birches and alders. The desolate hills around are partially covered with snow, the pastures are drenched with the rains, the brown torrents scum the heathy slopes, and the little birds have long ceased to enliven those deserted thickets with their gentle songs. Margining the waters, extends a long muddy beach, over which are scattered blocks of stone, partially clothed with dusky and olivaceous weeds. Here and there a gull floats buoyantly in the shallows; some oyster-catchers repose on a gravel-bank, their bills buried among their plumage; and there, on that low shelf, is perched a solitary heron, like a monument of listless indolence,—a bird petrified in its slumber. At another time, when the tide has retired, you may find it wandering, with slow and careful tread, among the little pools, and by the sides of the rocks, in search of small fishes and crabs; but, unless you are bent on watching it, you will find more amusement in observing the lively tringas and turnstones, ever in rapid motion; for the heron is a dull and lazy bird, or at least he seems to be such; and even if you draw near, he rises in so listless a manner, that you think it a hard task for him to unfold his large wings and heavily beat the air, until he has fairly raised himself. But now he floats away, lightly, though with slow flapping, screams his harsh cry, and tries to soar to some distant place, where he may remain unmolested by the prying naturalist.

"Perhaps you may wonder at finding him in so cold and desolate a place as this dull sea-creek on the most northern coast of Scotland, and that, too, in the very midst of winter; but the heron courts not society, and seems to care as little as any one for the cold. Were you to betake yourself to the other extremity of the island, where the scenery is of a very different character, and the inlands swarm with ducks and gulls there, too, you would find the heron, unaltered in manners, slow in his movements, careful and patient, ever hungry and ever lean; for even when in best condition, he never attains the plumpness that gives you the idea of a comfortable existence."

In 1841 Mr. Macgillivray was appointed by the Crown to the Professorship of Natural History in Marischal College, Aberdeen, solely on account of his acknowledged merit, for he had no interest whatever; and the zeal, ability, and success with which he discharged his duties amply justified the nomination. He was an admirable lecturer,—clear, simple, and methodical, laboring to lay securely the foundations of knowledge in the minds of his pupils. He imbued them with the love of science, and communicated to them—as every successful lecturer cannot fail to do—a portion of his own enthusiasm.

In·the autumn of 1850 he made an excursion to Braemar, with the intention of writing an account of the natural history of Balmoral (which was ready for publication at the time of his death); and he afterwards extended his excursion to the central region of the Grampians, in pursuit of the materials for another work. The fatigue and exposure which he underwent on this occasion seriously affected his health; and he removed to Torquay, in Devon, in hopes of renewed vigor. But he never rallied. A severe calamity befell him while in Devon, through the sudden death of his wife, to whom he was tenderly attached. Nevertheless, he went on steadily with his work, which even his seriously impaired health would not permit him to interrupt. We can conceive him in such a state to have written the following passage, which appears in the preface to his last work, published in the week of his death:

"As the wounded bird seeks some quiet retreat, where, freed from the persecution of the pitiless fowler, it may pass the time of its anguish in forgetfulness of the outer world, so have I, assailed by disease, betaken myself to a sheltered nook, where, unannoyed by the piercing blasts of the North Sea, I had been led to hope that my life might be protracted beyond the most dangerous season of the year. It is thus that I issue from Devonshire the present volume, which, however, contains no observations of mine made there, the scenes of my labors being in distant parts of the country.

"It is well that the observations from which these descriptions have been prepared, were made many years ago, when I was full of enthusiasm, and enjoyed the blessings of health, and freedom from engrossing public duties ; for I am persuaded that now I should be in some respects less qualified for the task,—more, however, from the failure of physical than of mental power. Here, on the rocky promontory, I shiver in the breeze, which, to my companion, is but cool and bracing. The east wind ruffles the sea, and impels the little waves to the shores of the beautiful bay, which presents alternate cliffs of red sandstone and beaches of yellow sand, backed by undulated heights and gentle acclivities, slowly rising to the not distant horizon ; fields and woods, with villages and scattered villas, forming—not wild nor altogether tame—a pleasing landscape, which, in its summer and autumnal garniture of grass and corn, and sylvan verdure; orchard blossom and fruit, tangled fencebank, and furze-clad common, will be beautiful indeed to the lover of nature. Then, the balmy breezes from the west and south will waft health to the reviving invalid. At present, the cold vernal gales sweep along the Channel, conveying to its haven the extended fleet of boats that render Bircham, on the opposite horn of the bay, one of the most celebrated of the southern fishing-stations of England. High over the waters, here and there, a solitary gull slowly advances against the breeze, or shoots athwart, or, with a beautiful gliding motion sweeps down the aerial current.

At the entrance to Torquay are assembled many birds of the same kind, which, by their hovering near the surface, their varied evolutions, and mingling cries, indicate a shoal, probably of atherines or sprats. On that little pyramidal rock, projecting from the water, repose two dusky cormorants; and far away, in the direction of Portland Island, a gannet, well known by its peculiar flight, winnows its exploring way, and plunges headlong into the deep."

And, speaking of the conclusion of his great work, on the last page, he says of it :—

"Commenced in hope, and carried on with zeal, though ended in sorrow and sickness, I can look upon my work without much regard to the opinions which contemporary writers may form of it, assured that what is useful in it will not be forgotten, and knowing that already it has had a beneficial effect on many of the present, and will more powerfully influence the next, generation of our home ornithologists. I had been led to think that I had occasionally been somewhat rude, or at least blunt, in my criticisms; but I do not perceive wherein I have much erred in that respect, and I feel no inclination to apologize. I have been honest and sincere in my endeavors to promote the truth. With death, apparently not distant before my eyes, I am pleased to think that I have not countenanced error through fear or favor; neither have I in any case modified my statements so as to endeavor thereby to conceal or palliate my faults. Though I might have accomplished more, I am thankful for having been permitted to add very considerably to the knowledge previously obtained of a very pleasant subject. If I have not very frequently indulged in reflections on the power, wisdom, and goodness of God, as suggested by even my imperfect understanding of his wonderful works, it is not because I have not ever been sensible of the relation between the Creator and his creatures, nor because my chief enjoyment when wandering among the hills and valleys, exploring the rugged shores of the ocean, or searching the cultivated fields, has not been in a sense of His presence.   'To Him who alone doeth great wonders' be all the glory and praise. Reader, farewell!"

Mr. Macgillivray was able to return to Aberdeen—to die. He expired on the 5th of September, 1852, at the age of fifty-six, leaving a large family behind him, for whom he had been unable (through the slenderness of his means throughout life) to make any provision. His eldest son, however, had already distinguished himself as a naturalist, having been employed by the late Earl of Derby to accompany the expedition sent by him round the world; and he was subsequently appointed Government Naturalist on board the *Rattlesnake*, to complete the exploration of the Eastern Archipelago and Southern Pacific. We may, therefore, expect to have considerable accessions to our knowledge of the natural history of these interesting regions from his already experienced pen.

JOHN STERLING.

A pard-like, spirit, beautiful and swift.

JOHN STERLING seems to have been one of those beautiful natures that carry about with them a charm to captivate all beholders. They are full of young genius, full of promise, full of enthusiasm; and seem to be on the high road towards honor, fame, and glory, when suddenly·their career is cut short by death, and their friends are left lamenting. Just such another character was Charles Pemberton,—a man of somewhat kindred genius to Sterling, —who had *done* comparatively little, but had excited great hopes among a circle of ardent friends and admirers, whom he had riveted to him by certain indefinable personal and intellectual charms; when he was stricken down by death, and, like Sterling, left only a few scattered "Remains" to be judged by. Poor Keats, too, died just as he had given to the world the promise of one of its greatest men, but not before he had sent down into the future strains of undying poesy. Shelley, too! What a loss was there! What glorious promise of a man did he not offer! But the names of the great, who have died in youth, are more than can be told: as Shelley sang,

> The good die first,
> While they whose hearts are dry as summer's dust
> Burn to their socket.

But what of Sterling? What did he do? What has he left as a legacy to us by·which to know and remember him?

We have now two lives of him, written by two of his many intimate friends and devoted admirers,—Archdeacon Hare and Thomas Carlyle. That two such men should have written a life of Sterling would argue of itself something in his character and career more than ordinary. Archdeacon Hare's came first: his work was in two volumes, containing the collected Essays and Tales of John Sterling, with a memoir of his life. On reading that life, interesting and

beautiful though it was, one could not help feeling that there was a
good deal remaining untold, and that the tone adopted in speaking
of John Sterling's opinions on religious subjects was unnecessarily
apologetic. It seems to have been this circumstance which has
drawn forth the life by Carlyle. "Archdeacon Hare," says Carlyle,
"takes up Sterling as a clergyman merely. Sterling, I find, was a
curate for exactly eight months. But he was a man, and had relation to the universe for eight and thirty years; and it is in this latter
character, to which all the others were but features and transitory
hues, that we wish to know him. His battle with hereditary church-
formulas was severe; but it was by no means his one battle with
things inherited, nor indeed his chief battle; neither, according to
my observation of what it was, is it successfully delineated or summed up in this book." And so Carlyle determined to give his por-
traiture of his deceased friend.

Sterling was born at Kaimes Castle, in the island of Bute, Scotland,
in 1806, of Irish parents, who were both of Scotch extraction. The
mother was somewhat proud of being a descendant of Wallace, the
Scottish hero. Edward Sterling, the father, pursued farming; he
had been a militia captain, and took to it as a calling, by way of
helping out the family means. From Bute he removed to Llan-
blethian, in Glamorganshire, in 1809. Here the young Sterling's
childhood was nurtured amid forms of wild and romantic beauty.
But his father, the captain, was an ardent-minded, active man, and
could ill confine himself to the small details of Welsh farming. His
thoughts were abroad. He corresponded with newspapers. He
wrote a pamphlet. He sent letters to the Times, signed "Vetus,"
which were afterwards thought worthy of being collected and re-
printed. The captain went further. He left his farm in Wales, and
proceeded to Paris, with the object of acting as foreign correspondent for the Times newspaper. His family accompanied him to Paris,
where they stayed some eight months, until the sudden return of
Napoleon from Elba, when they had to decamp to England on the
instant. Captain Sterling returned to London, where he settled;
and before long became a very notorious, if not a distinguished, per-
sonage. His connection with the Times newspaper grew closer;
until at length he became extensively known as "The Thunderer,"
and was publicly lashed by O'Connell in that character; Sterling, on
his part, returning the great agitator's compliments with full interest.

The boy was schooled in London, and grew up as boys like him will
grow; he was quick, clever, cheerful, gallant, generous, self-willed,
and rather difficult to manage. From a little letter of his to his
mother, which has been preserved, written when he was twelve years
old, it appears that he "ran away" from his home at Blackheath,
to Dover. The cause was some slight or indignity put upon him
which he could not bear. But he was brought home, and, like other

child's "slights," it was soon forgotten. As a boy, he was a great reader in the promiscuous line; reading Edinburgh Reviews, and cart-loads of novels. At sixteen he was sent to Glasgow University, where he lived with some of his mother's relations. Then, at nineteen, he proceeded to Trinity College, Cambridge, where he had for his tutor Julius Hare, the archdeacon, one of his biographers.

Though not an exact scholar, Sterling became well and extensively read, possessing great facilities of assimilation for all kinds of mental diet. His studies were irregular and discursive, but extensive and encyclopædic. At Cambridge he was brought into friendly connection with Frederick Maurice, Richard Trench, John Kemble, Charles Buller, Monckton Milnes, and others, who were afterwards in life his fast friends. Sterling was a frequent and a brilliant speaker at the Union Club; and already began to exhibit strong "Radical" leanings, displaying no small daring in his attacks upon established ideas and things.

It was Sterling's intention to take a degree in law at Cambridge, but, like many other of his intentions, it came to nothing ; and after a two years' residence, his university life ended. What to do next? He has grown into manhood, and must have a " profession." What is it to be? Is it to be the Law, or the Church? or is he to enter the career of trade, and make money in it, thereby to secure "the temporary hallelujah of flunkeys." His "Radical" notions gave him a deep aversion to the pursuit of the law ; and as for the church, at that time, it was clear that his leanings were not that way. The true career for Sterling, in Carlyle's opinion, was Parliament, and it was possibly with some such ultimate design in view that Sterling engaged himself as secretary to a public association of gentlemen, got up for the purpose of opening the trade to India. But the association did not live long, and the secretaryship lapsed.

One other course remained open for Sterling,—the career of literature,—and he plunged into it. Joining his friend Maurice, the copyright of the Athenæum (which Silk Buckingham had some time before established) was purchased ; and there he printed his first literary effusions,—crude, imperfect, yet singularly beautiful and attractive papers, as, for instance, "The Lycian Painter," containing seeds of great promise. Yet, as Carlyle observes, "a grand melancholy is the prevailing impression they leave ; partly as if, while the surface was so blooming and opulent, the heart of them was still vacant, sad and cold. The writer's heart is indeed still too vacant, except of beautiful shadows and reflexes and resonances ; and is far from joyful, though it wears commonly a smile." He himself used afterwards to speak of this as his "period of darkness."

The Athenæum did not prosper in Sterling's hands. He did not understand commercial management, which is absolutely necessary for the success even of a literary journal. So the Athenæum was transferred to other hands, under which it throve vigorously. But the Athenæum had introduced Sterling into the literary life of London, which tended to confirm him in his pursuit. Among the celebrities with whom he now had familiar intercourse was Coleridge, whose home at Highgate Hill he often visited, and there he listened to that eloquent talker playing the magician with his auditors, — "a dusky, sublime character, who sat there as a kind of Magus, girt in mystery and enigma, whispering strange things, uncertain whether oracles or jargon." The influence which Coleridge exercised upon the religious thinking of his day was unquestionably great, dreamy and speculative though he was; but whether it will survive, whether the religious life of the world will be advanced in any way by Coleridge's lofty musings, is matter of great doubt to many; because, glorious though the rumbling of his sonorous voice was, you too often felt that it died away in sound, leaving no solid, appreciable, practicable, intelligible meaning behind it. But on this wide question we shall not enter. Certain it was that Sterling, notwithstanding his "Radical" notions, was for the time deeply influenced by his intercourse with Coleridge, and by what Carlyle calls his "thrice-refined pabulum of transcendental moonshine." This sufficiently appears in the novel of "Arthur Coningsby," which Sterling wrote in 1830,—his only prose book.

About this time, Sterling deeply interested himself in the fate of some poor Spanish emigrés, driven out of their own country by some revolution there, and then vegetating about Somer's Town and frequently beating with their feet the pavement in Euston Square. Their chief was General Torrijos, with whom Sterling had become intimate, and in whose fortunes he took a warm interest. Torrijos was zealous in the cause of his country; he would effect a landing, revolutionize and liberalize Spain; but he wanted money. Sterling was interested by the romance of the thing, and he also warmly sympathized with the sentiments of the old general. He proceeded to raise money among his friends; money was collected; arms were bought; a ship was provided by Lieutenant Boyd, an Irishman; the ship was in the Thames, taking in its armament, when, lo! the police suddenly appeared on board, and the vessel was seized and its stores confiscated. Torrijos, Boyd, and some others, did afterwards manage to land in Spain; where they met with an exceedingly tragical ending.

But something else issued from this Spanish misadventure, of interest to Sterling. He had become acquainted with the Misses Barton, the daughters of Lieutenant-General Barton, of the Life Guards,—very delightful young ladies. He seems to have excited something more than merely friendly feelings in Susannah's bosom; for when he went to take leave of her, to embark in the projected Spanish invasion, a scene occurred from which it appeared clear that he had won the girl's heart, and then marriage was the result.

But scarcely was he married ere he fell seriously ill,—so ill that he lay utterly prostrate for weeks, and his life was long despaired of. His career after this was a constant alternation of health and illness, rampant good spirits and prostrate feebleness. His lungs were affected, and consumption began to show indications of its coming. The doctors, however, gave hopes of him,—only it was necessary he should remove to a warmer climate. His family had inherited a valuable property in the West Indies, at St. Vincent, whither he went to reside in 1831, and remained in that beautiful island, under the hot sun of the tropics, for about fifteen months, returning to England greatly improved in health, From thence he went to Bonn, in Germany, where he met with his old friend and quondam tutor, the Rev. Julius Hare, and with him Sterling had much serious talk on religious matters.

Still under the influence of the Coleridgean views which had been working within him at St. Vincent and since, Sterling expressed to Mr. Hare a wish to enter the church as a minister, which Mr. Hare "strongly urged" him to do, offering to appoint him to his own curacy at Herstmonceux, which was then vacant. Shortly after, he returned to England, was ordained deacon at Chichester in 1834, and was appointed curate immediately after, entering earnestly on the duties of that calling. He occasionally preached in the metropolis, and Carlyle described his appearance on two of such occasions:

" It was in some new college chapel in Somerset House ; a very quiet small place, the audience student-looking youths, with a few elder people, perhaps mostly friends of the preacher's. The discourse, delivered with a grave sonorous composure, and far surpassing in talent the usual run of sermons, had withal an air of human veracity, as I still recollect, and bespoke dignity and piety of mind ; but gave me the impression rather of artistic excellence than of unction or inspiration in that kind. Sterling returned with us to Chelsea that day ; and in the afternoon we went on the Thames Putney-ward together, we two with my wife ; under the sunny skies, on the quiet water, and with copious, cheery talk, the remembrance of which is still present enough to me.

"This was properly my only specimen of Sterling's preaching. Another time, late in the same autumn, I did indeed attend him one evening to some church in the City,—a big church behind Cheapside, 'built by Wren,' as he carefully informed me ;—but there, in my wearied mood, the chief subject of reflection was the almost total vacancy of the place, and how an eloquent soul was preaching to mere lamps and prayer-books ; and of the sermon I retain no image. It came up in the way of banter, if he ever urged the duty of 'Church extension,' which already he very seldom did, and at length never, what a specimen we once had of bright lamps, gilt prayer-books, baize-lined pews, Wren-Built architecture ; and how, in almost all directions, you might have fired a musket through the church, and hit no Christian life. A terrible outlook, indeed, for the apostolic laborer in the brick-and-mortar line !"

For reasons which Archdeacon Hare does not clearly state, but which Carlyle in a rather mystical way indicates, Sterling left his curacy at Herstmonceux, and removed to London, where he took a house at Bayswater. At this time he was, in personal appearance, thin and careless-looking,—his eyes kindly, but restless in their glances,—his features animated and brilliant when talking,—and he was always full of bright speech and argument. He did not give you the idea of ill-health; indeed, his life seemed to be bounding, and full of vitality; his whole being was usually in full play;—it was his vehemence and rapidity of life which struck one on first seeing him.

Carlyle says, that he *wore holes* in the outer case of his body by this restless vitality, which could not otherwise find vent. He seems now to have been in the thick of doubts and mental discussions,—probing the foundations of his faith,—and, it is to be suspected, losing one by one the pillars on which it had rested. It is a terrible "valley of the shadow of death," this which so many young minds have to pass through in these days of restless inquiry into all subjects,—religious, social, and political. As Shelley writes,—

> If I have erred, there was no joy in error,
> But pain and insult, and unrest and terror.

Sterling's views began to diverge more and more from those formerly held by him, yet this never interfered with a single one of his friendships. Tolerant and charitable, there was an agreement to differ; and certainly it is better for men to differ openly and honestly, than hypocritically to agree and conform,—even for "peace's sake." And why should men quarrel about such matters, respecting which no one man can have more positive or certain knowledge than any other man? Says Tennyson:

> What am I ?
> An infant crying in the night:
> An infant crying for the light;
> And with no language but a cry!

Sterling read many German books at this time, such as Tholuck and Schleiermacher, from which he diverged into Goethe and Jean Paul Richter. But his health was still delicate, and a residence in the south of France was determined on.

He reached Bordeaux, and while there worked at various literary enterprises. Poetry occupied his attention, and he there wrote "The Sexton's Daughter;" he also stored up a number of notes and memoranda respecting Montaigne, whose old country-house he visited,

BIOGRAPHIES 4

and these shortly after appeared, in a very able article from his pen, in the London and Westminster Review. After a year's stay, he returned to England, and occupied himself in writing occasional articles for Blackwood's Magazine. His health being still delicate, he wintered at Madeira in 1837; speaking of it in one of his letters, he says that, "as a temporary refuge, a niche in an old ruin, where one is sheltered from the shower, the place has great merit." He continued writing papers for Blackwood, of which the best was "The Onyx Ring." Wilson early recognized Sterling's merit as a writer, and lavished great praise upon him in his editorial comments. Indeed, he seems to have possessed the gift of literary improvising to a great extent. He was a swift genius: Carlyle likened him to "sheet-lightning." He had an incredible facility of labor, flashing with most piercing glance into a subject, and throwing his thoughts upon it together upon paper with remarkable felicity, brilliancy, and general excellence. While at Madeira Sterling busied himself with reading Goethe, of whom he gives the following striking opinion, in many respects true: "There must, I think, have been some prodigious defect in his mind, to let him hold such views as his about women and some other things; and in another respect, I find so much coldness and hollowness as to the highest truths, and feel so strongly that the heaven he looks up to is *but a vault of ice,*—that these two indications, leading to the same conclusion, go far to convince me he was a profoundly immoral and irreligious spirit, with as rare faculties of intelligence as ever belonged to any one."

His health improved by Madeira, he returned to England, still fragile, but radiant with cheerfulness; "both his activity and his composure he bore with him, through all weathers, to the final close; and on the whole, right manfully he walked his wild, stern way towards the goal, and like a Roman wrapped his mantle round him when he fell." He went on writing for Blackwood, contributing the "Hymns of a Hermit," "Crystals from a Cavern," "Thoughts and Images," and other papers of this sort. Then he engaged as contributor to the London and Westminster Review, for which he wrote several fine papers. The raw winter air of England proving too much for his weak lungs, he went abroad again,—this time to Italy,—where he reveled in its picture-galleries and collections of fine art. He did not like the religious aspect of things there, and spoke freely about it. He was home again in 1839, considerably improved in health; but still he continued to lead a nomadic life, for the sake of his health. Now at Hastings, then at Clifton; and again he had to fly before worse symptoms than had yet shown themselves,—spitting of blood and such like,—taking flight late in the season for Madeira. But when he reached Falmouth, the weather was so rough that he could not set sail; so he rested there for the winter, the mild climate suiting his feeble lungs better than Clifton had done. By this time, during his residence in the last-named place, he had written his fine paper on "Carlyle," for the Westminster Review, and also published a little volume of poems, containing some noble pieces. Carlyle speaks in rather a slighting strain of poetry in general, and has a strong dislike to what he calls the "fiddling talent." "Why *sing*," he asks, "your bits of thoughts, if you *can* contrive to speak them? By your *thought*, not by your mode of delivering it, you must live or die." Besides, he denies to Sterling that indispensable quality of successful poetry,—depth of *tune;* his verses "had a monotonous rub-a-dub, instead of tune: no trace of music deeper than that of a well-beaten drum." But let any one read Sterling's "Dœdalus," and they will be satisfied of his tunefuless, as well as his true poetic feeling. We know no verses fuller of music in every line. These are a few stanzas:

> Wail for Dœdalus, all that is fairest,
> All that is tuneful in air or wave!
> Shapes whose beauty is truest and rarest,
> Haunt with your lamps and spells his grave.
>
> Statues, bend your heads in sorrow,
> Ye that glance 'mid ruins old,
> That know not a past, nor expect a morrow,
> On many a moonlit Grecian wold!
>
> By sculptured cave, and speaking river,
> Thee, Dædalus, oft the nymphs recall;
> The leaves, with a sound of winter, quiver,
> Murmur thy name, and murmuring fall.
>
> Ever thy phantoms arise before us,
> Our loftier brothers, but one in blood;
> By bed and table they lord it o'er us,
> With looks of beauty and words of good.

The volume of poems, however, attracted no notice ; yet Sterling labored on, determined to conquer success. He met with some delightful friends at Falmouth, among others, with John Stuart Mill and an intelligent Quaker family,—the Foxes,—with whom he spent many happy hours. In the following spring he was by his own hearth again at Clifton, now engaged on a long poem called "The Election," which was published; he had also commenced his tragedy, of "Strafford," when he went to winter at Torquay. Thus he journeyed flying about from place to place for life. Then to Falmouth again, where he delivered an excellent lecture on "The Worth of knowledge," before the Polytechnic Institution of that place. Soon after, he was off to Naples and the sunny south, his health still demanding warmth. He was home again in 1843 ; and one day, while helping one of the servants to lift a heavy table, he was seized with sudden hemorrhage, and for long lay dangerously ill. By dint of careful nursing, he recovered, but the seeds of death must have been planted in him by this time. This year his mother died, and in a few days after his beloved wife,—terrible blows to him. But weak and worn as he was, he bore up manfully, making no vain repinings, and with pious valor fronting the future. He had six children left to his charge, and he felt the responsibility deeply. Falmouth, associated as it now was in his mind with calamity and sorrow, he could endure no longer; so he purchased a house at Ventnor, in the Isle of Wight, and removed thither at once. Sterling visited London for the last time in 1843, when Carlyle dined with him. "I remember it," says he, "as one of the saddest of dinners ; though Sterling talked copiously, and our friends—Theodore Parker one of them—were pleasant and distinguished men. All was so haggard in one's memory, and half consciously in one's anticipations ; sad, as if one had been dining in a ruin, in the crypt of a mausoleum."

Carlyle saw Sterling afterwards at his apartments in town, and the following is the conclusion of his last interview with him : "We parted before long ; bed-time for invalids being come, he escorted me down certain carpeted back-stairs, and would not be forbidden ; we took leave under the dim skies ; and, alas ! little as I then dreamed of it, this, so far as I can calculate, must have been the last time I ever saw him in the world. *Softly as a common evening, the last of the evenings had passed away, and no other would come for me forevermore.*"

Sterling returned to Ventnor, and proceeded with his "Cœur-de-Lion. But the light of his life had gone. " I am going on quietly here, rather than happily," he wrote to his friend Newman; "sometime quite helpless, not from distinct illness, but from sad thoughts, and a ghastly dreaminess. *The heart is gone out of my life.*" The brittle existence of his was at length about to be shivered. Another breakage of a blood-vessel occurred, and he lay prostrate for the last time. The great change was at hand,—the final act of the tragedy of life. He gathered his strength together to quit life piously and manfully. For six months he had sat looking at the approaches of the foe, and he blanched not nor quailed before him. He had continued working, and setting all his worldly affairs in order. He wrote some noble letters to his eldest boy, then at school in London, full of affectionate counsel. "These letters," says Carlyle, "I have lately read; they give beyond any he has written, a noble image of the intrinsic Sterling, — the same face we had long known; but painted now as on the azures of eternity, serene, victorious, divinely sad; the dusts and extraneous disfigurements imprinted on it by the world now washed away."

About a month before his death, he wrote a last letter to Carlyle, of "Remembrance and Farewell," wherein he says : "On higher matters there is nothing to say. I tread the common road into the great darkness, without any thought of fear, and with very much of hope. Certainty, indeed, I have none. With regard to You and

Me, I cannot begin to write; having nothing for it but to keep shut the lid of those secrets with all the iron weights that are in my power. Toward me it is still more true than toward England, that no man has been and done like you. Heaven bless you ! If I can lend a hand when there, that will not be wanting. It is all very strange, but not one-hundredth part so sad as it seems to the standers-by."

"It was a bright Sunday morning when this letter came to me," says Carlyle, "and if in the great Cathedral of Immensity I did no worship that day, the fault surely was my own. Sterling affectionately refused to see me; which also was kind and wise. And four days before his death, there are some stanzas of verse for me, written as if in star-fire and immortal tears; which are among my sacred possessions, to be kept for myself alone. His business with the world was done; the one business now to await silently what may lie in other grander worlds. 'God is great,' he was wont to say: 'God is great.' The Maurices were now constantly near him; Mrs. Maurice (his sister) assiduously watching over him. On the evening of Wednesday, the 18th of September, his brother—as he did every two or three days—came down; found him in the old temper, weak in strength, but not very sensibly weaker; they talked calmly together for an hour ; then Anthony left his bedside, and retired for the night, not expecting any change. But suddenly, about eleven o'clock, there came a summons and alarm; hurrying to his brother's room, he found his brother dying; and in a short while more, the faint last struggle was ended, and all those struggles and strenuous, often foiled, endeavors of eight-and-thirty years lay hushed in death."

LEIGH HUNT.

WHAT reader of books is there who does not feel that he owes a debt of gratitude to Leigh Hunt, for his many beautiful thoughts, his always cheerful views of life, and his generous efforts, extending over a period of half a century, on behalf of the freedom and happiness of the human family ? His name is associated in our minds with all manner of kindness, love, beauty, and gentleness. He has given us a fresh insight into nature, made the flowers seem gayer, the earth greener, the skies more bright, and all things more full of happiness and blessing, By the magical touch of his pen, he " kissed dead things to life." Age, which dries up the geniality of so many, brought no change to him. To the last he was spoken of as the " gray-haired boy,"—"the old-young poet, with gray hairs on his head, but youth in his eyes,"—and the perusal of his Autobiography, written in his old age, serves to bring out charmingly the prominent features of his life.

Leigh Hunt's temperament doubtless owed something to the warm, sunshiny clime in which his progenitors lived, that of Barbadoes, in the West Indies. His grandfather was a clergyman there, and his grandmother an O'Brien,—very proud of her alleged descent from certain mythical Irish kings of that name. Their son (Leigh Hunt's father) was sent to Philadelphia, then belonging to the English American colonies, to be educated ; and there he married and settled. But on the war of the American Revolution breaking out, he entered so warmly into the cause of the British government that he was mobbed, narrowly escaped tarring and feathering, and ultimately fled to England, his wife and little family following him. He was there ordained a clergyman by the Bishop of London, and became famous as a preacher of charity sermons. He was fond, however, of pleasurable living; drank more than was good for him; got into pecuniary difficulties, from which he never escaped; and lived a life of shifts and expedients, always trusting, like Mr.

134

Micawber, to "something turning up." He found a brief friend in Marquis of Chandos, and was engaged by him as tutor for his nephew, Mr. Leigh, after whom Leigh Hunt was subsequently named.

To be tutor in a duke's family is often a sure road to a bishopric, or some other high promotion in the church: but the tutor in this case had no such good fortune: his West Indian temperament spoiled all: he had ceased to think the British government perfect, and he did not hesitate to express his opinions freely thereon. So, after leaving this situation, he lapsed again into difficulties, and afterwards into distress and debt. Still his happy and joyous nature bore him up, even though he was haunted by duns and became familiar with prisons. "Such an art had he," said his son, "of making his home comfortable when he chose, and of settling himself to the most tranquil pleasures, that, if she could have ceased to look forward about her children, I believe, with all his faults, those evenings would have brought unmingled satisfaction to her, when, after settling the little apartment, brightening the fire, and bringing out the coffee, my mother knew that her husband was going to read Saurin or Barrow to her, with his fine voice, and unequivocal enjoyment."

Leigh Hunt's mother was of American birth, a Philadelphian; she had "no accomplishments but the two best of all, a love of nature and a love of books." She was a woman of great energy of principle, though timid and gentle almost to excess. Her husband's great dangers at Philadelphia, and the imminent risk of shipwreck which she, with her family, ran on the voyage to England, had shaken her soul as well as frame. Her son said of her: "The sight of two men fighting in the streets would drive her in tears down another road; and I remember, when we lived near the park, she would take me a long circuit out of the way, rather than hazard the spectacle of the soldiers. Little did she think of the timidity with which she was inoculating me, and what difficulty I should have, when I went to school, to sustain all those pure theories, and that unbending resistance to oppression, which she inculcated. However, perhaps it ultimately turned out for the best. One must feel more than usual for the sore places of humanity, even to fight properly in their behalf. One holiday, in a severe winter, as she was taking me home, she was petitioned for charity by a woman, sick and ill-clothed. It was in Blackfriars Road, I think, about midway. My mother, with the tears in her eyes, turned up a gateway, or some such place, and beckoning the woman to follow, took off her flannel petticoat and gave it to her. It is supposed that a cold which ensued fixed the rheumatism upon her for life. Her greatest pleasure, during her decay, was to lie on a sofa, looking at the setting sun. She used to liken it to the door of heaven; and fancy her lost children there waiting for her." As a man is but his parents, or some other of his ancestors, drawn out, so Leigh Hunt, in his own life and history,

was but a repetition of his father and mother, and an embodiment,
of their character in about equal proportions; inheriting from the
one a happy and joyous temperament, and from the other tenderness
and a deep love of nature and books.

Leigh Hunt was born at Southgate, in the parish of Edmonton, on
the 19th of October, 1784, in the midst of the beautiful pastoral
scenery which he afterwards loved to paint in his works. During
his infancy he was delicate and sickly, and was watched over with
great tenderness by his mother. To assist his recovery, he was
taken to the coast of France for a short time, and returned improved
in health. He was very nervous, and easily frightened by his elder
brothers, who delighted to terrify him by ghost-stories and pretended
apparitions.

The great events which were passing in Hunt's childhood rose up
afterwards in his mind like a dream,—the American Revolution
completed, the French Revolution beginning; the eloquence of
Burke, and the rivalries of Pitt and Fox; the poetry of Cowper and
Young, and the novels of Miss Burney and Mrs. Inchbald; the
violent politics of Wilkes, and the gallantries of the young Prince
of Wales. These were the days of pigtails and toupees, when ladies
wore hoops, and lay all night with their hair three-stories high,
waiting for the spectacle of next day,—a very different style of
living and dressing from the present.

The boy went to school at Christ Church Hospital, where Lamb
and Coleridge were also educated about the same time. The thrash-
ing system, which was then in vogue in all schools, horrified him;
his gentle spirit made him the sport of the other boys, and he " went
to the wall" till he gained strength and address to stand his own
ground. Even as a boy he had the reputation of a romantic enthu-
siast. He fought only once, beat his opponent and made a friend
of him.

While only a school-boy, Leigh Hunt fell in love with the Muses,
—with Collins and Gray passionately,—and he already began to
write verses. He also fell in love in another way,—with a charming cousin, Fanny Dayrell. "Fanny was a lass of fifteen, with
little laughing eyes, and a mouth like a plum. I was then (I feel
as if I ought to be ashamed of it) not more than thirteen, if so
old; but I had read Tooke's Pantheon, and came of a precocious race.
My cousin came of one, too; and was about to be married to a handsome young fellow of three-and-twenty. I thought nothing of this,
for nothing could be more innocent than my intentions. I was not
old enough, or grudging enough, or whatever it was, even to be
jealous. I thought everybody must love Fanny Dayrell; and if she
did not leave me out in permitting it, I was satisfied. It was
enough for me to be with her as long as I could; to gaze on her with
delight as she floated hither and thither; and to sit on the stiles in
the neighboring fields, thinking of Tooke's Pantheon. Three-

fourths of my heart was devoted to friendship; the rest was in a vague dream of beauty, and female cousins, and nymphs and green fields, and a feeling which, though of a warm nature, was full of fear and respect." In course of time Fanny married, and his first passion died away, but was not forgotten.

At Christ Church, Hunt formed intimacies with men afterwards famous in literature. There was Wood, afterwards Fellow of Pembroke College, Cambridge; Mitchell, the translator of Aristophanes, and a Quarterly Reviewer; and Barnes, the future editor of the Times. With the last named he learned Italian, and the two went shouting Metastasio together, as loud as they could bawl, over the Hornsey fields.

At fifteen he took leave of his school-books and school friends, and after going about eight years bareheaded, put on the fatal hat. He set about writing verse and haunting book-stalls,—the occupation of no small part of his future life. The first verses he wrote were collected and published by subscription. These, he confesses, were but "a heap of imitations, all but absolutely worthless." The book was, however, successful, particularly in the metropolis; and the author found himself a kind of "Young Roscius" in verse. His grandfather in America, sensible of the young author's fame, wrote to him that, if he would come to Philadelphia he would "make a man of him;" to which his answer was, that "men grew in England as well as America."

After joining as a private in the volunteers, who were called into existence by the rumor of Bonaparte's coming, and going the round of the London theaters, taking his full of pleasures, Leigh Hunt appeared, for the first time, as a prose essayist, in the columns of the Traveler, now the Globe, newspaper, under the signature of "Mr. Town, Junior, for which he received as his reward some five or six copies of each paper in which his essays appeared. He wrote a long mock heroic poem about the same time, and made several attempts at farce, comedy, and tragedy ; reading largely in Goldsmith, Voltaire, novels and history, promiscuouly. His brother, John Hunt, set up a paper called The News, in 1805, on which the subject of our memoir, then in his twentieth year, went to live with him; and wrote the theatricals for the journal. He there commenced the system of independent criticism, and adhered to it, though he afterwards frankly admitted that he then knew nothing of either actors or acting. In the midst of his labors, he fell into ill-health and melancholy ; palpitations, hypochondria, dyspepsia—in other words, the "literary disease" had attacked him. He recovered, by ceasing his occupation for a time and taking exercise ; but he gained more than a cure. "One great benefit," he says, "resulted to me from this suffering. It gave me an amount of reflection such as, in all probability, I never should have had without it ; and if readers have derived any good from the graver portion of my writings, I attribute it to this experience of evil. It taught me patience ; it taught me charity (however imperfectly I may have exercised either) ; it taught me charity even towards myself ; it taught me the worth of little pleasures, as well as the utility and dignity of great pains ; it taught me that evil itself contained good ; nay, it taught me to doubt whether any such thing as evil, considered in itself, existed ; whether things altogether, as far as our planet knows them, could have been so good without it ; whether the desire, nevertheless, which nature has implanted in us for its destruction, be not the signal and the means to that end; and whether its destruction, finally, will not prove its existence, in the meantime, to have been necessary to the very bliss that supersedes it." We could not, perhaps, have selected a passage from Leigh Hunt's writings that embodies his philosophy more completely than than this does.

The year 1808 saw him and his brother John afoot with an important enterprise,—the establishment of the since famous Examiner newspaper. It started as a Radical print,—a bold thing in those perilous times, when a man dared scarcely say the thing he would without risk of Horsemonger Jail, or worse. The new paper attracted attention, and brought around it many choice and kindred spirits. Leigh Hunt now mixed among literary men, whom he has described in his Autobiography. Of Theodore Hook, Thomas Campbell, Horace Smith, Fuseli, Matthews, Godwin, Bonnycastle, Byron, Shelley, Keats, Wordsworth, and others, he furnishes many recollections. Horace Smith (one of the authors of the "Rejected Addresses") he speaks of as "delicious." "A finer nature than Horace Smith's, except in the single instance of Shelley, I never met with in man ; nor even in that instance, all circumstances considered, have I a right to say that those who knew him as intimately as I did the other, would not have had the same reasons to love him. Shelley said to me once : 'I know not what Horace Smith must take me for, sometimes ; I am afraid he must think me a strange fellow ; but it is so odd, that the only truly generous person I ever knew. who had money to be generous with, should be a stock broker. And he writes poetry, too,' continued Shelley, his voice rising in a fervor of astonishment.—'he writes poetry and pastoral dramas, and yet knows how to make money, and does make it, and is still generous !'"

Here is an odd outline of a man ! "Bonnycastle was a good fellow: he was a tall, gaunt, long-headed man, with large features and spectacles, and a deep, internal voice, with a twang of rusticity in it, and he goggled over his plate like a horse. I often thought that a bag of corn would have hung well on him. His laugh was equine, and showed his teeth upwards at the sides." This was the famous algebraist.

The Examiner. in which the brothers were boldly discussing the politics of the day, very soon drew upon it the keen eyes of men in power, who waited for an opportunity of pouncing upon it. The remarks on a pamphlet published by Major Hogan, in which the notorious Mrs. Clarke's dispensation of the Duke of York's patronage in return for hard cash was broadly hinted, excited marked attention, and the government commenced an action against the proprietors of the paper, from which they were only saved by a member of the House of Commons (Colonel Wardle) taking up the subject, and bringing up Mrs. Clarke (whose relation to the Duke of York was well known) for examination at the Bar of the House, when the whole thing was exposed by her, with barefaced effrontery. Before another year was out, the government instituted a second prosecution, for a sentence in an article which, at this time of day, would look exceedingly mild, if appearing in the daily Times. The Morning Chronicle was first prosecuted for having copied the article, but the jury pronounced an acquittal, and the action against the Examiner again fell to the ground. A third prosecution was shortly commenced by the government against the proprietors, for having copied an article from the Stamford News, against military flogging ; but on a trial, the jury acquitted them.

About this time, John Hunt started a quarterly magazine, called The Reflector, which Leigh Hunt edited, and of which only four numbers appeared. Charles Lamb, Barnes (afterwards of the Times), and some other Christ Church Hospital men, were amongst its contributors. In it first appeared Leigh Hunt's "Feast of the Poets," in which he satirized many of his Tory contemporaries,—amongst others Gifford, the editor of the Quarterly, the only man for whom he seems to have entertained a thorough dislike. Amongst the poetical effusions in the Reflector also appeared one on a famous dinner given by the Prince of Wales to a hundred and fifty of his particular friends. The Prince had just deserted the Whig party, and gone over to the Tories, so that there was a strong savor of political gall in the piece. About the same time, an article on the Prince, in connection with the annual dinner on St. Patrick's Day, was inserted in the Examiner, and on this the government fastened, as the means of crushing the paper and its proprietors. The point in the article at which the Prince was understood to have taken violent offense was, that he whom his adulators styled "an Adonis in loveliness," should be plainly designated as "a corpulent man of fifty," which he was. The government prosecution succeeded. The proprietors of the paper were fined one hundred pounds, and condemned to two years' imprisonment each, in separate jails!

Leigh Hunt's prison-life was thoroughly characteristic of him. He was in a very delicate state of health when first imprisoned in Horsemonger Jail, but he determined to make the best of it. His wife and friends were allowed to be constantly with him. Owing to his delicate state of health, the doctor proposed he should be removed into the infirmary, and the proposal was granted. And now see how a happy mind and a sound conscience can make even a prison-house a place of joy.

" The infirmary was divided into four wards, with as many small rooms attached to them. The two upper wards were occupied, but the two on the floor had never been used; and one of these, not very providently (for I had not yet learned to think of money) I turned into a noble room. I papered the walls with a trellis of roses; I had the ceiling colored with clouds and sky; the barred windows I screened with Venetian blinds; and when my book-cases were set up with their nests, and flowers and a piano-forte made their appearance, perhaps there was not a handsomer room on that side the water. I took a pleasure, when a stranger knocked at the door, to see him come in and stare about him. The surprise on issuing from the borough, and passing through the avenues of a jail, was dramatic. Charles Lamb declared there was no other such room, except in a fairy-tale.

" But I possessed another surprise, which was a garden. There was a little yard outside the room, railed off from another belonging to the neighboring ward. This yard I shut in with green palings, bordered it with a thick bed of earth from a nursery, and even contrived to have a grass-plot. The earth I filled with flowers and young trees. There was an apple-tree, from which we managed to get a pudding the second year. As to my flowers, they were allowed to be perfect. Thomas Moore, who came to see me with Lord Byron, told me he had seen no such heart's-ease. Here I wrote and read in fine weather, sometimes under an awning. In autumn, my trellises were hung with scarlet runners, which added to the flowery investment. I used to shut my eyes in my armchair, and affect to think of myself hundreds of miles off.

" But my triumph was in issuing forth of a morning. A wicket out of the garden led into the large one belonging to the prison. The latter was only for vegetables; but it contained a cherry-tree which I saw twice in blossom. I parceled out the ground, in imagination, into favorite districts. I made a point of dressing myself as if for a long walk; and then, putting on my gloves, and taking my book under my arm, stepped forth, requesting my wife not to wait dinner if I was too late. My eldest little boy to whom Lamb addressed some charming verses on the occasion, was my constant companion, and we used to play all sorts of juvenile games together. It was, probably, in dreaming of one of these games (but the words had a more touching effect on my ear) that, he exclaimed one night in his sleep, 'No, I'm not lost; I'm found.' Neither he nor I were very strong at the time; but I have lived to see him a man of forty, and wherever he is found, a generous hand and a great understanding will be found together."

The two years slowly passed, during which the visits of many friends, Hazlitt, Lamb, Shelley, Hentham, and others, cheered

Leigh Hunt's captivity. He read and wrote verses; composed the principal part of the "Story of Rimini;" furnished articles and critcisms for the Examiner; and anxiously looked forward to the hour of his release. Meanwhile, there were generous friends who volunteered to pay the fine for hfm, but their offer was declined. The Hunts would bear their own burdens, and maintain their own independence while they could. At length, on the 3d of February, 1805, they were free.

"It was now thought I should dart out of my cage like a bird, and feel no end in the delight of ranging. But, partly from ill-health and partly from habit, the day of my liberation brought a good deal of pain with it. An illness of a long standing, which required a very different treatment, had by this time been burnt in upon me by the iron that enters into the soul of the captive, wrap it in flowers as he may; and and I am ashamed to say, that, after stopping a little at the house of my friend Alsager, I had not the courage to continue looking at the shoals of people passing to and fro as the coach drove up the Strand. The whole business of life seemed a hideous impertinence. The first pleasant sensation I experienced was when the coach turned into the Few Road, and I beheld the old hills of my affection, standing where they used to do, and breathing me a welcome.

"It was very slowly that I recovered anything like a sensation of health. The bitterest evil I suffered was in consequence of having been confined so long in one spot. The habit stuck to me on my return home, in a very extraordinary manner, and made, I fear, some of my friends think me ungrateful. This weakness I have outlived; but I have never thoroughly recovered the shock given to my constitution. My natural spirits, however, have always struggled hard to see me reasonably treated. Many things give me exquisite pleasure, which seem to affect other men in a very minor degree; and I enjoyed, after, such happy moments with my friends, even in prison, that, in the midst of the beautiful climate which I afterwards visited, I was sometimes in doubt whether I would not rather have been in jail than Italy."

The "Story of Rimini" was published shortly after Leigh Hunt's release from prison. It was greatly and deservedly admired, but it could not prove very remunerative to him. In order to meet demands which had been accruing upon him, he also published "The Indicator," but want of funds prevented the publication being advertised and pushed as it deserved. The Examiner was now declining in circulation and receipts, for the party against which it struggled was entirely in the ascendant. We fear, also, that its business management must have suffered from the long imprisonment of the two proprietors, as well as from the acknowledged deficiency of at least one of them in business capacity. "I had never attended," says Leigh Hunt, "not only to the business part of the

Examiner, but to the simplest money matter that stared at me on the face of it. I could not tell anybody who asked me what was the price of its stamp! Do I boast of this ignorance? Alas! Alas! I have no such respect for the pedantry of absurdity as that. I blush for it; and I only record it out of a sheer, painful movement of conscience, as a warning to those young authors who might be led to look on such folly as a fine thing; which, at all events, is what I never thought it myself. I did not think about it at all, except to avoid the thought; and I only wish that the strangest accidents of education, and the most inconsiderate habit of taking books for the only end of life, had not conspired to make me so ridiculous. I am feeling the consequences at this moment, in pangs which I cannot explain, and which I may not live long to escape."

In the winter of 1821 Leigh Hunt set sail, with his wife and seven children, on a voyage to Italy, to join Byron and Shelley, then residing there. After a tremendous storm the vessel in which they sailed was driven into Dartmouth, where they re-landed, and passed on to Plymouth, where they waited until May, 1822, and from thence sailed to Leghorn. The residence in Italy was not pleasant; it was embittered by the death of Shelley and of Keats, and the obvious alienation of Byron. The tedium was not relieved by the pleasures which opulence supplies, for, from this time, Leigh Hunt seems to have been haunted by the ghost of poverty. Everything that he touched failed. The Liberal, a quarterly publication brought out by him while in Italy, reached only the fourth number, though Byron, Shelley, and Hazlitt wrote for it, as well as himself, The Literary Examiner, a new publication set up by his brother, also failed; and the political Examiner, the newspaper, was now in the crisis of its difficulties; it shortly after passed into other hands, when it prospered. Leigh Hunt, in the midst of these failures, grew sick of Italy." "I was ill, unhappy, and in a perpetual low fever," he says. He longed for the sight of English hedge-rows and green fields, to wander through paths leading over field and stile, across hay-fields in June, and through woods full of wild flowers. "To me," he says, "Italy had a certain hard taste in the mouth. The mountains were too bare, its outlines too sharp, its lanes too stony, its voices too loud, its long summer too dusty. I longed to bathe myself in the grassy balm of my native fields."

He reached home in 1823, and commenced anew a struggle with difficulties. Perhaps "struggle" is too strong a word. Leigh Hunt seems to have been playing with life, even with its sorrows, all the way through. He was not a man to grapple with a difficulty and overcome it; but to float alongside of it rather carelessly, and say pleasant things about it. He had a good deal of his father's West Indian temperament in him, and loved to lie basking in the sun, building castles in the air. He wrote occasional essays and poems from time to time, for monthly magazines; and, for a bookseller, who had assisted him to return to England, a novel called "Sir alph Esher." He also obtained pecuniary assistance from friends, and struggled on the best way he could. He started a new periodical, The Companion, which did not live long; then the Tatler, a daily literary and theatrical paper, which nearly killed him, as he wrote it all; Chat of the Week was tried, and failed too. A subscription list was got up for a new edition of his poems, which helped him somewhat. Then he wrote for the True Sun, which also died; next he edited the Monthly Reporter, which did not survive long. The London Journal lived through two volumes, and then gave up the ghost; it was too literary, too refined and recherché, for the mass of cheap readers; it aimed too high above their heads. And yet it contains some of Leigh Hunt's best writings, which will perhaps live the longest. Next he wrote "Captain Sword and Captain Pen," the "Legend of Florence" (a play), and several other plays not yet printed. All this mass of literary work barely enabled him to live, eked out though it was by frequent writings in the reviews. The "Legend of Florence" was his most profitable work, bringing him in about two hundred pounds; and perhaps, too, it helped him to his pension. He had, before this, on two occasions received two hundred pounds from the Royal Bounty Fund, to enable him to live. His more recent works were "The Palfrey," "Imagination and Fancy," "Wit and Humor," "Stories from the Indian Poets," the "Jar of Honey," the "Book for a Corner," and "The Town." Several of these originally appeared as contributions to the magazines and newspapers. His book entitled "Lord Byron and his Contemporaries" was published many years ago, and it was one that its author himself wished to be forgotten, and we say no more of it here.

Notwithstanding the life of ill-health, and of difficulty, which Leigh Hunt led, it may be pronounced on the whole to have been a happy life. It is the heart that makes life sweet, not the purse,—it is pure and happy thoughts, a well-stored mind, and a genial nature, full of sympathy for human kind. In all these respects, a happy lot has been Leigh Hunt's, though wealth has been denied him. There are few men who could say, like him, towards the close of life: "I am not aware that I have a single enemy, and I accept the fortunes, good and bad, which have occurred to me, with the same disposition to believe them the best that could have happened, whether for the correction of what was wrong in me, or for the improvement of what was right. I have never lost cheerfulness of mind or opinion. What evils there are, I find to be, for the most part, relieved with many consolations; some I find to be necessary to the requisite amount of good; and every one of them I find come to a termination, for either they are cured and live, or are killed and die; and in the latter case I see no evidence to prove that a little finger of them aches any more."

HARTLEY COLERIDGE.

Nor child, nor man,
Nor youth, nor sage, I find my head is gray,
For I have lost the race I never ran;
A rathe December blights my lagging May;
And still I am a child; though I be old,
Time is my debtor for my years untold.

SONNETS.

THE life of Hartley Coleridge reminds me of a painful dream. There was little health or soundness in it. The man was conscious of this himself, and was full of lamentations as to his want of purpose and self-control, which he took no pains to amend. That he had great talents will be conceded,—that he had what is called genius is not so clear. But what powers he had he grievously misused. He was always calling on Jupiter, but would not help himself. In his poems he preached purity, and in his life he practiced self-indulgence. Is such a career excusable in any man,—in a day-laborer or a shopkeeper? then how much less excusable in one who was competent to be a great teacher, and whose talents were equal to the highest vocation?

We hold that the literary man or poet is as much under obligation to lead a pure and virtuous life as any other man, and that the fact of his talent or his genius is not a palliation, but an aggravation, of offenses committed by him against public morality. Intellectual powers are gifts committed to men to subserve their own happiness, as well as to promote the enlightenment of their kind. Poetic powers, if employed by the possessor merely in dreamy indolence, and in the indulgence of the luxury of imaginative thinking, are not rightfully, but wrongfully, applied. In such a case the poet's enjoyment is sensual and selfish. He may spend his time in ar-

144

ranging phrases,—embodying beautiful ideas it may be; but all the while he is not so much discovering, enforcing, or disseminating truth, as luxuriating in his own tastes. If he spends his life in the meantime wastefully and hurtfully, his great gifts are naught, and might as well not have been. · What is thought or thinking worth, unless it help forward the life, and is illustrated in the life? What are poetic dreams or imaginings if the man's daily conduct be at constant variance with them?

It used to be too much the case with the poets of a former age, to claim a kind of immunity from the ordinary laws of life. The poet used to be pictured as a man out at elbows. This old notion might be a vulgar one, but it must have been formed on some basis of experience. Hogarth's picture of the "Distressed Poet" probably was not far from the truth. The literary character has become greatly elevated since then, and the lives of Wordsworth, Southey, Moore, Rogers, and others, amply prove that poetic gifts are not incompatible with a fair share of ordinary worldly prudence; that authors, as a class, are not necessarily poor, hungry, and drunken. But there are still to be met with, here and there, young dapperlings of poets, apt at stringing phrases together about unrequited genius, and ready to cite the fate of Burns, Savage, and Chatterton,—perhaps even to contemplate with sympathy, if not with feelings akin to admiration, the lives of such as Hartley Coleridge. Their sentimental reveries are full of despair, sighs, cries of revolt, and hopelessness; and if you say a word in deprecation of such a strain, they cry out, "Be still! I am a poet;—you! you are only flesh and blood; you don't comprehend me:—leave me to my illusions." But really intelligence and poetry are not to be regarded apart from morality. It is not enough that a man is intelligent, and writes delicious verse. If he is a drunkard or immoral, we cannot excuse him any more than an ordinary man. Genius affords no palliation in such a case; where a man's talents are great, his blame is only the more if he egregiously misuses them.

And yet we admit that much is to be said in palliation of the life of Hartley Coleridge. Doubtless, our constitution and character in no small degree depend upon the originators of our being,—and not only so, but our tastes, idiosyncrasies, sympathies, habits, and even modes of thought. Samuel Taylor Coleridge, with his abounding gifts, was improvident, feeble of purpose, and self-indulgent to excess; and his son seems to have inherited all his frailties, together with a considerable portion of his genius. The child was born in dreams, he lived in dreams, and in dreams he died. He is said to have puzzled himself, when a child, about the reality of existence! Sitting on the knee of old Jackson, Southey's humble friend, he would pour out the most strange speculations, and weave the wildest inventions. When only eight years old, he found a spot upon the globe, which he peopled with an imaginary nation, to whom he gave an imaginary name, imaginary language, imaginary laws, and an imaginary senate. These day-dreams he is said to have in course of time believed as real; and his relations encouraged the dreamy boy, and made a wonder of him. His dreams even became a more real world to him than the actual world in which he lived. Then his father early crammed him with Greek, beginning at ten years old, though his instruction in this, as in other branches of knowledge, was interrupted and desultory. He had always abundant time to build his castles in the air, and to carry on the affairs of his dream-land, which he called Ejuxria. He was constantly forming "plans,"—dreaming of doing things which were never to be done,—until the practice became at length habitual with him, and was gradually welded into his life.

Living in this dream-land of his, the boy became morbidly shy. He never played with his fellows. He passed his time in reading, walking, dreaming to himself, or telling his dreams to others. His uncle, Southey, used to tell him that he had *two left hands*. He lived not the life of other boys, but spun romances and tales for them of immense length, and kept them awake for hours together, when they lay in bed at night, during their recital. For the boy had already the gift of extraordinary powers of speech,—another inheritance from his gifted father. But he never took a high place at school. Boys of very commonplace talents, but with application and industry, rarely failed to take the lead of him. "Unstable as water, thou shalt not excel," might be said of his whole life. "While at school," says his brother, "a certain infirmity of will, the specific evil of his life, had already shown itself. His sensibility was intense, and he had not wherewithal to control it. He could not open a letter without trembling. He shrank from mental pain,—he was beyond measure impatient of constraint. He was liable to paroxysms of rage, often the disguise of pity, self-accusation, or other painful emotion,—anger it could hardly be called,—during which he bit his arm or finger violently. He yielded, as it were unconsciously, to slight temptations,—slight in themselves, and slight to him,—as if swayed by a mechanical impulse apart from his own volition. It looked like an organic defect,—a congenital imperfection. I do not offer this as a sufficient explanation. There are mysteries in our moral nature upon which we can only pause and doubt.

Hartley went to college at Oxford, where he was supported by his father's friends and relatives,—for his father was at the time in embarrassed circumstances, and could not afford the expense, could scarcely even maintain himself. He there distinguished himself chiefly by his extraordinary powers as a converser at "wine-parties," where he would hold forth by the hour on any subject that offered. He spent his vacations at Highgate or Keswick, where he had the advantages of association with many distinguished literary men.

He was still living in dreams,—reading Wordsworth more than the classics, and fitting himself rather for the career of a dreamer, than for the life of a working, active man. He succeeded, however, in obtaining a fellowship at Oriel, which was the source of no small joy to his friends. But he enjoyed his position only for a very short time. "At the close of his probationary year, says his brother, "he was judged to have forfeited his Oriel Fellowship, on the ground, mainly, of intemperance." This, we shall find, was the great blemish of his after-life.

Then he went to London, to maintain himself by his pen; but his dreamy, purposeless character accompanied him: he failed to exert himself,—wanted industry,—made plans, which remained such,—procrastinated from day to day,—and of course he failed. The successful literary man must be a hard worker, and not a mere dreamer; but this young man had never trained himself to habits of industry, nor had any one else so trained him; so he failed,—taking refuge in intoxication, and often disappearing for days together. For about two years he resided in London, occasionally contributing small pieces to the London Magazine; but this scrambling life only served to aggravate his weaknesses, and the scheme was then proposed of taking a school for him in the north of England. Hartley's "genius" revolted at the proposal, but at last he consented, commenced the work without heart, without purpose, and failed again. That was at Ambleside, whither his friends had thought it advisable now to remove him. His habits remained the same, and he occasionally, though undesignedly, led others into the same excess with himself. Yet he was not without bodily and intellectual strength, had he but chosen to use it. In one of his letters to his brother he says: "I cannot find that either my cares or my follies have materially diminished my bodily or intellectual vigor." He was perfectly conscious of the folly and unworthiness of the course he was pursuing, and often overflowed with wise moral reflections on the subject. But he would make no effort to rise, and only sunk to lower depths. One of the most eminent of his friends on the Lakes relates that he latterly ceased to call on him,—"it was so ridiculous and pitiable to find the poor, harmless creature, amid the finest scenery in the world, and in beautiful summer weather, dead drunk at ten o'clock in the morning."

A publisher at Leeds having engaged him to write a book on the "Worthies of Yorkshire," found that the work proceeded so slowly,— Hartley procrastinating from day to day, as was his wont,—that he induced him to go over to Leeds and write it there. While at Leeds, his life was of the usual description, fitful in labor, irresolute, often desponding, and as often breaking off into fits of dissipation and wandering. He would disappear for days together, and the printer's boys were sent scouring about the country in search of him,— sometimes finding him in a hedge-bottom, at other times in an obscure beer-shop. When, after one of these wanderings, he retraced his steps home by himself, he would hang about the house at the end of the street, not having the courage to enter, until some messenger, sent out to watch for his return, would lead him back,—often in a pitiable state. All this was very lamentable: and what is the more extraordinary, during this time his brain was teeming with fancy, with poet's dreams, with beautiful thoughts, such as an angel of purity might have entertained. Never, perhaps, was there a life more utterly at variance with his thoughts than that of Hartley Coleridge.

It was so to the end. He deplored his habits, but did not change them. He lamented his indolence, but would not work. His poetry breathed aspirations after purity, but his life remained impure and groveling. And yet he was beloved by all,—loved because of his amiability, his inoffensiveness, his almost helplessness. He remained (to use his own words)

> Yet to the last a rugged wrinkled thing.
> To which young sweetness did delight to cling.

Children doted on Hartley Coleridge,—himself a child. Nature in him appeared reversed; for in his infancy he was a man in the maturity of his fancy, and in his advanced years he was as a helpless child among men,—a child with gray hairs, for his head early became silver-white, though the gray hairs brought no wisdom with them. And yet his literary culture was great; his knowledge of books was immense; and the elegant manner in which he would dilate upon lofty themes charmed all hearers. In the aspect of nature, his converse was like that of a god.

The only after incidents that occurred worthy of note in Hartley Coleridge's life were his temporary occupation as a schoolmaster at Sedburgh, and his appearance as a contributor to Moxon's edition of some of the older British poets,—for which, after great procrastination, he wrote the introduction to the works of Massinger. A similar introduction to the works of Ford was committed to him, and was in hand for years, but he had not sufficient industry nor application to complete it. But he occasionally contributed a paper to Blackwood's Magazine, when the fit of writing came upon him. A collection of these articles, with his "Marginalia," written by him in books while reading them, has recently been published.

Such is a brief outline of this blurred and blotted life. A few months before his death, he wrote the following lines in a copy of his poems, alluding to his intention of publishing another volume, which he had bound himself under bond to furnish, and, we have been informed, had even been paid for, but which was never furnished. The lines are entitled

FOLLOWED BY ANOTHER.

O woful impotence of weak resolve,
Recorded rashly to the writer's shame!
Days pass away, and Time's large orbs revolve
And every day beholds me still the same;
Till oft-neglected purpose loses aim,
And hope becomes a flat unheeded lie,
And conscience, weary with the work of blame,
In seeming slumber droops her wistful eye,
As if she would resign her unregarded ministry.

It only remains to note the death of this poor fellow-being. It occurred on the 6th of January, 1849, when in his fifty-third year. " He died the death of a strong man, his bodily frame being of the finest construction, and capable of great endurance." The following incident relative to Wordsworth is related in the biography by Hartley Coleridge's brother :

"'The day following Hartley's death, Wordsworth walked over with me to Grasmere, to the churchyard,—a plain inclosure of the olden time, surrounding the old village church, in which lay the remains of his wife's sister, his nephew, and his beloved daughter. Here, having desired the sexton to measure out the ground for his own and Mrs. Wordsworth's grave, he bade him measure out the space of a third grave, for my brother, immediately beyond.

"'When I lifted up my eyes from my daughter's grave,' he exclaimed, 'he was standing there!' pointing to the spot where my brother had stood on the sorrowful occasion to which he alluded. Then, turning to the sexton, he said, ' Keep the ground for us,—we are old people, and it cannot be for long.'

"In the grave thus marked out my brother's remains were laid on the following Thursday, and in little more than a twelvemonth his venerable and venerated friend was brought to occupy his own. They lie in the southeast angle of the churchyard, not far from a group of trees, with the little beck, that feeds the lake with its clear water, murmuring by their side. Around them are the quiet mountains. . . . . . . It was a winter's day when my brother was carried to his last home, cold, but fine, as I noted at the time, with a few slight scuds of sleet and gleams of sunshine, one of which greeted us as we entered Grasmere, and another smiled brightly through the church window. May it rest upon his memory!"

We can add nothing to this. The recital is very touching, and is done throughout with the extremest delicacy and grace by his brother, who would lovingly palliate the errors of the departed. He sleeps well by Wordsworth's side, Wordsworth having been the model of all his poetry, and standing to him instead of a father through the greater part of his unhappy life.

Hartley Coleridge's poetry reminds the reader of Wordsworth in nearly every line, though it is Wordsworth diluted ; and at its best, the Lake poetry cannot bear much dilution. Excepting in the sonnets which relate to his own personal unhappiness, the poems sound like the echoes of other poets, rather than welling warm from the writer's own heart. And though, in the personal sonnets referred to, he paints his purposeless life and blighted career in terse and poetic language, it were perhaps better that they had not been written at all. His poems addressed to childhood are perhaps the most charming things in the collection. For poor Hartley loved children, and they returned his love. He loved women, too, but at a distance; and his despondency at his own want of personal attractions for them is a frequent theme of his poetry.

The melancholy history of Hartley Coleridge is not without its moral. It was perhaps his misfortune to be the son of a poet, who gave little heed to the healthy training of his children. The child's endowment of fancy, though a rare one, proved only a source of unhappiness in after-life, having been cultivated, as it was, to the entire disregard of those other practical qualities which fit a man for useful intercourse with the world. Living in a state of dreaminess and abstraction, his mind became unnerved, and his manly powers fatally impaired. He indulged in poetic thought rather as an effeminate luxury than as a means of self-culture or a relaxation from the severer toils and duties of life. He was, however, fully aware of the wrongness of his course, as appears from his numerous melancholy plaints in stanza and sonnets. But he made no effort at self-help; he met adversity and temptation half-way, and laid himself down at their feet, a willing victim. Though we ought to be tolerant of the frailties of genius, we cannot overlook its sins and follies, which are but too often seized upon as excuses for excess by those who are less gifted. We must bear in mind that high powers are committed to man for noble uses,—that from him to whom much is given much shall be required,—that however poetic may be a man's thoughts, he is not thereby absolved from the observance of the practical virtues of life, or from living soberly, purely, and religiously ; on the contrary, the man of high thinkings is expected to live thus daily, and to make his life the practical record of his thoughts. Though there were many things to love about Hartley Coleridge, we trust his sad career may not be without its lesson and its warning to others.

DR. KITTO.

NOT long since, we were attracted by the announcement in a second-hand book catalogue, of "Essays and Letters, by Dr. Kitto, written in a Workhouse." As one of the celebrities of the day, the editor of the "Pictorial Bible," "Cyclopædia of Biblical Literature," and many other highly important works, which have obtained an extensive circulation, and are greatly prized, we could not but feel interested in this little book, and purchased it accordingly. It has proved full of curious interest, and from it we learned, that, besides having endured from an early age the serious privation of hearing, the author has also suffered the lot of poverty, and, by dint of gallant perseverance and manly courage, he was enabled to rise above and triumph over both privations.

It is indeed true that Dr. Kitto's first book was "written in a workhouse." And we must here tell the reader something of his early history. The father of Dr. Kitto was a working mason at Plymouth, whither he had been attracted by the demand for laborers of all descriptions at that place, about the early part of the present century. John Kitto was born there in 1804. In his youth he received very little school education, though he learned to read, and had already taken some interest in books, when the serious accident occurred which deprived him of his hearing. At that time his parents were in very distressed circumstances, and, though little more than twelve years of age, the boy was employed by his father to help him as a laborer, in carrying stones, mortar, and such like. One day in February, 1817, when stepping from the ladder to the roof of a house undergoing repair in Batter street, the little lad, with a load of slates on his head, lost his balance, and, falling back, was precipitated from a height of thirty-five feet into the paved court below!

Dr. Kitto has himself given a most vivid account of the details of the accident in the interesting work by him, on "The Lost Senses,—Deafness," some time since published by Charles Knight.

"Of what followed," says he, "I know nothing. For one moment, indeed, I awoke from that deathlike state, and then found that my father attended by a crowd of people, was bearing me homeward in his arms ; but I had then no recollection of what had happened, and at once relapsed into a state of unconsciousness.

"In this state I remained for a fortnight, as I afterwards learned. These days were a blank in my life; I could never bring any recollections to bear upon them; and when I awoke one morning to consciousness, it was as from a night of sleep. I saw that it was at least two hours later than my usual time of rising, and marveled that I had been suffered to sleep so late. I attempted to spring up in bed, and was astonished to find that I could not even move. The utter prostration of my strength subdued all curiosity within me. I experienced no pain, but I felt that I was weak; I saw that I was treated as an invalid, and acquiesced in my condition, though some time passed—more time than the reader would imagine—before I could piece together my broken recollections, so as to comprehend it.

"I was very slow in learning that my hearing was entirely gone. The unusual stillness of all things was grateful to me in my utter exhaustion; and if, in this half-awakened state, a thought of the matter entered my mind, I ascribed it to the unusual care and success of my friends in preserving silence around me. I saw them talking, indeed, to one another, and thought that out of regard to my feeble condition, they spoke in whispers, because I heard them not. The truth was revealed to me in consequence of my solicitude about a book ("Kirby's Wonderful Magazine") which had much interested me on the day of my fall..... I asked for this book with much earnestness, and was answered by signs which I could not comprehend.

"'Why do you not speak?' I cried; 'pray let me have the book.'

"This seemed to create some confusion; and at length some one, more clever than the rest, hit upon the happy expedient of writing upon a slate, that the book had been reclaimed by the owner, and that I could not in my weak state be allowed to read.

"'But,' said I, in great astonishment, 'why do you write to me, why not speak? Speak, speak!'

"Those who stood around the bed exchanged significant looks of concern, and the writer soon displayed upon his slate the awful words, 'You are deaf.'"

Various remedies were tried, but without avail. Some serious organic injury had been done to the auditory nerve by the fall, and hearing was never restored; poor Kitto remained stone-deaf. The boy, thus thrown upon himself, devoted his spare time—his time was now all spare time—to reading. Books gradually became a source of interest to him, and he soon exhausted the small stocks of his neighbors. Books were then much rarer than now, and reading was regarded as an occult art, in which few persons of the working class could venture to indulge.

The circumstances of Kitto's parents still continued very poor. This, with other sources of domestic disquietude, rendered his position for some years very unfortunate. At length, in 1819, about two years from the date of his accident, on an application for relief from the guardians of the poor of Plymouth, young Kitto was taken from his parents and placed among the boys of the workhouse. There he was instructed in the art of shoemaking, with the view of enabling him thus to obtain his livelihood. He was afterward bound apprentice to a poor shoemaker in the town, where his position was very miserable; so much so, that an inquiry as to the apprentice's treatment was instituted before the magistrates, the result of which was that they discharged Kitto from his apprenticeship, and he was returned to the workhouse, where he continued his shoemaking. He found a warm friend in Mr. Bernard, the clerk to the guardians, and also in Mr. Nugent, the master of the school. From these gentlemen he obtained loans of books, mostly of a religious character.

He remained in the workhouse about four years; his deafness condemned him to solitude; for, deprived of speech and hearing, he had not the means of forming friends among his companions, such as they were. At the same time, it is possible enough that his isolation from the other occupants of the workhouse may have preserved his purity, and encouraged him to cultivate his intellectual powers to a greater extent than he might otherwise have been disposed to do. Thrown almost exclusively upon his visual perceptions, he enjoyed with an intensity of delight the beautiful face of nature,—the sun, the moon, the stars, and the glories of earth. In after life he said: "I must not refuse to acknowledge that, when I have beheld the moon 'walking in brightness,' my heart has been 'secretly enticed' into feelings having perhaps a nearer approach to the old idolatries than I should like to ascertain. I mention this because, at this distant day, I have no recollecton of earlier emotions connected with the beautiful than those of which the moon was the object. How often, some two or three years after my affliction, did I not wander forth upon the hills, for no other purpose in the world than to enjoy and feed upon the emotions connected with the sense of the beautiful in nature. It gladdened me, it filled my heart, I knew not why or how, in view 'the great and wide sea,' the wooded mountain, and even the silent town under that pale radiance; and not less to follow the course of the luminary over the clear sky, or to trace its shaded pathway among and behind the clouds." An exquisitely keen perception of the beautiful in trees was of somewhat later development, as Plymouth, being by the sea-side, is not favorable to the growth of oaks, and had nothing to boast of but a few rows of good elms. Another great source of enjoyment with him, at that early period, was to wander about the printsellers' and picture-framers' windows, and learn the pictures by heart, watching anxiously from day to day for the cleaning out of the windows, that he might enjoy the luxury of a new display of prints and frontispieces. He scoured the whole neighborhood with this view, going over to Devonport, which he divided into districts and visited periodically, for the purpose of exploring the windows in each, with leisurely enjoyment at each visit.

A young man so peculiarly circumstanced, and with such tastes, could not remain altogether overlooked; and he was so fortunate as to attract the notice of two worthy gentlemen, who, when he had reached the age of about twenty years, used every exertion to befriend him. One of these was Mr. Harvey, a member of the Society of Friends, well known as an accomplished mathematician, who supplied young Kitto with books of a superior quality to anything he had before had access to. Mr. Harvey, when one day in a bookseller's shop, saw a lad of mean appearance enter, and begin writing a communication to the master on a slip of paper. On inquiry, he found him to be a deaf workhouse boy, distinguished by his desire for reading and thirst for knowledge of all kinds; and that he had come to borrow a book which the bookseller had promised to lend him. Inquiries were made about him, interest was excited in his behalf, and a subscription was raised for his benefit. He was supplied with books, paper, and pens, to enable him to pursue his literary occupations; and in a short time, having secured the notice of Mr. Nettleton, one of the proprietors of the Plymouth Journal, and also a guardian of the poor, several of his productions appeared in the columns of that journal. The case of the poor lad became the subject of general conversation in the town; several gentlemen associated themselves together as the guardians of the youth; after which Kitto was removed from the workhouse, and obtained permission to read at the public library. A selection of his writings, chiefly written in the workhouse, was shortly afterward published by subscription, and the young man found himself in the fair way of advancement. He made rapid progress in learning, acquiring a knowledge of Hebrew and other languages, which he imparted to pupils whom he shortly after obtained, the sons of a gentleman into whose house he was taken as tutor. He read largely on all subjects, but his early bias toward theological literature clung to him, and he soon acquired an extensive and profound knowledge of scriptural and sacred lore. At length he was enabled to turn his stores of learning to rich account, in his Pictorial Bible and Cyclopedia of Biblical Literature, which many of our readers may have seen. In his day, Dr. Kitto has also been an extensive traveler; having been in Palestine, in Egypt, in the Morea, in Russia, and in many countries of Europe.

"For many years," he says, "I had no views towards literature beyond the instruction and solace of my own mind; and under these views, and in the absence of other mental stimulants, the pursuit of it eventually became a passion which devoured all others. I take no merit for the industry and application with which I pursued this object,—none for the ingenious contrivances by which I sought to shorten the hours of needful rest, that I might have the more time for making myself acquainted with the minds of other men. The reward was great and immediate, and I was only preferring the gratification which seemed to me the highest. Nevertheless, now that I am in fact another being, having but slight connection—excepting in so far as 'the child is the father to the man'—with my former self ; now that much has become a business which was then simply a joy; and now that I am gotten old in experiences, if not in years,— it does somewhat move me to look back upon that poor and deaf boy, in his utter loneliness, devoting himself to objects in which none around him could sympathize, and to pursuits which none could even understand. There was a time—by far the most dreary in that portion of my career—when an employment was found for me [it was when he was apprenticed to the shoemaker,] to which I proceeded about six o'clock in the morning, and from which I returned not until about ten at night. I murmured not at this, for I knew that life had grosser duties than those to which I would gladly have devoted all my hours; and I dreamed not that a life of literary occupations might be within the reach of my hopes. This was, however, a terrible time for me, as it left me so little leisure for what had become my sole enjoyment, if not my sole good. I submitted ; I acquiesced; I tried hard to be happy; but it would not do ; my heart gave way, notwithstanding my manful struggles to keep it up, and I was very thoroughly miserable. Twelve hours I could have borne. I have tried it, and know that the leisure which twelve hours might have left would have satisfied me ; but *sixteen hours, and often eighteen,* out of the twenty-four, was D than I could bear. To come home weary and sleepy, and then . ve only for mental sustenance the moments which by self-imposed tortures, could be torn from needful rest, was a sore trial ; and now that I look back upon this time, the amount of study which I did, under these circumstances, contrive to get through, amazes and confounds me, notwithstanding that my habits of application remain to this day strong and vigorous.

"In the state to which I have thus referred, I suffered much wrong; and the fact that, young as I then was, my pen became the instrument of redressing that wrong, and of ameliorating the more afflictive part of my condition was among the first circumstances which revealed to me the secret of the strength which I had, unknown to myself, acquired. The flood of light which then broke in upon me not only gave distinctness of purpose to what had before been little more than dark and uncertain gropings ; but also, from that time, the motive to my exertions became more mixed than it had been. My ardor and perseverance were not lessened ; and the pure love of knowledge, for its own sake, would still have carried me on ; but other influences, the influences which supply the impulse to most human pursuits, *did* supervene, and gave the sanction of the judgment to the course which the instincts of mental necessity had previously dictated.   I had, in fact, learned the secret, 'that knowledge is power ; and if, as is said all power is sweet, then, surely, that power which knowledge gives is, of all others, the sweetest."

In conclusion, we may add, that Dr. Kitto continued to lead a happy and a useful life, cheered by the faces of children around his table,—though alas ! he could not hear their voices.   He resided until his death, in 1854, in the beautiful environs of London, that he might be *within sight of old trees*, without which his heart could scarcely be satisfied.   Indeed, with such love and veneration did he regard them, that the felling of a noble tree caused him the deepest emotion.   But he delighted in the faces of men, too, and nothing gave him greater delight than to walk or drive through the crowded thoroughfares of the metropolis.   In this respect he resembled the amiable Charles Lamb, to whom the crowd of Fleet Street was more delightful than all the hills and lakes of Westmoreland.   "How often," said Dr. Kitto, "at the end of a day's hard toil, have I thrown myself into an omnibus, and gone into town, for no other purpose in the world than to have a walk from Charing Cross to St. Paul's on the one hand, or to the top of Regent Street on the other ; or from the top of Tottenham Court Road to the Post-office.   I know not whether I liked this best in summer or in winter.   I could seldom afford myself this indulgence but for one or two evenings a week, when I could manage to bring my day's studies to a close an hour or so earlier than usual.   In summer there is daylight, and I could better enjoy the picture-shops and the street incidents, and might diverge so far as to pass through Covent Garden, and luxuriate among the finest fruits and most beautiful flowers in the world.   And in winter it might be doubted whether the glory of the shops, lighted up with gas, was not a sufficient counterbalance for the absence of daylight.   Perhaps 'both are best,' as the children say ; and yield the same kind of grateful change as the alternation of the seasons, offers."   Thus, what we, who have our hearing entire, regard as a great calamity, in Dr. Kitto ceased to be regarded as such.   The condition became natural to him, and his sweet temper and steady habits of industry enabled him to pass through life honorably and usefully.   His life was a noble and valuable lesson to all young men.

EDGAR ALLAN POE.

RICHTER, writing from Weimar, whither he had gone to see, eye to eye, the great men with whose fame all Europe was ringing, said: "On the second day I threw away my foolish prejudices about great authors; they are like other people. Here, every one knows that they are like the earth, which looks from a distance, from heaven, like a shining moon; but when the foot is upon it, it is found to be made of Paris mud (boue de paris)."

Alas! it is so. Those lofty gods whom we have worshiped and bowed down before,—those gifted children of genius whose eyes gazed eagerly into the unseen, and penetrated its depth far beyond our ken,—when we approach them closer, and know them more intimately, become stripped of their halo glory. We find that they are but men,—fallible, frail, and erring,—tempest-tosed by passion and desire,—stumbling and halt, and often blind and decrepit. We worship no more. The earth which seen from a distance, looks a beautiful moon, when the foot is on it, is but rocks, clods, and "Paris mud!"

Sad is the impression left on the mind by reading the brief records some of these unhappy children of genius; gifted, but unhappy; loftily endowed, but fitful and capricious; with the aspirations of an angel, but the low appetites of a brute; daringly speculative, but grovelingly sensual ;—such, in a few words, was the life of Edgar Allan Poe: a being full of misery, but all beaten out upon his own anvil; a man gifted as few are, but without faith or devotion, and without any earnest purpose in life.

You have read his "Raven." You see the gloom and despair of that unhappy youth's life written there. What a dismal, tragic, remorseful transcript it is !—the croaking raven, bird of ill omen, perched above its master's chamber-door, responding with his doleful "Nevermore" to all his deep questions and impatient feelings :

" Prophet," said I, " thing of evil ! Prophet still, if bird or devil !
  Whether Tempter sent, or whether tempest tossed thee here ashore,
Desolate yet all undaunted, on this desert land enchanted,
  On this home by horror haunted,—tell me truly, I implore,
Is there—*is* there balm in Gilead? Tell me, tell me, I implore !"
              Quoth the raven,—" Nevermore !"

" Be that word our sign of parting, bird or fiend !" I shrieked, upstart-
          ing ;
  "Get thee back into the tempest. and the Night's Plutonian shore !
Leave no black plume as a token of that lie thy soul hath spoken !
  Leave my loneliness unbroken ! quit the bust above my door !
Take thy beak from out my heart, and take thy form from off my
          door !"
              Quoth the raven,—"Nevermore !"

And the raven, never flitting, still is sitting, still is sitting,
  On the pallid bust of Pallas, just above my chamber-door ;
And his eyes have all the seeming of a demon's that is dreaming,
  And the lamplight o'er him streaming throws his shadow on the
          floor ;
And my soul from out the shadow that lies floating on the floor,
              Shall be lifted—nevermore !

By this light, read the following brief record of the poet's blurred
and blotted life.

Edgar Allan Poe was born at Baltimore, in 1811, of an old and respectable family. His father was a lawyer, but having become en-
amored of an English actress, he married her, and followed her
profession for some years, until his death, which shortly followed.
Poe's mother died about the same time, and three children were left
destitute. But a wealthy gentleman, named Allan, who had no
children of his own, adopted Edgar, it was understood with the intention of leaving him his heir. In 1816 Mr. Allan took the boy to
England with him, and placed him in a boarding-school at Stoke
Newington, near London, where he remained some four or five
years, under the Rev. Dr. Bransby, returning to America in 1822.

It will be obvious that the circumstances of Poe's early life were
very unfavorable to his healthy moral development. Deprived of
the blessings of maternal nurture, without a home, brought up
among strangers, there is little cause to wonder at the subsequent
heartlessness towards others which he displayed, and the excesses
in which he indulged. Returned to America, he entered the University of Charlottesville, in Virginia, in 1825. Unfortunately, the
students of that University were then distinguished for their disso-
luteness and their excesses in many ways; and Edgar Poe was one
of the most reckless of his class. Although his talents were such as
to enable him to master with ease the most difficult studies, and to
take the highest honors of his year, his habits of gambling, intemperance, and general dissipation were such as to cause his expul-
sion from the University.

Mr. Allan, his benefactor, had made him a liberal allowance; but Poe nevertheless ran deeply into debt, chiefly to his gambling friends; and when his drafts were presented to Mr. Allan for payment, he declined to honor them; on which Poe wrote him an abusive letter, left his house, abandoned his half-formed plans of life, and suddenly left the country to take part as a volunteer, like Byron, in the Greek Revolution. But he never reached Greece. Whither he wandered, Heaven knows. Nothing was heard of him until, after the lapse of a year, the American Minister at St. Peterburgh was one morning summoned to save him from the penalties incurred in a drunken debauch over night. Through the Minister's intercession, he was set at liberty and enabled to return to the United States.

His friend, Mr. Allan, was still willing to assist him, and, at his request, Poe was entered as scholar in the Military Academy at West Point; but again his dissipated habits displayed themselves. He neglected his duties and disobeyed orders, on which he was cashiered, and once more returned to Mr. Allan's house, who was still ready to receive him and treat him as a son. But a circumstance shortly occurred which finally broke the connection between the two. Mr. Allan married a second time, and the lady was considerably his junior. Poe quarreled with her, and, it is said, ridiculed Allan. The lady's friends have averred that the real cause of the rupture was, that Poe made disgraceful overtures to the young wife, which throws another dark stain upon his character. Whatever the real cause may have been, certain it is, that he was now expelled from his patron's house in anger, and when Mr. Allan died, some years after, he left nothing to Poe.

The young man had in the meanwhile published a small volume of poetry, when he was not more than eighteen years of age. This was very favorably received, and a little perseverance might have enabled him to maintain himself creditably as a literary man. But in one of his hasty and reckless fits, he enlisted as a private soldier. He was recognized by some of his old fellow-students at West Point, and they made efforts to obtain him a commission, which promised to be successful; but, fitful in everything, before the result of their kind application could be known, he deserted !

We next find Poe a successful competitor for certain prizes offered by the proprietor of the Baltimore Visitor for the best story and the best poem. Poe competed for both, and gained both. The author was sent for, and made his appearance in due time. He was in a state of the utmost destitution, pale, ghastly, and filthy. His seedy frock-coat, buttoned up to his throat, concealed the absence of a shirt, and his dilapidated boots disclosed his want of stockings. Mr. Kennedy, the author of "Horseshoe Robinson," who was the adjudicator of the prize, took an immediate interest in the young man, then only twenty-two years old ; and accompanied him to a clothing-store, where he provided him with a respectable suit, with changes of linen, and, after taking a bath, Poe once more appeared in the restored guise of a gentleman.

Mr. Kennedy further used his influence in obtaining for Poe some literary employment, and he was shortly engaged as joint editor of the Southern Literary Messenger, published at Richmond. He was now a literary man, living by his pen. The literary profession is an honorable one, even noble, inasmuch as it is identified with intellectual culture and high manly gifts. The literary man exercises much power in the world. He helps to form the opinions of other men; indeed, he makes public opinion. All other powers have in modern times become weaker, while this has been waxing stronger from day to day. Kings are being superseded by books, priests by magazines, and diplomatists by newspapers. Perhaps bookmen and editors now wield more intellectual power than all the other crafts combined. Literary men have taken the place of the feudal barons, and the pen has become the ruling instrument instead of the sword. The man of letters is an altogther modern product, the like of whom was unknown to former ages. Never, before the last century, was there any class of men in society who made a profession of thinking for others, or who earned a subsistence by writing and publishing their thoughts in books and journals. Soldiers, law-givers, and priests may have taken up the pen to write and give an account of their lives and times, or have written books of philosophy or meditation, but never before has there been a special class of men who made it their sole business and profession to write for the general public.

The question has been discussed whether this purely professional literary life is compatible with the simple and straightforward duties of a man. His position is certainly very different from that of the great non-professional writers of former times,—the Homers, Shakespeares, Miltons, Bossuets, Pascals, Bacons, Fenelons; these wrote to satisfy an earnest desire, in answer to some strong inward call,—to do a certain work, though not for money,—that was not their main work,—but to fulfill a duty,—it might be, to fill up a vacant hour. Modern literary men may, however, have no special, distinct, or well-defined call to write; with them it is a business, a calling, a craft, self-chosen. They write that they may live. There may be no sense of responsibility as to what they write; and the gift may thus be abused as well as used. To enter upon what is called a "literary career," may even be a merely instinctive and irrational act, performed without deliberation, the choice being determined by taste rather than by reflection. In other professions experience and character are required; but in this profession they are not regarded as at all requisite. The literary man may be dissolute, spendthrift, without any business habits or any moral stamina; and yet he may succeed as a public writer. This must be regarded as a curious feature of the literary character.

Here we have Edgar Poe installed at twenty-two as a public teacher through the medium of the press; a young man incompetent to manage a small store, unable to manage himself, and yet a public writer. Not many months pass before he lapses into his old habits of drunkenness. Fatal bottle! What manifold curses have been poured from that narrow neck of thine! Poe fell a victim like thousands more. For a whole week he was drunk and unable to write; then he was dismissed. Next followed entreaties, intercessions, pleadings, professions of abstinence for the future from the fatal bottle. He was taken back for a time; but the habit had become rooted; the character was formed, and, the demon had wound his fetters about the doomed man. Finally dismissed from his situation, he went from Richmond to Baltimore, and thence to Philadelphia, where he proceeded to lead the life of a literary "man about town."

It was while he resided at Philadelphia, in 1839, that Poe published his two volumes of "Tales of the Grotesque and the Arabesque." These tales exhibit extraordinary metaphysical acuteness, and an imagination which delights to dwell in the shadowy confines of human experience, among the abodes of crime, gloom, and horror. They exhibit a subtle power of analysis, and a minuteness of detail and refinement of reasoning remarkable in so young a writer. He anatomizes mystery, and gives to the most incredible inventions a wonderful air of reality.

While Poe was engaged in writing these striking tales, he was pursuing his old round of dissipation. To his other imprudences he had added that of marrying,—the most imprudent thing a determined drunkard can do. For, instead of one miserable person, there are two, following in whose wake are usually a train of little miseries, at length becoming agonies, eating into a man's flesh as it were fire,—that is, if he have any sense of responsibility still surviving within him. The woman Poe married was his cousin, Virginia Clemm, amiable and lovely, but poor and gentle, quite unfitted to master the now headstrong passion of her husband for drink.

Poe managed to eke out a slender living for himself and wife by writing for the magazines and the newspapers. For a time it seemed that he would reform; he wrote to one friend that he had quite "overcome the seduction and dangerous besetment" of drink, and to another, that he had become a "model of temperance." But shortly after, he again fell off as before into his old habits, and for weeks was regardless of everything but the ways and means of satisfying his morbid and insatiable appetite for drink. All this shows how little intellectual power avails without moral goodness, and of how small worth is genius without the common work-a-day elements of sober, manly character. For it is *life*, not scripture, that avails,—character, not literary talents, that brings a man happiness, and tells on the betterment of the world at large.

Poe could appreciate the glorious thoughts contained in books, yet he failed to apply their precepts of wisdom. He could rejoice in his own thoughts, but had not learned to respect his own life. His mind was full of riches, yet, wanting in moral good, he remained poor and without resources. His life did not embrace duty, but pleasure. Intoxicated with essences and perfumes, he neglected wisdom, which is the true balm of life. Poor unfortunate, thus worthlessly eating and drinking out of the sacred vessels of knowledge! Many and poignant must have been the distresses suffered by poor Poe in the dreary and miserable state in which he lived,—distress not only about money and worldly well-being, but about God and duty. Then followed new catastrophes, family disasters, domestic misery,—teaching him, if he would but learn, the same lessons of duty, but of which, through life, he seemed to be altogether ignorant. Man cannot lead an egotistic and selfish life without suffering. For life, from time to time, tells him that he is *not* alone, and that he owes much to those of his own blood and household. Love itself, smiling and celestial love, in such a case, becomes a source of torments and calamities to him. The brave only, live through this state; the heartless despair, utter loud cries of revolt, blaspheme, and precipitate themselves into extreme courses. Their originality and genius may astonish the world, but originality is nothing unless it includes the realities of life; they are but dreamers, unless poets, they also do the daily living of true men. But you are a poet! Well, show me the practical issue of knowledge and beauty in your life and character. Unless you do, I say you have adopted the profession merely to indulge in the luxury and fascination of thinking,—not so much to discover and propagate truth as to gratify your own selfish tastes.

We wish there had been no more than this in Poe's case; but there was positive dishonor in the course of life he pursued. While admitted into the confidence of Mr. Burton, proprietor of the Gentleman's Magazine, at Philadelphia, at the very time that he was neglecting his own proper work of writing for the Magazine, he was nevertheless engaged in preparing the prospectus of a new rival monthly, and obtaining transcripts of his employer's subscription and account books, to be used in a scheme for supplanting his periodical. Of course, on this scurvy trick being discovered, Poe was at once dismissed; but only to start a rival Graham's Magazine, with which he was connected for a year and half, leaving it, as usual, because of his drunken habits. While writing in Graham's Magazine, Poe published several of his finest tales, and some of his most trenchant criticisms. These last were disfigured, however, by a tone of morbid bitterness, such as a man who misconducts himself towards the world so often affects. In his capacity of critic, Poe not unfrequently assumed an air of bitter sarcasm, and made the air blatant with his cries of rage and his implacable anathemas. Burton, his

former employer, often expostulated with him because of the havoc
which he did upon the books of rival authors, and tried to tame
down his severity to a moderate tone, but without avail.

In 1844 Poe removed to New York, where he published his wonderful poem, "The Raven,"—perhaps the very finest and most
original single poem of its kind that America has yet produced. It
indicates a most wayward and subtle genius. It takes you captive
by its gloomy, weird power. Of his other poems, "Annabel Lee"
and "The Haunted Palace" are especially beautiful. But the radiance which they give forth is lurid; and the fire which they contain
scorches, but does not warm. As in his "Haunted Palace," we

> Through the red-litten windows see
> Vast forms, that move fantastically,
> To a discordant melody ;
> While, like a ghastly rapid river,
> Through the pale door,
> A hideous throng rush out forever
> And laugh—but smile no more.

At New York, Poe was admitted into the best literary circles, and
might have made for himself a position of influence, had he possessed ordinary good conduct. But his usual failing again betrayed
him. What was worse, he was poisoned in his principles : indeed,
he had no principles. He was false, and a coward. Take this instance : he had borrowed fifty dollars from a lady, on a promise given
by him that he would return the money in a few days. He did not
return it; and was then asked for a written acknowledgment of the
debt; his answer was a denial that he had ever borrowed the money,
accompanied with a threat, that, if the lady said anything more
about the subject, he would publish a correspondence of hers, of an
infamous character, which would blast her forever. Of course, there
was no such correspondence in existence; but when Poe heard that
the lady's brother was in search of him for the purpose of obtaining
the satisfaction considered necessary in such cases, he sent a friend
to him with a humble apology and retraction, and an excuse that he
had been "out of his mind at the time."

His habits of intoxication increased, and his pecuniary difficulties,
as might have been expected, became more urgent. Often, after a
long-continued debauch, he was without the ordinary necessaries of
life. His wife, and mother-in-law, who were dependent upon his
exertions for their means of living, went a-begging for help. Not
improbably, the distress which his wife suffered from the irregular-
ity of her husband's career, and the frequent privations which she
endured, had something to do with causing the illness from which
she eventually died. A number of friends voluntarily contributed
towards the support of the distressed family when their case became
known through the newspapers, but the help came too late to be of
any service to Mrs. Poe.

In 1848 Poe delivered a public lecture on the Cosmogony of the Universe,—an extraordinary rhapsody, very imaginative, but quite unscientific. His object was to raise money for the purpose of establishing a monthly magazine, and we believe several numbers were published; but his unsteady habits soon proved its ruin. He also quarreled with the editors of the principal magazines for which he had formerly written, and made enemies all round. About the same time, he formed the acquaintance of one of the most brilliant women of New England, sought her hand, and the day of marriage was fixed. They were not married, and the breaking of the engagement affords a striking illustration of his character. His biographer thus relates the circumstances connected with it:

"Poe said to a female acquaintance in New York, who congratulated him upon the prospect of his union with a person of so much genius and so many virtues, 'It is a mistake; I am not going to be married.' 'Why, Mr. Poe, I understand that the banns have been published!' 'I cannot help what you have heard, my dear madam, but, mark me, I shall not marry her!' He left town the same evening, and the next day was reeling through the streets of the city which was the lady's home; and in the evening that should have been the evening before the bridal, in his drunkenness he committed at her house such outrages as made necessary a summons of the police."

He pursued a course of reckless dissipation for some time, after which he went to Virginia, on means raised from the charity of his few remaining friends. He delivered some lectures there; then he joined a temperance society, and professed a determination to reform his evil habits. But it was too late; his bad genius prevailed over all his better resolutions. Again he contracted an engagement to marry a lady whom he had known in his youth, and returned to New York to fulfill a literary engagement, and prepare for his marriage. In a tavern he casually met some of his old acquaintances, who invited him to drink. He drank until he was deplorably drunk. He was afterwards found in the streets, insane and dying, and was carried to the public hospital, in which he expired on the 7th of October, 1849, in his thirty-eighth year.

Thus miserably perished another of the most gifted of earth's sons. What a torn record of a life it is! more sorrowful by far than that of our own Otway or Chatterton. Alternately a seraph and a brute,—an inspired poet and a groveling sensualist,—a prophet and a drunkard,—his biography unfolds a tale of mingled admiration and horror, such as has been told of very few literary men. It is painful to think of it: but it is right that such a history should be known, were it only as a beacon to warn susceptible youth from the horrible fascination of drink, which lures so many to their destruction.

THEODORE HOOK.

T HE unhappy career of Edgar A. Poe is not without its counter-
part in English literary biography. Johnson, in his painful
memoir of Savage, has told a similar story of genius and misfortune, or rather genius and misconduct ; for it is a mistake to
suppose that the possession of genius in any way conduces to misfortune, except through the misconduct of its possessor. Poetry and·
a garret used at one time to be identified ; but life in a garret may be.
as noble as life in a palace, and a great deal purer. As Sir Walter
Raleigh once wrote in the little dungeon in the Tower, still pointed
out as the place of his confinement,

My mind to me a kingdom is!

It is the mind that makes the man, and not the place,—call it a hovel,
a garret, or a palace,—in which the body lives. Even Johnson has
summed up the ills of the scholar's life in these words: "Toil, envy,
want, the patron, and the jail." But Johnson, doubtless, bitterly
remembered the day when he signed himself Impransus, or *Dinner-
less*, and received the anonymous alms of a pair of shoes. Johnson
must have been in one of his ungenial moods when he penned
those bitter words.

The fate of Chatterton, also, was a hapless one, Proud, impulsive,
ardent, and full of genius, like Poe, his career was short, unhappy,
and mournfully concluded. That of Otway, the author of "Venice
Preserved," who perished for want of bread, also springs to mind.
Nor are other equally mournful examples a-wanting, which it would
be painful to relate. These instances are apt to be dwelt upon too
much, and cited from time to time as illustrations of the unhappy lot
of genius; whereas they are merely exceptional cases, not at all
characteristic of literary men in general.

Poets and authors are often charged with being improvident, as
a rule. But are there no improvident lawyers, divines, merchants,
and shopkeepers? The case of Theophilus Cibber is sometimes
cited, who begged a guinea and spent it on a dish of ortolans; and
perhaps of poor Goldsmith, who, when preserved from a jail by
the money received for "The Vicar of Wakefield," forthwith celebrated the circumstance by a jollification with his landlady. But
authors have their weaknesses and their frailties, like other men;
and some of them are drunken, and some improvident, as other
men are. As a class, however, they are neither generally improvident nor out at elbows. But we are usually disposed to think
much more of the "calamities of authors" than we do of the calamities of other men. A hundred bankers might break, and ten
thousand merchants ruin themselves by their improvidence, but
none would think it worth their while to record such events in
books; nor, except as a mere matter of news for living men, would
any one care to read of such occurrences. But how different in
the case of a poet? Biographers eagerly seize the minutest matter
of detail in the history of a man of genius. Johnson tells us the
story of Savage, Southey relates the career of Chatterton, Cun-
ningham recounts the life of Burns, and every tittle of their history
is carefully gathered up and published for the information of contemporary and future readers.

The late Thomas Hood, in one of his prose works, little known,
well observed that:

"Literary men, as a body, will bear comparison in point of conduct with any other class. It must not be forgotten that they are
subjected to an ordeal quite peculiar, and scarcely milder than the
Inquisition. The lives of literary men are proverbially barren of
incident, and consequently the most trivial particulars, the most
private affairs, are unceremoniously worked up, to furnish matter
for their bald biographies. Accordingly, as soon as an author is
defunct, his character is submitted to a sort of Egyptian post mortem
trial; or rather, a moral inquest with Paul Pry for the coroner, and
a judge of assize, a commissioner of bankrupts, a Jew broker, a
Methodist parson, a dramatic licenser, a dancing-master, a master
of the ceremonies, a rat-catcher, a bone-collector, a parish clerk,
a schoolmaster, and a reviewer for a jury. It is the province of
these personages to rummage, ransack, scrape together, rake up,
ferret out, sniff, detect, analyze, and appraise, all particulars of the
birth, parentage, and education, life, character, and behavior, breed-
ing, accomplishments, opinions, and literary performances of the
departed. Secret drawers are searched, private and confidential
letters published, manuscripts intended for the fire are set up in
type, tavern-bills and washing-bills are compared with their receipts.
copies of writs re-copied, inventories taken of effects, wardrobe
ticked off by the tailor's accounts, bygone toys of youth—billets-doux,

snuff-boxes, canes—exhibited,—discarded hobby-horses are trotted out,—perhaps even a dissecting surgeon is called in to draw up a minute report of the state of the corpse and its viscera; in short, nothing is spared that can make an item for the clerk to insert in his memoir. Outrageous as it may seem, this is scarcely an exaggeration. For example, who will dare to say that we do not know at this very hour more of Goldsmith's affairs than he ever did himself? It is rather wonderful than otherwise, that the literary character should shine out as it does after such a severe scrutiny."

It is not enough, however, that literary men will bear comparison in point of conduct with any other class. We think the public are entitled to expect *more* than this; and to apply to them the words, "Of those to whom much is given, much shall be required." They are men of the highest culture, and ought to be men of the highest character. As influencing the minds and morals of our readers,—and the world is daily looking more and more to the books which men of genius write, for instruction,—they ought to cultivate in themselves a high standard of character,—the very highest standard of character,—in order that those who study and contemplate them in their books may be lifted and lighted up by their example. At all events we think the public are not over-exacting when they require that the great gifts with which the leading minds among men have been endowed shall not be prostituted for unworthy purposes, nor employed for merely selfish and venial ends. Genius is a great gift, and ought to be used wisely and uprightly for the elevation of the moral character and the advancement of the intelligence of the world at large. If not so employed, genius and talent may be a curse to their possessor, and not a blessing to others,—they may even be a fountain of bitterness and woe, spreading moral poison throughout society.

We do not say that Theodore Hook was an author of this latter class; but we do think that a perusal of his life, as written by one of his own friends and admirers,* cannot fail to leave on the reader's mind the impression, that here was a man gifted with the finest powers, in whom genius proved a traitor to itself, and false to its high mission. With shining abilities, a fine intellect, sparkling wit, and great capacity for work, Hook seemed to have no higher ambition in life than to sit as an ornament at the tables of the great,—to buzz about their candles, and consume himself for their merriment and diversion. In the houses of titled men, who kept fine company and gave great dinners, he did but play the part of the licensed wit and jester,—wearing the livery of his entertainers, not on his person, indeed, but in his soul; bartering the birthright of his superior intellect for a mess of pottage,—as Douglas Jerrold has said, "a mess of pottage served up at a lord's table in a lord's platter."

* Theodore Hook: a Sketch. Murray.

Theodore Hook was the son of a musical composer of some note in his day, and born in Bedford Square, London, in 1788. He had an only brother, James, who afterwards became Dean of Worcester, and whose son, Dr. Hook, Dean of Chichester, survives to do honor to the talents and reputation of the family.   Theodore was, in early life, petted by his father, who regarded him as a prodigy.   He was sent to school at Harrow, where he was the school-fellow of Byron and Peel, though not in the same form.   But on the death of his mother, Mr. Hook took the boy from school, partly because he found his society an amusing solace, and also because he had discovered that he could turn the youth's precocious talents to profitable account.   Already, at the age of fourteen, Theodore could play expertly on the piano, and sing pathetic as well as comic songs with remarkable expression.   One evening he enchanted the father especially by singing, to his own accompaniment, two new ballads, one grave and one gay. Whence the airs,—whence the words? It turned out that the verses and the music were both Theodore's own! Here was a mine for the veteran artist to work! Hitherto he had been forced to borrow his words: now the whole manufacture might be done at home.   So young Hook was taken into partnership with his father, at the age of sixteen; and straightway became a precocious man, admired of musicians and players, the friends and boon companions of his father.   Several of his songs "took" on the stage, and he became the pet of the green-room.   Night after night he hung about the theaters, with the privilege of admission before the curtain and behind it.   Popular actors laughed at his jokes, and pretty actresses would have their bouquets handed to them by nobody but Theodore.

An effort was made by his brother—then advancing in the Church —to have the youth removed from this atmosphere of dissipation and frivolity; and, at his urgent remonstrance, Theodore was entered a student at Oxford. But he carried his spirit of rebellious frolic with him.   When the Vice-Chancellor, noticing his boyish appearance, said, "You seem very young, sir; are you prepared to sign the *Thirty-nine Articles ?*" "O yes, sir," briskly answered Theodore,— "quite ready,—*forty*, if you please!" The dignitary shut the book; the brother apologized, the boy looked ·contrite, the articles were duly signed, and the young scape-grace matriculated at Alma Mater. He was not yet to reside at Oxford, however, but returned to London to go through a prescribed course of reading. Under his father's eye, however, no serious study could go forward; besides, the youth's head was full of farce.   At sixteen, he began to write vaudevilles for the stage, the music adapted to which was supplied by his father. These trifles succeeded, and the clever boy became a greater green-room pet than ever. He thus made the acquaintance of Mathews and Liston, for whom he wrote farces. Hook was not over particular about the sources from whence he cribbed his "points;"

borrowing unscrupulously from all quarters. In the course of four years, he wrote more than ten plays, which had a considerable run at the time, though they are now all but forgotten. Two of them have, nevertheless, been recently revived, namely, "Exchange no Robbery," and "Killing no Murder." Had he gone on writing plays, he would certainly have established a reputation as a first-rate farce-writer. But, in his volatile humor, he must needs try novels; and forthwith, at twenty years old, he wrote "Musgrave,"—a novel of ridiculous sentimentality, but sparkling and clever: yet it was a failure. About the same time, his life was a succession of boisterous buffooneries, of which his "Gilbert Gurney" may be regarded as a pretty faithful record. Unquestionably, Hook wrote that novel chiefly from personal recollections ; it is virtually his autobiography ; and in his diary when speaking of its progress, he uses the words, "working at my life."

Hook often used to tell the story—which he gives in detail in "Gilbert Gurney"—of Mathews and himself, when one day rowing to Richmond, being suddenly smitten by the sight of a placard at the foot of a Barnes garden.—"*No body permitted to land here—Offenders prosecuted with the utmost rigor of the Law.*" The pair instantly disembarked on the forbidden paradise; the fishing-line was converted into a surveyor's measuring-tape; the wags paced to and fro on the beautiful lawn,—Hook, the surveyor, with his book and pencil in hand,—Mathews the clerk, with the cord and walking-stick, both soon pinned into the exquisite turf. Then suddenly opened the parlor-window of the mansion above, and forth stepped, in blustering ire, a napkined alderman, who advanced with what haste he could against the intruders on his paradise. The comedians stood cool, and scarcely condescended to reply to his indignant inquiries. At length oozed out the gradual announcement of their being the agents of a New Canal Company, settling where the new cut was to cross the old gentleman's pleasure-ground. Their regret was extreme at having "to perform so disagreeable a duty," but public interests must be regarded. Then came the alderman's suggestion that the pair had better "walk in and talk the matter over;" their reluctant acquiescence,—"had only a quarter of an hour to spare, —feared that it was of no use" their endeavoring to avoid the beautiful spot,—the new cut must come through the grounds. However, in they went; the turkey was just served, an excellent dinner followed, washed down with madeira, champagne, claret, and so on. At length the good fare produced its effect,—the projected branch of the canal was reconsidered,—the city knight's arguments were acknowledged to be more and more weighty. "Really," says the alderman, "this cut must be given up; but one bottle more, dear gentlemen." At last when it was getting dark—they were eight miles from Westminster Bridge—Hook burst out into song, and narrated in extempore verse the whole transaction, winding up with—

> And we greatly approve of your fare,
> Your cellar's as prime as your cook,
> And this clerk here is Mathews the player,
> And my name, sir, is—Theodore Hook!"

The adventure forms the subject of a capital chapter in "Gilbert Gurney," which many of our readers may have read.

But the maddest of Hook's tricks was that known as the "Berners Street Hoax," which happened in 1809, as follows: Walking down Berners Street, one day, Hook's companion (probably Mathews) called his attention to a particularly neat and modest house, the residence—as was inferred from the door-plate—of some decent shop-keeper's widow. "I'll lay you a guinea," said Theodore, "that in one week that nice quiet dwelling shall be the most famous in all London." The bet was taken, and in the course of four or five days, Hook had written and posted *one thousand* letters, annexing orders to tradesmen of every sort within the bills of mortality, all to be executed on one particular day, and as nearly as possible at one fixed hour. From "wagons of coals and potatoes, to books, prints, feathers, ices, jellies, and cranberry tarts," nothing in any way whatever available to any human being but was commanded from scores of rival dealers, scattered all over the city, from Wapping to Lambeth, from Whitechapel to Paddington. It can only be feebly imagined what the crash and jam and tumult of that day was. Hook had provided himself with a lodging nearly opposite the fated house, where, with a couple of trusty allies, he watched the progress of the melodrama. The mayor and his chaplain arrived,—invited there to take the death-bed confession of a peculating common-councilman. There also came the Governor of the Bank, the Chairman of the East India Company, the Lord Chief Justice, and the Prime Minister,—above all, there came his Grace the Archbishop of Canterbury, and His Royal Highness the Commander-in-Chief. These all obeyed the summons, for every pious and patriotic feeling had been most movingly appealed to. They could not all reach Berners Street, however,—the avenues leading to it being jammed up with drays, carts, and carriages, all pressing on to the solitary widow's house; but certainly the Duke of York's military punctuality and crimson liveries brought him to the point of attack before the poor woman's astonishment had risen to terror and despair. Most fierce were the growlings of doctors and surgeons, scores of whom had been cheated of valuable hours. Attorneys, teachers of every kind, male and female, hair-dressers, tailors, popular preachers, Parliamentary philanthropists, had been alike victimized. There was an awful smashing of glass, china, harpsichords, and coach-panels. Many a horse fell, never to rise again. Beer-barrels and wine-barrels were overturned and exhausted with impunity amidst the press of countless multitudes. It was a great day for the pickpockets; and a great godsend to the newspapers.

Then arose many a fervent hue and cry for the detection of the wholesale deceiver and destroyer. Though in Hook's own theatrical world he was instantly suspected, no sign escaped either him or his confidants. He found it convenient to be laid up a week or two by a severe fit of illness, and then promoted reconvalescence by a few weeks' country tour. He revisited Oxford, and professed an intention of commencing his residence there. But the storm blew over, and Hook returned with tranquillity to the green-room. This was followed by other tricks and hoaxes,, in one of which he made Romeo Coates his victim. These may be found detailed at some length in "Gilbert Gurney," and in Mrs. Mathews's Memoirs of her husband, who was usually Hook's accomplice in such kinds of mischief.

One of Hook's extraordinary talents—which amounted in him to almost a genius—was his gift of singing. improvised songs on the spur of the moment, while under the influence of excited convivial feelings. He would sit down to the piano-forte, and, quite unhesitatingly, compose a verse upon every person in the room, full of the most pointed wit, and with the truest rhyme, gathering up, as he proceeded, every incident of the evening, and working up the whole into a brilliant song. He would often, like John Parry, sport with operatic measures, in which he would triumph over every variety of meter and complication of stanza. But John Parry's exhibitions are carefully studied, whereas Hook's happiest effects were spontaneous and unpremeditated. The effect he produced on such occasions was almost marvelous. Sheridan frequently witnessed these exhibitions, and declared that he could not have believed such power possible, had he not witnessed it. Of course, Hook was usually stimulated by wine or punch when he ventured on such exploits; and it is recorded, that during one of his songs, at which Coleridge was present, every pane in the room window was riddled by the glasses flung through them by the guests, the host crowning the bacchanalian riot by demolishing the chandelier with his goblet.

Hook's fame as a wit, a jester, a talker, and an improvisatore singer, shortly reached aristocratic circles; and he was invited to their houses to make sport for them. Sheridan mentioned him to the Marchioness of Hertford as a most amusing fellow, and he was shortly after called upon to display his musical and metrical facility in her ladyship's presence; which he did. He was called, in like manner, to minister to the amusement of the Sybarite Prince Regent at a supper in Manchester Square, and he so delighted his Royal Highness, that, on leaving the room, he said, "Mr. Hook I must see you and hear you again." Hook was only too glad to play merry-andrew to the Prince; and, after a few similar evenings, his Royal Highness was so good as to make inquiry about Hook's position, when, finding he was without a profession or fixed income of any sort, he signified his opinion that "something must be done for

Hook." As the word of the Prince was equivalent to a law, and quiet jobs were easily done in those days, Hook's promotion followed as a matter of course. He was almost immediately after appointed Accountant-General and Treasurer to the Colony of the Mauritius, with an income of £2,000 a year. Hook had no knowledge of accounts; but he had the Prince Regent's good word, and that was enough. He stayed five years in the Mauritius, paying no attention to the duties of his office, living in great style, a leading man on the turf, the very prince of Mauritian hospitality. But it came to a sad end. In March, 1818, Hook was arrested, while supping at a friend's house, and dragged, by torchlight, through crowded streets, to the common prison of the town, on a charge of embezzling the public moneys in the colonial treasury to a large amount! From thence he was conveyed to England, tried before the law officers of the crown, and brought in as defaulter to the extent of £12,000. This debt he never paid; though his earnings by his pen, for many years after, were very large. Into the merits of the case against Hook we shall not here enter; but as the government which brought him to book was friendly to him, and under the influences of many of his personal friends, we must presume the charges to have been well founded. The most favorable view of his case that can be taken is this: that *somebody* embezzled the colonial moneys; but as Hook had no knowledge of accounts, and rarely took any concern in the treasury business, spending his £2,000 a year in the manner of a gentlemanly sinecurist, the colonial funds were "mumbled away," and Hook, being the responsible party, was saddled with the blame.

On reaching London again, to wait the issue of the government investigation, he was set at liberty, on the Attorney-General's report, that there was no apparent ground for a criminal procedure; and the case was treated as one of defalcation and civil prosecution only. In order to live in the meanwhile, Hook had recourse to his ever-ready pen. First, he wrote for magazines and newspapers; then he tried a shilling magazine, called The Arcadian, of which only a few numbers were issued, when the publisher lost heart. In 1820, Sir Walter Scott accidentally met Hook at a dinner-party at Daniel Terry's, and was delighted, as everybody could not help being, with Hook's brilliant conversation. Hook, notwithstanding the affair of his colonial defalcations, and the prosecution of him by the Audit Board, still held his "good old Tory" views of politics; and gratefully remembered his personal obligations to the Prince Regent, now the reigning monarch. He was consequently violently opposed to the pretensions and partisans of Queen Caroline. The strong color of his politics induced Scott to mention Hook to a gentleman who shortly after applied to him to recommend an editor for a newspaper about to be established. To this circumstance his connection with the famous "John Bull" is probably to be attributed.

At all events, the John Bull shortly after came out, with Hook for its editor. But he preserved his incognito carefully for many years; which was the more necessary in consequence of the thick cloud which still hung over his moral character in connection with his colonial affair. Hook threw himself with great fury into the ranks of the Georgites, and published many violent squibs against Queen Caroline and her friends, which excited a storm of popular indignation. The John Bull was generally admitted to be the most powerful, unscrupulous, and violent advocate of the king's cause; whether it was the better for the advocacy, we shall not here venture to determine. The paper was well supported with money,—as was surmised, from "headquarters;" and for some years Hook's income from the John Bull alone, amounted to as much as £2,000 a year. At length it began to ooze out that Hook was the editor of the John Bull. Though furnishing nearly the whole of the articles and squibs which appeared in it, he at once indignantly denied the imputation in a letter, "the editor," in which he disclaimed and disavowed all connection with the paper. But, by slow degrees, the truth came out and at last all was known. The John Bull was denounced by many as a reckless," "venomous," "malignant," "lying" publication; and by others it was defended as a "spirited," "courageous," "loyal," and "admirable" defender of the church, crown, and constitution.

In 1823 Hook was arrested for the sum of £12,000, which the authorities had finally decided that he stood indebted to the public exchequer. He was then confined in a sheriff's house in Shire Lane,—a miserable, squalid neighborhood. He remained there for several months, during which his health seriously suffered. While shut up in Shire Lane he made the acquaintance of Dr. William Maginn, who had recently come over from Ireland, a literary adventurer, but had fallen into the sheriff's officer's custody. It was a lucky meeting for both, however, as Maginn proved of great assistance to Hook, in furnishing the requisite amount of "spicy" copy for the columns of the John Bull. Hook was transferred to the rules of the King's Bench, where he remained for a year, and afterwards succeeded in getting liberated; but was told distinctly that the debt must hang over him until every farthing was paid. He then took a cottage at Putney, and re-entered society again. He had for companion here a young woman whom he ought to have married; that he did not—that he left upon the heads of his innocent offspring by her a stigma and a stain in the eyes of the world—was only, we regret to say, too much in keeping with the character and career of the reckless, unscrupulous, and feeble-conscienced Theodore Hook.

While living in his apartments at Temple Place, within the rules of the King's Bench, Hook had begun his career as a novelist. His first series of "Sayings and Doings" was very successful, and yield-

ed him a profit of £2,000. The second and third series were equally
successful. His other novels, entitled "Maxwell," "The Parson's
Daughter," "Love and Pride," were also successful, and paid
him well. In 1836 he became the editor of the New Monthly Magazine, in which he published "Gilbert Gurney" (perhaps the raciest
of all his novels, being chiefly drawn from his own personal experiences), and afterwards "Gurney Married," "Jack Brag," "Births,
Deaths, and Marriages," "Precepts and Practice," and "Fathers and
Sons." These were all collected and republished afterwards in separate forms. The number of these works,—thirty-eight volumes,
—which he wrote within sixteen years, at the time when he was
editor and almost sole writer for a newspaper, and for several years
the conductor of a Magazine, argue a by no means idle disposition.
Indeed, Hook worked very hard; the pity is that he worked to so
little purpose, and that he squandered the money with which he
ought to have paid his debts (and he himself admitted that he was
in justice responsible for £9,000) in vying with fashionable people
to keep up appearances, and live a worthless life of dissipation,
frivolity, and burlesque "bon ton." For many years Hook must
have been earning from £4,000 to £5,000 a year by his pen, and
yet he was always poor! How did he spend his earnings? Let the
friend who has written the sketch of him in the Quarterly Review
explain the secret:

"In 1827 (after leaving his house at Putney) he took a higher
flight. He became the tenant of a house in Cleveland Row,—on the
edge, therefore, of what, in one of his novels, he describes as the
'real London,—the space between Pall Mall on the south, and Pic-
cadilly on the north, St. James's Street on the west, and the Opera
House to the east.' The residence was handsome, and, to persons
ignorant of his domestic arrangements, appeared extravagantly too
large for his purpose; we have since heard of it as inhabited by a
nobleman of distinction. He was admitted a member of diverse
clubs; shone the first attraction of their House dinners; and, in such
as allowed of play, he might commonly be seen in the course of his
protracted evening. Presently he began to receive invitations to
great houses in the country, and, for week after week, often traveled
from one to another such scene, to all outward appearance in the
style of an idler of high condition. In a word, he had soon entangled
himself with habits and connections which implied much curtailment
of the time for labor at the desk, and a course of expenditure more than
sufficient to swallow all the profits of what remained. To the upper
world he was visible solely as the jocund convivialist of the club,—
the brilliant wit of the lordly banquet,— the lion of the crowded assembly,—the star of a Christmas or Easter party in a rural palace,—
the unfailing stage-manager, prompter, author, and occasionally excellent comic actor, of the private theatricals, at which noble guards-
men were the valets, and lovely peeresses the soubrettes."

Thus did the brilliant Hook flutter like a dazzled moth around the burning taper of aristocracy, scorching his wings, and at length sinking destroyed by the seductive blaze, when he was at once swept away as some unsightly object.

It was a feverish, miserable, unhealthy life, with scarcely a redeeming feature in it. To make up for the time devoted by him to the amusement of aristocratic circles, and to raise the money wherewithal to carry on this brilliant dissipation, as well as to relieve himself of the pressure of his more urgent pecuniary embarrassments. Hook worked day and night when at his own house, often under the influence of stimulants, and thus increased the nervous agonies of a frame prematurely wasted and exhausted. Meanwhile he was pressed by his publisher, into whose debt he had fallen ; and publishers, in such a case, are exacting, like everybody else in similar circumstances. Debts—debts—forever debts—accumulated about Hook, each debt a grinning phantom, mocking at him even in the midst of his gayest pleasures. "Little did his fine friends know at what tear and wear of life he was devoting his evenings to their amusement. The ministrants of pleasure with whom they measured him were almost all as idle as themselves,—elegant, accomplished men, easy in circumstances, with leisure at command, who drove to the rendezvous after a morning divided between voluptuous lounging in a library chair and healthful exercise out of doors. But he came forth, *at best*, from a long day of labor at his writing-desk, after his faculties had been kept on the stretch,—feeling, passion, thought, fancy, excitable nerves, suicidal brain, all worked, perhaps well-nigh exhausted,—compelled, since he came at all, to disappoint by silence, or to seek the support of tempting stimulants in his new career of exertion. And we may guess what must have been the effect on his mind of the consciousness, while seated among the revelers of a princely saloon, that next morning must be, not given to the mere toil of the pen, but divided between scenes in the back-shops of three or four eager, irritated booksellers, and weary prowlings through the dens of city usurers for the means of discounting this long bill, staving off that attorney's threat; not less commonly—even more urgently—of liquidating a debt of honor to the grandee, or some of the smiling satellites of his pomp.

"There is recorded (in his diary) in more than usual detail, one winter visit at the seat of a nobleman of almost unequaled wealth (Marquis of Hertford?), evidently particularly fond of Hook, and always mentioned in terms of real gratitude,—even affection. Here was a large company, including some of the very highest names in England; the party seem to have remained together for more than a fortnight, or, if one went, the place was filled immediately by another not less distinguished by the advantages of birth and fortune ; Hook's is the only untitled name, except a led captain and chaplain or two, and some misses of musical celebrity. What a struggle he has to maintain! Every Thursday he must meet the printer of the John Bull to arrange the paper for Saturday's impression. While the rest are shooting or hunting, he clears his head as well as he can, and steals a few hours to write his articles. When they go to bed on Wednesday night, he smuggles himself into a post-chaise, and is carried fifty miles across the country, to some appointed Blue Boar, or Crooked Billet. Thursday morning is spent in overhauling correspondence,—in all the details of the editorship. He, with hard driving, gets back to the neighborhood of the castle when the dressing-bell is ringing. Mr. Hook's servant has intimated that his master is slightly indisposed; he enters the gate as if from a short walk in the wood; in half an hour, behold him answering placidly the inquiries of the ladies,—his headache fortunately gone at last,—quite ready for the turtle and champagne,—puns rattle like a hail-shower,—'that dear Theodore' had never been more brilliant. At a decorous hour the great lord and his graver guests retire; it is supposed that the evening is over,—that the house is shut up. But Hook is quartered in a long bachelor's gallery, with half-a-dozen bachelors of far different caliber. One of them, a dashing young earl, proposes what the diary calls 'something comfortable' in his dressing-room. Hook, after his sleepless night and busy day, hesitates,—but is persuaded. The broiled bones are attended by more champagne, Roman punch, hot brandy and water, finally; for there are plenty of butlers and grooms of the chamber ready to minister to the delights of the distant gallery, ever productive of fees to man and maid. The end is, that they play deep, and that Theodore loses a great deal more money than what he had brought with him from town, or knows how to come at if he were there. But he rises next morning with a swimming, bewildered head, and, as the fumes disperse, perceives that he must write instantly for money. No difficulty is to be made; the fashionable tailor (alias, merciless Jew) to whom he discloses the case, must on any terms remit a hundred pounds by return of post. It is accomplished,—the debt is discharged. Thursday comes round again, and again he escapes to meet the printer. This time the printer brings a payment of salary with him, and Hook drives back to the castle in great glee. Exactly the same scene occurs a night or two afterward. The salary all goes. When the time comes for him at last to leave his splendid friend, he finds that he has lost a fortnight as respects a book that *must* be finished within a month or six weeks; and that what with traveling expenses hither and thither (he has to defray the printer's, too), and losses at play to silken coxcombs,—who considered him an admirable jack-pudding, and also as an invaluable pigeon, since he drains his glass as well as fills it,—he has thrown away more money than he could have earned by the labor of three months in his own room at Fulham. But then the rumble of the green chariot is seen well-stocked with pheasants and hares, as it pauses in passing through town at Crockford's, the Carlton, or the Athenæum; and as often as the Morning Post alluded to the nobler peer's Christmas court, Mr. Theodore Hook's name closed the paragraph of 'fashionable intelligence.'"

But at last the end of all came, and the poor jester and bon-viant strutted off the stage. To the last, even when positively ill, he could not refuse an invitation to dine with titled people. To the last,—padded-up old man,—he tried to be effervescent and gay. He died in August, 1841, and the play was ended. Some may call such a life as this a tragedy, and a painful one it seems. To look at it now, there appears little genuine mirth in it; the laughter was all hollow. As for the noble and titled friends for whom Hook had made so much merriment during his unhappy life, they let him die overburdened with debt, and go to his grave unwept and unattended. They did nothing for his children,—it is true they were such as the respectable world usually disown; and they did not, so far as we know, place a stone over the grave in which their jester was laid to sleep. Notwithstanding Theodore Hook's naturally brilliant powers,—his sagacity, his humor, his genius,—we fear that the verdict of his survivors and of posterity will be, that here was the life of a greatly gifted man worse than wasted.

DR. ANDREW COMBE.

THE life of Andrew Combe was quiet and unostentatious. It was chiefly occupied by the investigations and labors incident to the calling which he had chosen,—that of medicine; —a profession which, when followed successfully, leaves comparatively little leisure for the indulgence of literary tastes. Yet we do not exaggerate when we say, that there are few writers who have effected greater practical good, and done more to beneficially affect the moral and physical well-being of mankind, than the subject of this memoir. He was one of the first writers who directed public attention to the subject of physiology, in connection with health and education. There had, indeed, been no want of writers on physiology previous to this time; but they addressed themselves mainly to the professional mind; and their books were, for the most part, so full of technical phrases, that, so far as the public was concerned, they might as well have been written in an unknown tongue. As Dr. Combe grew up towards manhood, and acquired habits of independent observation, he perceived that the majority of men and women were, for the most part, living in habitual violation of the laws of health, and thus bringing upon them debility, disease, premature decay, and death; not to speak of generations unborn, on whom the penalty of neglect or violation of the physiological laws inevitably descends. He conceived the idea of instructing the people in those laws, in a simple and intelligible manner, and in language divested of technical terms. And there are words enough in the English tongue in which to utter common sense to common people upon such subjects as air, exercise, diet, cleanliness, and so on, as affecting the healthy lives of human beings, without drawing so largely as had been customary upon Greek and Latin terminology for the purpose.

Dr. Combe's first book, on "The Principles of Physiology applied to the Preservation of Health, and to the Improvement of Physical and Mental Education," was written in this rational and common-sense style.   In that work Dr. Combe appealed to the ordinary, average understandings of men.   He explained the laws which regulate the physical life,—the conditions necessary for the healthy action of the various functions of the system ; and directed par-ticular attention to those habits and practices which were in viola-tion of the natural laws, pointing out the necessity for amendment in various ways, in a cogent, persuasive, and perspicuous manner. We remember very well the appearance of the book in question. It excited comparatively small attention at first,—the subject was unusual, and up to that time deemed so unattractive.   People were afraid then, as they often are now, to look into their own physical system, and learn something of its working.   There is alarm to many minds, in the thought of the heart beating, and the lungs blowing, and the arteries contracting upon their red blood.   The consideration of such subjects used formerly to be regarded as strictly professional: and people were for the most part satisfied to leave health, and all that concerned it, to the exclusive charge of "the doctors."   And, truth to say, medical men were disposed to regard the publication of Dr. Combe's "Physiology" as somewhat "infra dig."; for it looked like a revealing of the secrets of the pro-fession before the eyes of the general public.   But all such feeling has long since disappeared, and medical men now find that they have in the readers of good works on popular physiology more in-telligent patients to deal with,—more able to co-operate with them in their attempts to subdue disease and restore the bodily functions to health,—than when they have mere blank ignorance and blind prejudice to encounter.   Where there is not sound information, there will always be found prejudice enough,—the most difficult of all things to contend against.   It is not improbable, also, that to the growing popular knowledge of physiological conditions we are, in a great measure, to attribute the improvement in the medical profession which has taken place of late years.   For medical men are the better for knowing that, in order to make good their influence and to advance as a profession, they must keep well ahead of the intelligence of their employers.   Everybody knows that questions of health,—as affecting the sanitary condition of towns,—are among the leading questions of this day; and we cannot help attributing much of the active concern which now exists among legislators, philanthropists, and all public-spirited men, for the improvement of the physical condition of the people, to the impulse given to the subject by the publication of Dr. Combe's admirable books.

Dr. Combe was himself a serious sufferer through neglect of the laws of physical health; and it was probably this circumstance which early directed his attention to the subject, and induced him to give it the prominency which he did in nearly all his published works. He was the fifteenth child of respectable parents, living in Edinburgh: his father was a brewer at Livingston's Yards, a suburb of the Old Town, situated nearly under the southwest angle of Edinburgh Castle rock. Seventeen children in all were born to the Combes in that place; but the neighborhood abounded with offensive pools and ditches, the noxious influence of which (in conjunction with defective ventilation in small or over-crowded sleeping apartments) must have been a potent cause of the disease and early mortality which prevailed in the family. Very few of the seventeen children grew up to adult years; and although the parents, who were of robust constitution, lived to an old age, those of the children who survived grew up with feeble constitutions, and, in Andrew's case, containing within them the seeds of serious disease. Nor was the mental discipline of the children of a much healthier kind. As an illustration, George Combe, in the life of his brother, recently published, gives the following picture of the Sabbath, as spent in a Scotch family:

"The gate of the brewery was locked, and all except the most necessary work was suspended. The children rose at eight, breakfasted at nine, and were taken to the West Church at eleven. The forenoon service lasted till one. There was a lunch between one and two. The afternoon's service lasted from two till four. They then dined; and after dinner, portions of the Psalms and of the Shorter Catechism with the 'Proofs' were prescribed to be learned by heart. After these had been repeated, tea was served. Next the children sat round a table and read the Bible aloud, each a verse in turn, till a chapter for every reader had been completed. After this, sermons or other pious works were read till nine o'clock, when supper was served, after which all retired to rest. Jaded and exhausted in brain and body as the children were by the performance of heavy tasks at school during six days of the week, these Sundays were no days of rest to them."

From a private school, Andrew Combe proceeded to the high school, and then he was placed apprentice to an Edinburgh surgeon. He was singularly obstinate in connection with his entry upon his profession. Although he had chosen to be "a doctor," when finally asked "what he would be," his answer in the vernacular Scotch was, "I'll no be naething." He would give no further answer; and after all kinds of "fleechin" and persuading were tried, he at length had to be *carried* by force out of the house, to begin his professional career. His father and brother George, afterwards his biographer, with a younger brother, James, performed this remarkable duty. George thus describes the scene.

A consultation was now held as to what was to be done; and again it was resolved that Andrew should not be allowed to conquer, seeing that he still assigned no reason for his resistance.

He was, therefore, lifted from the ground; he refused to stand; but his father supported one shoulder, George carried the other, and his younger brother, James, pushed him on behind; and in this fashion he was carried from the house, through the brewery, and several hundred yards along the high road, before he placed a foot on the ground. His elder brother John, observing what was passing, anxiously inquired, "What's the matter?" James replied, "We are taking Andrew to the doctor." "To the doctor! what's the matter with him,—is he ill, James?" "O, not at all,—we are taking him to *make* him a doctor." At last, Andrew's sense of shame prevailed, and he walked quietly. His father and George accompanied him to Mr. Johnson's house; Andrew was introduced and received, and his father left him. George inquired what had passed in Mr. Johnson's presence. "Nothing particular," replied his father; "only my conscience smote me when Mr. Johnson 'hoped that Andrew had come quite willingly!' I replied, that I had given him a solemn promise that, if he did not like the profession after a trial, he should be at liberty to leave it." "Quite right," said Mr. Johnson; and Andrew was conducted to the laboratory. Andrew returned to Mr. Johnson's the next morning without being asked to do so; and to the day of his death he was fond of his profession.

In a touching letter to George, written nearly thirty years after the above event, he thanked him cordially for having been instrumental in sending him to a liberal profession; and he confesses that he really "wished and meant to be a doctor," notwithstanding his absurd way of showing his willingness. Always ready, as both he and his brother were, to account for everything phrenologically, he attributed the resistance on the occasion to wit and secretiveness. "I recollect well," he says in the letter referred to, "that my habitual phrase was, 'I'll no be naething.' This was universally construed to mean, 'I'll be naething.' The true meaning I had in view was what the words bore. 'I will be *something*;' and the clew to the riddle was, that my wit was tickled at school by the rule that 'two negatives make an affirmative,' and I was diverted with the mystification their use and *literal truth* produced in this instance. In no one instance did mortal man or woman hear me say seriously (*if ever*) 'I'll be naething.' All this is as clear to me as of yesterday's occurrence, and the double entendre was a source of internal chuckling to me. You may say, Why, then, so unwilling to go to Mr. Johnson's? That is a natural question, and touches upon another feature altogether. I was a dour [stubborn] boy, when not taken in the right way, and for a time nothing would then move me. Once committed, I resolved not to yield, and hence the laughable extravaganza which ensued."

At the age of fifteen, Andrew Combe went to live with his elder brother George, who, in 1812, began practicing as writer to the Signet. This was an advantage to Andrew, in point of health, and was a convenience to him in attending his place of business, and also the medical lectures in the University. In his letters to his brother, written in after life, Andrew often referred with regret to the neglect of ventilation, ablution, and bathing, in his father's family; to which he attributed the premature deaths of the greater number, and impaired constitutions of the few who survived.

"Our parents," he said in one letter, "erred from sheer ignorance; but what are we to think of the mechanical and tradesman-like views of a medical man who could see all the causes of disease existing, and producing these results year after year, without its ever occurring to him that it was part of his solemn duty to warn his employers, and try to remedy the evil? All parties were anxious to cure the disease, but no one sought to remove its cause; and yet so entirely were the causes within the control of reason and knowledge, that my conviction has long been complete, that, if we had been properly treated from infancy, we should, even with the constitutions we possessed at birth, have survived in health and active usefulness to a good old age, unless cut off by some acute disease." But nearly all medical men were alike empirical in those days. They merely attacked the symptoms which presented themselves; and when these were overcome, their task was accomplished. That medical men are now so careful in directing their measures toward the prevention as well as the cure of disease, we have to thank Dr. Combe, Edwin Chadwick, and other popular writers and laborers in the cause of public health.

At the early age of nineteen, Andrew Combe passed at Surgeons' Hall. He used afterwards to say, that it would have better for him had he been then only commencing his studies. Shortly after, Dr. Spurzheim, the phrenologist, visited Edinburgh, and attracted many ardent admirers, of whom George Combe, then a young man, shortly became one. Andrew, like most of the medical men of the day, was at first disposed to laugh at the new science; but before many years had passed, he too became an ardent disciple of Dr. Spurzheim. He afterwards attributed much of the improvement of his mind and character to his study of this science, and to the practical application of its principles to his own case. In 1817 he went to Paris, where he studied under Dupuytren, Alibert, Esquirol, Richerand, and other celebrated men. He also cultivated the frendship of Dr. Spurzheim, and pursued his observations and studies in phrenology. From Paris he proceeded with a friend on a walking tour through Switzerland and the north of Italy. Disregarding the laws of health, he injured his delicate constitution by exposure, irregular diet, and over-fatigue; and on his return to Edinburgh, shortly after, he was seized with a serious illness, the beginning of long-continued lung disease. He removed for a season to the south of England, and then proceeded to Italy, wintering at Leghorn. There his cough left him, and he regained his health and strength so far as to be enabled to practice for a time as a physician among the English in that town and Pisa. Returning to Edinburgh in 1823, he regularly settled down in that city as a medical practitioner.

In this profession he was very successful. His quiet manner, suavity, and kindness, good sense, attention, professional abilities, and gentlemanly demeanor, secured him many friends; and he won them to his heart by his truthful candor, and by the manner in which he sought to obtain their intelligent co-operation in the remedial measures which he thought proper to employ. He deemed it as much a part of his duty to instruct his patients as to the conditions which regulate the healthy action of the bodily organs, as to administer drugs to them for the purpose of curing their immediate ailments. But he found great obstacles in his way, in consequence of the previous ignorance of most people—even those considered well educated—as to the simplest laws which regulate the animal economy. Hence he very early felt the necessity of improving this department of elementary instruction; and with that view he set about composing his works on popular physiology. His first appearance as an author was in the pages of the Phrenological Journal,— an excellent periodical now defunct. To the subject of phrenology he devoted considerable attention, and soon became known as one of its ablest defenders. Some of his friends told him that he would injure his professional standing and connection by the prominency of his advocacy of the new views; but he persevered, nevertheless, "firmly trusting in the sustaining power of truth;" and he afterwards found that, instead of being professionally injured, he was greatly benefited by the labor which he bestowed upon the study and exposition of the science. To phrenology he attributed, in a great measure, the direction of his attention to the subject of hygienic principles ; and after his mind had been fairly opened to the importance of those principles, he not only reduced them to practice in his own personal habits, but labored to disseminate a knowledge of them among the public generally.

In the midst of the arduous duties of his 'profession, Dr. Combe was more than once under the necessity of leaving home and going abroad for the benefit of his health. Disease had fixed upon his lungs, and he felt that his life could only be preserved by removing to a milder air. He traveled to Paris, to Orleans, to Nantes, to Lyons, to Naples, to Rome, returning rather improved, but with his lungs full of tubercles. For many years his life hung as by a thread, and it was by his careful observance of the laws of health that he was enabled to survive. In his work on "The Principles of Physiology," speaking of the advantages experienced in his own person of paying implicit obedience to the physiological laws, he says: "Had he not been fully aware of the gravity of his own situation, and from previous knowledge of the admirable adaptation of the physiological laws to carry on the machinery of life, disposed to place implicit reliance on the superior advantages of fulfilling them, as the direct dictates of Divine Wisdom, he would never have been able to persevere in the course chalked out for him, with that ready and long-enduring regularity and cheerfulness which have contributed so much to their successful fulfillment and results. And, therefore, he feels himself entitled to call upon those who, impatient at the slowness of their progress, are apt after a time to disregard all restrictions, to take a sounder view of their true position, to make themselves acquainted with the real dictates of the organic laws; and having done so, to yield them full, implicit, and persevering obedience, in the certain assurance that they will reap their reward in renewed health, if recovery be still possible; and if not, that they will thereby obtain more peace of mind and bodily ease than by any other means which they can use." ·

Dr. Combe's first published book was on "Phrenology applied to the Treatment of Insanity." It was given to the world in 1831, and proved very successful, being soon out of print. His second book was on "The Principles of Physiology," some chapters of which were first published in the Phrenological Journal. This book was published in 1834. Among the booksellers it was regarded with aversion. It was one of the successful books which booksellers sometimes reject. The first edition, of 750 copies, and a second edition, of 1,000 copies, both printed at the author's expense, were sold off; when Dr. Combe offered to dispose of the copyright to John Murray, without naming terms. Mr. Murray, and all the other London publishers who were applied to, declined to have anything to do with the purchase of the copyright; and the author went on publishing the book at his own expense. We need scarcely say that the book had a great run: about 30,000 copies were sold in England, besides numerous editions in the United States.

Although Dr. Combe was enabled at intervals to resume his practice in Edinburgh, he found it necessary to leave it from time to time for the benefits of a Continental residence; until, in 1836, he was induced to accept the appointment of physician to the King of the Belgians, believing that a residence at Brussels might possibly suit his constitution. But his health again gave way on reaching Brussels, and he was shortly under the necessity of giving up the appointment,—preserving, however, the honorary office of consulting physician to the Belgian Court. During the leisure which the cessation from professional pursuits afforded him, he prepared his next work, on "The Physiology of Digestion," another highly successful book. And in 1840 appeared his last work, on "The Physiological and Moral Management of Infancy." All these books have had a large circulation in England and in America, besides having been translated and circulated largely in Continental countries.

In 1841 Dr. Combe was again attacked with hæmoptysis, or discharge of blood from the lungs, and fell into a state of gradual and steady decline. As he himself said, "I believe I am going slowly and gently *down hill.*" He continued, however, to live for several years. In 1842 and 1843, he paid two visits to Madeira, and spent some time in Italy; and in the two following years he was enabled to travel about, a pallid invalid, taking a deep interest meanwhile in all useful public and social movements. His judgment seemed to grow stronger, and his insight into men and things clearer, as his bodily powers decayed. On all topics connected with education, as his correspondence shows, he took an especially lively interest. In 1847 he made a voyage to New York, chiefly for the purpose of visiting his brother William, who had long been settled in the States; but the heat of the climate proved too trying for his enfeebled constitution, and he almost immediately took ship again for England. The last literary labor in which he occupied himself was thoroughly characteristic of the man. While in the States, he had been sickened by the accounts of the ravages which the ship-fever had made among the poor Irish of emigrants, and he determined to bring the whole subject before the public in an article in the Times. Writing to a corn merchant in Liverpool, on his return home, for information as to the regulations of emigrant ships, he said : "I have not yet regained either my ordinary health or power of thinking, and, consequently, find writing rather heavy work; but my spirit is moved by the horrible details from Quebec and New York, and *I cannot rest without doing something in the matter.*" The letter in which this passage occurred was the last that Dr. Combe wrote. His article had meanwhile been hastily prepared, and it appeared in the Times of the 17th of September, 1847, occupying nearly three columns of that paper. He was interrupted, even while he was writing it, by a severe attack of the diarrhea, from which he died, after a few days' illness, on the 9th of August, 1847. His dying hours were peaceful, and the last words he uttered, when he could scarcely articulate, were, "Happy, happy !"

Such is a brief outline of the life of an eminently useful man, who, without the aid of any brilliant qualities, and merely by the exercise of industry, good sense, and well-cultivated moral feelings, was enabled to effect a large amount of good during his lifetime, and beneficially to influence the condition of mankind, it may be for generations to come.

ROBERT NICOLL.

THE name of Robert Nicoll will always take high rank among the poets of Scotland. He was one of the many illustrious Scotchmen who have risen up to adorn the lot of toil, and reflect honor on the class from which they have sprung,—the laborious and hard-working peasantry of their land. Nicoll, like Burns, was a man of whom those who live in the poor men's huts may well be proud. They declare, from day to day, that intellect is of no class, but that even in abodes of the deepest poverty there are warm hearts and noble minds, wanting but the opportunity and the circumstances to enable them to take their place as honorable and zealous laborers in the work of human improvement and Christian progress.

The life of Robert Nicoll was not one of much variety of incident. It was, alas! brought to an early close; for he died almost ere he had reached manhood. But in his short allotted span, it is not too much to say, that he lived more than most men have done who reach their three-score-years-and-ten. He was born of hard-working, God-fearing parents, in the year 1814, at the little village of Tullie-belton, situated near the foot of the Grampian Hills, in Perthshire. At an early period of his life, his father had rented the small farm of Ordie-braes; but having been unsuccessful in his farming, and falling behind with his rent, his home was broken up by the laird, the farm-stock was sold off by public roup ; and the poor man was reduced to the rank of a common day-laborer.

Robert was the second of a family of seven children, six sons and one daughter, the "sister Margaret" of whom the poet afterward spoke and wrote so affectionately. Out of the bare weekly income of a day-laborer, there was not, as might be inferred, much to spare for schooling. But the mother was an intelligent, active woman, and assiduously devoted herself to the culture of her children. She taught them to read, and gave them daily lessons in the Assembly's Catechism; so that before being sent to school, which they all were in due course, this good and prudent mother had laid the foundations in them of a sound moral and religious education.

"My mother," says Nicoll, in one of his letters, "in her early years, was an ardent book-woman. When she became poor, her time was too precious to admit of its being spent in reading, and I generally read to her while she was working; for she took care that the children should not want education."

Robert's subsequent instruction at school included the common branches of reading, writing, and accounts; the remainder of his education was his own work. He became a voracious reader, laying half the parish under contribution for books. A circulating library was got up in the neighboring village of Auchtergaven; which the lad managed to connect himself with, and his mind became stored apace.

Robert, like the rest of the children, when he became big enough and old enough, was sent out to field-work, to contribute by the aid of his slender gains towards the common store. At seven he was sent to the herding of cattle. an occupation, by the way, in which many distinguished Scotchmen—Burns, James Ferguson, Mungo Park, Dr. Murray (the Orientalist), and James Hogg—spent their early years. In winter Nicoll attended the school with his "fee." When occupied in herding, the boy had always a book for his companion; and he read going to his work and returning from it. While engaged in this humble vocation he read most of the Waverley novels. At a future period of his life, he says, "I can yet look back with no common feelings on the wood in which, while herding, I read Kenilworth." Probably the perusal of that beautiful fiction never gave a purer pleasure, even in the stately halls of rank and fashion, than it gave the poor herd-boy in the wood at Tulliebelton.

When twelve years of age, Robert was taken from the herding, and went to work in the garden of a neighboring proprietor. Shortly after, when about thirteen, he began to scribble his thoughts, and to string rhymes together. About this time also, as one of his intimate friends has told us, he passed through a strange phasis of being. He was in the practice of relating to his companions the most wonderful and incredible stories as facts,—stories that matched the wonders of the Arabian Tales,—and evidencing the inordinate ascendency at that time of his imagination over the other faculties of mind. The tales and novel literature, which, in common with all other kinds of books, he devoured with avidity, probably tended to the development of this disease (for such it really seemed to be) in his young and excitable nature. As for the verses which he then wrote, they were not at all such as satisfied himself; for, despairing of ever being able to write the English language correctly, he gathered all his papers together and made a bonfire of them, resolving to write no more "poetry" for the present. He became, however, the local correspondent of a provincial newspaper circulating in the district, furnishing it with weekly paragraphs and scraps of news, on the state of the weather, crops, etc. His return for this service was an occasional copy of the paper, and the consequence attendant on being the "correspondent" of the village. But another person was afterwards found more to the liking of the editor of the paper, and Robert, to his chagrin, lost his profitless post.

Nicoll's next change was an important one to him. He left his native hamlet and went into the world of active life. At the age of seventeen he was bound apprentice to a grocer and wine-merchant in Perth. There he came in contact with business, and activity, and opinion. The time was stirring with agitation. The Reform movement had passed over the face of the country like a tornado, raising millions of minds to action. The exciting effects of the agitation on the intellects and sympathies of the youth of that day are still remembered; and few there were who did not feel more or less influenced by them. The excitable mind of Nicoll was one of the first to be influenced; he burned to distinguish himself as a warrior on the people's side; he had longings infinite after popular enlargement, enfranchisement, and happiness. His thoughts shortly found vent in verse, and he became a poet. He joined a debating-society, and made speeches. Every spare moment of his time was devoted to self-improvement,—to the study of grammar, to the reading of works on political economy, and to politics in all their forms. In the course of one summer, he several times read through with attention Smith's Wealth of Nations, not improbably with an eye to some future employment on the newspaper press. He also read Milton, Locke, and Bentham, and devoured with avidity all other books that he could lay hands on. The debating-society with which he was connected proposed to start a periodical, and Nicoll undertook to write a tale for the first number. The periodical did not appear, and the tale was sent to Johnstone's Edinburgh Magazine, where it was published under the title of "Jessie Ogilvy," to the no small joy of the writer. It decided Nicoll's vocation,—it determined him to be an author. He proclaimed his Radicalism,—his resolution to "stand by his order," that of "the many. His letters to his relatives, about this time, are full of political allusions. He was working very hard, too,—attending in his mistress's shop, from seven in the morning till nine at night, and afterwards sitting up to read and write; rising early in the morning, and going forth to the North Inch by five o'clock, to write or to reap until the hour of shop-opening. At the same time he was living on the poorest possible diet,—literally on bread and cheese, and water,—that he might devote every possible farthing of his small gains to the purposes of mental improvement.

Few constitutions can stand such intense labor and privation with impunity; and there is little doubt but Nicoll was even then undermining his health, and sowing the seeds of the malady which in so short a time after was to bring him to his grave. But he was eager to distinguish himself in the field of letters, though but a poor shop-lad; and, more, than all, he was ambitious to be independent, and have the means of aiding his mother in her humble exertions for a living; never losing sight of the comfort and welfare of that first and fastest of his friends. At length, however; his health became seriously impaired, so much so, that his Perth apprenticeship was abruptly brought to a close, and he was sent home by his mistress to be nursed by his mother at Ordie Braes,—not, however, before he had contributed another Radical story, entitled "The Zingaro," a poem on "Bessy Bell and Mary Gray," and an article on "The Life and times of John Milton,' to Johnstone's Edinburgh Magazine. An old friend and schoolfellow, who saw him in the course of his visit to his mother's house, thus speaks of-him at the time: "Robert's city life had not spoiled him. His acquaintance with men and books had improved his mind without chilling his heart. At this time he was full of joy and hope. A bright literary life stretched before him. His conversation was gay and sparkling, and rushed forth like a stream that flows through flowery summer vales."

His health soon became re-established, and he then paid a visit to Edinburgh, during the period of the Grey Festival, —and there met his kind friend Mrs. Johnstone, William Tait, Robert Chambers, Robert Gilfillan, and others known in the literary world, by all of whom he was treated with kindness and hospitality. His search for literary employment, however, which was the main cause of his visit to Edinburgh, was in vain, and he returned home disappointed, though not hopeless.

He was about twenty when he went to Dundee, there to start a small circulating library. The project was not very successful; but while he kept it going, he worked harder than ever at literary improvement. He now wrote his Lyrics and Poems, which, on their publication, were extremely well received by the press. He also wrote for the liberal newspapers of the town, delivered lectures, made speeches, and extended his knowledge of men and society. In a letter to a friend, written in February, 1836, he says: "No wonder I am busy. I am at this moment writing poetry; I have almost half a volume of a novel written; I have to attend the meetings of the Kinloch Monument Committee; attend my shop; write some half-dozen articles a week for the Advertiser; and, to crown all, I have fallen in love." At last, however, finding the library to be a losing concern, he made it entirely over to the partner who had enjoined him, and quitted Dundee, with the intention of seeking out some literary employment by which he might live.

The Dundee speculation had involved Nicoll, and through him his mother, in debt, though to only a small amount. This debt weighed heavily on his mind, and he thus opened his heart in a highly characteristic letter to his parent about it; "This money of M's [a friend who had lent him a few pounds to commence business with] hangs like a millstone about my neck. If I had it paid, I would never borrow again from mortal man. But do not mistake me, mother; I am not one of those men who faint and falter in the great battle of life. God has given me too strong a heart for that. I look upon earth as a place where every man is set to struggle, and to work, that he may be made humble and pure-hearted, and fit for that better land for which earth is a preparation,—to which earth is the gate. Cowardly is that man who bows before the storm of life, —who runs not the needful race manfully, and with a cheerful heart. If men would but consider how little of real evil there is in all the ills of which they are so much afraid,—poverty included,—there would be more virtue and happiness, and less world and mammon worship on earth than there is. I think, mother, that to me has been given talent; and if so, that talent was given to make it useful to man. To man it cannot be made a source of happiness unless it be cultivated; and cultivated it cannot be unless, I think, little [here some words are obliterated]; and much and well of purifying and enlightening the soul. This is my philosophy; and its motto is,

> Despair, thy name is written on
> The roll of common men.

Half the unhappiness of life springs from looking back to 'griefs which are past, and forward with fear to the future. That is not my way. I am determined never to bend to the storm that is coming, and never to look back on it after it has passed. Fear not for me, dear mother,; for I feel myself daily growing firmer, and more hopeful in spirit. The more I think and reflect,—and thinking, instead of reading is now my occupation,—I feel that, whether I be growing richer or not, I am growing a wiser man, which is far better. Pain, poverty, and all the other wild beasts of life which so affright others, I am so bold as to think I could look in the face without shrinking, without losing respect for myself, faith in man's high destinies, and trust in God. There is a point which it costs much mental toil and struggling to gain, but which, when once gained, a man can look down from, as a traveler from a lofty mountain, on storms raging below, while he is walking in sunshine. That I have yet gained this point in life, I will not say, but I feel myself daily nearer it."

About the end of the year 1836, Nicoll succeeded, through the kind assistance of Mr. Tait, of Edinburgh, in obtaining an appointment as editor of an English newspaper, the Leeds Times. This was the kind of occupation for which he had longed; and he entered upon the arduous labors of his office with great spirit. During his year and a half of editorship his mind seemed to be on fire; and on the occasion of a Parliamentary contest in the town in which the paper was published, he wrote in a style which to some seemed bordering on frenzy. He neither gave nor took quarter. The man who went not so far as he did in political opinion was regarded by him as an enemy, and denounced accordingly. He dealt about his blows with almost savage violence. This novel and daring style, however, attracted attention to the paper, and its circulation rapidly increased, sometimes at the rate of two or three hundred a week. One can scarcely believe that the tender-hearted poet and the fierce political partisan were one and the same person, or that he who had so touchingly written

> I dare not scorn the meanest thing
> That on the earth doth crawl

should have held up his political opponents, in the words of another poet,

> To grinning scorn a sacrifice,
> And endless infamy.

But such inconsistencies are, we believe, reconcilable in the mental histories of ardent and impetuous men. Doubtless, had Nicoll lived, we should have found his sympathies becoming more enlarged, and embracing other classes besides those of only one form of political creed. One of his friends once asked him why, like Elliott, he did not write political poetry. His reply was he could not : when writing politics, he could be as *wild* as he chose; he felt a vehement desire, a feeling amounting almost to a wish, for vengeance upon the oppressor; but when he turned to poetry, a softening influence came over him, and he could be bitter no longer.

His literary labors while in Leeds were enormous. He was not satisfied with writing from four to five columns weekly for the paper; but he was engaged at the same time in writing a long poem, a novel, and in furnishing leading articles for a new Sheffield newspaper. In the midst of this tremendous labor, he found time to go down to Dundee to get married to the young woman with whom he had fallen in love. The comfort of his home was thus increased, though his labors continued as before. They soon told upon his health. The clear and ruddy complexion of the youth grew pallid; the erect, manly gait became stooping; the firm step faltered; the lustrous eye dimmed; and health gave place to debility: the worm of disease was already at his heart and gnawing away his vitals. His cough, which had never entirely left him since his illness, brought on by self-imposed privation and study while at Perth, again appeared in an aggravated form; his breath grew short and thick; his cheeks became shrunken; and the hectic flush which rarely deceives, soon made its appearance. He appeared as if suddenly to grow old; his shoulders became contracted; he appeared to wither up, and the sap of life to shrink from his veins. Need we detail the melancholy progress of a disease which is, in this country, the annual fate of thousands?

As Nicoll's illness increased, he expressed an anxious desire to see his mother, and she was informed of it accordingly. She was very poor, and little able to afford an expensive journey to Yorkshire by coach; nevertheless she contrived to pay the visit to her son. Afterwards, when a friend inquired how she had been able to incur the expense, as poor Robert was in no condition to assist her even to the extent of the coach fare, her simple but noble reply was, "Indeed, Mr. ——, I shore for the siller." The true woman, worthy mother of so worthy a son, earned as a reaper the means of honestly and independently fulfilling her boy's dying wish, and the ardent desire of her own loving heart. So soon as she set eyes on him on her arrival at Leeds, she felt at once that his days were numbered.

It almost seemed as if, while the body of the poet decayed, his mind grew more active and excitable, and that, as the physical powers become more weakened, his sense of sympathy became more keen. .When he engaged in conversation upon a subject which he loved,—upon human progress, the amelioration of the lot of the poor, the emancipation of mind,—he seemed as one inspired. Usually quiet and reserved, he would on such occasions work himself into a state of the greatest excitement. His breast heaved, his whole frame was agitated, and while he spoke, his large lustrous eyes beamed with unwonted fire. His wife feared such outbursts, which were followed by sleepless nights and the aggravation of his complaint.

Throughout the whole progress of his disease, down to the time when he left Leeds, Nicoll did not fail to produce his usual weekly quota of literary labor. They little know, who have not learned from experience, what pains and anxieties, what sorrows and cares, lie hid under the columns of a daily or weekly newspaper. No galley-slave at the oar tugs harder for life than the man who writes in newspapers for the indispensable of daily bread. The press is ever at his heels, crying, "Give, give!" and well or ill, gay or sad, the editor must supply the usual complement of "leading article." The last articles poor Nicoll wrote for the paper were prepared whilst he sat up in bed, propped about by pillows. A friend entered just as he had finished them, and found him in a state of high excitement; the veins on his forehead were turgid and his eyes bloodshot; his whole frame quivered, and the perspiration streamed from him. He had produced a pile of blotted and blurred manuscript, written in his usual energetic manner. It was immediately after sent to press. These were the last leaders he wrote. They were shortly after followed by a short address to the readers of the paper, in which he took a short but affectionate farewell of them, stating that he went "to try the effect of his native air, as a last chance for life."

Almost at the moment of his departure from Leeds, an incident occurred which must have been exceedingly affecting to Nicoll, as it was to those who witnessed it. Ebenezer Elliott, the "Corn-Law Rhymer," who entertained an enthusiastic admiration for the young poet, had gone over from Sheffield to deliver a short course of lectures to the Leeds Literary institution, and promised himself the pleasure of a kindly interview with Robert Nicoll. On inquiring about him, after the delivery of his first lecture, he was distressed to learn the sad state to which he was reduced. "No words," says Elliott, in his letter to the writer of this memoir, "can express the pain I felt when informed, on my return to my inn, that he was dying, and that if I would see him I must reach his dwelling before eight o'clock next morning, at which hour he would depart by railway for Edinburgh, in the hope that his native air might restore him. I was five minutes too late to see him at his house, but I followed him to the station, where about a minute before the train started he was pointed out to me in one of the carriages, seated, I believe, between his wife and his mother. I stood on the step of the carriage and told him my name. He gasped—they all three wept; but I heard not his voice."

The invalid reached Newhaven, near Leith, sick, exhausted, distressed, and dying. He was received under the hospitable roof of Mrs. Johnstone, his early friend, who tended him as if he had been her own child. Other friends gathered around him, and contributed to smooth his dying couch. It was not the least of Nicoll's distresses, that towards his latter end he was tortured by the horrors of destitution; not so much for himself as for those who were dependent on him for their daily bread. A generous gift of £50 was forwarded by Sir William Molesworth, but Nicoll did not live to enjoy the bounty; in a few days after, he breathed his last in the arms of his wife.

The remains of Robert Nicoll rest in a narrow spot in Newhaven churchyard. No stone marks his resting-place; only a small green mound that has been watered by the tears of the loved he has left behind him. On that spot the eye of God dwells; and around the precincts of the poet's grave, the memories of friends still hover with a fond and melancholy regret.

Robert Nicoll was no ordinary man; Ebenezer Elliott has said of him, "Burns at his age had done nothing like him." His poetry is the very soul of pathos, tenderness, and sublimity. We might almost style him the Scottish Keats; though he was much more real and lifelike, and more definite in his aims and purposes, than Keats was. There is a truthful earnestness in the poetry of Nicoll, which comes home to the universal heart. Especially does he give utterance to that deep poetry which lives in the heart, and murmurs in the lot of the poor man. He knew and felt it all, and found for it a voice in his exquisite lyrics. These have truth written on their very front;—as Nicoll said truly to a friend, "I have written my heart in my poems; and rude, unfinished, and hasty as they are, it can be read there."

"We are lowly," "The Ha' Bible," "The Hero," "The Bursting of the Chain," "I dare not scorn," and numerous other pieces which might be named, are inferior to few things of their kind in the English language. "The Ha' Bible " is perhaps not unworthy to take rank with "The Cotter's Saturday Night" of Robert Burns. It is as follows:

THE HA' BIBLE.

Chief of the Household Gods
    Which hallow Scotland's lowly cottage homes!
While looking on thy signs,
    That speak, though dumb, deep thought upon me comes,—
With glad yet solemn dreams my heart is stirred,
Like Childhood's when it hears the carol of a bird!

The Mountains old and hoar,—
    The chainless Winds,—the Streams so pure and free,—
The God-enameled flowers,—
    The waving forest,--the eternal Sea,—
The Eagle floating o'er the mountain's brow,--
Are Teachers all; but oh! they are not such as thou!

O, I could worship thee!
    Thou art a gift a God of love might give;
For Love and Hope and Joy
    In thy Almighty-written pages live!—
The Slave who reads shall never crouch again;
For, mind-inspired by thee, he bursts his feeble chain!

God! Unto Thee I kneel,
    And thank Thee! Thou unto my native land—
Yea, to the outspread Earth--
    Hast stretched in love Thy Everlasting hand,
And Thou hast given Earth and Sea and Air,--
Yea, all that heart can ask of Good and Pure and Fair!

And, Father, Thou hast spread
    Before men's eyes this Charter of the Free,
That all Thy Book might read,
    And Justice love, and Truth and Liberty.
The Gift was unto Men,—the Giver God!
Thou Slave! it stamps thee Man,—go spurn thy weary load,

Thou doubly precious Book!
    Unto thy light what doth not Scotland owe?--
Thou teachest Age to die,
    And Youth in Truth unsullied up to grow!
In lowly homes a Comforter art thou,—
A sunbeam sent from God,—an Everlasting bow!

O'er thy broad ample page
    How many dim and aged eyes have pored?
How many hearts o'er thee
    In silence deep and holy have adored?
How many Mothers, by their Infants' bed
Thy Holy, Blessed, Pure, Child-loving words have read!

And o'er thee soft young hands
 Have oft in truthful plighted Love been joined,
And thou to wedded hearts
 Hast been a bond,--an altar of the mind!--
 Above all kingly power or kingly law
May Scotland reverence aye the Bible of the Ha' !!

SARAH MARGARET FULLER.

FEW women of her time have created a livelier interest throughout the literary world than Margaret Fuller, of Boston, has done. The tragic circumstances connected with her death, which involved at the same time the destruction of her husband and child, have served to deepen that interest; and therefore it is that the memoirs of her life and labors, edited by Emerson and Ellery Channing, have been hailed in England as among the most welcome books which have come across the Atlantic for many a day.

Margaret Fuller had not done much as a writer; but she had given great promise of what she could do. Her "Woman in the Nineteenth Century," and a collection of papers on Literature and Art, originally published in the American periodical called "The Dial," with the book entitled "A Summer on the Lakes," include her principal writings, and even these are of a comparatively fragmentary character; it was chiefly through her remarkable gifts of conversation that she was known and admired among her contemporaries; it was to this that her great influence among them was attributable; and, like John Sterling, Charles Pemberton, and others of kindred gifts, the wonder to many who never came within the reach of her personal influence is how to account for the literary reputation she had achieved, upon a basement of writings so slender and so incomplete. It was the individual influence, the magnetic attraction, which she exercised over the minds within her reach, which accounts for the whole.

From early years Margaret Fuller was regarded as a kind of prodigy. Her father, Mr. Timothy Fuller, who was a lawyer and a representative of Massachusetts in Congress, from 1817 to 1825, devoted great pains —far too great pains—to the intellectual culture of the little girl. Her brain was unmercifully taxed, to the serious injury of her health. In after-life she compared herself to the poor changeling, who turned from the door of her adopted home, sat down on a stone, and so pitied herself that she wept. The poor girl was kept up late at her tasks, and went to bed with stimulated brain and nerves, unable to sleep. She was haunted by spectral illusions, nightmares, and horrid dreams; while by day she suffered from headaches, weakness and nervous affections of all kinds. In short, Margaret Fuller had *no natural childhood.* Her mind did not grow,—it was forced. Thoughts did not come to her,—they were thrust into her. A child should expand in the sun, but this dear little victim was put under a glass frame, and plied with all manner of artificial heat. She was fed, not on "milk for babes," but on the strongest of meat.

Thus Margaret Fuller leaped into precocious maturity. She was petted and praised as a "prodigy." She lived among books.—read Latin at six years old, and was early familiar with Virgil, Horace, and Ovid. Then she went on to Greek. At eight years of age devoured Shakespeare, Cervantes, and Moliere! Her world was books. A child without toys, without romps, without laughter; but with abundant nightmare and sick-headaches! The wonder is, that this monstrously unnatural system of forced intellectual culture did not kill outright! "I complained of my head," she said afterwards; "for a sense of dullness and suffocation, if not pain, was there constantly." She had nervous fevers, convulsions, and so on; but she lived through it all, and was plunged into still deeper studies. After a course of boarding-school, she returned home at fifteen to devote herself to Ariosto, Helvetius, Sismondi, Brown's Philosophy, De Stael, Epictetus, Racine, Castilian Ballads, Locke, Byron, Sir William Temple, Rousseau, and a host of other learned writers!

Conceive a girl of fifteen immersed in all this farrago of literature and philosophy! She had an eye to politics, too; and in her letters to friends notices the accession of Duke Nicholas, and its effect on the Holy Alliance and the liberties of Europe! Then she goes through a course of the Italian poets, accompanied by her sick-headache. She lies in bed one afternoon, from dinner till tea, "reading Rammohun Roy's book, and framing dialogues aloud on every argument beneath the sun." She had her dreams of the affections, too,—indulging largely in sentimentality and romance, as most young girls will do. She adored the moon,—fell in love with other girls, and dreamed often the other subject uppermost in most growing girls' minds.

This wonderfully cultivated child, as might be expected, ran some risk of being spoiled. She was herself brilliant, and sought equal brilliancy in others. She had no patience with mediocrity, and regarded it with feelings akin to contempt. But this unamiable feeling she gradually unlearned, as greater experience and larger-heartedness taught her wisdom,—a kind of wisdom, by the way, which

is not found in books. The multitude regarded her, at this time, as
rather haughty and supercilious,—fond of saying clever and sarcas-
tic things at their expense,—and also as very inquisitive and anxious
to "read characters." But it is hard to repress or dwarf the loving
nature of a woman. She was always longing for affection, for sympathy, for confidence, among her more valued friends. She wished to be
"comprehended,"—she looked on herself as a "femme incomprise,"
as the French term it. Even her sarcasm was akin to love. She was
always making new confidants, and drawing out their heart-secrets,
as she revealed her own.

The family removed from Cambridgeport, where she was born, to
Cambridge, where they remained till 1833, when they went to reside
at Groton. Margaret had by this time written verses which friends
deemed worthy of publication, and several appeared. But her spirit
and soul, which gave such living power to her conversation, usually
evaporated in the attempt to commit her thoughts to writing. Of
this she often complains. "After all," she says in one of her letters,
"this writing is mighty dead. O for my dear old Greeks, who talked
everything! Again she said : " Conversation is my natural element.
I need to be called out, and never think alone without imagining
some companion. Whether this be nature, or the force of circumstances, I know not; it is my habit, and bespeaks a second rate
mind."

But she was a splendid talker;—a New England Corinne,—an im-
provisatrice of unrivaled powers. Her writings give no idea of her
powers of speech,—of the brilliancy with which she would strike a
vein of happy thought, and bring it to the daylight. Her talk was
decidedly masculine, critical, common-sense, full of ideas, yet withal,
graceful and sparkling. She is said to have had a kind of prophetic
insight into characters, and drew out, by a strong attractive power
in herself, as by a moral magnet, all their best gifts to the light.
"She was," says one friend, "like a moral Paganini : she played
always on a single string, drawing from each its peculiar music,—
bringing wild beauty from the slender wire no less than from the
deep-sounding harpstring."

In 1832 she was busy with German literature, and read Goethe,
Tieck, Körner, and Schiller. The thought and beauty of these works
filled her mind and fascinated her imagination. She also went
through "Plato's Dialogues." She began to have infinite longings for
something unknown and unattainable, and gave vent to her feelings
in such thoughts as this : "I shut Goethe's 'Second Residence in
Rome,' with an earnest desire to live as he did,—always to have
some engrossing object of pursuit. I sympathize deeply with a
mind in that state. While mine is being used up by ounces, I wish
pailfuls might be poured into it. I am dejected and uneasy when
I see no results from my daily existence, but I am suffocated and
lost when I have not the bright feeling of progression." ____.

But she was always full of projects, which remained such. She meditated writing "six historical tragedies, *the plans* of three of which are quite perfect." She had also "a favorite *plan*" of a series of tales illustrative of Hebrew history. She also meditated writing a life of Goethe. She tried her hand on the tragedies. Alas! what a vast difference is there, she confesses, between conception and execution! She proceeded, as Coleridge calls it, "to take an account of her stock," but fell back again almost in despair. "With me," she says, "it has ended in the most humiliating sense of poverty; and only just enough pride is left to keep your poor friend off the parish." But in this confession you will find the germs of deep wisdom. She now, more than ever, felt the need of self-culture. "Shall I ever be fit for anything," she asked, "till I have absolutely re-educated myself? Am I, can I make myself, fit to write an account of half a century of the existence of one of the master-spirits of this world? It seems as if I had been very arrogant to dare to think of it." She nevertheless proceeded to accumulate materials for the life of Goethe, which, however, was never written.

Yet often would the woman come uppermost? She longed to possess *a home for her heart.* Capable of ardent love, her affections were thrown back upon herself, to become stagnant, and for a while to grow bitter there. She could not help feeling how empty and worthless were all the attainments and triumphs of mere intellect. A woman's heart must be satisfied, else there is no true, deep happiness of repose for her. She longed to be loved *as a woman,* rather than as a mere human being. What woman does not? The lamentation that she was not so loved broke out bitterly from time to time. She knew that she was not beautiful; and, conceal her chagrin as she might, she felt the defect keenly. There was weakness in this, but she could not master it.

In her journal is a bitter sentence on this topic, the meaning of which cannot be misunderstood. She is commenting on the character of Mignon, by Goethe: "Of a disposition that requires the most refined, the most exalted tenderness, without charms to inspire it, poor Mignon! fear not the transition through death; no penal fires can have in store worse torments than thou art familiar with already." Again she writes, in the month of May: "When all things are blossoming, it seems so strange not to blossom too,—that the quick thought within cannot remold its tenement. Man is the slowest aloe, and I am such a shabby plant of coarse tissue. I hate not to be beautiful, when all around is so." She writes elsewhere: "I know the deep yearnings of the heart, and the bafflings of time will be felt again; and then I shall long for some dear hand to hold. But I shall never forget that my curse is nothing, compared with those who have entered into these relations, but not made them real; who only seem husbands, wives, and friends." But she endeavors to force herself to feel content: "I have no child; but now, as I look on these lovely children of a human birth, what low and neutralizing cares they bring with them to the mother! The children of the Muse come quicker, and have not on them the taint of earthly corruption." Alas! It is evidently a poor attempt at self-comfort.

Her personal appearance may be noted. A florid complexion, with a tendency to robustness, of which she was painfully conscious, and endeavored to compress by artificial methods, which did additional injury to her already wretched health. Rather under the middle size, with fair complexion, and strong, fair hair. She was near-sighted, from constant reading when a child, and peered oddly, incessantly opening and shutting her eyelids with great rapidity. She spoke through the nose. From her passionate worship of Beauty in all things, perhaps she dwelt with the more bitterness on her own personal short-comings. The first impression on meeting her was not agreeable; but continued intercourse made many fast friends and ardent admirers,—that is, intellectual admirers. An early attack of illness destroyed the fineness of her complexion. "My own vanity," she said of this, "was severely wounded; but I recovered, and made up mind to be bright and ugly. I think I may say, I never loved. I but see my possible life reflected in the clouds. The bridal spirit of many a spirit, when first it was wed, I have shared, but said adieu before the wine was poured out at the banquet."

The Fuller family removed to Groton in 1833, and two years after Margaret's father died suddenly of cholera. He left no will behind him; there was little property to will,—only enough to maintain the widow and educate the children. Margaret was thrown into fresh lamentations,—wished she had been a man, in order to take charge of the family; but she "always hated the din of such affairs." About this time she had made the acquaintance of Miss Martineau, then in the States, and clung to her as an "intellectual guide," hoping to be "comprehended" by her. She had strongly desired to accompany Miss Martineau back to England, but the sad turn in the family affairs compelled her to give up the project; and she went to Boston instead, to teach Latin, Italian, and French, in Mr. Alcott's school. She afterwards went to teach, as principal, in another school at Providence. She still read tremendously,—almost living upon books, and tormented by a "terrible feeling in the head." She had a "distressing weight on the top of the brain," and seemingly was "able to think with only the lower part of the head." "All my propensities," she once said "have a tendency to make my head worse; it is a bad head,—as bad as if I were a great man."

Amid all this bodily pain and disease, she suffered moral agony, —heartache for long days and weeks,—and on self-examination, she was further "shocked to find how vague and superficial is all my knowledge." Some may say there is a degree of affectation in all this; but it is the fate of the over-cultivated, without any solid basis of wisdom; they are ever longing after further revelations, greater light,—to pry into the unseen, to aim after the unattainable. Hence profound regrets and life-long lamentations. The circlet which adorns the brow of genius, though it may glitter before the gazer's eye, has spiked thorns for the brow of her who wears it, and the wounds they make bleed inwards. Poor Margaret!

Emerson's memoir of his intercourse with Margaret Fuller is by far the most interesting part of the volume. He was repelled by her at first, being a man rather given to silence; but she gradually won upon him as upon others, and her bright speech at length reached his heart. He met her first in the society of Miss Martineau, and often afterward in the company of others, and alone. He was struck by the *night side* of her nature;—her speculations in mythology and demonology; in French Socialism; her belief in the ruling influence of planets; her sympathy with sortilege; her notions as to the talismanic influence of gems; and her altogether mystic apprehensions. She was strangely affected by dreams, was a somnambule, was always full of presentiments. In short, as Emerson says, "there was somewhat *a little pagan* about her." She found no rest for the sole of her restless foot, except in music, of which she was a passionate lover. Take a few instances of her strange meditations. "When first I met with the name Leila," she said, "I knew from the very look and sound, it was music; I knew that it meant night,—night, which brings out stars as sorrow brings out truths." Later on, she wrote: "My days at Milan were not unmarked. I have known some happy hours, but they all lead to sorrow, and not only the cups of wine, but of milk, seem drugged with poison for me. It does not seem to be my fault, this destiny. I do not court these things,—they come. I am a poor magnet, with power to be wounded by the bodies I attract.

But Emerson, like everybody else, was especially attracted by Margaret's powers of conversation. "She wore her circle of friends, as a necklace of diamonds about her neck. The confidences given her were their best, and she held to them. She was an active, inspiring correspondent, and all the art, the thought, and the nobleness in New England seemed at that moment related to her, and she to it. Persons were her game, especially if marked by fortune, or character, or success; to such was she sent. She addressed them with a hardihood,—almost a haughty assurance,—queen-like. She drew her companions to surprising confessions. She was the wedding-guest to whom the long-pent story must be told ; and they were not less struck, on reflection, at the suddenness of the friendship which had established, in one day, new and permanent covenants. She extorted the secret of life, which cannot be told without setting mind and heart in a glow; and thus had the best of those she saw; the test of her eloquence was its range. It told on children and on old people; on men of the world, and on sainted maids.

She could hold them all by the honey tongue. The Concord stage-coachman distinguished her by his respect; and the chambermaid was pretty sure to confide to her, on the second day, her homely romance." But she lived fast. In society she was always on the stretch. She was in jubilant spirits in the morning and ended the day with nervous headache, whose spasms produced total prostration. She was the victim of disease and pain. "She read and wrote in bed, and believed she could understand anything better when she was ill. Pain acted like a girdle, to give tension to her powers." Her enjoyment consisted of brief but intense moments. The rest was a void. Emerson says: "When I found she lived at a rate so much faster than mine, and which was violent compared with mine, I foreboded a rash and painful crisis, and had a feeling as if a voice had said, *Stand from under!* as if, a little farther on, this destiny was threatened with jars and reverses, which no friendship could avert or console."

There was one very prominent feature in Margaret Fuller, which she could never conceal, and that was her intense individuality,— some would call it self-esteem: she was always thoroughly possessed by herself. She could not hide the *"mountainous me,"* as Emerson calls it. In enumerating the merits of some one, she would say, "He appreciates me." In the coolest way, she boasted, "I now know all the people worth knowing in America, and I find no intellect comparable to my own." She idealized herself as a queen, and dwelt upon the idea that she was not her parents' child, but a European princess confided to their care. "I take my natural position always," she said to a friend; "and the more I see, the more I feel that it is regal. Without throne, scepter, or guards, still a queen." In all this there was exhibited a very strong leaning towards a weak side.

Yet, at other times, she was strongly conscious of her imperfections. She was impatient of her weakness in production. "I feel within myself," she said, "an immense force, but I cannot bring it out." Notwithstanding her "arrogant talk," as Emerson called it, and her ambition to play the Mirabeau among her friends, she felt her defect in creative power. Her numerous works remained projects. She was the victim of Lord Bacon's idols of the cave. She was a genius of impulse, but wanted the patience to elaborate. "How can I ever write," she asked, "with this impatience of detail? I shall never be an artist; I have no patient love of execution; I am delighted with my sketch; but if I try to finish it I am chilled. Never was there a great sculptor who did not love to chip the marble." And then she attributed her inability to sex. Speaking of the life of thought, she said: "Women, under any circumstances, can scarce do more than dip the foot in this broad and deep river; they have not strength to contend with the current. It is easy for women to be heroic in action; but when it comes to interrogating God, the

universe. the soul, and, above all, trying to live above their own
hearts, they dart down to their nest like so many larks, and if they
cannot find them, fret like the French Corinne." A little later she
says: "I shall write better, but never, I think, so well as I talk; for
then I feel inspired. The means are pleasant; my voice excites me,
my pen never. I want force to be either a genius or a character."

She had, however, a genuine fund of practical benevolence about
her. She visited the prisons and penitentiaries on many occasions,
for the purpose of restoring to new life and virtue the poor, degraded
women confined there. Behind all her wit, there was always a
fountain of woman's tears ready to flow. She had a passionate love
of truth, and ardent thirst for it. "In the chamber of death I prayed in early years, 'Give me Truth; cheat me by no illusion.' O,
the granting of this prayer is sometimes terrible to me! I walk on
the burning plowshares, and they sear my feet. Yet nothing but
Truth will do." And she might be said almost to worship beauty,—
in art, in literature, in music. "Dear Beauty!" she would say,
"where, where, amid these morasses and pine-barrens, shall we make
thee a temple? where find a Greek to guard it,—clear-eyed, deep-
thoughted, and delicate enough to appreciate the relations and gra-
dations which nature always observes?"

We can only notice very briefly the remaining leading events in
Margaret Fuller's life. There was not much dramatic character in
them, except towards their close. The student's story is generally a
quiet one; it is an affair of private life, of personal intimacies and
friendships. She went on teaching young ladies, conducting con-
versation-classes, and occasionally making translations from the
German for the booksellers. The translation of Eckermann's "Conversations with Goethe" was by her, as also that of the "Letters of
Gunderode and Bettine." In 1843 she traveled into Michigan, and
shortly afterwards published her "Summer on the Lakes." She then
became a writer for "The Dial," an able Boston review, chiefly supported by Emerson, Brownson, and a few more of the "Transcendental writers of America. There she reviewed German and English
books, and first published "The Great Lawsuit, or Woman in the
Nineteenth Century," an eloquent expression of discontent at the
social position of woman. Her criticisms of American books were
not relished and often gave great offense. The other critics said of
her, that she thought that books, like brown stout, were improved
by the motion of a ship, and that she would praise nothing unless
it had been imported from abroad. She certainly gave a less hearty
recognition to merit in American than in German or English books.
Afterwards, she went to New York, to perform an engagement on
Mr. Horace Greeley's newspaper, the New York Tribune. But she
had a contempt for newspaper writing, saying of it: "What a vul-
garity there seems in this writing for the multitude! We know not
yet, have not made ourselves known, to a single soul, and shall we
address those still more unknown?"

The deep secret of her heart again and again comes uppermost in her communications to her bosom friends. A living female writer has said, that, though few may confess it, the human heart may know peace, content, serene endurance, and even thankfulness ; but it never does and never can know *happiness*, the sense of complete, full-rounded bliss, except in the joy of a happy love. The most ardent attachment of woman for others of their own sex cannot supply the want. Margaret Fuller tried this, but it failed, as you may see from her repeated complaints. "Pray for me," she said, "that I may have a little peace,—some green and flowery spot amid which my thoughts may *rest;* yet not upon fallacy, but upon something genuine. *I am deeply homesick, yet where is that home?* If not on earth, why should we look to heaven? I would fain truly live wherever I must abide, and bear with full energy on my lot, whatever it is. Yet my hand is often languid, and my heart is slow. I would be gone; but whither? I know not. If I cannot make this spot of ground yield the corn and roses, famine must be my lot forever and ever, surely." *This* is the dart within the heart, as well as I can tell it : "At moments the music of the universe, which daily I am upheld by hearing, seems to stop. I fall like a bird when the sun is eclipsed, not looking for such darkness. The sense of my individual law—that lamp of life—flickers. I am repelled in what is most natural to me. I feel as, when a suffering child, I would go and lie with my face to the ground, to sob away my little life." "Once again I am willing to take up *the cross of loneliness.* Resolves are idle, but the anguish of my soul has been deep. It will not be easy to profane life by rhetoric." In a pathetic prayer, found among her papers, she says : "*I am weary of thinking.* I suffer great fatigue from living. O God, take me! Take me wholly. It is not that I repine, my Father, but I sink from want of rest, and none will shelter me. Thou knowest it all. Bathe me in the living waters of thy love."

Thus the consciousness of an unfulfilled destiny hung over the poor sufferer, and she could not escape from it ; she felt as if destined to tread the wine-press of life alone. To hear the occasional plaintive tone of sorrow in her thought and speech, Mr. Channing beautifully says, was ' like the wail of an Æolian harp, heard at intervals from some upper window." And amid all this smothered agony of the heart, disease was constantly preying on her. Headache, rooted in one spot,—fixed between the eyebrows,—till it grew real torture. The black and white guardians, depicted on Etruscan monuments, were always fighting for her life. In the midst of beautiful dreams, the "great vulture would come, and fix his iron talons on the brain,"—a state of physical health which was not mended by her habit of drinking strong potations of tea and coffee in almost limitless quantities.

At length, in search of health, Margaret resolved to accomplish her long-meditated, darling enterprise, of a voyage to Europe;—to the Old World, where her thoughts lived—to England, France, Germany, and Rome. She left New York in the summer of 1846, in the *Cambria*, and on reaching England sent home many delightful, though rapid, sketches of the people she had seen, and the places she had visited. These letters are, to us, the most delightful part of the volumes; perhaps because she speaks of people who are so much better known to us than her American contemporaries. In England and Scotland, she saw Wordsworth, De Quincey, Dr. Chalmers, Andrew Combe, the Howitts, Dr. Southwood Smith, and, above all, Carlyle, of whom she gives an admirable sketch, drawn to the life. In England, also, she first formed an acquaintance with Mazzini, which she afterwards renewed, amid most interesting circumstances, at Rome, during the tumult of the siege. At Paris she made the personal acquaintance of George Sand, of whom she gives a lifelike description, and saw many other notorieties of that time.

But she longed to be at Rome; and sped southward. She seems immediately to have plunged into the political life of the city. But her means were cramped, and she longed for a little money." Yet what she had, she was always ready to give away to those who were more in need than herself. "Nothing less than two or three years," she says, ' free from care and forced labor would heal my hurts, and renew my life-blood at its source. Since destiny will not grant me that I hope she will not leave me long in the world, for I am tired of keeping myself up in the water without corks, and without strength to swim. I should like to go to sleep and be born again into a state where my young life should not be prematurely taxed."

All the great events of 1847 and 1848 occurred while Margaret Fuller remained in the Eternal City. She was there when the Pope took the initiative in the reforms of that convulsed period; witnessed the rejoicings and the enthusiasm of the people; then the reaction, the tumult, the insurrection, and the war. Amidst all this excitement, she is "weary." "The shifting scenes entertain poorly. I want some scenes of natural beauty; and, imperfect as love is, I want human beings to love, as I suffocate without." Then came the enthusiastic entrance of Gioberti into Rome, then Mazzini, then ensued the fighting. Margaret looked down from her window on the terrible battle before St. Angelo, between the Romans and the French. Mazzini found her out of her lodgings, and had her appointed by the "Roman Commisison for the succor of the Wounded" to the charge of the hospital of the Fata-Bene Fratelli. She there busied herself as a nurse of those heroic wounded,—the flower of the Italian youth. But the French entered, and she had to fly. "I cannot tell you," she writes, "what I endured in leaving Rome; abandoning the wounded soldiers; knowing that there is no provision made for them, when they rise from the beds where they have been thrown by a noble courage, where they have suffered with a noble patience. Some of the poorer men, who rise bereft even of the right arm,—and one having lost both the right arm and the right leg,—I could have provided for with a small sum. Could I have sold my hair, or blood from my arm, I would have done it. These poor men are left helpless, in the power of a mean and vindictive foe. You felt so oppressed in the slave states ; imagine what I felt at seeing all the noblest youth, all the genius of this dear land, again enslaved."

. So the battle was lost! Margaret Fuller fled from Rome to her child at Rieti. Her child? yes. She had married! The dream of her life had ended, and she was now a wife and a mother. But in this sweet, new relationship, she enjoyed but a brief term of happiness. Her connection with Count Ossoli arose out of an accidental meeting with him in the church of St. Peter's, after vesper service. He waited upon her to her dwelling; returned; cultivated her acquaintance; offered her his hand, and was refused. But Ossoli was a Liberal, and moved in the midst of the strife. He had frequent opportunities of seeing Margaret, pressed his suit, and was finally accepted. There did not seem to be much in common between them. He was considerably her junior; but he loved her sincerly, and that was enough for her.

The marriage was kept secret for a time, because the Marquis's property might have gone from him at once, had his marriage with a Protestant become known while the ecclesiastical influence was paramount at Rome. But when the Liberal cause had suffered defeat, there was no longer any need of concealment. Ossoli had lost all; and the marriage was confessed. Margaret had left her child in safety at Rieti, to watch over her husband, who was at Rome, engaged in the defense of the city against the French; and we have seen how she was engaged while there. She returned to her child, whom she found ill, and half starved; but her maternal care made all right again. Writing to her mother, she said: "The immense gain to me is my relation with the child. I thought the mother's heart lived within me before, but it did not; I knew nothing about it." "He is to me a source of ineffable joy,—far purer, deeper, than anything I ever felt before,—like what Nature had sometimes given, but more intimate, more sweet. He loves me very much; his little heart clings to mine."

Margaret is at length happy; but how brief the time it lasted! The poor Marquis, with his wife and child, must leave Florence, where they for a brief time resided after their flight from Rome; and they resolved to embark for the United States in May, 1850. Writing beforehand, she said: "I have a vague expectation of some crisis,—I know not what. But it has long seemed that in the year 1850 I should stand on a plateau in the ascent of life, where I should be allowed to pause for a while, and take more clear and commanding views than ever before. Yet my life proceeds as regularly as the fates of a Greek tragedy, and I can but accept the pages as they turn." And at the close of a letter to her mother, she said: "*I* hope we shall be able to pass some time together yet in this world. But if God decrees otherwise,—here and hereafter, my dearest mother, I am your loving child, Margaret." Ossoli had never been at sea before, and he had an undefined dread of it. A fortune-teller, when he was a boy, had uttered a singular prophecy of him, and warned him to "beware of the sea."

The omens prove true. Everything went amiss on the ill-fated voyage. The captain sickened and died of small-pox. The disease then seized the child, Angelino, whose life was long despaired of. But he recovered, and the coast of America drew nigh. On the eve of the landing, a heavy gale arose, and the ship struck on Fire Island Beach, on the Long Island shore.

"At the first jar, the passengers, knowing but too well its fatal import, sprang from their berths. Then came the cry of 'Cut away,' followed by the crash of falling timbers, and the thunder of the seas, as they broke across the deck. In a moment more the cabin skylight was dashed in pieces by the breakers, and the spray, pouring down like a cataract, put out the lights; while the cabin-door was wrenched from its fastenings, and the waves swept in and out. One scream—one only—was heard from Margaret's state-room; and Sumner and Mrs. Hasty, meeting in the cabin, clasped hands, with these few but touching words: 'We must die.' 'Let us die calmly, then.' 'I hope so, Mrs. Hasty.' It was in the gray dusk, and amid the awful tumult, that the companions in misfortune met. The side of the cabin to the leeward had already settled under water; and furniture, trunks, and fragments of the skylight were floating to and fro, while the inclined position of the floor made it difficult to stand; and every sea, as it broke over the bulwarks, splashed in through the open roof. The windward cabin-wall, however, still yielding partial shelter, and against it, seated side by side, half-leaning backwards, with feet braced upon the long table, they awaited what next should come. At first, Nino, alarmed at the uproar, the darkness, and the rushing water, while shivering with the wet, cried passionately; but soon his mother, wrapping him in such garments as were at hand, and folding him to her bosom, sang him to sleep. Celeste, too, was in an agony of terror, till Ossoli, with soothing words, and a long and fervent prayer, restored her to self-control and trust. Then calmly they rested, side by side, exchanging kindly partings, and sending messages to friends, if any should survive to be their bearer."

A long night of agony passed, and at last the tragedy drew to a close :

"It was now past three o'clock, and as, with the rising tide, the gale swelled once more to its former violence, the remnants of the bark fast yielded to the resistless waves. The cabin went by the board, the after-parts broke up, and the stern settled out of sight. Soon, too, the forecastle was filled with water, and the helpless little band were driven to the deck, where they clustered round the fore-mast. Presently, even this frail support was loosened from the hull, and rose and fell with every billow. It was plain to all that the final moment drew swiftly nigh. Of the four seamen who still stood by the passengers, three were as efficient as any among the crew of the *Elizabeth*. These were the steward, carpenter and cook. The fourth was an old sailor, who, broken down by hardship and sickness, was going home to die. These men were once again per-suading Margaret, Ossoli, and Celeste, to try the planks, which they still held ready in the lee [of the ship ; and the steward by whom Nino was so much beloved, had just taken the little fellow in his arms, with the pledge that he would save him or die, when a sea struck the forecastle, and the foremast fell, carrying with it the deck and all upon it. The steward and Angelino were washed upon the beach, both dead, though warm, some twenty minutes after. The cook and carpenter were thrown far upon the foremast, and saved themselves by swimming. Celeste and Ossoli caught for a moment by the rigging, but the next wave swallowed them up. Margaret sank at once. When last seen, she had been seated at the foot of the foremast, still clad in her white night-dress, with her hair fallen loose upon her shoulders. It was over,—that twelve hours' com-munion, face to face, with death ! It was over ! and the prayer was granted, 'that Ossoli, Angelino, and I may go together, and that the anguish may be brief !'

"The only one of Margaret's [treasures which reached the shore was the lifeless form of little Angelino. When the body, stripped of every rag by the waves, was rescued from the surf, a sailor took it reverently in his arms, and, wrapping it in his neckcloth, bore it to the nearest house. There, when washed, and dressed in a child's frock found in Margaret's trunk, it was laid upon a bed ; and as the rescued seamen gathered round their late playfellow and pet, there were few dry eyes in the circle. The next day, borne upon their shoulders in a chest, it was buried in a hollow among the sand-bills."

And thus terribly ended the tragedy of Margaret Fuller's life.

SARAH MARTIN.

A MONG the distinguished women in the humble ranks of society, who have pursued a loving, hopeful, benevolent, and beautiful way through life, the name of Sarah Martin will long be remembered. Not many of such women come into the full light of the world's eye. Quiet and silence befit their lot. The best of their labors are done in secret, and are never noised abroad. Often the most beautiful traits of a woman's character are confided but to one dear breast, and lie treasured there. There are comparatively few women who display the sparkling brilliancy of a Margaret Fuller, and whose names are noised abroad like hers on the wings of fame. But the number of women is very great who silently pursue their duty in thankfulness, who labor on,—each in their little home circle,—training the minds of growing youth for active life, molding future men and women for society and for each other, imbuing them with right principles, impenetrating their hearts with the spirit of love, and thus actively helping to carry forward the whole world towards good. But we hear comparatively little of the labors of true-hearted women in this quiet sphere. The genuine mother, wife, or daughter is good, but not famous. And she can dispense with the fame, for the doing of the good is its own exceeding great reward.

Very few women step beyond the boundaries of home and seek a larger sphere of usefulness. Indeed, the home is sufficient sphere for the woman who would do her work nobly and truly there. Still, there are the helpless to be helped, and when generous women have been found among the helpers, why should not we rejoice in their good works, and cherish their memory? Sarah Martin was one of such,—a kind of Elizabeth Fry, in a humbler sphere. She was born at Caister, a village about three miles from Yarmouth, in the year 1791. Both her parents, who were very poor people, died when she was but a child; and the little orphan was left to be brought up under the care of her poor grandmother. The girl obtained such education as the village school could afford,—which was not much,—and then she was sent to Yarmouth for a year, to learn sewing and dressmaking in a very small way. She afterwards used to walk from Caister to Yarmouth and back again daily, which she continued for many years, earning a slender livelihood by going out to families as an assistant dressmaker at a shilling a day.

It happened that, in the year 1819, a woman was committed to the Yarmouth jail for the unnatural crime of cruelly beating and ill-using her own child. Sarah Martin was at this time eight-and-twenty years of age, and the report of the above crime, which was the subject of talk about the town, made a strong impression on her mind. She had often, before this, on passing the gloomy walls of the borough jail, felt an urgent desire to visit the inmates pent up there, without sympathy, and often without hope. She wished to read the Scriptures to them, and bring them back lovingly—were it yet possible—to the society against whose laws they had offended. Think of this gentle, unlovely, ungifted, poor young woman taking up with such an idea! Yet it took in her, and grew within her. At length she could not resist the impulse to visit the wretched inmates of the Yarmouth jail. So one day she passed into the dark porch with a throbbing heart, and knocked for admission. The keeper of the jail appeared. In her gentle low voice, she mentioned the cruel mother's name, and asked permission to see her. The jailer refused. There was "a lion in the way,"—some excuse or other, as is usual in such cases. But Sarah Martin persisted. She returned; and at the second application she was admitted.

Sarah Martin afterwards related the manner of her reception in the jail. The culprit mother stood before her. She was "surprised at the sight of a stranger." "When I told her," says Sarah Martin, "the motive of my visit, her guilt, her need of God's mercy, etc., *she burst into tears, and thanked me!*" Those tears and thanks shaped the whole course of Sarah Martin's subsequent life.

A year or two before this time Mrs. Fry had visited the prisoners in Newgate, and possibly the rumor of her labors in this field may have in some measure influenced Sarah Martin's mind; but of this we are not certain. Sarah Martin herself stated that, as early as the year 1810 (several years before Mrs. Fry's visit to Newgate), her mind had been turned to the subject of prison visitation, and she had then felt a strong desire to visit the poor prisoners in Yarmouth jail, to read the Scriptures to them. These two tender-hearted women may, therefore, have been working at the same time, in the same sphere of Christian work, entirely unconscious of each other's labors. However this may be, the merit of Sarah Martin cannot be detracted from. She labored alone, without any aid from influential quarters: she had no persuasive eloquence, and had scarcely received any education; she was a poor seamstress, maintaining herself by her needle, and carried on her visitation of the prisoners in secret, without any one vaunting her praises : indeed, this was the last thing she dreamed of. Is there not, in this simple picture of a humble woman thus devoting her leisure hours to the comfort and improvement of outcasts, much that is truly noble and heroic ?

Sarah Martin continued her visits to the Yarmouth jail. From one she went to another prisoner, reading to them and conversing with them, from which she went on to instructing them in reading and writing. She constituted herself a schoolmistress for the criminals, giving up a day in the week for this purpose, and thus trenching on her slender means of living. "I thought it right," she says, "to give up a day in the week from dressmaking to serve the prisoners. This regularly given, with many an additional one, was not felt as a pecuniary loss, but was ever followed with abundant satisfaction, for the blessing of God was upon me."

She next formed a Sunday service in the jail, for reading of the Scriptures, joining in the worship as a hearer. For three years she went on in this quiet course of visitation, until, as her views enlarged, she introduced other ameliorative plans for the benefit of the prisoners. One week, in 1823, she received from two gentlemen donations of ten shillings each for prison charity. With this she bought materials for baby-clothes, cut them out, and set the females to work. The work, when sold, enabled her to buy other materials and thus the industrial education of the prisoners was secured ; Sarah Martin teaching those to sew and knit who had not before learned to do so. The profits derived from the sale of the articles were placed together in a fund, and divided amongst the prisoners on their leaving the jail to commence life again in the outer world. She, in the same way, taught the men to make straw hats, men's and boys' caps, gray cotton shirts, and even patchwork,—anything to keep them out of idleness, and from preying upon their own thoughts. Some also she taught to copy little pictures, with the same object, in which several of the prisoners took great delight. A little later on, she formed a fund out of the prisoners' earnings, which she applied to the furnishing of work to prisoners upon their discharge; "affording me," she says, "the advantage of observing their conduct at the same time."

Thus did humble Sarah Martin, long before the attention of public men had been directed to the subject of prison discipline, bring a complete system to maturity in the jail of Yarmouth. It will be observed that she had thus included visitation, moral and religious instruction, intellectual culture, industrial training, employment during prison hours, and employment after discharge. While learned men at a distance, were philosophically discussing these knotty points, here was a poor seamstress at Yarmouth, who in a quiet, simple and unostentatious manner had practically settled them all ! —

In 1826 Sarah Martin's grandmother died, and left her an annual income of ten or twelve pounds. She now removed from Caister to Yarmouth, where she occupied two rooms in an obscure part of the town; and from that time devoted herself with increased energy to her philanthropic labors in the jail. A benevolent lady in Yarmouth, in order to allow her some rest from her sewing, gave her one day in the week to herself, by paying her the same on that day as if she had been engaged in dressmaking. With that assistance, and a few quarterly subscriptions of two shillings and sixpence each, for Bibles, Testaments, tracts, and books for distribution, she went on, devoting every available moment of her life to her great purpose. But her dressmaking business—always a very fickle trade, and at best a very poor one—now began to fall off, and at length almost entirely disappeared. The question arose, Was she to suspend her benevolent labors, in order to devote herself singly to the recovery of her business? She never wavered for a moment in her decision. In her own words, "I had counted the cost, and my mind was made up. If, whilst imparting truth to others, I became exposed to temporal want, the privation so momentary to an individual would not admit of comparison with following the Lord, in thus administering to others." Therefore did this noble, self-sacrificing woman go straightforward on her road of persevering usefulness.

She now devoted six or seven hours in every day to her superintendence over the prisoners, converting what would otherwise have been a scene of dissolute idleness into a hive of industry and order. Newly-admitted prisoners were sometimes refractory and unmanageable, and refused to take advantage of Sarah Martin's instructions. But her persistent gentleness invariably won their acquiescence, and they would come to her and beg to be allowed to take their part in the general course. Men old in years and in crime, pert London pickpockets, depraved boys, and dissolute sailors, profligate women, smugglers, poachers, the promiscuous horde of criminals which usually fill the jail of a seaport and county town,—all bent themselves before the benign influence of this good woman; and under her eyes they might be seen striving, for the first time in their lives, to hold a pen, or master the characters in a penny primer. She entered into their confidences, watched, wept, prayed, and felt for all by turns; she strengthened their good resolutions, encouraged the hopeless, and sedulously endeavored to put all, and hold all, in the right road to amendment.

What was the nature of the religious instruction given by her to the prisoners may be gathered from Captain Williams's account of it, as given in the "Second Report of the Inspector of Prisons" for the year 1836:

"Sunday, November 29, 1835.—Attended divine service in the morning at the prison. The male prisoners only were assembled. A female resident in town officiated; her voice was exceedingly melodious, her delivery emphatic, and her enunciation extremely distinct. The service was the Liturgy of the Church of England; two Psalms were sung by the whole of the prisoners, and extremely well, —much better than I have frequently heard in our best-appointed churches. A written discourse, of her own composition, was read by her; it was of a purely moral tendency, involving no doctrinal points, and admirably suited to the hearers. During the performance of the service, the prisoners paid the profoundest attention and the most marked respect; and, as far as it was possible to judge, appeared to take a devout interest. Evening service was read by her, afterwards, to the female prisoners."

Afterwards, in 1837, she gave up the labor of writing out her addresses, and addressed the prisoners extemporaneously, in a simple, feeling manner, on the duties of life, on the connection between sin and sorrow on the one hand, and between goodness and happiness on the other, and inviting her fallen auditors to enter the great door of mercy which was ever wide open to receive them. These simple but earnest addresses were attended, it is said, by very beneficial results; and many of the prisoners were wont to thank her, with tears, for the new views of life, its duties and responsibilities, which she had opened up to them. As a writer in the Edinburgh Review has observed, in commenting on Sarah Martin's jail sermons: "The cold, labored eloquence which boy-bachelors are authorized by custom and constituted authority to inflict upon us; the dry husks and chips of divinity which they bring forth from the dark recesses of the theology (as it called) of the fathers, or of the Middle Ages, sink into utter worthlessness by the side of the jail addresses of this poor, uneducated seamstress."

But Sarah Martin was not satisfied merely with laboring among the prisoners in the jail at Yarmouth. She also attended in the evenings at the workhouse, where she formed and superintended a large school and afterward, when that school had been handed over to proper teachers, she devoted the hours so released to the formation and superintendence of a school for factory-girls, which was held in the capacious chancel of the old Church of St. Nicholas, And after the labors connected with the class were over, she would remain among the girls for the purpose of friendly intercourse with them, which was often worth more than all the class lessons. There were personal communications with this one and with that, private advice to one, some kindly inquiry to make of another, some domestic history to be imparted by a third; for she was looked up to by these girls as a counselor and friend, as well as schoolmistress. She had often visits also to pay to their homes; in one there would be sickness, in another misfortune or bereavement; and everywhere was the good, benevolent creature made welcome. Then, lastly, she would return to her own poor, solitary apartments late at night, after her long day's labor of love. There was no cheerful, ready-lit fire to greet her there, but only an empty, locked-up house, to which she merely returned to sleep. She did all her own work, kindled her own fires, made her own bed, cooked her own meals. For she went on living upon her miserable pittance in a state of almost absolute poverty, and yet of total unconcern as to her temporal support. Friends supplied her occasionally with the necessaries of life, but she usually gave away a considerable portion of these to people more destitute than herself.

She was now growing old; and the borough authorities at Yarmouth, who knew very well that her self-imposed labors saved them the expense of a schoolmaster and chaplain (which they were now bound by law to appoint) made a proposal of an annual salary of £12 a year! This miserable renumeration was, moreover, made in a manner coarsely offensive to the shrinkingly sensitive woman; for she had preserved a delicacy and pure-mindedness throughout her life-long labors which, very probably, these Yarmouth bloaters could not comprehend. She shrank from becoming the salaried official of the corporation, and bartering for money those labors which had throughout been labors of love.

"Here lies the objection," she said, "which oppresses me: I have found voluntary instruction, on my part, to have been attended with great advantage; and I am apprehensive that, in receiving payment, my labors may be less acceptable. I fear, also, that my mind would be fettered by pecuniary payment, and the whole work upset. To try the experiment, which might injure the thing I live and breathe for, seems like applying a knife to your child's throat to know if it will cut...... Were you so angry," she is writing in answer to the wife of one of the magistrates, who said she and her husband would "feel angry and hurt" if Sarah Martin did not accept the proposal,—"were you so angry as that I could not meet you, a merciful God and a good conscience would preserve my peace; when, if I ventured on what I believed would be prejudicial to the prisoners, God would frown upon me, and my conscience too, and these would follow me everywhere. As for my circumstances, I have not a wish ungratified, and am more than content."

But the jail committee savagely intimated to the high-souled woman: "If we permit you to visit the prison, you must submit to our terms;" so she had no alternative but to give up her noble labors altogether, which she would not do, or receive the miserable pittance of a "salary" which they proffered her. And for two more years she lived on, in the receipt of her official salary of £12 per annum,—the acknowledgment of the Yarmouth Corporation for her services as jail chaplain and schoolmaster!

In the winter of 1842, when she had reached her fifty-second year, her health began seriously to fail, but she nevertheless continued her daily visits to the jail,—"the home," she says, "of my first interest and pleasure,"—until the 17th of April, 1843, when she ceased her visits. She was now thoroughly disabled; but her mind beamed out with unusual brilliancy, like the flickering taper before it finally expires. She resumed the exercise of a talent which she had occasionally practiced during her few moments of leisure,—that of writing sacred poetry. In one of these, speaking of herself on her sick-bed, she says:—

> I seemed to lie
> So near the heavenly portals bright,
> I catch the streaming rays that fly
> From eternity's own light.

Her song was always full of praise and gratitude. As artistic creations, they may not excite admiration in this highly critical age; but never were verses written truer in spirit, or fuller of Christian love. Her whole life was a noble poem,—full also of true practical wisdom. Her life was a glorious comment upon her own words:

> The high desire that others may be blest
> Savors of Heaven.

She struggled against fatal disease for many months, suffering great agony, which was partially relieved by opiates. Her end drew nigh. She asked her nurse for an opiate to still her racking torture. The nurse told her that she thought the time of her departure had come. Clasping her hands, the dying Sister of Mercy exclaimed, "Thank God! thank God!" And these were her last words. She died on the 15th of October, 1843, and was buried at Caister, by the side of her grandmother. A small tombstone, bearing a simple inscription written by herself, marks her resting-place; and, though the tablet is silent as to her virtues, they will not be forgotten:

> Only the actions of the just
> Smell sweet, and blossom in the dust.

THE END.